I0822549

ONCE WE WERE KINGS

DAWN TREADER PRESS
Titles by
Joshua Graham

Award Winning Titles

Beyond Justice

International Book Award 2011
Suspense Magazine Best of 2010
Barnes & Noble #1 bestseller
Amazon Kindle bestseller
2008 Amazon Breakout Novel Award Competition Semi-Finalist

The Door's Open

2010 Authonomy Christmas Story Competition

The Accidental Series

The Accidental Existentialist
The Accidental Exorcist
The Accidental Acquittal (Death and Taxes)
The Accidental Healer
The Accidental Hero
The Accidental Rebel
The Accidental Poltergeist

Historical and Fantasy

Four Gifts for Aria
Legend of the Tiger's Throne

ONCE WE WERE KINGS

Joshua Graham
writing as

IAN ALEXANDER

DAWN TREADER PRESS

Visit Dawn Treader Press' exciting website at www.dawntreaderpress.com
For the latest on Joshua Graham's work visit: www.joshua-graham.com
Visit Ian Alexander's Official website: www.ianalex.com

Cover art by Anna Steinbauer

Library of Congress Cataloging-In-Publication Data

Alexander, Ian
Once We Were Kings / Ian Alexander
ISBN 0-9844526-1-3 (hardcover)
I. Alexander, Ian II. Title.

Praise for ONCE WE WERE KINGS

...a page-turning epic fantasy adventure..."
"...right out of the Golden Age of fantasy..."
"...elements of Tolkien...the Belgariad, the 'Adept' trilogy by Piers Anthony, and a healthy dollop of C.S. Lewis' Narnia Chronicles."
"...Ian Alexander provides a spark, a momentum often absent in other epic fantasies."
"...Compulsively readable..."
"...an admirable debut novel."
~Michael Bellomo, Amazon Bestselling Author

"...an epic fantasy tale of pure delight..."
"Joshua Graham transitions from writing suspense and thrillers to the fantasy realm as Ian Alexander with flying colors."
"...invokes awe in the reader that I've only felt with J.R.R. Tolkien, David Eddings and before them both, C.S. Lewis."
"..a page turner with a very driven plot...
"What doesn't this book have? Magic, shapeshifters, powerful deities and characters that you love and love to hate..."
"...will stay with you long after you've gotten to the end and leave you wanting more."
"This is one of those books that you cannot miss in 2011 if you're a fantasy lover."
~The Top shelf

"...an amazing adventure..."
"...a fast-paced, action-packed adventure that hooked me from the start and kept me glued to the pages until the very end."
"...incredible action, adventure and characters..."
"...The characters practically leap off the page, they are so vivid and real! "

"... rich symbolism with a great message..."
"...values and a message that you can feel good about..."
"...I would definitely be the first one in line for more Ian Alexander novels!"
~Life in Review

"...an amazing epic adventure that will take the reader on an unforgettable journey like no other.
"... I was immediately sucked into the story..."
"...absorbing me and surrounding me with amazing imagery, emotion and distinctiveness like none other I had ever read before."
"...truly poetic."
"...a generation bridging epic fantasy that is sure to span and hold strong through the test of time as well as our ever changing society and circumstances of readers everywhere."
"...I often found my heart gripped within sadness, as well as bursting with joy."
"...action, adventure, intrigue, romance and even shape-shifting spirits."
"...the ending is the perfect segue into future books.
"A true classic in the making."
~Cafe of Dreams Book Reviews

"Ian Alexander's ONCE WE WERE KINGS sets new standards for epic fantasy."
"ONCE WE WERE KINGS transcends the qualities found in such great works as "The Chronicles of Narnia" to "The Lord of the Rings".
"... a true master of the written word."
"...a thoroughly magical story filled with memorable characters, danger, hope,inspiration and romance."
"Alexander's ONCE WE WERE KINGS should sit on the highest shelf of your library."
"A sparkling story that will leave the reader breathless and

wanting more."
~Susan Wingate, author of DROWNING and the award-winning BOBBY'S DINER series

"...[Ian Alexander] delivers a very pleasing fantasy epic."
"...seems to parallel some of our own socio-political climates, in regards to terrorism, racial and cultural biases, religious biases..."
"...many pleasant surprises..."
"...definitely recommend it, especially to those who are fans of novels such as Narnia"
"...I look forward with great anticipation to see what occurs next with some of the characters from this [book]."
"...You won't be disappointed."
~Rhodes Review

For Alexander and Madeleine,
My beloved children

FORE WORD

GATHERED ROUND the wide and level stump of the Great Ancients' Tree, the Twelve Elders of the Sojourner's Council stood within the stone walls of the courtyard and rejoiced that the fulfillment of Shamis the Stargazer's prophecy was now at hand.

By the alignment of the northern constellations they knew that the time of deliverance drew nigh. By the anomalous tide shifts and the unprecedented lunar phases, they knew that the dark reign of Malakandor would soon come to an end.

What they knew not was that a traitor lurked amongst them.

Oreus, the chief elder stood and raised his chalice. "Brethren, you have honored the name of Valhandra with longsuffering and steadfast hope." He turned to the elder on his right. "Hephesta the Wolf-Hearted, you have endured three wars over the course of five hundred years."

With deep humility, Hephesta arose and inclined his head.

"And Bereus, the Tiger-Hearted." He too arose. "Thy service as the stalwart protector of the royal line beyond three hundred years has not gone unnoticed." This continued until he turned his attention to the final elder. At seventy-nine years of age, she was the youngest, most spry of them all.

At seventy-nine years of age, she was the youngest, most spry of them all.

"And you, dear youngling—Lucretia, Raven-Heart." At the very mention of her name, the council began to applaud to such effect that a flock of wild night birds flew blackly from tree branches into the deep and purple sky. A fleeing cloud. "Unto thee do we bestow special honor. For fearlessly have you employed the gifts bestowed by Valhandra for a cause predating even your own birth." Once again Oreus regarded the entire council. "Would that we possessed such faith as our beloved sister, when we ourselves were but fledglings."

Completely aware of the effect her beauty had upon all who beheld her, the impostor who had killed the true Lucretia and taken on her likeness now feigned a smile and inclined her head.

"Rejoice brethren, for our redemption is nigh," declared Oreus. "And now, among the faithful, in the villages of Talen Wood, in the great Citadel of Valdshire Tor, yea, verily, in thine own hearts," once again he lifted his chalice and cleared his throat, "Prepare ye the way for the beneficent reign of the Great Deliverer!"

They all responded lifting their chalices. "The Great Deliverer!"

"The Deliverer." The false Lucretia scoffed quietly as she tapped her cup against those of the other council members. She smiled again at the old men as they imbibed of the ceremonial Dragon'sblood Wine. Noble warriors though they were, able-bodied and powerful though they were, she could not help but laugh at the pathetic manner in which they would meet their demise.

First, Hephesta fell. Clutching his throat, his eyes widened with something entirely alien to those who'd known him and certainly to himself:

Fear.

A chorus of confused cries filled the courtyard. All gathered around the fallen Hephesta. The impostor did not join in. Rather, she watched with satisfaction as the pulverized Shikar stone mixed in the wine began to take its toll.

One by one, they fell. Ancient warriors who had arrogantly considered themselves immortal. Just like Hephesta, now writhing, now frothing. A most pleasing sight indeed.

Now, the impostor did not even attempt to restrain her smile.

Having witnessed the violent throes of death and realizing what was happening, three of the surviving Elders—Oreus amongst them—stopped short of drinking the poisoned bloodwine. They saw her laughing and charged forward, swords and crossbows at the ready.

"Lucretia, what have you done?" cried Oreus.

Timena and Cerbeas trained their weapons upon her.

"You have not only betrayed us, but all Sojourners," said Cerbeas as he drew his crossbow.

"And it is you who have betrayed the true ruler of this world!" Her hands trembled. If only she could fly this very moment. But she had prepared for this, trained her reflexes, her mind.

"You have turned against Valhandra, Himself," said Timena.

"Valhandra is dead!" The impostor stood defiant. One hand still in her pocket, she fingered the razor-stars fashioned out of smooth Shikar stone. Their very presence weakened her, but not for long.

Oreus lifted his staff. The orb atop glowed blue and white. The impostor knew better than to hesitate. "Would you compound the pain of this betrayal by compelling me to deal with you as I must?" His eyes now brimming azure pools, Oreus pointed his staff.

"But I am not Lucretia, old fool!"

Stunned, Oreus hesitated.

The impostor let out a feral cry and leapt into the air. She forced her eyes shut and invoked utter blackness around her entire being. In one swift motion, she flung the three Shikar razor-stars at Oreus, Timea and Cerbeas.

The first struck and lodged itself into Oreus' forehead. He let out a roar and fell to the ground, convulsing and howling in pain.

The second caught Timea in the leg just as he began to transform. He cried out and fell to one side, trembling and foaming.

The third grazed Cerbeas just as he completed his equine transformation and flew from the slaughter and bounded clear over the stone wall.

Unhampered by the fetters of a human body, the impostor flew up and looked for him. But to her dismay the night did not betray her quarry. Even from this vantage point high above the courtyard, she could not see him, though he had galloped into the night in the form of a mighty stallion.

It mattered not. Cerbeas had been grazed. If he survived, it would not be for long. She would simply report that the mission was prosperous. And this would more than suffice, unless her master condescended to having the bodies counted.

Alighting on the Great Table of the Ancients, the impostor smiled with satisfaction. The only remaining testament to their existence would be the carcasses, whatever had not yet been picked apart by vultures.

CHAPTER ONE

Six Months Prior

IN THE BLACKEST OF NIGHTS, a fortnight before the seventeenth birthday of a slave named Render, the moon, full and blood-red glared down upon Talen Wood, a ways from the Citadel walls of Valdshire Tor. Three boys bent upon nothing good approached the lad as he lay down, trying to sleep. Render's master—last seen with his beard bathed in drivel—reclined in his chair, a drunken stupor barely veiling his cherry-nosed countenance.

Outside the damp broom closet better known as Render's room, in that fetid cottage in which he and his master dwelled, one of the boys tapped furtively on the wall.

"Render. Hssst! Render."

"What? Who's there?" So poor was his vision he could barely see the fingers before his face, for the sands of slumber had encrusted his eyes.

"Come on, Render. Are you going join us or not?" He recognized the voice of Kaine, his elder brother. He too was a slave belonging to an old master on the other side of Talen Wood. Some two years his senior, Kaine led this band of mongrels who, despite all their capers, had always eluded capture. They were the closest thing to a family he had.

Atop the ledge of the window sat a black cat, not unlike the one he had seen a day or two prior. It ceased licking its paw and washing its face. With turquoise eyes, it stared straight into Render's. Throughout Render's life, black cats appeared frequently, though he had never been able to take one as a pet. The cat looked over to Kaine and his companions, then back at Render. It leapt down from the ledge, almost daring Render to follow.

Kaine appeared in the window and grinned. "Coming or not, Rend?"

"After last time? I shouldn't go anywhere with you again." But something about that cat drew Render's curiosity. The way it regarded him, as if it knew of something interesting, an adventure or a pirate's chest full of gold and trinkets. Perhaps a magical sword.

Render stole past his snoring master and out the door.

"Come now, you old tortoise," said Kaine, the oldest of the boys. He stood at least a head taller than Render. Kaine brushed his fire-red hair out of his eyes, smiled and slapped a heavy hand onto Render's shoulder. "Hungry?"

"Do birds fly?" Render's master afforded him but one meal each day, though he toiled without respite in his stables and fields and barnyard from the rising of the sun till dusk.

"Well, they're hungry." Kaine tossed a glance to Folen and Stewan, the twins. When they faced each other, they looked like reflections. Beneath the dirt lay bespeckled cheeks which in the daylight took the hue of apples. This more than betrayed their tender age of eight years.

How diverse a band.

Yet one thing bound them in common. They were orphans, all of them. And all of them slaves.

Searing pain like a branding iron scathed Render's back when he stretched his arms to yawn. Wounds from yesterday's lashing reopened. He winced and groaned but dared not reach back to touch it. "You'd better go on without me," he said. "If Bobbington catches me..."

"On then," Kaine said, raising up fistful of tree branches fashioned into spears. "I heard dinner grunting by the stream."

Render's eyes opened wider, though it brought no clearer vision in the gloom. "You don't mean—?"

"A boar," whispered Stewan, excitedly.

"Wild, fat boar." Kaine handed Render one of his spears.

"Do let's go," Folen said, pulling Render's sleeve. He held up a glinting dagger which he'd undoubtedly stolen from a traveler who'd taken pity on him, and stopped to give him a piece of bread.

"Yes, do let's," Stewan echoed.

"I don't know."

Kaine leaned down and whispered, "Big. Fat. Juicy boar."

Charging into the wood, Render joined in and let out a mighty cry of ancient hunters. The thought of fresh meat teased the tips of his tongue.

Less than half an hour later, and arguably twice as hungry and frustrated than before, they returned. The entire village now lay quiet as a graveyard. The boar had proven a most crafty beast indeed, and escaped. Grunting merrily into the bush, it seemed to mock them.

Bested by a pig.

The shame.

Thankfully, darkness blanketed the night. Not a soul stirred. But this did nothing to prevent Render's stomach from making a formidable growl. At that very moment, amidst Folen and Stewan's giggles, the black cat climbed up onto a barrel just outside the door and mewed.

"Hello," Render said and walked over, with confidence.

"Wait," Kaine whispered. "Don't frighten it. We can cook it."

"Not to worry. I've got a way with cats. They trust me." Render took pity on it, however. It was but a bag of fur and bones. From deep within his pocket he pulled out a scrap of salted fish, stolen from his master's cupboard, and put it under her nose.

Mroooow! The cat hissed and scratched his hand.

"Ow! You horrid little beast!" A pale beam of moonlight revealed three dark lines growing deeper and wider on Render's hand. Straight across the oddly shaped birth mark which to him always looked like an ancient symbol. Like those found in the archeology books he'd liberated from Bobbington's shelves.

Render sucked the salty blood from the wound and glared at the vicious creature. It sat quite satisfied with itself on its hindquarters. Glowering down at the dried fish scrap, the cat knocked it off the barrel and into the dirt with its paw.

Render huffed. "There's gratitude for you."

Laughing and slapping his thighs, Kaine said, "You've got quite a way with cats, indeed." He raised his spear.

"You're not serious," Render said.

"Quite." He crouched low, pointed the spear at the cat. It arched its back, flattened its ears, and with a hiss, bore tiny white fangs.

"Come on, she's hardly worth the effort." Render

grabbed Kaine's arm. Folen and Stewan had raised their spear and dagger as well.

Kaine huffed. "It nearly tore your hand off, and you mean to defend it? Stand aside, we're going to have dinner if I have anything to do with it."

"No!" Render's shout echoed through the hills rousing the barks of several dogs. A chill ran through his blood when he heard Bobbington snort and awaken inside the cottage.

"Render! REN - DER!" he roared. "By the scrolls of Malkor, where are you!"

"Now you've done it," Kaine said and gathered the two younger boys. "Better run with us."

"And when I return?" Sweat seeped through the opening in his scabs and burned. "You know what he'll do to me."

"Suit yourself." And with that Kaine flew off with the boys.

The door blasted open.

The cat leapt off the barrel and into Render's arms.

The sight of Bobbington, his lardy, hairy belly hanging over his pants, and the whip in his fist made Render's hands tremble. Had he the stature or strength, he might well stand up to the brute.

Render had neither. Nor did he possess the fortitude to escape for orphaned as a babe and sold as a slave, this was the only home he knew.

"Wretched vermin!" Bobbington said, his foul breath steaming up into the night. "You dare run? In the middle of the night? Have you so soon forgotten the last time you tried?"

The wounds on his back permitted no such relief. "Sir, I—"

"And what is that, eh?"

Render glanced down at the warm, furry creature of destruction, sitting in his arms and purring. "It... it's a cat."

"I can see that, you fool! Bring it here so that I can gut it and sell its innards to the fiddle maker."

Render turned the cat away from him, as if she might be offended by Bobbington's words. "What a ghastly thought!"

"It's just a mangy cat. Bring it here, boy!"

"No!"

That was the moment that changed everything. Bobbington's lips shook, his right eye twitched. With great malice, he uncoiled the whip. Render had been lashed many times before, but now he feared for the cat.

"Go," he said, and placed it on the ground. "Run!"

Bobbington blinked, his mouth gaping in surprise. "Why you...you insolent little—! Stand still and receive your due!"

The cat ran a few steps towards the wood, then stopped and turned around. With its back arched it watched.

"Five lashes now," Bobbington said, "then ten more after I drag you back inside!"

Teeth clenched, eyes unblinking, Render stood there, gazing into Bobbington's inebriated countenance.

He was prepared.

Bobbington lifted the handle of his whip, wound back his arm as far as he could without falling.

Render mustered all his courage.

His shoulders crept up. His neck tensed.

And then...

He ran.

"What—?" Bobbington sputtered and lashed out. But Render was out of reach. Bobbington, surprised as Render, fell forward landing face first into the dirt.

The cat flew into the thicket.

Render followed, arms and face clawed by dry branches. The frigid air seared his lungs as he ran.

Bobbington gave a great shout. "Come back here, boy!" His heavy footfalls grew nearer. "I'll flay you and that flea-ridden cat!" In his condition however, it was doubtful he could ever catch him. Nevertheless, Render ran faster still.

Letting out a growl befitting a creature many times its size, the cat raced over to the only possible hiding place.

"Not there!"

For lack of a better plan, Render followed. Straight into the black cave, which neither he, nor Kaine, nor anyone with half a brain dared set foot.

In he charged, following the lunatic cat.

CHAPTER TWO

PALLID MOONLIGHT entered from between the vines which dangled over the cave's mouth like the fingers of a hag. Sliding his hand along the rough, damp wall, Render continued to step deeper inside. The air hung thick and old. It reeked of moss and other decaying things which he hoped not to discover.

"Boy!" Bobbington's voice boomed into the cave. Again he called, but this time a bit quieter. "Render?"

Just then, something rather large and heavy brushed past Render's hand. He gasped and braced himself against the cave wall as the firm, sinewy form, covered with bristly fur pressed up against him.

He saw nothing, but felt the creature's warmth and heavy footfalls thumping ahead. Then, the rumble of a deep growl filled the entire cave, like that of a great lion or bear. A cold tingle danced up Render's back.

"If...if you think this is amusing...." Bobbington's voice broke. "You'd best quit this foolery right now and come out."

He dared not move.

The growl started again.

"What in all that is—? Render come out at once!"

Render's heart pounded so loud in his ears he feared it

would betray him. Just when he could stand it no longer, the growl sprang up into a terrible roar.

Bobbington let out a girlish scream.

A mad rush of leaves and branches.

His quickly fading cries.

Bobbington fled. Faster than one could have imagined, considering his weight and condition.

With his ear turned to the cave's entrance, Render listened to the roar once again echoing into the wood. Whatever beast had frightened Bobbington away would surely return for Render.

And the cat.

Where was that foolish little animal, anyway?

Better the monster eat her than me, he thought. But then, from the front of the cave came a tiny sound. Something that struck him as both odd and alarming.

"Meow?"

If he didn't already suspect delirium, Render would have remained completely still, within the cave until dawn. But how was it that the cat stood there, near that dreadful monster? And alive?

Unless...

Render approached the cave opening, standing as tall as he could for he had heard that if one were to confront a bear or a mountain lion, one must stand as erect as possible and shout loudly.

Steady now.

Ready to shout....

He waited a moment, then leapt out into the open.

"HYAH!"

But there was no monster. Had it hidden behind a rock? A tree? Waiting to pounce and shred him to ribbons? To the left, he directed his eyes. Then to the right. Above and behind. Nothing.

No monster.

And then...

"Meow?" Warm, and furry, the cat rubbed against his bare ankle, just above his shoe. Render jumped back and gasped. "Oh, it's you."

"Mrow." The little rascal. With a tilt of its head, it gazed up at Render as if he had gone completely insane. But then it continued to circle his legs, leaning in and rubbing warmly against them. Had it no fear, no sense?

He scooped the cat up into his arms and stared down the hill. Below, oil lamps mounted on cottage walls flickered. The hinges on his master's door—his former master—squeaked. Bobbington had a habit of complaining such that his neighbors could hear of his woes and perhaps commiserate. Instead, they took to avoiding him.

He could be heard now, muttering on about how Render had become more trouble than he was worth. Bobbington rushed in and shut his door with a heavy slam that reverberated throughout the village.

"Well then," Render said, rubbing the cat behind its ears, "We'll not be going back, I suppose." It purred as he slipped it inside his leather vest, sharing some much appreciated warmth.

From the top of Smyth's Hill, Render's shadow stretched down to the bottom and made him look enormous. He gave the farming village, the place he'd called home for as long as he could remember, one last look, then turned to face the moon. Amber light, brighter than he'd ever seen before, almost made him shade his eyes. Within his vest, the cat moved. It too stared at the strangely bright, strangely hued moon. To Render's surprise, it turned its eyes to his, as if to speak.

"I've never seen anything like it before, either," Render said, and scratched gently under the cat's chin. Its throat trilled as it leaned its head down in the crook of his thumb and forefinger. From where he stood, Talen Wood ended behind him. Before him however, an open plain stretched for about a mile and dropped off.

A howling wind chilled Render to the bone and nearly threw him off balance. He held cat tighter and reestablished his footing. "You all right?"

Its claws dug into his forearm.

And as quickly as the gust came, it passed, swaying tree branches below. Like ripples in a lake, the tops of the trees shivered.

He'd never wandered this far from the village before. But up ahead, he knew of a rocky precipice—the largest of several—which dropped so far, no one had ever returned to say just how high it stood over the plain. Further East, miles past the white desert valley, a battalion of mountains lined the wasteland like sentries. The Handara Mountain Range. The tallest summit, towered far above the others like a commander inspecting warriors under his command. Render's pulse quickened at the sight, for he had never gotten such a clear view before.

What lay on the other side?

Lacking proper education afforded only to the genteel people of Valdshire Tor's grand citadel, all he'd heard were tales, legends and rumors.

An escaped slave now, Render imagined life as an exile, crossing to the East. As far from Valdshire Tor as he could get. After all, to return meant certain capture—or recapture, rather. He'd heard rumors of young slaves being turned over to the traders because they either displayed defect or were not particularly useful. And as he'd now proven himself a useless slave, Bobbington would probably have him hunted down, hauled off, and killed. Like the runt of a litter.

"Sort of like you, eh, cat?"

It buried its head deeper into his vest. At least he would not travel alone. He was glad of the company. But how would he traverse such a distance and so treacherous a terrain?

As if the ground had heard his question, a rumbling underfoot drew his attention to the wood. The cat stiffened as the whinnying of horses and the thunder of their hooves approached.

Render tried to run. But with nowhere to go but down, he froze in place. Three riders wearing red tunics over chainmail shirts and hoods approached from all sides.

With all his might, Render dashed into the fast closing space between two of the horsemen. The sickening sound of scraping steel filled the air as the dark riders unsheathed their swords.

Glints of reflected moonlight flashed.

Render was stopped in his tracks by the cold, sharp edge of a sword under his chin.

CHAPTER THREE

HALT, if you fancy the head upon your neck," said the mounted rider. "Or continue and leave it behind as a token." From her tone and the shining decorations on her armor, Render gathered she was the leader.

She scoffed. "What's your name, boy?"

Not a word escaped Render's clenched throat.

"Seems to've misplaced his tongue," the rider to her right said.

"Speak boy," said the leader, leaning down so that the ends of her dark hair touched Render's face. "Or I'll find that tongue of yours with my dagger."

"Please, ma'am. My name is Render." The cat squirmed. He held it tight and out of view.

"Where're your parents?"

"Dead, Ma'am."

She let out a hearty laugh and the others joined. "Perfect." Pointing her sword down to the foot of the hill, she said to the rider behind Render, "Bring him back with the others. That ought to be the last of them."

"Yes my lady," he said in a gravelly voice. Between Render's shoulders, the point of the soldier's sword urged him downwards.

"If he resists, cut off his ears," the leader said, all humor gone from her tone. "If he tries to strike you, cut off his hands. If he tries to run cut off his feet. And if he tries to call for help..."

"I understand."

"As best you should," the leader said. "The wagon is nigh full by now. You know where to bring them."

"Aye."

"Hyah!" With slaps on their horses' rumps and a clinking of spurs, the dark rider and her remaining subordinates rode off.

Down the hill, Render now saw a horse drawn wagon, covered with a heavy canopy. Its driver sat at the reins, waiting.

When he stepped in, or rather, was shoved in, Render's captor forced him to sit upon a bench. "I won't hesitate to dice you into vittles if ye try anything," the horseman said. He then shackled Render's feet which were chained to those of some other unfortunate souls, whose faces were obscured in the pitch black wagon.

Like his fellow prisoners, Render dared not speak.

The door slammed shut. A thin beam of light stole in from the small square windows around the top of the door and walls. Immediately, the wagon lurched forward. Every bump in the path jarred him.

From the stuttering breaths, drawn through clenched teeth, Render could tell that there were children around him in that cramped space.

"I want to go back," came a pitiful murmur.

"Me too."

"Quiet!" hissed a familiar voice.

Render blinked in surprise. He sat up straight and inclined forward and whispered, "Kaine?"

"Keep to yourself, whoever you are, or I swear, I'll knock you down, kick open the door and toss you out. Then you'll be dragged to death, or they'll think you're trying to escape and...and—"

"Kaine you idiot, it's me, Render!"

All went quiet. Save for the rolling of the wheels, the blowing and snorting of the horses and the humming of the driver.

"Render?"

"It is you then, isn't it?" Render's heart leapt.

"Over to the light where I can see you," Kaine said.

"You first."

"Bother! Isn't it just like you to quarrel so?" Kaine exhaled sharply. "All the same, let's go to the edge so that we can see each other in the light."

"Right."

There at the end of the wagon, their eyes met and lit up.

"Why, it is you."

"Of course it is," Render said and grabbed his arm. He could not help but smile. "We're going to be killed!"

"Yes! Isn't it fantastic?"

If there was any joy at being taken prisoner by dark knights and horsemen, or whatever they were, it was in finding his brother and the twins. Not that Render wished ill upon them. It was just better not to face this alone. He asked the twins if they were all right. They were, but felt frightened. Though he had no basis for saying so, Render assured them that all would be fine.

Kaine stared down at Render's vest. "And what have we here?" At the opening of his vest, the cat rested with one paw casually draped over the other. It glared at Kaine with flattened ears. "How in the world did that happen?" He asked.

Render lifted it out and placed it on his lap, soothing it with strokes along its stiff back and tail. "As I said, I have a way with cats." Still staring at Kaine, her claws gripped

Render's pant legs. "Anyway...I think she likes you."

"She?" Kaine scoffed. "That beast is too fierce to be a she."

"What do you know of cats?"

"What do you? I'll wager my slingshot that it's a boy."

"That so?" Not about to back off from a challenge, especially one which he knew he could most certainly win, Render held the cat up and lifted her tail.

"Reeeow!" She swung around and swatted Render in the face. Then she jumped out of his hands and went into the dark part of the wagon.

"You win," said Kaine.

"I told you so. Now, if you would be so kind and hand over your slingshot."

"Of course. As soon as I get back to retrieve it from my master's home."

Home.

The very word caused a twinge in Render's chest. Never had he known such a place that he could truly call home. Growing up a slave robbed him of something so important, so fundamental to being human: a sense of belonging.

Oh, of course he belonged. He belonged to Master Bobbington, as did cattle or sheep or any other livestock: property. But Render envied children who went home to warm dinners, whose fathers took them hunting, taught them their wares, whose doting grandparents served as purveyors of forbidden confections. Such things he beheld only from a distance, remembered only as a dream.

The carriage came to an abrupt stop. A great deal of yelling and commanding alerted Render. The cat returned to sit upon his lap.

Kaine, pulling the slack between his shackles and Render's, stood on his bench and peered through the slits in the wagon cover.

"What is it?"

He didn't answer.

"Kaine!"

"Shhh!"

Folen and Stewan whimpered, the chains of their fettered feet scraped the floor. The cat, back on Render's lap, sat up and inclined her ears towards the window.

"By the decree of The Lord Mooregaard, Lord Duke of Talen Wood, advisor to King Corigan, open the gate!" It was the horseman who threw Render into the wagon.

"Where are we?" Render whispered. A cold drop of perspiration rolled down his spine.

"You're as observant as you are good with cats." Kaine clicked his tongue. "A blind man could see."

"See what?"

"That we're at the gate."

"What gate!"

"The Citadel, moss-brain."

The cat stiffened and leapt from Render's lap. She then climbed up and squeezed through the window in the door.

"Hey!" Render didn't bother trying to stop her. So distracted was he by sounds outside. They were so alien, he hardly noticed that she'd gone. Without realizing, he held his breath.

Heretofore, he had only heard stories of the great Citadel, where streets were paved with gold, where the highest forms of art, science and heraldry flowed. And where those unfortunate enough to be deemed criminals suffered unspeakable horrors.

"Don't you understand?" said Kaine, excitement hanging on every syllable, "We've been appropriated."

"Appro...?" said Stewan.

"It means," Render said, "we no longer belong to our

masters."

Folen leaned over and whispered. "You mean, we're free?"

"I mean we're being sold."

CHAPTER FOUR

The Empire of the East

IN THE EASTERN EMPIRE of Tian Kuo, during the rule of the Lohng Dynasty, the greater part of the population lived in rural villages outside the capital walls, without the amenities of the Emperor's city. This had not been the intention of the Emperor, but rather that of his widow, the Empress Dowager, soon after his demise.

Though they were afforded marginal protection by imperial troops during wars, for the most part these villagers were left to their own devices. This is not to say that they were what one might consider provincial, uneducated or uncultured. On the contrary, much of Tian Kuo's fading cultural, scientific and spiritual wisdom found its roots in the written and oral traditions of outcast cultures such as that of Xingjia.

Towards the Western border of Tian Kuo, between the Myng River and the Lohngdi desert, lay a peaceful hamlet set within tall palms and flowing silvery brooks. The inhabitants of Xingjia were an uncomplicated people. But many of them had once been scholars or government officials, and possessed an ancient wisdom, from which many a great storyteller and seer had emerged.

And then put to death.

For their beliefs were considered the dangerous superstition of the wealthy land owners, the so called "oppressors of the masses." But that was over two centuries ago. Ancient history.

Now, to the Tianese Empress, the people of Xingjia were nothing more than a backwards people that had best keep to themselves.

"Ahndien," Mother called, cutting vegetables at the stone table in their wooden house. "Father will return soon. Go out and fetch those Kai roots."

Barely hearing, Ahndien carefully turned a withering page from the Book of Didactic Songs in Praise of Falun Darah and attempted to recite Song Number One Hundred and Six, The Fall of Mah LhaKor, in the ancient tongue.

"Ahndien!" Mother called again.

"Yes, Ma! I'm coming." Still holding her book, her face buried in its pages, she began walking back towards her house. Before she could complete the final line, the book was yanked from her hands. Her mother's annoyed eyes took its place.

"Ai! You are just like your father! Nose in book, head in clouds! Don't you know that we need to have dinner prepared for his return?"

"But Ah-Ma," Ahndien said, grabbing at the old leather-bound book which she had taken without permission from Ah-Bah's library.

"Go get the roots now," she said, and shook her head. "Always talking superstition like your father."

"But Ah-Bah says that everyone has a spirit, a potential

to—"

"Ai! Enough! You are nearly a grown woman. How will you ever find a husband if you keep going on with these childish fairy tales?" She handed Ahndien a satchel packed with nuts, dried pork, a steamed bun, and a flask of water for the journey to the Huangtoa hills, where the Kai roots grew. "Where is the spirit potential to put rice on the table? Hmm?"

"I'm hungry," said Shao-Bao, her little brother.

"Yes Ah-Ma." Ahndien lowered her head, tied the pack around her waist and shouldered the empty buckets. "May I at least take Ah-Bah's book with me?"

"When would you have time to read?"

"Please, Mother?"

Her stone carved countenance softened. A smile emerged from Ah-Ma's features and she lowered her arched shoulders. "I tell you. You'll end up an eccentric word-eater like your father." She handed her the book and huffed. "If you are lucky, you'll end up with a husband who will put up with all this..." she waved her fingers dismissively. "This nonsense!"

Ahndien bounced on her toes and clapped her hands. "I won't waste any time. I promise."

"You can read while you take your lunch."

"Yes." Ahndien rummaged through the closet making an extraordinary amount of noise. There she found father's antique sword and made sure Ah-Ma wasn't looking when she strapped it to her waist. She winked at Shao-Bao and went to the door.

"Be home before dusk," said Ah-Ma.

She was already out the door and on her way.

The midday sun began its indolent ascent into the sky and warmed Ahndien's shoulders. She took a sip from her flask and wiped her brow. With a red ribbon she tied up her long, ink-black hair and gazed out at her surroundings.

How lovely the mountains were this time of the year. Green with life, intoxicating jasmine blossoms, new life emerging all around. Taking it all in with a deep breath, Ahndien felt a profound connection to the very land on which she stood.

Directly above her in a tree branch, nested eagle chicks cheeped for their mother. Perhaps it was the great bird's shadow among several that had flown over Ahndien several times since she reached the hill. A shrill cry told her that this was the case. The eagle returned with a small rodent in its beak and alighted in the nest to feed her young.

Ahndien reached into her satchel and pulled out a small wooden flute which she only played when she left the village, for the old songs grandfather had taught her vexed mother so.

Five notes. In improvised sequences, she created a song which originated from her heart in reaction to the inspiring landscape. At the first piercing note which split the air and echoed down to Xingjia below, she expected the birds to fly off in surprise.

Indeed, the birds flew.

But instead of flying away, they all gathered around her, some on the branches, some at her feet, and some on her shoulders—a secret pleasure Ahndien had enjoyed since her eighth birthday when Ah-Yeh (grandfather) gave her his flute.

Her otherworldly pentatonic song filled the mountain and she began to march around a fallen tree trunk. A procession of sparrows, rainbow finches and even a wild goose followed.

When she stopped, the birds cocked their heads to the side. Down below the people in her village went about their business. She felt a twinge of guilt. They are all working so hard at their chores, and here I am enjoying myself. But her heart took flight when she looked down into the village and saw a broad shouldered man entering the village gates.

"Ah-Bah!"

Mother and Shao-Bao, ran up to greet him. He had returned from the symposium earlier than expected.

"Little brothers and sisters," Ahndien announced to her winged friends. "Thank you for gracing me with your company. But now I must make haste."

The birds, now encircling her, stood perfectly still. As she unpacked her food, preparing to give her entire meal to her avian friends, a rustling in the bush caught her attention.

Chittering into the sky, every bird flew off.

Ahndien called into the thicket. "Hello?" There was no wind, so someone or something must have been there. "Please, show yourself." She reached for her waist and unsheathed the sword that mother did not know she'd taken. Her mouth grew dry. The rustling drew closer.

CHAPTER FIVE

AH-BA!" SHAO-BAO CRIED OUT, ran and leapt into his father's open arms. For all his shortcomings as a husband, Myanwu conceded that he always redeemed himself many times over as a father.

"Shao-Bao, be careful. You'll hurt your father's back."

"Beloved," her husband said wrapping his free arm around her shoulder. He kissed her forehead. "Forgive me for arriving early without sending word."

"Nonsense, Bai Juang," Myanwu said, her ears warming and not from the midday sun. "How was the symposium?"

Bai Juang set his son down and pulled a toy bird made of bright colored feathers and handed it to him. Shao-Bao squealed in delight when his father pulled a string and the bird began flapping its wings.

He turned to Myanwu, and though his smile remained, the light in his eyes was dimming. "I have been away from my family for two weeks. I don't want to bore you with matters which do not concern you."

"Husband," Myanwu said, slightly hurt. "I only meant to—"

He stood and regarded her sharply, then moved his eyes to Shao-Bao. For a moment, Myanwu could not understand his reticence. Apprehension hollowed her stomach. He only acted that way when—

"But where is my little Empress?" said Bai Juang, a warm smile washing away the tension. Myanwu let out the breath she'd been inadvertently holding.

"Ahndien has gone to gather Kia roots. Did you not hear her flute?"

"Ah, I thought that might be her," he said and put his pack of books down. "Perhaps I should go join her."

"Ah-Ba?" Shao-Bao said, now whimpering. He was facing down into his cupped hands, sniffling in little hiccups. When he looked up at his father, two large tear drops rolled down his plump cheeks.

"What is it, little warrior?" he said and knelt down to open his hands.

"It's broken," he sobbed. "Won't fly anymore."

"Ai!" Myanwu scowled. "You always break every new toy your father—"

Bai Juang held up a hand, took his son into his arms and let him bury his face into his shirt. "Do not fret. Nothing that has been damaged is beyond repair."

Would he spoil his son as he had Ahndien?

"Run along, son. I will repair this for you later." From his bag, he produced a small picture book and handed it to Shao-Bao. "I believe I made you a promise before I left?"

His wet eyes opened wide and his frown inverted. "The Dragon Adventures of Kronis the Great!" The boy hugged his father's neck and ran into the house. "Thank you, father!"

Bai Juang straightened up and smoothed the wrinkles in his cloak. He turned to Myanwu and shrugged with repentant eyes. "I know what you are going to—"

"Bai Juang," she said, sharply curbing her indignance. "Would you simply fix everything for your son, rather than teach him to take care of his property?"

"He will learn."

"Not at this rate."

"He needed comfort."

"You always chose the heart over the head."

Bai Juang put his elbow in his hand, rubbed his dark beard and pondered this. His eyes deepened and his lips pulled thin. Then he stepped over to his wife and put a strong arm around her waist. "I choose the heart over the head because it was the only way I could win your hand." From behind his back he pulled out a Golden Fire Orchid.

And the walls fell.

She wanted to remain angry at him for leaving her with the children for weeks at a time, for being more devoted to his cause—a dying one at that—than to his own wife. But what stopped her were these two things:

First, deep down, she too believed in his cause; because she believed in him. Never had she met a man of such integrity and conviction. If Bai Juang believed something, it must be true. And second, he always knew the paths of diplomatic warfare when it came to their conflicts.

"Where did you...?" She took hold of the flower and wanted to cry.

"My bride. How soon you have forgotten. "Twenty years ago today," he pointed to the hills, "at the foot of that very mountain where our daughter gathers Kai roots, you and I met for the first time and—"

"Bai." Myanwu took the flower and sank into her husband's embrace. "I will never forget."

She remained there, holding him tight, glad that he was home. Even if it was only until his next three week trip to and back from the symposium. He was a good man. And she treasured these moments.

Then, at the sound of something she hadn't heard since

she was a child, Bai's body went stiff.

"No."

From the outskirts of Xingjia, atop the sentry towers, a clarion call resounded. "Shao-Bao," Bai Juang's eyes darted to the village gates. Myanwu dropped the Orchid and ran to the house not realizing that she had trampled and torn the delicate petals on the ground.

Frantic, she vaguely heard her husband shouting to the men running back into the gates, calling all men to arms, "How far off? How far off!"

The only reply she heard was, "How can this be! Where are the imperial guards?"

Already inside the house, Myanwu found her son, rushed him down into the hidden room beneath the house, and held him close.

Out in the courtyard, someone cried out, "Torians!"

She winced. Above them, someone was overturning chairs, ransacking the cabinets and dropping dishes and utensils to the ground.

Shao-Bao let out a gasp.

She covered his mouth. Held up a finger.

The crashing of furniture and items being kicked aside onto the floor grew closer. Louder.

Then, the worst thing that could have happened, did.

The door hinges above them squealed. Where was Bai Juang?

The door to the hidden room flung open.

Myanwu and her son screamed, their eyes squeezed shut.

"Where is it?" Bai Juang said, his eyes round with panic."

"What?

"Where is my sword!"

CHAPTER SIX

"COME OUT." Affecting all the courage she could, Ahndien grasped the hilt of her father's sword tighter still. "Show yourself...and...and I won't hurt you."

The rustling in the bush stopped. Curiosity overtook caution and Ahndien stepped forward, ready to strike, though Father's sword felt a bit too heavy to swing with any effect. When she reached the place from which the rustling sounds came, she took a deep breath, held it, and with her foot, pushed away some of the branches.

"Please," she whispered. "Answer me." Father had warned her not to wander off to the top of the hill. There are vicious mountain lions that devour little children, he had always said. Her heart beat like the festival drums of the New Year, yet fear had not seized her. Not entirely.

She pulled the branches aside. "Aha!"

Just then, a small man, slightly hunched in the back and wearing the white garb of a monk, turned around and gasped. "Ai!" He lifted his walking stick as if to strike. But when he saw Ahndien's face, he lowered it. "What do you mean, startling an old man like that? Why, I might have..." he coughed, sputtered, pounded his chest. "I might have mistook you for... for a bandit!"

"I'm sorry," she said and rushed to his side. "You didn't answer."

"Eh?"

"You didn't answer me when—"

"Eh?" he turned his head. "Speak into this ear, my child. The hearing's not what it once was."

"Never mind." She helped the old man out into the clearing where she had set her things down. "Have you eaten yet?"

"My food is knowledge, wisdom...and truth!" From behind the white beard that stretched down to his chest, a smile pulled at the corners of his mouth. The monk bore a striking resemblance to Ah-Yeh, her grandfather who lived with her family until he passed away last winter.

Ahndien thought his bones would surely creak as he sat on the tree trunk and rested both hands on his cane. "Was that you, playing the song of the Fenghuang?"

"Feng...what?" This had always been her secret, not so much the music, but her way with the birds. "I don't know what you are talking about."

"Of course you don't." His round belly rolled like grass jelly when he laughed. "And yet, you do."

She should have felt apprehensive speaking to a stranger, alone on the mountain like this, but for some reason she did not. He was too frail to be any sort of threat. Perhaps it was the way he spoke, the way he laughed. Just like Ah-Yeh.

"My name is Lao-Ying." He leaned forward on his cane.

"I am honored to make your acquaintance, sir," she replied. "I am—"

"Ahndien, daughter of Xing Bai Juang," he said. His hazel-green eyes sparkled. They seemed unusually sharp for a man of his age. "I have waited long to meet you."

"But how do you know me?"

Before he could answer, a strange sound rang out into the mountains from below—the sound of horns, rapid and urgent. Lao-Ying arose and bounded to the edge of the hill. With a hand he shielded his eyes. "And so it begins."

"What is it?"

"Something that should not have happened for another ten years."

Ahndien came to his side and looked down at her village. Her heart sank at the sight of the trebuchets, large monstrosities on wheels, pushed by soldiers in red vested chainmail and armor. Flying high with the army's advance, a flag with the image of a crimson, winged creature stood tall on a pole.

"What are they doing?"

Lao-Ying took her elbow and tried to lead her away. "Come along, child. Come."

"Wait." Just then, the three trebuchets stopped a good distance from the village walls. She looked harder at the flag, the soldiers and realized. "Are those...?"

Lao-Ying lowered his gaze and shut his eyes. "Soldiers of Valdshire Tor."

"Western Demons!"

The Torian soldiers lit the cauldrons in the center of the slings and flames burst upwards. In swift succession the trebuchet's massive arms swung forward, hurling the flaming projectiles at the village.

"No!" Ahndien tried to run. But something restrained her with alarming force. She looked down at her arm. Lao-Ying had taken hold of it.

In a low and regretful voice, he said, "It is too late."

A thunderous explosion erupted from the center of the village. Cries of terror arose with plumes of fire and billowing black smoke. Like a swarm of red fire ants, Torian soldiers with swords, crossbows and all manner of weaponry charged into the village.

Ahndien broke free and ran down the path. Even at her best speed, the village was at least half an hour away.

"Please," shouted Lao-Ying, "You mustn't!"

CHAPTER SEVEN

THE SHARP SOUND of curtain rings ripping across a rod, followed by a blinding light jarred Render from his sleep.

"Arise!" boomed a husky voice.

Render rubbed his eyes. Had Bobbington fallen ill of the throat? Had he dreamt the entire thing last night? But when he saw Kaine waking up in the bed across the chamber, and Folen and Stewan as well, Render knew it was not a dream.

"Up now, you den of sloths. All of you!" A rather large and rotund man with flaxen hair stood at the door. Dressed in a brown cloak, he very much resembled one of those Malkoran scholars, illustrations of which he'd seen in the moldering books of Bobbington's library.

Folen yawned and nudged Stewan who, laying next to him, was still asleep. "Come on, sleepy head, wake up."

"Who are you?" Kaine said to the scholar. "And where are we?"

"You will address me as Sir Edwyn," he said gazing down the side of his considerable nose. "And you have three minutes to clean up and change into those." He pointed to the neatly folded bundles at the foot of each of their beds and then gestured to the basins and pitchers at the end tables. Sir Edwyn clapped his hands, making Render wince. The sound of it resounded throughout the cavernous stone walls of their chamber, which, when compared to his room in Bobbington's cottage, seemed more like a cathedral. "Quickly now. When I return you had best be ready."

When he shut the door, a profound echo thundered through the chamber. Render looked about. Smooth stone walls decorated with intricate tapestries, shimmering curtains which must have been made of exotic Eastern fabric. His bare feet stood cushioned upon a thick rug of violet and blue and gold. But where were the shackles?

"Are you certain, Render?" Stewan said.

"Of what?"

"That we've been appo...appro-pee-ated?"

"Of course we have," Render removed his shirt and splashed water over his face from the gold rimmed basin on his bedside table. The other boys followed his example. Then to his brother: "Haven't we?"

"I'm not quite so certain now, truth be told." Kaine dabbed his face with a towel. Then with a wicked grin, he said, “I wonder if they might be preparing us for a brutal execution."

The twins gasped. Their eyes grew the size of plums.

"Stop it Kaine," said Render. "Must you frighten them so?"

"I'm merely saying..." Kaine shrugged. "I mean, who's to say we're not going to have our heads lopped off and stuck on the points of spears and marched through Talen Wood as an example to other slave boys who try to run away."

"Do stop it," Folen said. "Please!"

Render agreed. "Enough, Kaine."

But on he went. "Or perhaps we'll be thrown into an arena with hungry mountain lions, and be mauled for royal sport. You know, like those Sojourner zealots, ages ago. That's what happened to them, you know." He pointed to his spotless white shirt. Render knew too well where his brother meant to go with all this. When he was the twins' age and they'd steal into the wood to share stolen food, Kaine would try to frighten him with drivel as this. "The blood shows much better against this pure white shirt. All the better for spectators at a distance who—"

"I said, enough!" Render's shout came as a surprise to all, not the least of whom, himself. But it wasn't clear if it had been irritation at his brother's teasing or the actual fear it instilled.

Kaine smirked. "Well, aren't you the pickled puss?"

Render pulled his belt tight. For once in his life, he wore new, clean clothes that didn't reek of sweat. He smiled at the twins. "Bother him," then went over to help Stewan with a clasp on the back of his vest. Fine trappings indeed for slaves. "We should just do as Sir Edwyn says." He turned to help Folen tie up a lace on his shoe.

"Oh yes," Kaine said. "He seems nice enough, don't you think?"

Render didn't bother to look up when neither of them answered. When he stood up and turned around, however, there at the now open door stood Sir Edwyn, a scowl etched into his brow. He clapped his hands twice and motioned for the hallway.

"Where are we going?" Folen said, clinging to Render's arm. "We want to go back!"

"Your life as you have hitherto known it..." Edwyn

heaved a dour gaze upon them all, "...is over."

CHAPTER EIGHT

SIR EDWYN walked before Render, Kaine and the twins and would have appeared harmless if not for the armed guards with longswords marching beside him.

Flecks of dust floated in the morning beams of sunlight which entered through the windows above. The corridor stretched eternal and turned not even once before they finally arrived at a large wooden door. There, two armor clad sentries stood with pikes crossed over the entrance. Above the archway hung a sculpture. A pair of winged creatures—difficult to discern without staring unduly—one of them black, the other red. Both of their talons clutched an auric orb. With bat-like wings and scales, Render decided they must be dragons.

Edwyn clapped his hands twice. The pikemen slapped their hands to their sides, stomped a foot, and uncrossed their weapons affording passage through the slowly opening door.

Edwyn gestured forth.

As Render and his companions stepped forward, dread filled his thoughts. His throat became so parched that he wanted to cough. But so frightened was he that he resisted the urge. If this was the end, would it be an execution by beheading, or a mauling by wild beasts?

No one dared utter a word.

They entered, and for a moment the light inside was so bright his eyes could not adjust. When they did, he would no doubt find himself before an executioner, or a tormentor, or mountain lions or tigers ready to make a meal of them all. Render took a deep breath, resolved to stand in place until he felt the point of a sword in his back.

"Welcome, my young friends!" A strong and familiar voice said, just as Render's vision cleared. Standing before them, a lady dressed in an extravagant scarlet gown embroidered with intricate aureate piping and patterns smiled and with a welcoming hand stretched out. Her raven hair struck a stark contrast with paper-white face. Her lips shone with such a deep shade of crimson they stood in stark contrast to her hair and eyes, which were dark as midnight.

She stood there in the center of a vast courtyard with the morning sun shining down from a blue sky, in which barely a lambswool cloud floated.

"I trust you've a healthy appetite?" She waved her slender fingers with red, claw-like nails toward the dining tables behind her. Scores of children, all finely dressed, sat on benches along these tables. Their ages ranged from about Folen and Stewan's to as old as Render himself. "My fine young men," the lady said, "do join us for breakfast."

The aroma of freshly baked bread, boiled eggs, and cooked meat made Render's mouth water. But a thought soured his mood. "What are they doing?" he whispered to

Kaine, "fattening us for the kill?"

"Does it matter, really?"

Folen and Stewan had already taken their seats, their eyes large with hunger before the feast, the likes of which none of them had ever seen, much less partaken of.

"And now," she said, a bright smile widening across her face, "With the compliments of his Majesty, Corigan, High King of Valdshire Tor, enjoy this, your first of many such meals, as the adopted children of his kingdom."

Without hesitation, Kaine and all the other children let out a cheer and dug into their food, forks and knives barely employed.

"Rejoice children! For the High King has turned his countenance upon you. He has bestowed his favor upon you and liberated you from the yoke of superstition, the oppressive hand of slavery."

It was then that Render realized who she was. The harsh, yet fetching tone of her voice, the way her ebony hair fell over one of her eyes when she tilted her head as she emphasized a word, or scrutinized some of the children. He nudged Kaine's arm with his elbow. "It's her."

"What are talking about?" Kaine said, his mouth so full he was barely intelligible.

"Dear children," she said, her voice rising above the din of happy, hungry slaves now proclaimed royal wards. "I am Lady Volfoncé, advisor to King Corigan."

Kaine put his fork down and took a harder look. "Well, I think she's lovely."

"You would." Hadn't he heard the brutal threats she made prior to throwing Render into the wagon last night?

"Who is she then?"

"Don't you see? She's the one who abducted us last night."

CHAPTER NINE

TO THIS VERY DAY, the gentrification decree which had been issued years before Sir Edwyn's birth continued to bring rescued children of all ages from round the kingdom into the citadel walls. In fact, Edwyn himself had been one of those refugees from the zealot insurrections, to which King Corigan had finally brought an end and along with it, "The Age of Inscience."

Edwyn sniffed with disdain as the children ravaged their meals like a pack of famished dogs. None of them displayed the slightest modicum of civility. This, and no doubt many other things, would have to be taught.

Amongst this last litter—orphans, alleged Sojourner children and slaves—was to be his class of pupils. The boy called Render and his friends already seemed troublesome. According to the registration records, Render's former master Bobbington had kept, the lad might have been a child of Sojourner parents who had died in a preemptive raid on insurgent soil.

The very thought brought a sharp twinge between Edwyn's ribs. He was only slightly older than Render when his own parents had died because of Sojourner superstition. Consequently, Edwyn had become an orphan.

So, as was the case for these children slopping down their fine breakfast like pigs at a trough, Edwyn had been brought up a ward of the King.

A disguised blessing, perhaps.

Lady Volfoncé continued to lecture the children on their assignments, while Edwyn and the other mentors stood by the walls observing their new charges. Scarcely a child lifted his head when their name was called and matched with their tutor.

But Render did.

Though his older brother and two young friends continued eating with their bare hands in spite of the proper utensils within easy reach, Render stopped and attended when Volfoncé called.

"Render, Stewan and Folen of lower Talen Wood," she announced. "You shall henceforth submit to the care and authority of Sir Edwyn. Your tutor."

Render stood up. "What about my brother?"

"Shut up!" Kaine hissed, and pulled him back down to the bench.

Volfoncé smiled. "As Master Kaine is the only one of this class near the age of cultivation, he shall be under the tutelage of The Lord Mooregaard."

Across the courtyard, the wickedly handsome Don raised a black-gloved hand ever so slightly and half turned it, indicating his presence to his sole pupil. He then turned and bowed to Lady Volfoncé. As he straightened up, from behind his dark goat-like mustache and beard, a smile whiter than snow emerged.

Never one to admit it, Edwyn had always envied Mooregaard's status as a knight of the Order of the Scarlet Pendragon. What was it about him? His sword, his chainmail, his commanding stature?

Inclining her head in response, Lady Volfoncé continued with the introductions. Edwyn stood patiently awaiting his trio of students. This time, he thought, for once in my seven years as a royal tutor, please let them be different. Not just sheep incapable of independent thought.

By the time Volfoncé finished the introductions and all thirty-one students had been matched with their tutors, she clasped her hands together and said, "Now then. Any questions?"

"Yes, Milady." A girl at the far end of the courtyard stood. She may have been about nine or ten years old and didn't notice that she had put her splendid red gown on backwards.

Volfoncé covered her mouth to suppress a laugh. "Yes, dearest."

"Besides mathematics, astronomy, literature and physi...phizzi.."

"Physical Sciences, precious one," Volfoncé assisted, endearment beaming from her countenance, "among other disciplines."

"Yes, physical sciences. Aside from those, will we be taught....uhm...Oh, bother, what is it called...? Oh yes! Will we be taught magic?"

Volfoncé retained her smile, but her eyes dimmed under arched brows. She stood silent for a moment. The backwards dressed girl blanched and sat right down with a wordless apology on her face.

"If by magic," Volfoncé said, low and foreboding, "you mean, illusionism, and sleight of hand, as performed by court entertainers, you've clearly misunderstood the elevation of your station."

"I'm sorry, ma'am," said the girl, "I... I just meant—"

"There is no other kind of... of... magic!" Volfoncé glared

down her upturned nose. "Never forget that you have been called to royalty. The future of this great kingdom is with you, oh blessed children. And in this future, there shall be no trace of that terror imposed upon the gentle and learned people of Valdshire Tor by those fanatical Sojourner zealots. Do I make myself clear?" Slowly, her gaze swept across the courtyard scrutinizing every eye, now affixed to hers. "To all of you?"

Not a sound.

"Very well, then." Volfoncé spread open a fan and flapped it at herself. The warmth in her tone and demeanor returned. "There shall be time enough for all questions, dear ones. But you shall take them up with your tutors."

Even Edwyn breathed a sigh of relief. It had been nearly twenty years ago when Edwyn himself sat at those tables and received his orientation by Lady Volfoncé. And while she seemed only to grow more beautiful with the passage of time, her formidable presence never abated.

"Now, children," she said, sharp as the tip of a dirk. "Line up before your tutors. Your orientation begins presently."

An excited commotion ensued as each of the children got up and went about finding their assigned mentors. Edwyn stood tall and haughty as his three new students gathered around.

"Folen?" he read from a list written on vellum.

"That's me."

"Stewan?"

"Here, sir."

"And finally," he looked down at the last boy, whose face was turned and watching his brother walking off with Lord Mooregaard. "Render."

The boy did not turn his head.

"Render!"

"Yes!" Jolted, he spun around with a gasp. He bumped into Folen, who shoved him back nearly causing him to trip over his own feet.

Hapless.

A pair of whelps and a day dreaming youth. Edwyn sighed. The coming year promised to be every bit as stimulating as those prior. He rolled his eyes. "Follow me."

CHAPTER TEN

THE OLD MAN'S WARNING continued to resound within Ahndien's mind. But nothing could stop her from flying down the mountain trail and back to her home.

As she came to the foot of the hill, less and less of her burning village could be seen above the tall palms and bamboo leaves. But the acrid smell of burning huts and the dark tendrils of smoke clawing into the sky was more than enough a signpost.

Branches and leaves scraped her arms. Father's sword rattled against her side as she ran down the dirt path. Foolish! Why had she taken the sword, to protect herself from rabbits? How would Father defend the family?

She must have been running for at least fifteen minutes. Burning air filled her lungs with each breath. Her legs defied the pain. Each step brought her closer to the fumes. But the shouting, the commotion, the sound of struggle diminished as she got nearer.

Tears blurred her vision.

Gasping, choking, knees failing.

No! Keep running.

Soon, too winded to continue, Ahndien stopped.

Still in the distance, now with the sun setting behind black, billowing clouds of smoke, she saw the village a bit further down the path. If only she could run for another minute. Then she'd arrive. But what then?

Doubled over, hands on her thighs, Ahndien leaned back against the smooth striped trunk of a bamboo tree and wept bitterly. The old man up at the mountain top had been right. It was too late.

Now, the only sound she heard over her own sobs and coughs were those of the Torian soldiers. Laughing and swearing in that accursed accent, that twisted dialect of the common tongue which represented the demons of the West. It could mean only one thing:

They were leaving.

On the tips of her toes, she stepped forward taking care not to make a sound. Between the trees she now could see the entire village burning. Except for the remaining Torian soldiers poking through the ashes, no one stirred.

Ahndien tried in vain to swallow the tension lodged in her throat. Where were Ah-Ma and Ah-Ba and Shao-Bao? And everyone else for that matter? If only she could get past the leaves and branches. But she dared not move. She held her breath as a pair of Torians walked by, not a stone's throw from her.

Just then, a loud shriek rang out above.

Ahndien let out a gasp.

Immediately she covered her mouth and braced herself behind a tree.

"What was that?" one of the soldiers said.

"You fool," the other said and pointed upwards into the sky. He laughed. "It's just a bird. See?"

"You're the fool! It's a vulture. Coming to pick the bones clean."

For fear she might wretch, Ahndien held her mouth tighter.

"By its marking, you idiot," said the first. "A blind man could see that it's an eagle."

The second soldier did not reply. He kept staring up. His lips started to move, but now words came out. Then he began to point. Finally, he said, "Whatever it is, it's coming at us!"

At that, they both ran, cowards that they were, and mounted their horses, just as the bird—the size of a horse—landed on the ground where they had fled. The magnificent creature tilted its head, jerked it side to side, surveying the destruction. It almost looked sad.

The eagle was every bit as terrible as it was beautiful. But Ahndien dared not move. Its razor sharp talons and beak were more frightening than a Torian sword. It let out a piercing cry, which caused the fleeing soldiers to blubber as they fled. Then the eagle itself spread its massive wings and sent a strong gust that bent the tree branches to the point of breaking as it flew off into the sky.

Finally, after it had vanished, Ahndien drew a deep breath. It was time. Tears stinging her eyes and the hilt of Ah-Ba's sword shaking between her fists, she descended the path to the burning village.

"Ah-Ba?" she whimpered, entering the gates. "Ah-Ma?" Neither responded. "Shao-Bao?"

Nothing.

She pushed the draping palms aside. All at once her heart sank. Strewn all over the ground were men, women and their children. All dead. Some of their clothes continued to burn. Others lay in pools of blood. None moved.

Every hut, burned to the ground or in the process. Carts overturned, fruits and vegetables scattered and crushed.

The hideous stench of what Ahndien could only imagine was burning flesh made her stomach twist. The word "no" kept repeating silently on her lips.

Then something arrested her steps, her very breath.

Past the south wall, which had been smashed open, the clinking gears and grinding wheels of those monstrous siege engines and trebuchets pulling away caused the hair on the back of her neck to prickle. Ahndien dropped behind a fallen cart and gasped. Her entire body quaked. Every breath stuttered between clenched teeth. Her knuckles went pale, as she strangled the hilt of Ah-Ba's sword.

A large shadow from above passed over. The giant eagle.

The Torian soldiers' voices faded into the forest along with their monstrosities. It could not have taken but a few minutes, but to Ahndien it was an eternity.

Now came the dreadful task of looking for her family through the bodies and debris.

Let them be alive. Please.

When she arrived at the well, where ten paces to the south her house should have been, her knees grew weak. She fell upon them. The sword dropped from her hands and clanked against the rocks.

"Ah-Ma!" she cried out. "Shao-Bao!" In the fallen doorway of her hut, Mother lay still, face down with her arm draped over Shao-Bao. Arrows protruded from their backs and smoke continued to rise from their clothes. "No!"

She tried to get up, to run to them. But it was no good. Instead, she fell on her face and cried out in anguish. Like everyone else around, her family was dead.

She wanted to scream. Release the horror, the dagger of sorrow and regret that impaled her heart. But, for fear of betraying her presence, she held her hands tightly over her mouth as she rocked back and forth, shaking her head.

No amount of sobbing could dislodge the pain in her chest, her knotted innards.

"Ah-Ma!" The words caught. "Ah-Ma. I'm so sorry."

And finally, the sight of poor little Shao-Bao, clutching a toy bird, would have overcome her utterly. But she noticed that Ah-Ba was not present.

"Ah-Ba!" she cried, abandoning any care or reason. Where was he? Again she cried out, "AH-BA!"

If only she could just lie down and die there, with her mother and brother. She would have spent the rest of the day, on her knees, sobbing.

If not for the feral snarls of a wild animal, approaching from behind.

CHAPTER ELEVEN

THE LOW-PITCHED GROWL vibrated in the ground through Ahndien's sandals. From the depth of the sound, it must have been that of a very large predator. Slow and steady, she reached for the handle of the sword, slipped her hand through its lanyard and grasped it.

All at once, the creature's furious roar flew above her, just as she spun around and swung the long, straight blade of Ah-Ba's sword. A wash of tawny brown flashed before her and she let out a shout. Before she could even complete the stroke, a deep and dull pain caught her forearm. Ahndien cried out in pain. Her eyes felt as if they'd bulge out of her head when she saw it.

Her arm, now about to be crushed or torn off, lay in the cruel grip of a mountain lion's jaw. Its glassy brown eyes fixed hard upon Ahndien's, not blinking, almost daring her to move.

Then, as if the shock were not complete, something even more freakish happened. With its jaws still clamped, the mountain lion gazed straight at Ahndien, as if it would speak to her. And that is exactly what happened.

// LITTLE GIRLS SHOULD NOT PLAY WITH SWORDS //

"What?" she cried out. The beast's fangs bore down harder, increasing the pain. Though she was aware of this pain, she was too confused to care. "What manner of evil is this?"

// YOU HAD BEST DROP IT...//

The mountain lion snarled, his otherworldly voice both aristocratic and sinister.

//...SOMEONE MIGHT GET HURT //

Two more mountain lions leapt over the burning ruins of Ahndien's neighbor's house and into the courtyard. Her blood went cold.

I must be going mad, she thought. How can this creature speak?

With her arm in the beast's jaw, neither its mouth nor tongue moved. Nevertheless, she would not relinquish Ah-Ba's sword.

The other two mountain lions stalked closer. The one biting down on her arm yanked and shook her arm.

// THE SWORD OR YOUR ARM? DECIDE! //

Ahndien shuddered. It was clear now. The creature did not speak aloud. Somehow, she could hear its thoughts. Whether or not the massive feline knew this, she couldn't be certain.

The beast clamped down harder still. Ahndien let out a sharp gasp.

Just then, a large shadow passed over them. What followed happened so quickly it was near impossible to recall the details.

A shrill cry from above.

With glassy eyes, the beast gazed into the sky, alerted with apprehension.

The two other mountain lions stepped back.

Ahndien's arm was free. Just as a swooping wind and flapping sound rushed down. A wash of brown and white surged past her eyes. She fell back and hit the ground.

When the dust cleared, she turned her gaze upwards. Well into the distance she discerned what appeared to be an eagle, the eagle, soaring high into the air and clutching a kitten in its talons.

Only, it was no kitten.

For on the ground, the mountain lion who had attacked her stared with its mouth agape. In the grasp of the bird's talons was one of the two mountain lions that had come to assist him.

Ahndien squeezed her eyes and blinked twice. How could this be? The eagle was enormous! Then screaming in terror, the mountain lion fell from the massive eagle's clutches and hit the rocky ground with a bone cracking thud.

Taking advantage of the momentary distraction, Ahndien bolted to her feet sword at the ready. The eagle returned causing the remaining two mountain lions to flee from the village gates and into the bush. Ahndien feared the colossal bird of prey would come for her next.

But it changed its course.

Instead, the eagle sailed over the tops of the green bamboo and palm trees. Leaves rustled with the passing wind.

And then it vanished into the thick of the woods.

Once again, it flew out with its quarry flailing about in its talons. Ahndien dropped behind the crumbling wall of a demolished house and peered out at the spectacle. As it did before, the great eagle dropped the second mountain lion to its death from a frightful height.

// BE STILL //

She jumped with a start.

Swung around.

Looked to the left. To the right. It was not the voice of the mountain lion. No, this voice rang with aged sagacity.

// FEAR NOT //

Right away, she lowered her arched shoulders. Let out a suspended breath.

Still clutching her father's sword, Ahndien kept her eyes on the woods just outside the gate. The eagle had flown out of view. But somewhere in the thick of the woods, she feared, one mountain lion lurked. The one that attacked her. Whether it had fled or if it lay in wait, she could not tell.

With her hands clutching the sword so tightly it shook, Ahndien waited an eternity. She dared not take her eyes from the fallen tree branches along the path outside the village gate. She remained so still the only sound she heard was the pounding of her heart. This did not subside with the passing of the time. Instead, as the stirring in the brush grew closer, her heart pounded louder, relentless.

Poised and ready to slash at whatever came through, Ahndien bit down on her lip. The crunching sound of pebbles and burnt twigs grew closer. She drew a profound breath; wanted to shut her eyes and swing blind and wild when it arrived.

A rustling in the distant branches caused her to stiffen. Something was coming.

CHAPTER TWELVE

THE RARE WORD or two spoken by Sir Edwyn barely left an impression in Render's mind. As they walked about the citadel, Render's jaw slackened. In awe, he gazed at the tall edifices made of smooth white stone, the spires of cathedrals which clutched at the sky. According to Edwyn, they, along with all other such buildings, had long since been converted from great houses of archaic superstition to the modern services of the government.

"As you can see, this is the center of commerce for—" Edwyn stopped, glanced down at his feet, where a black cat stood, its tail erect. It then circled and rubbed its face against his leg.

A warm, tingling sensation rushed through Render's body, up through his neck and to the top of his head.

"Away, vermin!" Edwyn shoved it away with his foot. Render tried to conceal his disappointment, though Folen and Stewan simply laughed.

They passed by a fountain in the middle of a public

square, which, as Edwyn informed them, was called Hawthern Fountain. A small crowd looked on as two young men fought. They were clad in armor, their swords and shields clanging with every strike. Each of their tutors, mounted on horses, held banners with their respective coat of arms emblazoned upon them. On occasion they would call out a short burst of exhortation.

"Behold," Sir Edwyn said. "When you have mastered a certain degree of proficiency in heraldry and combat, your training—all of it—the arts and letters, the martial arts, will culminate in a final exam, like the one these young men are taking."

"My word," said Folen. "Won't they get hurt?"

"There are rules to the combat exam," he said and turned to Render. "You shall learn soon enough."

Leaving the cheering crowd, the clashing weapons, Render and the twins followed their tutor past the fountain. Render kept looking back to see where the cat had run off to.

"As royal pages," said Edwyn, straightening his tunic, "you shall take residence in my lord, The Lord Agon's manor." He pointed to a walled castle to the left of the cathedral, the name of which escaped Render. The castle's outer boundaries stood by the very walls of the citadel. "Each of King Corigan's Lords take their official residency within the capital walls. Castle Mittelvald, there on the Eastern Wall of the citadel, is but one of several. It is there that you shall each receive your training."

When they arrived, a lancer clad in gray armor signaled the gate keeper. A moment later, the massive bars whined as they yawned open with reluctance.

"It's huge!" Folen craned his neck around as they proceeded up the paved promenade. Sweet jasmines, tall verdant trees and babbling fountains filled Render's senses. The grass must have been the greenest, most finely cut he had ever laid eyes upon. But surpassing all the grandeur of the courtyard, beyond the lush and perfectly level shrubs, a grand castle rose up from the ground. From the windows in the corner turrets hung banners with a coat of arms. Red, with the same dragon symbols Render had observed back at breakfast.

"For the duration of your training, you will study alongside with one other young squire," Edwyn said. "He is not your age, Render. But he is one or two years your elder, my twin pupils." Folen and Stewan barely nodded, so affixed were their eyes on the castle's open door.

When they entered, a young boy about thirteen years old came forward. He wore rich clothing, a small sword at his side, and a fine purple cap on his head. With an upturned nose he stood at the threshold with his arms crossed over his narrow chest. "Sir Edwyn, good day."

"And to you." Edwyn inclined his head.

"And what are these?"

"New students."

The young squire looked up at Render and frowned. "Students? These are provincial slaves. Why, I've never seen the likes of these here." He sneered at the twins. "Apart from slaves."

Render's ears grew hot. "I'm no slave!"

"Oh? Surely you don't mean to—"

"Nor am I a servant." Render stepped up such that the obnoxious little rat stood just beneath his nose. Neither of them moved.

"Do you know who I am?" said the squire, his white face now flushing like an apple. "I doubt you even know who you yourself are. But I'll tell you this: It's all about lineage. For you see, I am..." He turned to the tutor. "Sir Edwyn, would you be so kind?"

Edwyn's chest heaved. With lead-weighted words he announced, "Master Branson, son of the Lord Agon. The Lord Agon, who, thrice decorated for valor, is alone honored with the Scarlet Wreath." He turned to Render. "Master Branson is the son of your benefactor."

"How impressive," said Render, devoid of all sincerity.

Finally, with impassive eyes, Branson stepped away and gave a dismissive wave of his hand. "Quite. If the good Edwyn insists that you are to study with me..." he rolled his eyes at the don, "then so be it. Hmph. I could use the diversion."

"Branson," said Edwyn, "Shall The Lord Agon soon return from the campaign?"

"Cursed if I should know," the boy said in a tone far older than one would expect for an adolescent. "As if my father would condescend to telling me of his affairs."

"I only thought that—"

"You are here to instruct and prepare me for knighthood, though it ought to be mine by right of birth. It's bad enough that your attention is now divided between me and those...those mongrels."

"'Tis by royal decree, young Master. And by your father's wishes."

"I need not like it." Branson tilted his nose up and began to sniff around near the twins. "Do make certain they are bathed before dinner!"

"You stinking pile of cow dung!" Folen charged forward. Despite the shouts for him to stop, Folen leapt and toppled Branson. Straddling the young squire's chest, Folen repeatedly struck him.

Finally, Render and Edwyn grabbed his arms. Yanked him up.

Eyes wide with anger. Branson climbed to his feet. He drew his sword and rushed for Folen. But Sir Edwyn took hold of his wrist and restrained him.

"Unhand me! Unhand me now!"

"With all due respect, Master Branson, it was your discourteous disposition and words that entreated such a reaction."

"I demand satisfaction!"

"What would your father think of this? I am certain he would have a thing or two to say to you about your temper and woeful lack of decorum. These are, after all, royal wards and your father's guests."

Pulling his hand free, Branson huffed and sheathed his little sword. "Not a word, Sir Edwyn" he said. "On your honor."

"I am duty bound to report all to my Lord."

It was then that Branson's icy features thawed. More and more he began to look and talk like a boy of his age. "Edwyn, please. You mustn't. If father finds out, why he'll...Well, you know what he'll do."

Edwyn nodded gravely.

"It's not fair! I've worked so hard. And has he ever once said, well done, my son? No! He just drives me harder and harder. Can't you see why I am so ill-tempered?"

"Serves you right!" Folen said, rubbing his knuckles.

"Yes," Stewan said. "It does!"

Branson reached for his sword. Pulled it out partially. His mouth twisted open to speak—no doubt something foul. But Edwyn cleared his throat, which brought the petulant squire back under control. Branson smoothed his shirt and affected a proud look, eyes half open and glared down his nose at the twins. "Let us forget this unfortunate incident, shall we?"

None of them answered. Folen and Stewan looked to Render.

"We shall not speak of this matter again," said Render.

"Neither to each other nor to your father."

"Good. That's more like—"

"As long as you agree to one thing," said Render. Edwyn's eyes betrayed the smile hidden behind his hand.

Branson opened his eyes fully. "What is it?"

"As we are to be fellow students, you must treat us as fellow students. As equals." Render extended his hand.

For a moment longer than would have been polite, Branson stared at Render's hand as if it had just been pulled from a cesspool. But finally, he took it, smiled a crooked smile and said, "Fellow students."

"Fellow students."

Branson took his hand back and began walking inside. Mid-stride he stopped and looked back. "But equals?" He shook his head and scoffed as he left.

CHAPTER THIRTEEN

EXHAUSTED, Ahndien did not know if she had any strength left to defend herself against whatever was approaching. The soft but purposeful steps got closer. Trepidation gripped her heart tighter with each one.

"Ahndien."

She gasped, swung her sword back preparing to strike.

Held her breath.

Then from behind the bushes, he appeared.

Worn, ragged and limping.

At first she thought, Ah-Yeh? But then she realized he was not her grandfather at all. It was that voice. //BE STILL...FEAR NOT // The one she had heard in her head. Only stronger, more confident.

Still shaken from the mountain lion attack, Ahndien blinked and stood perfectly still. She dared not move. Then, when she saw who it was she lowered her sword and stepped forward. "Oh, it's you."

"Are you all right?" Lao-Ying hobbled over on his

gnarled walking stick. The question barely settled into her mind. Darkness enshrouded her thoughts. With disembodied awareness, she knew that overwhelming sorrow brewed within her, but somehow they failed to connect with her thoughts, her words.

They're gone, she tried to say, but no sound passed her lips.

"Yes, I am all right. I think."

Lao-Ying sighed wearily, took hold of her arm and turned it over. "You are bleeding."

"All of them. Gone."

Ahndien fixed her gaze upon the smoke rising from the village. Ah-Ma and Shao-Bao lay dead just ahead of her. A cold tear rolled down her face but she didn't move, barely breathed.

Lao-Ying muttered something, walked over to Ah-Ma and Shao-Bao and covered them with a large sackcloth. He turned around and searched Ahndien with concerned eyes. "I am truly sorry."

But her heart and her voice were entombed in ice. All she saw were ethereal images layered over of the hills. Flames shooting into the air, a few fleeing villagers running from the accursed Torian soldiers, who shot them with arrows. This echo-like vision seemed much more vivid than witnessing them firsthand. It disturbed her more than if it was actually happening before her eyes.

Lao-Ying returned and guided her to sit on a large rock. He ripped open her sleeve and with a strip torn from that sleeve tied it tight around her forearm, just above the puncture wounds. "What did the mountain lion say to you?"

The question echoed in her mind. But all she could think of was her village, her friends, her family. All gone. She continued to stare into the hills as the images continued to flood her consciousness, if it could be called consciousness. Her lips moved and, as if someone else had spoken, she answered the old man. "It wanted Ah-Ba's sword."

"Sword?" He pulled the ribbons tight. A sharp pain oozed from the holes in her arm. But Ahndien neither cried out, nor flinched. She didn't even blink. Lao-Ying rumbled. "Why would they...? Unless they thought that—"

All at once, like floodgates bursting, the reality of it all overcame her. She let out a painful cry that resounded through the woods.

"Ah-Ma!"

Ahndien tore herself from the old man's caring hands and rushed to the charred remains of her mother and little brother. "Ah-Ma!" All her cries melded into an unintelligible melisma of sobs and words and screams.

Tears mixed with soot and ash muddied her face. She fell to her knees over the bodies. Now, the only word she could utter was, "No." She choked back another sob. "No, no, no, no!"

She had only left for a short while. And in that time, her family, her village, her entire world had been destroyed.

"Ahndien," Lao-Ying said in a hushed tone. Gently, he placed his hands on her shoulders.

"No!" she bolted up, expecting the old man to lose balance and fall on his back. But instead, he straightened up and regarded her with empathy. This moved her little. "It is your fault!"

"My—?"

"You distracted me, delayed me! All the while my family was being murdered by the filthy Torians!"

"How could I have possibly—?"

"You knew! I don't know how, but you knew! That's

why you...Why I didn't..." She could not speak another word because the next wave of sobs and convulsions overtook her.

"Ahndien," Lao-Ying said, "To assign blame—"

"Ah-Ba!" Through her tears, anger arose. Where was he? When his family needed him most? She grabbed the sword and hacked at a tree branch over and over until the blade became lodged. "Where were you!"

Ahndien resheathed the sword andleaned an arm on the branch. Her tears fell and slapped against a fallen leaf. Sorrow, rage and despair boiled to the surface. When her vision cleared, something on the ground caught her eye. Glinting in the setting sun, it sent a tingle through her veins. Ah-Ba's pendant, the leather neck strap torn open. It never left his person. He had been here.

And to the side of the pendant, large drops of blood coagulated in the dirt. A trail dug into the ground suggested that he had been dragged on his knees up to a wagon, where tread marks from its wheels took over.

She spun around to Lao-Ying, standing erect, his walking stick abandoned behind him. "They've taken my father!"

He lowered his eyes and bowed his head.

"I've got to help him." Ahndien yanked the sword out of the tree branch and slung her satchel over her shoulder. She knelt by the cloth covering the remains of Ah-Ma and Shao-Bao. With reverence, she rested her hand on them. "For the honor of our family," she said in a grave voice. "I will avenge you."

"Ahndien, wait." Lao-Ying stepped forward and reached for her arm. "Do not act rashly."

Her sword flew out of the sheath and sang a ringing, metallic song just as its sharp edge found its way right before Lao-Ying's chest. "You will not impede me again, you frail, old coward of a man!" Her heart pounded like Lunar Festival drums, fire coursed through her blood. Her chest rose and fell, her teeth clenched. A single tear drop burned a trail down her cheek.

But Lao-Ying didn't so much as blink. He took a deep breath and stood taller than Ahndien could remember. "Kill me, and you will never know the answer."

"Answer?" She hadn't yet asked any question. "To what?"

"To the questions that arise from reading that." He pointed to her satchel. "Your father's book."

A cold wind passed over her and caused her to shiver. How did he know it was in there? She jutted her jaw out. Leaned forward and pressed the sword into his shirt. "I have no questions."

With the steadfast fortitude of a man half his age, Lao-Ying gazed right into her eyes and said, "But you shall."

CHAPTER FOURTEEN

"YOUR RIDDLES DO NOT INTEREST ME," Ahndien said, certain the blade would break the old man's frail skin if she pressed in any further.

"I offer answers, not riddles." He tried to back away, but Ahndien kept the edge of the sword against his chest.

"How do I know you are not in league with the Torians?"

"I am not."

"How can I be certain?"

"You cannot. At least not presently. You can only trust me. Or not."

Regardless of his age, this man could not be trusted. She would cut the tiresome old man's heart out. Ahndien let out a frustrated grunt and swung the sword.

Lao-Ying's only reaction came so quick Ahndien never saw it happen. Before the blade ever reached him, he was upon her, his hand grasping her right wrist with crushing force. All strength from her arm, her hand, her entire right side drained out of her. Instantly, she dropped the sword and it clanked twice on the ground.

"You are most assuredly your father's daughter."

"How did you—?" She would have completed her sentence if not for the transformation in the old man. Before her very eyes, he began to radiate with wisps of white light, its warmth spreading out and caressing her face.

"You have his fighting spirit, his heart of justice."

"He is a scholar."

"And the brash temper of his youth."

The white brilliance washed out Lao-Ying's features, his cottony beard, his winged eyebrows. This continued until all was light. And his voice began to envelop her thoughts.

// BUT IF YOU HUMBLE YOURSELF, YOU WILL LEARN GREAT THINGS. YOU WILL FULFILL ALL FOR WHICH YOU ARE DESTINED //

Like a roaring fire, Lao-Ying's brilliance rose above her. Ahndien stooped down and turned her eyes upward. "Is it you?" The sun had fallen behind the hills and the sky had turned to blood and wine. But Lao-Ying's radiance illuminated the entire village as though it were midday.

When she could see clearly again, she beheld a great figure directly above her, against the deep violet backdrop peppered with stars. A rush of wind blew down from the figure's wings.

"Was it—?"

// IT WAS AND IS //

The Eagle. The great bird of prey. The one who had snatched up the mountain lions and saved her from their deadly jaws. "But I...I don't understand."

As he descended, a cloud of dust floated up around her. Ahndien covered her face and backed away, yielding to the massive bird whose wingspan covered more than two huts.

// THERE IS MUCH TO BE DONE. WE MUST LEAVE THIS PLACE //

With as much caution as awe, she approached. Touched the dark, brassy plumage. His feathers were surprisingly velvet. And yet, they seemed stronger than iron. Lao-Ying—the eagle—lowered and turned his gold-crested head such that his black pearl of an eye gazed straight down at her. His beak seemed more powerful and deadlier than any sword a human could wield, his feathered legs ended with yellow rapier-like talons. And yet, she did not fear.

// THE PATH BEFORE US IS AS LONG AS IT IS ARDUOUS //

One final look to her ravished village.

One final glimpse into her past, all that she held dear.

Ahndien's knees faltered.

The entire world began to sway.

Lao-Ying leaned towards her. As Ahndien fell, she reached forward and with both hands grasped at one of the feathers in his wing, expecting to pluck it and drop to the ground.

Instead, she found it as firmly rooted as a Xuh-Suh tree in the rocky side of the mountains. And before she could fully appreciate what was happening, that feather, no, the entire wing yanked her upwards, sending her hurtling into the air.

Too awed to let out a cry, Ahndien's mouth gaped silently, though no breath passed through. She flew high above the tall bamboo trees. And then, a mass of brown, black and gold rushed past her. The next thing she felt, just as she began to fall from the apex of her ascent, was a swift tug on the back of her shirt. Her entire body jerked to a stop, father's sword rattling at her side. As quickly as she had been caught in Lao-Ying's formidable beak, she was lowered onto his back.

She let out a childish shriek. "You're flying!"

If ever a giant bird could smile, Ahndien believed she had just seen it. He nodded, turned to face forward and let out a fierce eagle call that resounded in the hills.

// HOLD FAST, AHNDIEN //

She attempted to wrap her arms around his neck, but could not clasp her hands together.

// Grasp the feathers of my nape //

"But, won't that hurt?" What followed was not so much words in her mind, but what could only be described as laughter from the great bird. Ahndien swallowed. "If you say so." She slipped her hands under the golden, leaf-shaped feathers and wrapped the shafts twice around her hands like rope. So strong, yet so flexible.

Presently, she became aware of the rising and dipping of her own body as she straddled Lao-Ying's tree trunk of a neck. As they floated up higher with each flap of his wings, the wind grew stronger. The village below grew smaller.

Clouds of black smoke arose from the center of her family's hut. A sharp pang twisted inside her chest.

Ah-Ma.

Shao-Bao.

Fading behind as they soared away.

Sharp blasts of wind streaked tears across her face. She sniffed wetly and wiped her eyes on her shoulder. One last look, please. Then stretched her neck back, but could not see her home. Her left hand releasing a feather, she twisted her trunk around. Right away, she lost her balance. Nearly slippped over the right side of Lao-Ying's neck. She shouted in terror.

// AHNDIEN! //

The entire horizon fell diagonally as Lao-Ying banked upwards on his right and reestablished Ahndien's balance. She spun around, leaned forward and grasped as many of his feathers as she could. As she leaned against his neck, her heart pounded so hard he must have felt it.

// ARE YOU ALL RIGHT? //

Silently, she nodded, her face buried in the silk and steel feathers.

// I'M SORRY, LAO-YING. I WANTED ONE A LAST LOOK //

He righted himself and soared towards the top of the Maw-Shuh Mountains. From his beak, a sound rose above the beating wind, like steam escaping a large and tightly covered cauldron. A sigh.

//LOOK BACK AND YOU SHALL SURELY FALL //

// I UNDERSTAND //

// AND NOW, DEAR FLEDGLING, THE TIME HAS COME TO LEAVE BEHIND THAT WHICH CANNOT BE RECOVERED, AND CONFRONT THAT WHICH CANNOT BE ESCAPED //

CHAPTER FIFTEEN

FOR THE MOST PART, aside from the occasional insult and jab, Render managed to remain distant from Branson, who kept to himself anyway. This suited Render well enough.

Under Sir Edwyn's tutelage, instruction had in earnest begun. No one was more surprised than Render when it was discovered that he possessed a multitude of talents in various disciplines.

Perhaps it was due to that unquenchable thirst for knowledge. The very thirst which over the years had driven him to liberate the multitude of books from Bobbington's dust-blanketed library—if you could even call it a library. They were probably artifacts he'd either inherited or found. Render had never actually seen Bobbington read.

Now, with unlimited resources at his disposal, Render devoured knowledge like a starved cat. Which did he enjoy most, Astronomy, History, Philology? And then, there were the arts: painting, sculpting, and music—the lute became his instrument of choice. There was always one more line of music to master, one more vista to paint. Sir Edwyn had to chase him from the classroom nearly every night.

After two and a half fortnights, the only discipline in which Render failed to excel was the one he cared for least: The Martial Arts. Weapons, armor, tactics, and mounted combat. Of what use were these to him in this enlightened society which was now his home? How much more satisfying to wield a paintbrush than a longsword.

"Daylight is fleeting, Render." Edwyn stood at the door to the Artist's Chamber. He stretched and yawned and said, "Need I remind you of the rules, again?"

"I'm almost finished," Render murmured, unsatisfied with the way the blazing amber hues of the setting sun illuminated the back of the mountains in his painting. At least, he presumed it was sunlight. Still, something in it resembled fire, a beautiful inferno behind the hills.

Sir Edwyn approached and peered over his shoulder. He then made that growling noise which meant he was trying to understand. He pointed at the painting "Surely you've never been there before."

"How could I? This place exists only in my thoughts, my dreams."

"Oh, no. No, no, no. I assure you, this place does indeed exist. But there is little chance you have been there. Perhaps you've seen other paintings? Though, I doubt—"

"I have been seeing it in my dreams, in my sleep and during my more contemplative waking moments. But never have I seen it with my eyes. Nor have I derived such a landscape from other paintings or drawings. It's original."

Edwyn rubbed his beard and squinted. "So real, though. Are you certain you haven't ever been there, beheld it?"

"I've been a slave since childhood. Aside from my little adventures with Kaine and the twins, I've never wandered far from Talen Wood. At a great distance have I seen the eastern mountain range, from the top of Smyth's Hill. But it looks nothing like this."

"No, it does not. The view from Talen Wood could not reveal this westward perspective." Edywn pushed his way in front of Render who, without question, stepped aside. "What you have depicted here, and with remarkable accuracy I might add, is not visible from Smyth's Hill. This here is the tallest of all mounts and deepest into the desert. It separates Valdshire Tor from the Eastern Kingdom."

"Tian Kuo?

"Yes." He pointed to the subject of the painting, lit up with a fiery glow. But the sun didn't set over the Western side of that mountain. That was what seemed wrong and caused Render to suspect that the light he painted was not in fact sunlight, but perhaps fire. Edwyn continued. "This is Mount Handara, subject of legend and lore. But more importantly, it is a natural barrier between us..." he pointed out the window to the east, "...and them."

How had he seen it so clearly? And why? Render gazed upon the painting which for some reason did not seem like something he could have created. Although he recalled the sensation of the brush in his hands, the strokes against the canvas, and the image coming to life before his very eyes, it all seemed oddly detached. As if someone or something else had painted it.

"In any case," said Edwyn, beginning to clean up the classroom, "it is late and you were supposed to have been in your room by now."

Render placed all his brushes in the can of solvent, washed his hands in a basin. As he wiped his hands on a cloth, he thought of the twins, whom he had not seen for the past two weeks.

"Sir Edwyn, how are Folen and Stewan?'

"They are well. Somewhat lacking in motivation, but that is understandable." He began leafing through Render's finished paintings, stopping every once in a while to gaze thoughtfully at those that caught his eye. "It is you with whom I am more concerned."

At this Render paused and regarded his tutor, though Edwyn, too engrossed in the paintings, did not reciprocate. "Am I not learning to your satisfaction?"

"Quite the contrary. I have never had a student that I needed to warn off from working so hard. You stay up at all hours, unless I find you and send you to bed. You drive yourself twice if not thrice as hard as most ordinary students. All this work is admirable, but—"

"I was a slave. Or have you so soon forgotten?" Edwyn looked up. Render smiled and pointed to his paintings, to his lute on the table next to his history books and his poetry. "This is not work. This is joy. Freedom."

His mentor returned the smile and clapped him on the shoulder. "Would that all my students took your view."

"All my life, Sir Edward, I have felt I was meant to be someone of worth. Not by fame or acclaim, mind you. Just something more than a slave. Someone who, before he dies, will have left some kind of mark, no matter how small, on this world. Of this I am certain: I wasn't destined to live and die without purpose."

"And just what purpose would that be, young squire?"

"It was my hope that you could help me discover this."

"Perhaps I shall." Edwyn stretched his hand to the open door. "But not tonight."

Only torch and candle light illuminated the stone hallways of the castle. The sweet smell of wax filled Render's senses as they walked. Their shoes made the only sounds other than their scarce words. Render spoke quietly if at all. "What of you, Sir Edywn?"

"What of me?"

"You never speak of yourself. Surely you have discovered your purpose in life by now." They reached Render's chamber, which thankfully he shared with no one. Edwyn unlatched the door and it creaked open. He gestured for Render to go inside. "Well?"

"Perhaps another time, Master Render."

"But—"

"Good night."

Trying to hide his disappointment, he took a deep breath and inclined his head. "Good night, Sir Edwyn."

Carefully, lest the ancient hinges awaken all nearby, Render shut the large wooden door. With his back against it, he took a deep breath and set his candle on the desk next to him. He went to light the lamp near the bed when he noticed the cool sheet of moonlight flooding through the open window. So pleasing was this light that he decided blow out his candle and gaze outside.

From his window he beheld the moon and stars above, and the high wall of the citadel below. Not long ago, he had lived outside the walls of this great and ever-expanding Torian capital.

A lifetime ago.

Now, he lived in the castle of the Lord Agon. Neither slave nor servant, nor a ragged boy scraping the floor for a morsel. He was Master Render, a knight in training, royal ward of the High King Corigan.

As he drew the curtains, shutting out all light, something dropped to the ground.

"Hello?" Instead of the lamp, he reached under the pillow for his dagger. Steadily, Render got to his feet. Squinted into the blackness as he drew his blade.

He was not alone.

CHAPTER SIXTEEN

THE EDGE of Sir Mooregaard's broadsword glinted in the moonlight. Just moments before it came slicing down over Kaine's neck. Letting out a terrified gasp, Kaine felt a surge of fear rush from the bottom of his feet straight up his mail-clad back.

"No!" Kaine fell onto his side and rolled.

Mooregaard's sword hit the pavement, a finger's width from his ear. Sparks flew as it scraped the stone, sending pebbles and dust into Kaine's face. The loud clang echoed in his head. He leapt to his feet and spun his own broadsword around his head and pointed it forward.

"Had I not been so charitable, Master Kaine, you would have stood a head shorter."

Kaine laughed nervously. "Not your charity, but my speed."

Pale beams from a very full moon painted the walls and floor of the courtyard, illuminating a vulnerable position on Mooregaard's left. With both hands, Kaine swung his broadsword for a swift cut at his opponent's forearms, sure to relieve the black knight of at least one of his hands.

If only things went as expected.

In an instant, Mooregaard parried the attack with such force it knocked Kaine off his feet and onto his side, then flat on his back.

Again.

Barely enough time to react, he felt the wind of a blade thrusting down into his face. A brutal way to die. He shut his eyes even as the blade came smashing down, crushing, piercing.

Mooregaard scoffed. "So much for speed!"

Kaine touched his forehead, felt around for the blade that must be impaling it. But the absences of wet, sticky blood and pain permitted him to open his eyes. He turned his face upon his left check and felt the rough stone surface of the floor as well as something cold and smooth. All he could see was the reflection of his own eyes in the sword, still wobbling as it stood stabbing the stone brick on the ground.

Sir Mooregaard grabbed Kaine by the wrist and pulled him to his feet with such force Kaine feared his arm would dislodge. "As I said, young squire," Mooregaard said, laughing heartily, "Charity."

"Considering you twice nearly relieved me of my head, I'll agree." Kaine bent down and retrieved his sword and sheathed it at his side. "But at this rate, your charity will be the only way I will ever become a knight."

"And you know this based upon what point of reference?" Mooregaard came over and put his arm over Kaine's shoulder. He thought he might collapse under the weight of his mentor's arm. "How long have you been training?"

"A month or so."

"Have I any other students in my court?"

"Well, Sir, I...No, you do not." He wondered about

Render, Stewan and Folen. So engrossed in his training, Kaine had only now thought of his brother and the twins.

"Have you ever tested your mettle against another?"

"I have not."

"Then all you know is that you are not superior to me." At last, Mooregaard took back his arm. He then clapped Kaine on the back, nearly tripping him face-first onto the ground. "Do you think it coincidence that you are my sole pupil?"

"The Lady Volfoncé said that it was because of my age."

"And what does age have to do with it?"

He didn't know, never thought to question it. Kaine shrugged.

"Your deductive facilities concern me more than your combat skills." Mooregard, who towered over Kaine, gestured to the fire pit in the center of the courtyard. To the fire he followed the Don, the chief knight of The Order of the Scarlet Pendragon. The knight's formidable shadow, cast from the dancing flames, took a strange form which barely resembled its owner. Kaine rubbed his eyes and blinked. But it stretched out of sight. He stopped at the fire and waved Kaine over with impatience.

"You exhibit the qualities of a fine leader in the army of the High King. Even so, you must prove your worth. Your loyalty. You must know all that is at stake before you commit to so noble an enterprise."

"And now, Master Kaine," Mooregaard grasped his shoulders, just as Kaine had imagined his own father might have. Mooregaard swelled with pride and gazed straight into his yes. "You are ready to know the truth."

CHAPTER SEVENTEEN

A COLD BEAD OF SWEAT crept down Render's back. Someone or something lurked in the room, of that there could be no doubt. A scraping sound caused the hairs on his neck to stand. If it were a rat, it must be of a monstrous size. And if it were a thief or assassin, it must be very light on his feet.

Render unsheathed his dagger and reached over for the curtain. The lamp and sword lay across the room.

Out of reach.

Even breathing felt too dangerous. With his dagger pointed blindly into the middle of the darkness he grasped the corner of the curtain between his fingertips. In just a moment he would flood the darkness with moon beams and confront the intruder.

Stillness.

It's probably the wind, he thought. But even as he exhaled, something hit the table knocking things onto the ground. Without wasting another second, Render threw open the curtain. In an instant, bright moonlight filled the room. He jabbed his dagger into the air, swung around, searched for the intruder.

Nothing.

No one.

"Hang it all!" It couldn't have been his imagination. Render tried to slow his shallow breaths. Sure enough, lying there on the cold stone floor was his candle, separated from its pewter stand. He bent down to pick it up and then thought he heard something behind him.

On his bed.

With his heart pounding in his chest, he tightened his grip on the handle of his dagger.

Behind him, a soft, rumbling sound pulsed. Slow, steady.

In one swift move Render spun around and thrust his dagger forward.

"Aha!"

There, resting on the pillow was the intruder. It's greenish-blue eyes calmly examining him.

"What? Where did you—?"

The black cat lifted her head and stood up on all fours. She then yawned, leaning downwards on her forepaws, tail pointed up, and stretched. Eyes affixed on Render, she moved just slightly above the pillow's edge.

"Wait," said Render approaching her. "Aren't you that cat...back at the cave at Smyth's Hill?" Again, she lifted her head and regarded him with such clear eye contact Render could have sworn she was answering him. He just knew.

Then she sat, coiled herself up again, looked at Render, down at the pillow, and again back at Render. The purring started again and she rested her head over her paws.

"What in all of creation?"

She must have climbed the wall and the tree just outside the window. A million speculations floated in his mind.

But Render found himself too tired to sift through them all. He sheathed his dagger and placed it on the table.

The cat, though she rested her head on his pillow, continued to eye him. As if she were waiting for him.

"What? You think I should get some rest? You're not my mother, you know." The expression never meant anything to him before. But this time it caused a twinge in his heart. He had never known his mother. What she looked like when she smiled, how she would speak tenderly to him. He whispered, "Not my mother..."

At that her ears flattened, eyes narrowed, and gave a guttural growl.

"Fine." He lifted the blanket and prepared to get into bed, but the cat did not move. "Oh, come on now." She shut her eyes and ignored him. Annoyed, Render tried to nudge her. Then he tried to lift her but strange as it seemed, he could not. Her eyes still shut, it almost seemed like she was smiling. Right. As if a cat could smile.

"Bother that." Render simply climbed in and put his head on the pillow just beneath the cat who, to his great annoyance, insisted on resting a warm paw on top of his head, no matter how many times he moved it away.

Even so, her presence came as a welcome surprise since he hadn't really seen anyone for weeks. Stewan and Folen lived and studied in an entirely different part of the castle. And Branson, thankfully was never around. Besides the weekly communal dinner, Render lived in solitude most of the day.

Despite his annoyance, the undulating purrs and warmth from the cat comforted him. Since his former life as a slave there hadn't been any of the ubiquitous cats to whom he'd grown so accustomed to, save for the one Sir Edwyn had shooed away the first day Render walked through the citadel.

To be completely honest, he missed them.

Perhaps I'll keep her.

Though, it seemed, she had already decided to keep him. Nevertheless, as fulfilling as these days of training and education were, a companion would be welcome now.

Only one concern surfaced as he drifted off. Something made painfully obvious the last time he went to the market with Sir Edwyn.

He detests cats.

CHAPTER EIGHTEEN

SEATED BY THE FIRE RING with The Lord Mooregaard, who had just nearly decapitated him, Kaine trembled in anticipation. "My Lord," he said, "For what truth am I ready?"

Mooregaard paced behind him, slowly, back and forth. "Before I tell you, you must answer a few questions. And with complete honesty. Can you do this?"

Kaine turned to face him. "I think so."

"Very well then." Mooregaard stopped, and stood before him with one hand resting on the hilt of his sword. "By our very nature, we are beings ruled by belief. Wouldn't you agree?"

"Well, Sir, I—"

"Belief, however subjective, is ruled by choice, by perception. For example, what do you believe yourself to be? A boy? Or a man?"

Kaine pondered the question, unsure of how best to answer. "Well, I am of age. So I suppose that would make me..."

"Quickly, think not too long upon it."

"A man. Yes, I am a man."

"And not a boy."

"A man, Sir."

Mooregaard's chest swelled as he took in a deep breath. "Had you answered any other way, I'd have been disappointed. Indeed, you are a boy no longer. Particularly because you have proven yourself an able fighter. And judging by your many victories in the game of Leit, you are most perceptive in the ways of strategy."

Though pleased by the affirmation, Kaine began to perspire. The heat from the fire ring grew increasingly uncomfortable. But he dared not move. Not just now.

"As a man, my dear Kaine you shall be defined not so much by your words, nor by the beliefs you profess. Nay, you shall be defined by your actions and choices. Particularly the difficult ones, the ones of ambiguous nature."

"I see." But all he really saw was the vision of himself a minute or two from now, burning as the flames melted his flesh. The flames from the fire ring were getting too hot. "Lord Mooregaard, if you don't mind terribly—"

"Do not interrupt. We discuss matters of grave importance. Now then. On to the questions."

"But sir—"

"Not now! We must press forward, for tomorrow your future will be determined. But first—"

"Sir, please!" Kaine stood up. The wind from rising and stepping away from the fire alone cooled him enough to afford some relief.

"Sit down, boy. Or I swear, I'll tie you down!"

"Yes, My Lord." Kaine obeyed but sat on a chair. Away from the fire ring. From this moment on, he'd be able to give his undivided attention.

Mooregaard cleared his throat. "Now, then. Kaine,

what is your purpose as a citizen of Valdshire Tor?"

"To serve my King, protect and defend my land from attacks both exotic and clandestine. But first and foremost, from the unseen enemy that is ignorance, superstition."

"Yes, yes. Any student can recite the pledge of royal fealty." Mooregaard pointed the tip of his sword straight at Kaine's heart. "What do you say your purpose is?"

Kaine tugged on his collar which suddenly felt tighter. "I'm not certain."

"I see in you valor, honor, all of which are hallmarks of a great leader, a leader of the next generation."

"But how do you know?"

"You will lead. But I must know if your priorities are in order. First: Given the choice of obeying your Lord, or commander in combat, or even your king, or obeying your conscience, your ideas of right and wrong, which would you chose?"

"My conscience."

"It is well spoken. Commanders, kings even, are all but mere men, all fallible. A true leader leads by conscience, not the approval of man. Now, second: Given the choice of obeying your conscience or violating it, to aid a friend or even, a loved one, which would you chose?"

Immediately, Kaine thought of the one person to whom this might one day, however hypothetical, apply. His reply was not as swift this time. Would that he'd never face this question in real life. "Well... I suppose, I'd still chose my conscience."

The ebony knight drew his lips into a taut line, set his eyes in an austere gaze. "Few have understood the implications of these questions. Fewer still have answered as well. And only they can be entrusted with the truth, because only they shall know how to act upon it. Verily, I say, you are indeed ready."

For the rest of the night, Kaine sat rapt in wonder at all Sir Mooregaard taught him. The history not only of Valdshire Tor, but of the world, all that could be known of it, from every aspect: Technology, culture, science and even an explanation of Valdshire Tor's ancient enemy.

"For as long as anyone can remember, before all written history," Mooregaard said, now seated before Kaine, "we have been at war with the Sojourners, those religious fanatics of the East In the name of their deity, Valhandra, these honorless cowards attack the innocent, sparing neither woman nor child. They employ terror where no decent warrior would imagine unsheathing a sword. They know no battle ground for their cowardice drives them to attack the unsuspecting during times of ostensible peace."

"Why do they war against us?" This was something he pondered since childhood. According to his former master, the Sojourners attacked the village of his parents and killed them. He and Render were not quite three and two years old, respectively, barely able to feed themselves. Both brothers were taken away, traveled westward for three days and sold to the people of Talen Wood into a life of slavery.

But now, to their great fortune, King Corigan's annexation of the backwards village had reversed all that. And it seemed fate had smiled upon Kaine, affording what might well be the chance to avenge his parents' death.

"Why do the Sojourners attack us?" Mooregaard huffed. "For our belief in universal freedom. Our way of life, some might argue."

"Might you expound on that, our way of life?"

Mooregaard sat back in his chair, rested his elbow on the hilt of his sword and cleared his throat. "Torians are rational, scientific, intellectually and culturally minded, we believe in tolerance of all people, despite our differences. But Tian Kuo is filled with fanatical zealots."

"Why have the Sojourners killed so many? What is it they want?"

"They wish to impose their superstitious ways on all. In the name of Valhandra, they hate, they terrorize, and they murder."

"My parents..." They too fell victim. For that reason had he been reminded and taught to fear, to hate the Sojourners, since childhood. Quickly, he pushed the grief into the recesses of his mind. "Do not all nations fight over religious ideals?"

Mooregaard straightened up, removed his helmet and placed a firm hand on his shoulder. "My young squire, if you have learned nothing else, mark this well: The people of this great kingdom are not beholden to any man-made superstition. Religion is but a walking stick for the feeble of mind. Any modern man with a sound head on his shoulders knows this. All this talk of magic, and the spirit realms, why, it's the stuff of fairy tales, nothing more."

"Lord Mooregaard," he said, his voice breaking. "Do you know anything about the attack on my parents' village?"

Mooregaard stood, sheathed his broadsword and held Kaine's own weapon out to him. "The hour grows late. You must be well-rested for your combat exams tomorrow."

"But I should like to know more about—"

"In due time. Remember, your knighthood, your very future depends on fulfilling this course of training. And as I have repeatedly said tonight, you are ready."

CHAPTER NINETEEN

THEY HAD FLOWN for two days away from the sun setting over the Eastern summits which stood like a fortress that separated the two great kingdoms. It had been Ahndien who wanted to stop and rest before entering the western mountain range, not so much because she felt tired, but because she was afraid.

Something about those snow covered peaks had always called to her, her sense of adventure. And at the same time, as she and Lao-Ying drew nearer, a cold dread darkened her heart like an overwhelming shadow. Such as when the moon stands before the sun and throws the entire world into darkness, when it ought to be light.

"We are not far from Handara," Lao-Ying said, now in his frail human form. The air was crisp and laced with the minty scent of pine. It sent a chill through Ahndien's body. The breeze, pure and clear, seemed to blow right through her body.

"I feel like we should wait." She sat upon a large rock, unbuckled and set her father's sword at her feet. "I'm not quite ready."

"In more ways than one, you are right." At some point, he must have started a fire, but Ahndien had not been paying attention. Her eyes and thoughts were drawn to the mountains with overwhelming ambivalence.

"I am going to get food, please fill the flask with water." He pointed to the glassy stream which flowed relentlessly down. Following its course, Ahndien saw how it ran all the way from the mountains down past this place. From the air, she had traced it past her village. This led to the Emerald River, which served as the main water supply for the great city of Tian Kuo.

"Are we having duck again?"

Lao-Ying grinned, his cottony eyebrows arching. "Would you prefer something heartier...mountain lion, perhaps?"

"No, thank you. Duck will be fine."

The old man laughed quietly and leapt into the air. "I won't be far."

"Are you sure?" The thought of being left alone made her heart beat forcefully.

"All can be seen from above, remember?" Before his body even began to fall, he transformed again. His gigantic wings kicked up leaves, branches and stones as he flew off with a piercing eagle's cry.

"I'll never get used to that." She stepped over father's sword and went to the babbling stream. With her hands cupped, she plunged them into the water. It was so pure, so cold she just had to take a drink before filling the flask. The first handful soothed her so much that she almost forgot about the lingering pain that she'd been carrying but stuffed away like too much clothing into a sack. Her mother, her little brother, she'd never see them again.

Oh, but the water did refresh her so.

It seemed to refresh her spirit as much as her thirst.

She would try not to cry for her family just now because if she did, she feared she would never stop. And how then would she go about finding Ah-Ba and return the sword?

His sword.

One of which she had taken without permission.

She could only hope that he'd been able to use the other one of the pair to defend himself against those Torian dogs. She had never felt so sad, so alone in all her life. Her vision blurred as a pang twinged the center of her chest. Quickly she wiped the tear before it could fall.

To soothe her thoughts, she took the flute from her pocket and began to play a cheerful song. But her own hiccupping breaths caused the melody to stutter. With a deep, wet breath, she sighed, wiped her upper lip and tried again.

For as long as she could remember, the only songs she ever played were simple tunes that Ah-Ba had taught her. Some of them she made up as the inspiration afforded. This time, the most beautiful melody she had ever played filled the hills. It was a long melodious line, still based on the five-note pentatonic scale so prevalent in the music of Tian Kuo, but its meter, phrasing and accents...there almost seemed to be words.

A patch of blue sky opened in the clouds and the sun shone warmly through. From the corner of her eye, she noticed that every tree branch—fallen or on the trees surrounding her—was filled with birds of many kinds. Sparrows, crows, doves, even owls and eagles (the normal-sized kind.) Each of them cocked their head at one point or another to get a better look at Ahndien as she played this song—a song that felt as familiar as a distant memory.

Four songbirds alighted on her shoulders and sang along while she played. Ahndien stood and began to stroll through the trees, an entourage of birds chirping, twittering, and fluttering gently around her.

This continued as she strolled by the side of the stream, delighted at her newfound friends. She'd always noticed that birds came to her when she played the flute, it was nothing particularly unusual to her. But this time, she felt a connection with them, a sort of kinship, for lack of a better term.

Turning back into the woods, Ahndien repeated the song, her eyes shut, taking in the sun on her face, the fresh pines, the harmonious bird songs, until something stopped her like a wall of ice.

Not even opening her eyes, she knew something was wrong.

The birds had stopped singing.

Ahndien lowered the flute from her lips.

Opened her eyes.

There, standing about a yard before her, stood a large gray wolf waiting to pounce, its sharp teeth snarling with malice.

CHAPTER TWENTY

FROM BEHIND A THICKET, three more wolves emerged. White drool dangled from their open jaws.

"Not again."

Careful not to make any sudden move, Ahndien slid her flute into her pocket and reached for her sword.

But it wasn't there.

She'd left it by the fire.

"Lao-Ying?" Barely a whisper. She was too afraid to raise her voice.

The undulating sound of four hungry wolves slowly closing in rumbled. She could feel the vibrations in her fingertips. A cold trickle of sweat rolled down the center of her back.

Part of her wanted to cry. But she pushed it back down to that place where she kept the sad memories of her family. "Lao-Ying?"

// YOUR FATHER'S SWORD...//

One of the wolves took a step forward, but turned

around and snapped at the wolf behind him who had gotten too close.

"Where are you?"

// I AM COMING, FIGHT THEM OFF! //

"How?"

// FROM YOUR HEART //

That made no sense. The sword lay on the ground, under the foot of the furthest wolf. Desperate, Ahndien took out her flute. She anticipated the wolves mocking her as the mountain lions had—somehow communicating their thoughts to her. They would laugh at the little wooden tube with eight holes, the choice weapon of a peasant girl.

But nothing like that happened.

These were common, witless beasts. And that made them seem even more dangerous.

From your heart.

Without a better choice than to trust the old eagle, she put the flute to her lips. And blew a fierce note so shrill, it made her teeth hurt.

Startled, the wolves stopped.

Blinked.

Shook their ears.

And continued to lurk forward.

How much would it hurt to be ripped to shreds by wolves? How far was Lao-Ying, if he wasn't already back to help? With nothing left to do but heed his advice, she began to play a song. Not a fast, angry song, but one that came from that place in her heart where all the fear, sorrow, and hopes lay waiting for her to unlock.

As she played, her eyes were shut but streaming with

emotion, ruffling sounds filled the air. The birds on her shoulders flew off. Terse growls and snarls mixed into the cacophony. Ahndien opened her eyes to find countless birds around her swarming around the lead wolf. Mercilessly, they flapped wings in its face, pecked at its eyes, its neck, until it fell to the ground thrashing about, snorting and trying to breathe.

Ahndien kept playing.

The lead wolf finally got up and ran into the woods, all the birds following. Two more, also engulfed in the avian attack followed it. Ahndien was so excited she stepped forward, as though chasing them away.

Just then, Lao-Ying landed in the form of a human. He crumpled to the ground, breathing heavily.

"Lao-Ying!"

"Stay alert!" He held up his hand trying to keep her back. His chest rose and fell rapidly. Struggling to keep himself upright, the old man could not seem to stand to his feet.

Without warning, one of the wolves of which Ahndien had lost track jumped and landed on Lao-Ying.

"No!" The old man put his arms up to shield his face and the wolf sunk its teeth into his wrist.

Ahndien whirled around and found the sword.

In three quick steps she grabbed it, unsheathed it and charged the wolf with a ferocious shout. She stopped right behind the wolf and lifted the sword. "Get off of him!"

In an instant, the wolf turned around and leapt onto Ahndien knocking her onto her back. The sword hit the dirt silently. The beast planted its forepaws on her chest and lowered its foul-smelling mouth over her neck.

It was all she could do to wrap her hands around its thick neck and keep its fangs away from her neck. Her thoughts scattered to every possible place: Lao-Ying on the ground—had he been injured? First mountain lions—now wolves, Father at the hands of Torian soldiers—what would they do to him?

// FROM YOUR HEART, AHNDIEN! //

Lao-Ying's thoughts seemed so much stronger than she'd expected. They brought her back to the moment. From your heart. Images of little Shao-Bao and Ah-Ma, at the hands of their attackers floated into her mind. An urgent need to defend them overwhelmed her thoughts.

Rancid breath flew into her face as the snarling wolf thrashed its head to the left and right, trying to free itself from her grip. Drops of its hot saliva fell on her face, fractions of an inch from her eyes.

And then it happened.

Something Ahndien could never have imagined.

At first it felt as though she had drank some very hot soup. The heat in her belly rose up, but instead of coming up her throat, it went through her limbs, out to her fingertips. When she opened her eyes, she could see nothing but golden light.

The wolf let out a painful whine and flew off of her body, as though someone very large had kicked it away. Not wasting a moment, in case the wolf attacked again, she grabbed the sword, leapt to her feet and swung around looking for the wolf.

Where was it? When she turned fully around she found it. Laying just a few feet from Lao-Ying. The wolf lay on its side, its entire body blackened. Smoke rose from it and small flames continued to lick up out of its scorched body. What now remained of its tail was nothing but a thin black crisp, twitching as black tendrils of smoke rose up into the air. The wolf whined in agony, pink and black flesh peeling off of its body.

"But how—?"

"Have mercy, Ahndien." As though nothing interesting had just happened, Lao-Ying stood up, brushed his sleeves and pants off. "Finish it off. It suffers in pain."

She lifted the sword.

"I...I've never..."

"For everything, there is an occasion. It would have killed and devoured you had you not defended yourself. You must now show it mercy by ending its suffering quickly."

The wolf, now breathing rapidly let out a mournful wail.

"Now, Ahndien."

She understood, even felt compassion for the wolf now. It was not evil, only hungry. In the clash for survival, she had won. Now she must help it before it suffered any longer. "I'm sorry." With one quick blow, she struck it in the heart. The wolf lurched in relfex, then let out a long, expiring breath.

Ahndien steadied herself on the hilt of the sword and sank to her knees. "I'm sorry." No matter what the reason, she hated killing. Yes, she was helping to end the pathetic beast's suffering, but it didn't make this task any more pleasant.

Lao-Ying came over and put his hand on her shoulder. "You have learned the first of many important lessons in warfare: A warrior cannot escape killing, but he must never forget to show mercy and honor."

So much death.

In the past few days she had gone from a carefree girl, simple in understanding, innocent about the ways of the world, to one whose life now had come into turmoil.

She put her hand upon Lao-Ying's and patted it. Then she stood and looked him over. "What happened to you?

Are you hurt?"

He frowned, looked down and shook his head. "No."

"Then why—? Well, you did help me with that last wolf."

"You underestimate your own combat skills."

"I didn't do anything. Was it not you who set the wolf on fire while—?" She looked into his eyes. A knowing smile creased the corners of his mouth and three distinct lines grooved his shiny forehead.

"From your heart, Ahndien. From there did you fight." He was gazing at her hands.

Even before she looked at them herself, she began to understand. She held up one hand, palm up. And from her fingertips, tiny flames continued to stream.

CHAPTER TWENTY-ONE

RENDER'S NEW LIFE so consumed his time and thoughts that he barely realized that three months had passed. Now that he and Kaine had found each other, on the rare occasion, they'd steal away in the middle of the night to explore—like they had back in Talen Wood—and find secluded locations such as rooftops, where they'd play tricks on passersby walking below, or just talk about their new lives.

Tonight, Render was not in the mood to pour water from the roof onto the people in the street. So Kaine suggested a contest to see who could knock over the most jars or earthen pots lined up on a tree branch, using nothing but small stones.

But even this didn't hold Render's interest. Something had been troubling him.

Thoughts.

Dreams.

"You're not concentrating." Kaine handed him another rock. "What's the matter with you?"

"Wrong? I don't know what you're talking about." Render tossed a stone at the first jar and it flew clear of the entire branch. "Sometimes, I just have this feeling that we'll see her again one day."

"Who?"

Render looked down at the rock in his hand. After a false start or two he answered. "Mother."

Kaine's smile remained for a while, but gradually faded. He threw a stone, missed a jar, and clicked his tongue. "Even if she were still alive, why would you want to see her?" Kaine took another shot. This time, with a crisp crack the pebble broke a tiny hole in the center of the smallest jar on the branch, and clinked around inside without so much as tipping it over.

"Good shot."

"I for one have no interest in even remembering her." A smug expression came over Kaine's face.

Render grabbed his shoulder and turned him. "But, she was our mother."

"It's your turn. Stop making excuses to cover your poor aim."

"I'm not joking. How can you speak that way of our mother?"

"I don't want to talk about her, all right? Now, throw your stupid rock or I'll throw you."

"Fine." He did, and this time it struck a large goblet. It made a ringing sound and fell over into the back alley where a cat shrieked in disapproval. "You never want to talk about her."

"A fair assessment."

"Why not?"

"We are not going to discuss it."

"But I want to."

"It doesn't matter what you want, this discussion is over." Kaine got up and climbed down from the roof, leaving Render beyond frustrated.

"Wait!"

But Kaine marched down the alley, not heeding him. By the time Render got to the ground, Kaine was halfway to the open street. "I said wait!"

When he caught up to Kaine, he shoved his shoulder.

"I'm in no mood for your annoyances." Kaine shoved Render back, sending him to the ground. As he turned around to walk off, Render hooked his foot and tripped him.

"I am sick of your arrogance—all these years, treating me like a child!"

Kaine got up, grabbed him by the shirt and pulled him up. "You blathering idiot!" He slammed Render's back against the wall so hard, it knocked the wind out of him. "You are a child!"

"You're...not...my father!" For the first time in his life, he felt such anger towards Kaine he actually did something about it. Render kicked him in the shin. "And you're certainly not my mother!"

With a furious grunt, Kaine wrestled him to the ground. They thrashed about, each trying to pin the other down or land a solid blow. But all they accomplished was kicking up clouds of dust and tiring themselves out.

Kaine pushed away and held up his hands. "What is the matter with you!"

"What's the matter with you?"

"I asked you first!"

Huffing and coughing, Render wiped the caked dirt from his mouth. "You're only a couple of years older than me. Why do you always have to treat me like you're my parent? I'm sick to death of it!"

"You want to know why? Really? Well, fine then. I'll tell you why!" Catching his breath, Kaine approached, despite his brother's defensive posture. His features softened and he stooped over, hands on his thighs like Render, and looked him in the eye. "Mother put me in charge of your safety when you were just a baby. I promised to look after you."

"But why are you so angry whenever I ask about her?"

His eyes became distant, as if foreseeing an impending disaster, but not being able to avert it. "Because...."

"Because what?"

The transformation of his demeanor came about so gradually, Render didn't recall when the tears actually began to fall from his brother's eyes. All that anger melted away like the wax of a candle, leaving behind an extinguished wick of sorrow.

"Because she left us."

Whatever it was that hit Render, it carried the weight of seventeen years of waiting and wondering, longing to know the truth of his origins. "No. You're lying! She wouldn't do that to us!"

Kaine sniffed sharply and wiped his face. "I'm sorry. I didn't want to tell you because....well... I was protecting you."

"I don't need your blasted protection!" Forgetting the trouble he had just caused by doing so, Render shoved his brother. "I'm not a child!"

But Kaine did not retaliate. Instead of anger or insult, only pity appeared in his eyes. "All these years you wanted to know about her, wanted to believe that one day we'd see her again. I'm sorry, I just couldn't— "

"You lied to me!" Now he was punching Kaine in the arm. But Kaine did not fight back.

"I wasn't lying, I just couldn't tell you the truth. For your own good."

"Don't ever protect me again! You will never again determine what is for my own good! Curse you, Kaine!

Why didn't you just tell me the truth from the beginning?"

Kaine only blinked.

"Why!"

"I don't know. Maybe deep down, I wanted to believe what you did. That we might see her again one day. That once we were loved."

Render sniffed away bitter tears. "How could she love us if she just left us like that? Defenseless children, to be raised as slaves?"

"That can't have been her intention."

"I hate her!"

"No, Render. Don't say that. This is precisely why I didn't want to tell you. You mustn't hate her."

"But you do!"

"I'm angry at her for leaving us. But...well, that doesn't mean I hate her."

They stood, staring at each other's bloodshot eyes, trying to look tough, not like pathetic children. Finally, not knowing what else to say to his brother, Render turned his back and whispered bitterly, "Just leave me alone."

"Come on, Rend–"

"Don't!" He held up a finger. "I said, Leave me alone!"

Kaine's feet dragged across the dirt until he was gone and all that could be heard was the busy goings about of the people in the square, getting ready to go home and eat dinner with their families. Children laughed and skipped down the streets, calling out, "Mother," or "Father." This dragged Render to the ground with his back against the wall. He lowered his face into his knees and wept.

"I don't hate you, Mother." In fact, more than ever, he wished he could see his parents. He would even settle for remembering her face, the sound of her voice, the smell of her perfume, which must surely be a sweet as honeysuckle.

And then, to his surprise, something warm pressed up against his leg. Without lifting his face, Render reached out and felt soft fur. "Hello?"

The black cat, stared up at him with those deep emerald eyes. Render smiled. "Oh, it's you again." She leaned her head against his hand and purred.

CHAPTER TWENTY-TWO

THE SUN HAD JUST BEGUN its ascent over the western hills, but Edwyn had already been awake and about the wood for two hours. For the most part, the guards at the citadel gates knew of his morning routine, or ritual, as one might call it.

No one else knew of his visits to the now barren wood that had long been abandoned since his childhood village had been annexed into the ever-expanding kingdom. And though for decades, nothing remained of his home, his past, his family, Edwyn continually returned to the ruins to think, to remember. Or perhaps to forget, he couldn't be sure which.

The sentry called down from his tower. "A fine morning, Sir Edwyn."

"Indeed." Edwyn pulled down his hood, turned his eyes upwards and nodded his thanks as the enormous iron gates opened for him. Render would soon be at the library awaiting his history lesson. And his combat exams thereafter, to be taken against the worst possible opponent. An opponent who by now was certainly an able swordsman under the tutelage of the King's premier military commander.

If he had survived the training.

Edwyn tightened his belt and hastened his steps past the merchants selling their wares, the farmers peddling their produce and livestock. Even in the fresh of the morning, the stench of rotting vegetables and yesterday's refuse hung in the air. But such was life in the citadel. If he hadn't been accustomed to it by now, he never would be.

As he continued, he noticed the haggard man who every day since the kingdom of Valdshire Tor had begun to expand its protectorate towards the Eastern borders, stood by Hawthern Fountain, pacing back and forth speaking quietly only to those that would stop and listen. Many mocked him and called him 'The Prophet.'

"Will you lend an ear today, Sir Edwyn?" The grimy prophet gently grasped his elbow. "It's about your—"

"My answer has remained steadfast for the past eleven years, old man. It shall not today change." Usually, The Prophet would release his arm and turn to another passerby. This time, he clutched it harder.

"The time is at hand," The Prophet said. "You of all people must hear my message."

"I think not. Kindly unhand me."

He did not.

Instead, The Prophet tightened his grip with alarming force. "Hear me, for I know all about you, your parents, what they—"

"Unhand me!" Edwyn shoved The Prophet with what should have only been adequate strength to gain release. But the old man fell back and landed with a weak grunt. His mouth remained agape as he lifted a finger and pointed at Edwyn. "Hear me, Sir Edwyn. I implore you."

"Defending the kingdom from the frail and elderly, I see." A voice from behind him said. Edwyn clenched his teeth. His face burned as he turned around to respond. "Mooregaard."

"Lord Mooregaard, if you please." He climbed down from his black steed, stepped past Edwyn and offered a hand to help the old man to his feet. The Prophet thanked him politely, never taking his oddly cautious eyes from him. Carefully, he backed away and bowed, then turned to the opposite side of the fountain.

"It is not as it seems," Edwyn said, as he started off for Castle Mittelvald. "I did not intend to... I merely tried to pry free from his grip."

"And a fine job you did of it," Mooregaard said, overtaking his stride. "For he did seem rather dangerous." Then, standing directly in his path, he bent down such that his nose nearly touched Edwyn's forehead and said, "Perhaps you are now ready to battle widows and small children."

"Not all battles are with flesh and blood," Edwyn replied, quoting the old book, the only tangible reminder of his parents, though he knew not why the words came to his lips.

"But those of significance...are."

"How reassuring that the High King has entrusted his military to those possessing such intelligence as yours."

Mooregaard stepped back a few steps, drew his broadsword and pointed at the dagger sheathed at Edwyn's belt. "But such belligerence does so betray your—shall we call it—weapon envy?"

Edwyn gave him a wry grin and shook his head. "I should like to say that your demise will come by the sword, but it is more likely that it come as a consequence of your folly and pride."

"What do you know of pride, you of questionable lineage?"

Edywn drew his dagger. For a brief moment, despite the impossible odds, he considered fulfilling the dream he'd dreamed since he and Mooregaard trained as fellow wards of the King: to rush him and cut his throat. Edwyn clutched the handle so hard the dagger shook in his hands.

"Now, now. Is that any way for a learned man to settle his differences?"

"I swear, if you ever mention my parents again, I'll... I'll—"

"You'll what?"

Reason returned along with the good sense to keep his limbs. Regaining his composure, Edwyn put his dagger away, took a deep breath and held his chin high.

A smile stretched across Lord Mooregaard's face as he too replaced his sword, and mounted his horse again. "Well then. Is your student ready for the exams?"

"You will be surprised at Render's swordsmanship."

"Little surprises me. We'll see you here by Hawthern Fountain, at the tenth hour."

"Why do you insist on making these exams a public spectacle?"

"Because my students—the highest rated to date, mind you—deserve recognition." He started riding off, then stopped to add, "And they never lose."

CHAPTER TWENTY-THREE

HOW UNLIKE SIR EDWYN to be tardy for lessons. Render stood at the balcony peering out into the courtyard with his books tied in a bundle and slung over his shoulder. Beyond the castle walls, people of the citadel were resurrected from an entombed slumber. Buyers, sellers, town criers, they all seemed to have a purpose, a vocation, simple though they might be.

Harsh as slavery had been, for Render, freedom opened the door for a new kind of despair. The uncertainty of one's purpose in life.

What shall I be? What shall be my lot in life? Unaccustomed to making choices for himself, the prospect of having to do so made him uneasy. Especially because of that troublesome feeling that he was meant to do something of great significance. What if he chose his path incorrectly?

He thought about his favorite activities and scoffed. "I don't suppose my paintings or music could have much of an impact on the world."

"Play me a song on your lute, and I'll tell you," said the familiar voice. Render turned around.

"Folen!" He could barely recognize the boy in the garb of a squire, a short sword at his hip.

"I've been searching all over this castle for you."

"Seems ages since I last saw you and your brother. Have you grown taller?" Render met him half way and gave him a one-armed embrace.

"We've had no opportunity to explore," he said. "You know Sir Edwyn."

"He's a task master, he is." But Render said this with a smile. "Whatever he may be, he's late today."

"And I seem to have misplaced my brother." Folen searched behind Render, as though Stewan might be hiding there.

Render wanted to know more about all they had been doing, or if they'd heard anything about Kaine recently. He tried to ask, but Folen's eyes kept wandering, searching around the balcony, back into the castle. "Folen, when did you last see your brother?"

"After breakfast. We were waiting in the library to receive our assignments from Sir Edwyn, when Branson—"

"Oh. Branson."

"Yes. He popped his flat little head in and told Stewan that Sir Edwyn wished to speak with him immediately and that he was sent to fetch him. So Stewan followed him out into the hallway."

"Bother that."

Folen nodded. "When too much time had passed, I went out to look for them. But I haven't found any of them yet. I'm worried." As he spoke, the faint, yet distinct sound of laugher, not the good-natured kind but more of a malicious variety, alerted Render. It came from the doorway.

"Branson!" Render called out. "Where is Stewan?"

"Wouldn't you like to know?"

Folen growled and whirled around and pulled out his sword. "You little beast!"

But Render held his arm and whispered, "If you hurt him, you'll have his father to reckon with, or worse, Edwyn."

"I was only planning on batting him with the flat side of the blade."

"Well," said Branson, pursing his lips, "Good day." And with that, he ran back into the castle.

"Come back here!" Immediately, Render gave chase. Folen followed directly behind. When they entered the hallway, Branson stopped at a corner, stuck out his tongue and made a flatulent sound. He stood there watching for a reaction.

"You would almost think he wanted to get caught," Folen said.

"Or he's setting a trap."

As soon as Render took a step forward, Branson reacted. "Ha! You'll never catch me!" He turned and bolted down another hallway.

"Come on!" Render grabbed Folen's arm and they raced towards the bend, footfalls echoing through the cavernous passageways. Again, the little rat turned a corner, taunting them.

"Not so clever as you thought, are you? Lowborn dungslingers!" Again, Branson vanished behind another corner.

"That's it!" Folen snarled and started after him again. "I don't care if his father is The Lord Agon, nor do I care what Sir Edwyn says, I am going to teach that brat a lesson."

"Not if I get to him first." Render said. They flew down

the hall with such determination that Render barely noticed the suit of armor, the tapestries and other art work on the walls and how they became increasingly sparse, as they proceeded deeper into unfamiliar regions of the castle.

They came upon their destination rather suddenly. About thirty paces away, the hallway ended and there stood Branson, the look on his face daring Render to come after him.

And, as Branson was the only person who seemed to know where Stewan was, that is exactly what Render did. But just as he came within striking distance, the little maggot slipped into a door that Render had not seen until the moment it slammed shut.

"Hey!" Oddly enough, Branson hadn't locked the door. Render pulled it open and what he saw inside arrested his breath.

Even Folen stood silent.

The sound of the door latches hung in the air like dust-flecks in slats of sunlight. Shelves filled with books and curios lined the walls, a table with parchments, quills and dark inkwells stood in the center of the vast chamber. And in the back room sat a bed, a pewter pitcher and a basin.

"It's a museum," Folen whispered, forgetting about their quarry.

"There must be thousands of them," Render strode over and reached up to touch one of the old leather bound tomes in the shelf.

As his fingertips touched it, a loud slam jolted him from his trance. When he swung around, he saw the large wooden door closed. The sound of keys and chains tinkled on the other side.

"You're in it deep, now." Branson said from the other side, as he locked them in.

CHAPTER TWENTY-FOUR

I'M IN HERE!" a muffled voice called out amidst repeated pounding. It came from within the bed chamber of this museum, or library, or whatever this odd place was. Render dashed over.

"Stewan?"

"In here!"

He turned around and went over to a closet door, removed the chair blocking it and opened it.

"I'll...I'll cut his ears off!" Stewan growled.

"Are you all right?" Render said.

"I'm fine, just very, very angry." Stewan bolted out of the bedchamber. But his footfalls stopped abruptly. "Where is that idiot Branson? I'll kill him!"

"I'm afraid it won't be that simple?" Render said.

"Why are you two just standing around?" Stewan demanded.

Folen shook his head. "He's locked us in."

While the twins complained and cursed Branson for his treachery, Render's eyes drifted to the multitude of books in the shelves. There were books on history, astronomy, philosophy, physical sciences and poetry. Perhaps being locked in here was not the worst imaginable fate.

Render ran his hand along the first row of books he came across and for some reason stopped on the spine of a book called Venerable Tales and Fables of the Handara. When he slid it out of the shelf, he noticed a glint of light reflecting from the space behind the books.

"Render!" Stewan called out. "How are we going to get out of here?"

But he didn't answer. Something about the object behind the books drew him deeper. Carefully, he removed two books on each side of the empty space left from the first book.

"We've missed our lesson with Sir Edwyn," Folen groaned. "He'll be exceedingly cross with us."

Not heeding, Render reached into the back of the bookcase and grasped the object which hung from a nail on a leather bootlace. A key.

"What's that for?" Stewan said, now at Render's side and peering over his arm. Folen continued to joggle the door and mutter.

"Something of great interest, I'm sure," Render said, searching the library. Nothing appeared to require a key so he stepped into the bedchamber. Found even less there. He scratched his chin. "If I had something to hide, where would I...?"

"Under the bed," Stewan said.

"Brilliant!" They both dropped to the ground, lifted the edge of the blanket and let out a excited shout.

Out from under the rickety wood frame, a blur of gray and black shot out, screeching and skittering on the ground.

"Rat!" Stewan leapt up but tripped over his own foot. He fell back on his rear and crawled back on his hands and feet, like a crab. Render gasped, but found it more amusing than frightening. The rodent scurried straight out to the library, between Folen's shoes and though the space at the bottom of the splintery door.

"Whoever lives here must not be very clean," Folen said, checking his feet.

"I'm just hoping he'll come back before we get gnawed to death!" Stewan said, shuddering.

"Or starve to death," said Stewan. "I haven't had breakfast yet."

"For all the both of you eat, it's amazing you're not a big as elephants," Render said. "I'm sure your master back in Talen Wood is glad that you've been liberated."

"I don't feel so liberated, now," Folen said, rattling the door. But Stewan's countenance darkened. His eyes became red and his lower lip quivered.

Render turned fully to face him. He grasped the boy's shoulder. "What is it?"

"I just—" He sniffed, holding back a sob. "They were so kind to us. Treated us like their children, not slaves. They were the closest we ever had to a mother or a father." Stewan buried his face into his arms draped over his knees and whimpered.

"I never knew that, Stew." Render slid over and put his arm fully around the boy's shoulders. "You must miss them terribly."

"I do."

"Well, maybe we can talk to Sir Edwyn. You know, arrange for some visitation time. After all, the government might treat you differently, knowing that you were more like adopted children than slaves. It's certainly worth a try."

At this, Stewan lifted his wet face and wiped his eyes with his sleeve. A hopeful smile shone through his tears. "You really think there's hope?"

"There's always hope."

"Do let's talk to him then."

"We shall," said Render.

"If we ever get out of this blasted death trap!" Folen said and kicked the door.

Render held up a hand. "Hold on, there, Folen. Let's not draw too much attention just yet."

Folen's eyes widened. "But I don't like it in here."

"Someone will find us soon enough." Render held up the key, which was entirely too small to fit the door's lock. "But first, let's see what this opens. I must know." He crawled on his hands and knees and stared under the bed. No disease-ridden vermin. Good. The only thing he found was an object wrapped in a dusty brown cloth.

"Hello, what have we here?" Render unwrapped the cloth to find a small wooden chest with brass hinges and a lock. "I wonder...."

"That's got to be it," Stewan said, wiping his nose. He sat up tall and peered over Render's shoulder. In no time, Folen stood behind his other shoulder. All eyes fixed upon the mysterious box.

"What do you think is inside?" Folen said.

"Only one way to know." Render slipped the key into the lock.

"Wait," said Stewan. Render and Folen both turned to him. "Hadn't we better leave that alone?"

"What's the harm?" Render didn't take his eyes from the box.

"Well, for one thing, isn't this like stealing?"

Folen shoved his brother in the arm. "Not like he's taking anything. We're just looking."

"One look," said Render. "I promise. Then I'll lock it up, and put the key back. They'll never know."

"I don't feel good about this."

"Don't be such a baby," said Folen.

Stewan let out a sigh. "I'm not a baby. Open it, for all I care. Just remember, I warned you not to." He crossed his arms and turned away.

Render turned the key.

It clicked and unlocked.

His pulse began to race.

He slipped his finger under the latch and flipped it open. Then, he opened the box.

"Why, it's—!"

"A book?" Folen said in a mixture of surprise and disappointment.

Stewan turned back and leaned over his brother's shoulders. "What kind of book?"

Render had already opened the blank cover with no title. The words on the page gave no indication of the book's subject, or even the type of work it might be. "I'm not certain."

"Well, why don't you just read something from it?"

"All right." He began with the top of the page to which he had turned. A spectral chill crawled up his spine. Depicted was a drawing of Mount Handara, familiar to him as when he'd seen it in his dreams, in his paintings. He blinked and looked closer at the page.

"What is it?" Folen said.

At first, Render could not form words. Though he had taken Edwyn at his word that the Mountain he'd seen and painted did in fact exist, this further confirmed it. He quickly turned the page and began to read.

w

And when Valhandra had finished, he wept, for his son had chosen the most painful path, one from which there was no redemption. But Malakandor had hardened his heart.

"I will rise up. Above my brother, above my father. I will take which was not given me, and rule as I please."

"You shall rule by power," Valhandra said. "But not with authority. Five and twenty millennia, shall I grant you this. And though you shall have liberty to choose to return to me, verily I say unto thee, you shall not."

Thus did Malakandor plunge the world into darkness, obscuring the true nature of its noble beings and—"

"What is this!"

All three jumped.

Render dropped the book on the floor and looked up.

There stood Sir Edwyn, his brow snarled and eyes ablaze, holding chain and lock which Branson had used to lock them in. "What are you doing in my quarters?"

CHAPTER TWENTY-FIVE

STANDING BY THE WAIST-HIGH WALL of the open terrace overlooking his dominion, The High King Corigan gnawed on his knuckle. The envoy should have arrived more than an hour ago. "Blast it, why does she insist on tormenting me so?"

"His majesty's reputation for patience does him no real justice," said Lord Mooregaard, Corigan's trusted advisor and friend. With a smile, he grasped his mail gauntlets with his right hand and gently rapped them against his left palm. Repeatedly. A most annoying habit.

"My Lord Mooregaard," Corigan said, "Have you been informed of any delay? Such tardiness is most atypical."

"I can offer no explanation, Majesty." More rapping of the mail gloves, which chafed the King. Corigan grabbed a polished Aluvium flagon and filled two ornate chalices with red Long-Xue, from the vineyards of the forbidden East, though nothing was forbidden the High King of Valdshire Tor.

"Drink, Mooregaard." Corigan offered him a chalice,

which he received with a grateful inclination of the head. They both peered out at the enormity of the citadel and over the massive walls which separated it from the peasant farms towards the edge of the continent. There, over Smyth's Hill, the land plunged straight down into miles of desolate sand only to be interrupted by the mountains which served as a natural barrier between his Kingdom and that of Tian Kuo. His stomach turned at the thought of the ruins the lay on the other side of the peaks, the fabled ruins of the Sojourners.

"Do you think we've seen the last of them, Mooregaard?"

"One can only hope."

"That any rational being could even entertain the idea that humans...spirit beings, all that rubbish! Would they kill innocents over such ideology, because we refuse to pretend? To indulge such childish fantasies?"

"Your father knew all too well."

"Indeed." The very mention of his father stung the center of Corigan's chest.

"As did the scribes of Malkor. Do not doubt, my young King. Your father died at my side, fighting to ensure your freedom. Freedom from religious tyranny. You do well to exterminate those radical, murderous zealots, as well as the very nation which harbors them."

Corigan set his chalice down. The Long-Xue burned a path down his throat and cooled it painfully as he spoke. "I have...concerns."

At this, Mooregaard stood tall, his dark countenance etched with care. "Your Majesty does well to remember: For more than a millennium, there has been no peace between the civilized world and those Tianese dogs. How, in all that is decent and true, can anyone give comfort to terrorists who murder defenseless innocents, women and children alike? Nay, my dear Corigan. This cannot be. Honor your father's charge, for they were his last words to you."

And it would have given Corigan nothing but pleasure to conquer all of Tian Kuo with force, had it not been for that seed of doubt planted in his mind, his heart.

"Where is that envoy!" He hurled his chalice such that the Long-Xue splashed against the stone wall and bled down in three slow trails. The dented chalice rocked back and forth on the ground on its rim, sending flashes of reflected sunlight into his eyes like daggers.

Just then, a voice intruded upon the moment. "Your Majesty."

Mooregaard and Corigan both turned and beheld her. Mooregaard bowed deeply as he took her gloved hand and kissed it. "My Lady."

"Lady Volfoncé, to what do I owe this pleasure?" Corigan spoke with measured acerbity, for he never liked nor trusted her much. Perhaps it was her eyes. Dark, almost hawk-liked, she seemed to peer straight into his soul. It so disturbed him that he rarely held her gaze, but instead concealed his apprehension behind a wall of regal haughtiness.

"I intercepted the envoy en route to Talen Wood." Now releasing Mooregaard's hand, Lady Volfoncé stepped forward and handed Corigan an envelope sealed with red wax. The seal of his dove. "The young Tianese feared for his life though I guaranteed him safe passage. But ultimately, he feared too much and after much cajoling on his part, pathetic as it had been, I agreed to take this letter to you personally."

"You have my gratitude." Corigan inspected the wax seal surreptitiously. It did not appear to have been tampered with. He lifted his eyes and found the lady gazing as if she expected something from him. "Yes?"

"Your majesty is aware, are you not, that such correspondence threatens the confidence, the stability of our nation, if word were to make it out that—"

"Have you any questions or remark of consequence, Lady Volfoncé?"

"Sire, I simply—"

"You are dismissed with my thanks, then."

A cold silence remained in the air like gray mist. Lady Volfoncé blinked once, or twice, Corigan could not tell, because it happened so quickly and her entire body stood perfectly still. That piercing gaze once again. It made the hairs on the back of his neck stand.

Finally, she took Mooregaard's proffered hand. They both bowed and backed away from the terrace and into the palace. Corigan noticed and called out, "My Lord! Pray tarry a while longer."

"Sire." He stopped, bowed and kissed The Lady's hand once again as she left. When he returned, he stood firm and severe. "Your Majesty?"

The sealed letter still in hand, Corigan approached his advisor with a purposeful stride. He felt along the stamped edge of the wax seal as he spoke. "You make little disguise of your sentiments for The Lady Volfoncé."

"She is a fine and worthy Lady, sire."

"No doubt."

"Do you disapprove?"

"Nay, I..." The envelope and its contents began to command Corigan's attention. "Nay, Mooregaard. I just..."

"Sire?"

"Something about her gives me pause."

Mooregaard smiled a broad, knowing smile.

"And this amuses you?"

"Please it your majesty to indulge your servant. But I daresay, I know what troubles you about The Lady, though she has never said but a kind or honorable word, nor done anything less than noble in your presence."

"Pray tell, my good Lord."

"Sire, I can tell you most assuredly that Lady Volfoncé reminds you of your mother, the queen mother, though you were of much too tender an age to remember her, before her untimely passing." At this, Mooregaard began to laugh, as though any apprehension Corigan felt had been the most childish folly.

"Yes, yes. It is well said. She reminds me of my mother!" Corigan laughed along, albeit half-heartedly and out of pride, lest he appear insecure. Yet, this was decidedly not the reason Volfoncé distressed him so.

Mooregaard continued to recite attributes of the deceased queen mother which ostensibly matched those of Lady Volfoncé. But Corigan's eyes floated to the envelope which he was presently opening.

Struggling to maintain but a shred of dignity, Corigan slid his finger carefully under the seal, though he wanted nothing more than to tear the envelope open and gaze lustfully at the bare letter within.

"...and then there is resemblance in her laugh," Mooregaard continued. "Oh, did the queen mother's laugh ever warble like the sweet music of a nightingale. So it is with that most noble of ladies, Volfoncé."

Not heeding the troubador's account of the "fair lady Volfoncé," Corigan lifted the folds of the letter with shortened breath and pounding heart. He reveled in the self-inflicted torture of opening it slowly. Then finally, he read its contents. As usual, his dove corresponded with enigmatic terseness.

A Fortnight, Your Highness.

The promise of her words, the anticipation, it all made Corigan's head swim in a sea of pulsing thoughts and urges. He didn't even notice that Mooregaard was calling his name.

"Sire!"

"Yes, yes. What is it Mooregaard?"

"Are you quite all right?"

"I am, thank you. Mooregaard, I require your counsel, your...perspective."

"As it has been with your father and mother, to serve is my honor, O my King."

"Right. Thank you. Mooregaard, do you not think it more wise to pursue less aggressive means of conquest. Was it not Ulrogh, Malkor's prized disciple, who said, "better to win over a kingdom slowly over the years, than with bloodshed over a night?"

The dark and tall knight rested his massive hand on Corigan's shoulder and the weight of it challenged him to stand still, lest he betray his own weakness under it. "Ah, but you extract these sayings from their true context. Ulrogh meant that in regards to economic warfare, not between two nations with an epic history of bloodshed and rivalry. Of such situations he said, "The quick spilling of royal blood, spares the manifold lives of both nations."

Corigan recoiled and twisted his brow. "The coldness with which you recite that gives me pause. How very uncivilized and coarse."

"Coarse, though it may be, this conflict with Tian Kuo will not soon end, nor shall it end easily. But end it must, and you must be the victor."

Here is where Corigan held the upper hand. Here is where for once, he held his trusted advisor at a disadvantage. "My good Lord, you may find many a surprise with me. I am aware that I lack my father's physical formidability and combat prowess, but I certainly possess all the cunning of my mother, if all you have told me of her is accurate."

"Truly?"

"Yea, verily."

This made Mooregaard stand just a little straighter. "How so, Your Majesty?"

"One word." Corigan's eyes grew wickedly dim. "Collaboration."

Mooregaard's smile hung artificially on his face. His eyes shifted to the side and back. "Surely you don't mean—"

"My dove. You know her not, and that must remain so. But suffice it to say, she has deeper connections, as the sinew and tendons of the Tianese society, the Tianese Government. She can assure that my diplomatic overtures are met with open arms—much to the relief of her people who, she says, are battle-worn and crave and end to the perpetual hostilities of our countries."

"Sire, I know not to whom you refer, but surely no one, no woman can—"

"Though I value your great counsel, pray do not underestimate me."

"I apologize, Sire."

"No need. But let me assure you, she has influence over the monarchy of Tian Kuo, the emperor himself. They will agree to a mutual cessation of hostilities. And before their soldiers have even put their barbarian swords away, I shall fall upon them with the full force of the mighty Torian army."

Mooregaard held his bearded chin in his hand but said not a word.

"You doubt me?" Corigan looked to him, not so much for approval, but for validation.

"It is not you that I doubt."

"Fear not. She has more influence than you can imagine. I have already implemented several stages of this plan, none of which you can know of until we make our final move. The empire of the accursed East will first join us in a common goal of ridding this world of those fanatical Sojourners—with our assistance of course. And when they are celebrating our new alliance, which you and I know is about as likely to exist as a ball of snow in the desert, we shall infiltrate their capital and take it by force."

He expected Mooregaard to congratulate him for his craftiness, his masterful strategy. But instead, Mooregaard shook his head.

"What now?" Corigan said. "Do you not agree this is the best way?"

"Not by my counsel, Sire. May Your Majesty be reminded that prior to your 'dove's' ascent in stature, she was—how to put it delicately—? A mere concubine."

"What good is your counsel, anyway! You are an old fool! You sit around training young recruits to fight battles which you are too old and cowardly to fight yourself."

"Sire, with respect..."

"Ah! That is why you disagree. By your words, you profess a desire to spare the innocents, and only spill the blood of their wicked monarchy. But in fact, you are a coward. Yes, that's what you are, a coward!"

Bristling at the charge, Mooregaard held his composure, drawing a tight line with his lips. Finally he said, calmly, "Please it Your Majesty, to indulge me as I speak my mind with candor."

"It pleases My Majesty to hear nothing less than the

truth!" Corigan was somewhat embarrassed at his own outburst, but too proud to let it show.

"Admittedly, I know not who this dove of yours is. But you can see why I am skeptical about anyone wielding such influence over the monarchy of the East. They are like stone, unmovable."

"And since when have you become such an expert at Tianese policy?"

"As you have permitted your servant to speak freely, may I remind Your Highness that I have many years more experience dealing with—"

"It matters not, old friend." Corigan placed his hand on Mooregaard's shoulders, unwilling to risk his friendship over something he knew Mooregaard would not dare oppose, regardless. "For all my years as king, I have trusted you."

"I am honored."

"And now, my dear Lord Mooregaard, trusted counselor, friend of my father and mother, I ask that you trust me."

He held Corigan's gaze with severity. And then a smile stretched like a stream across the barren wastelands of his countenance. "You have my trust, Sire."

"My dove will come to me soon, and all shall be set in place."

"How soon?"

"In a fortnight."

CHAPTER TWENTY-SIX

SIR EDWYN DROVE forward with angry steps. Render barely managed to step out of the way. The heavyset scholar brushed by and bent down to retrieve the book and the box.

"The key, if you please."

Render stared, standing still as a sculpture. Words failed. His back became drenched with perspiration.

"The key!"

Startled, Render stood, felt his pants and pockets. Finally, he found it and handed it to his mentor.

Sir Edwyn snatched it out of his hand. "You've no business going through my personal effects!"

Staring at his feet, Render said, "I didn't realize—"

"Had this been someone else's quarters, would it make ransacking and breaking open their locked belongings any more acceptable?"

"No, but—"

"Sir, Edwyn, please." Stewan stepped forward, his voice trembling. "It was my fault."

Render turned an incredulous eye to him. "You had no

part in this, Stew."

"Yes, I did."

Folen stepped forward. "If anyone is to blame, it's that idiot Branson."

"But I provoked him," Stewan said. "In fact, since we arrived at Castle Mittelvald...Oh, bother him! For all his nasty insults, he deserved it. But yesterday, I said something about his father not caring enough to stay home to raise him. And rather than strike me, he walked away and cried, I think."

Edwyn placed his book in the box and locked it. "I can hardly believe that."

"It's true. So today, he repays it by leading us here and locking us in. If I hadn't been so cruel to him, none of us would be here now."

"No," said Folen. "I am to blame. I chased the lout and made Render come with me. And I encouraged Render to open the box."

"You are all trying to take the blame for that which is my own doing." Render put his hands on their shoulders. "I let my curiosity get the best of me, Sir Edwyn. I ignored Stewan's warnings not to touch your belongings. I alone should be punished."

Without a word, Edwyn shoved his wrapped box under his bed, pocketed the key and went over to the library where he replaced the books that had been removed from the shelf. Render and the twins followed him and waited.

How he wished his mentor would say something. Chide him, berate him, anything but silence. Instead, Sir Edwyn went about tidying the library, inspecting his bedchamber.

When he could stand it no more, Render stood directly in Sir Edwyn's path and said, "You're angry. I understand."

"I am...disappointed."

If there were anywhere to crawl, Render would have preferred it than to face his mentor's downcast gaze. He waited until Edwyn finished pacing around before he spoke again.

"It shall never happen again," Render said. "I promise."

Sire Edwyn stared and said nothing. And then, with a deep breath he sat at the desk. "Render, it would be disingenuous of me to represent myself as one who had never made a youthful blunder or indiscretion. But you must never come into my quarters again, nor attempt to read my books, without my consent."

"Yes, sir."

"Very well, then. This matter is hereby laid to rest." He stood and turned to the twins, who out of instinct stepped back. "The two of you may report to Lady Justina for your music lessons."

They were gone before Render could bid them good day.

"Sir Edwyn," Render said, mustering up the courage to match his curiosity. "That book—"

Edwyn grunted in disapproval.

"It's special isn't it?" Render's voice began to rise with excitement. "I can tell, not just because how you guard it, but because of the pictures. Mount Handara. And the words. When I read the verses of Valhandra—"

"Quiet!" Edwyn rose to his feet and glanced over to the door which had been left ajar. He stepped over and with great care, shut it tight. "Do not ever utter that name again."

"Valhan-"

"I said, do not speak it."

"But why?"

The otherwise formidable scholar wiped the sweat from his upper lip and glanced around the room. Then out the window and then to the door.

"Your combat exams begin in ten minutes," Edwyn said and pointed out the window. "You'll go up against one of The Lord Mooregaard's best fighters."

"Who is Lord—? Sir Edwyn, please. Won't you tell me why the name of Valhandra—?"

"No!" Edwyn spun around with such tension in his face, Render thought he might scream. "Now get your armor and sword. You know full well what this exam means."

There could only be one victor in this match. And the one who lost would either be expelled from the training program, or worse, killed.

"I know what it means to you," Render said. "Your pride."

"If you fail, all I can do is appeal to the council that you be reassigned to train as a candlemaker or cobbler's apprentice. None of those tracks afford the opportunities for painting, music, or poetry."

Of course, Sir Edwyn was right, but Render felt he was at the cusp of a breakthrough. "I know what's at stake," he said. "I only want to know—"

"You must prepare for your exam."

"Not until you tell me."

"Now!"

So close. Edwyn would soon relent. Render could tell. "I'll keep repeating that name if you don't answer my question."

"Don't be a fool."

Render began with a whisper. "Valhandra."

Edwyn's face flushed red.

"Valhandra, Valhandra!"

Then to Render's astonishment, Edwyn grabbed him and slapped his hand over his mouth. "Stop it at once," he hissed.

Eyes wide, Render nodded. When Edwyn released him, Render said, "Please, at least tell me why that name is so terrible."

With no apparent recourse, Edwyn sighed and said, "It is because of Valhandra that my parents were killed."

CHAPTER TWENTY-SEVEN

EVEN AT THE TENTH HOUR, the sun beat down on Render through his chain mail shirt, which hung heavy on his shoulders. The shield he held bore the insignia of Castle Mittelvald, and made his hand sore even before arriving at the testing ground.

As he and Sir Edwyn approached Hawthern Fountain, Render noticed that a small crowd had gathered. "What are they all doing there?"

"Never mind them," Edwyn replied. "Fix your attention on your exam."

Render's ill-fitting helmet slipped down over his eyes. He adjusted it and realized just how slick his hand had become. No matter how much he'd practiced, combat was the last thing he wished to involve himself with. Alas, it was a compulsory examination for all who trained. Even Sir Edwyn, in his youth must have successfully passed it.

"Why won't you tell me who my opponent is?" Render said just as they arrived at the cobblestone plaza, where streams of water flowed from the sculpture of a large bird of prey, clutching a fish in its talons.

"You shall see soon enough." Edwyn fixed Render's belt, adjusted his breastplate and tried in vain to set the helmet such that it would not move with each turn of the head. "I did not wish to cause you any undue anxiety."

"The suspense has done wonders to calm me," Render said with an ironic grin.

"You're better off with suspense than fear."

"So I ought to be afraid?"

"That is not my point."

"Then what is—?"

"Render!" A voice which he had not heard for so long caused his heart to rush. He turned to see a young man, approaching with an aristocratic Lord clad in black sleeves under his chain mail. The young man removed his visor and right away, Render ran up to him.

"Kaine! I can't believe it's you!"

"And just look at you." Kaine grinned, and somehow looked different than he'd remembered. "You look a head taller in that armor." He wrapped one arm around Render's neck and rapped his fist on his helmet affectionately.

"What a surprise," Render said, freeing himself and shoving his older brother's shoulder. "What's it been, a month, two?" Guilt weighed his heart down like a wet cloak. He'd been such a beast the last time he'd seen him, blaming him for withholding the truth about Mother. Kaine had been right to protect Render's memories of her. As infuriating as he could so often be, Kaine had been a great brother.

"Well now," Lord Mooregaard said as he dismounted his horse, which to no one's surprise, was black, as well. He spread his hands wide and smiled. "I am loathe to disrupt this reunion, but as the esteemed Sir Edwyn would agree, we are here to conduct the combat exams for you both."

With that sobering statement, all the joy at seeing Kaine faded. Render began to feel ill at the realization.

"I have to fight Kaine?"

Edwyn nodded.

It should not be a fight to the death, nor to any significant injury, hopefully. But the thought of losing his chance to study the arts and letters? He must not fail. If only he'd devoted more time to his combat training.

"Well, Rend?" Kaine punched him in the arm. It hurt. "Ready to have your rump carved?"

Render bumped him back with his shield and laughed, trying to conceal his apprehension. "Just watch your own." He stepped back and saw that the crowd had pressed in closer. Eager faces looked on, some smiling with missing teeth, others refined and clean.

Lord Mooregaard's voice faded into the background as he announced the rules of engagement. An odd sensation coursed through Render's body. Sitting atop the sculptured hawk, was the black cat that had been sleeping on his pillow since the night she climbed into his room. She gazed intently with bright eyes.

Just then, interrupting the formalities and Lord Mooregaards endless words, a crazed voice broke through the crowd. "Oh, I am blessed!" shouted an old man in a tattered brown robe. He looked over to the plaza where Render and his brother stood, now facing each other. "At long last." He looked to Kaine, then to Render. "To see you! The two of you!" Before he could utter another sound, one of Mooregaard's guards quietly took him by the arm and led him away.

"On the third count," Mooregaard said, full of pomp, "You are to engage without pause until only one of you is left standing." He regarded Sir Edwyn as he continued.

"Limbs are fair game. You are to spare your opponent's life only. Understood?"

Render and Kaine nodded.

The crowd seemed to hold their collective breath.

Render had to win, it was as simple as that. He didn't know if Kaine shared the same ambitions or if any of this mattered to him as much. But it didn't matter. Render's future depended on this.

"On three." Mooregaard stood tall and began the count.

CHAPTER TWENTY-EIGHT

"...Two

...Three!"

On Mooregaard's mark, Kaine lunged at his brother and cut at his right arm with all his might. His lack of hesitation surprised him. But Render turned swiftly and blocked the blow with his shield.

The crowd cheered.

Render faltered.

As soon as he regained his footing, Render's sword came flying out at Kaine's face. Kaine parried the blow with his broadsword. Whirling his entire body around, he slammed his shield into Render's side.

Render fell on his side this time and groaned.

Without a moment to spare, Kaine stepped on Render's right hand.

Render's sword clanked onto the cobblestone.

"Come now, little brother," said Kaine, bending over his face. "That was too quick, too easy."

From beneath the shadow of Render's visor, a smile

emerged. Distracted, Kaine didn't see his brother swing his shield at his head.

Dizzied by the blow, Kaine reeled. For a moment he could not see a thing. His ears rang. Without thinking, he threw off his helmet and put a hand over the ear that had been struck.

A heavy blow caught him in between the shoulders.

Kaine lurched forward but remained on his feet.

Amidst the crowd's wild cheering and jeering, Mooregaard was shouting instructions. But Kaine didn't hear any of it.

A second blow didn't follow immediately.

Kaine took a breath, shook the flecks of light out of his head and turned around. There stood his little brother, smiling, holding up his shield and pointing his sword.

His strength returning, Kaine feigned exhaustion, held up a hand as if to request a respite. As soon as Render lowered his shield—ever so slightly—Kaine let out a shout and charged him with all this might.

Clang, clang, clang! His sword clashed against Render's, against his shield, his helmet. It was all Render could do to deflect, turn, gasp, shout and fall down upon his haunches.

With every crash of metal against metal, Kaine's fury increased in intensity. His control slipped away, yielding to that visceral desire to destroy, to conquer, to vanquish utterly.

And finally, it happened.

With Kaine's knee on his brother's chest, pinning him to the ground, with the sharp edge of his sword, drawing a pink line across the fair skin of his throat, Kaine's hand trembled. The impulse to press down and finish Render, who at the moment seemed more an enemy than his younger brother, felt irresistible. But Lord Mooregaard's words resonated within his mind. Follow your conscience.

Render's eyes began to well up. Through clenched teeth he said, "I surrender!"

CHAPTER TWENTY-NINE

FOR SEVERAL DAYS, Lao-Ying did not transform into an eagle. He and Ahndien continued their journey on foot, which didn't bother her so much. She had so many questions to ask and flying did not allow for discussion. Anyway, she liked climbing the hills.

What she didn't like was Lao-Ying's evasive answers. "In due time," he would say, in response to her most desperate questions such as, "Did I really burn that wolf back in the woods? You seemed perfectly capable when it attacked me. Why didn't you help me?"

She had managed to get one answer out of him, though it confused her more than helped her understand. "When those mountain lions tried to take Ah-Ba's sword from me, back in the village, why did it not simply kill me and take it?"

"Because it knew it could not."

"What do you mean?"

It struck her as an odd statement, but he was much too

old to be joking, at least he didn't appear to be, and much too wise to fabricate such an idea. "You mean, I can't die?"

Lao-Ying looked out at the sky, ablaze in red and amber. His eyes drooped and his entire countenance became dispirited. He let out a poignant sigh. "I only said, they cannot kill you."

They stopped at one last clearing in the hill, just before the ascent grew steep. Lao-Ying set his pack down and rubbed his back. In his human form, he looked to be a hundred years old, yet he never needed any more rest than Ahndien. When she looked at him, she could not help but see the sharp eyes and white crest of the eagle into which he had transformed several times now.

It was just as Ah-Ba had said, though in not so many words. There are some who manifest their full spirit potential. Lao-Ying was the first she'd ever beheld who fully embodied the spirit of an eagle. An enormous one, at that.

"Let us stop here," he said and sat on the green moss. "There are several things we must do and discuss before we make our ascent."

"I'm tired."

"First: Training."

"For what?"

Lao-Ying stared straight into her eyes as though examining her sincerity. But she had nothing to hide, she really didn't know. "Don't you want to know the answers to your questions?"

"Of course."

Lao-Ying reached up, grabbed a narrow limb of a Bakha Elm and snapped it like a twig. He began to wield it with the finesse of a seasoned swordsman. "Draw your sword."

"I'm tired. And hungry." To her surprise, Lao-Ying

swung the branch and swatted her swiftly on the left side of her rear. "Aiya!" It didn't hurt very much, but it did sting.

"Your sword."

Ahndien gritted her teeth. "I am in no mood—"

Another swat. This time on the right.

"Stop that!"

Lao-Ying wagged his finger at her, smiling and taunting. "You think me too old, eh? To slow, eh? I will teach you things you do not know." Another swat.

"I said stop!" More out of annoyance than compliance, Ahndien unsheathed Ah-Ba's sword. The mirror-like blade glinted in the sunlight. She didn't even take notice of the interesting carvings near the hilt.

Just then, Lao-Ying leapt high into the air in a frightful attack maneuver. He came down with the staff above his head, about to apply the full force of it to Ahndien's head.

Without thinking, she swung around and deflected the blow, just as he landed. Then he slashed at her three times, from three directions, in rapid succession.

But with equal swiftness, she deflected the blows. The sword whistled through the air with each swing. She didn't have time to wonder how she had gotten so deft with Father's sword.

She rather enjoyed it, though.

Lao-Ying continued his attack. But despite his speed and accuracy, Ahndien repelled every strike. The old man smiled, and narrowed his eyes. "Good. Very good!

The swordplay went on for a while until Lao-Ying finally stumbled, his hand on his back. Lifting one hand he said, "Respite. Please. I need to..." Then he clutched his chest and winced.

"Lao-Ying?" Ahndien dropped her sword and approached him fearing the worst.

"My...heart." He grimaced in pain.

CHAPTER THIRTY

AHNDIEN RUSHED OVER to Lao-Ying. As a small child, she had seen Ah-Yeh, her paternal grandfather, suddenly fall, clutching his chest as Lao-Ying was doing now. Ah-Yeh had died suddenly.

This could not be happening, not now. She stepped right up to him. "Lao-Ying!"

Then, quick as a flash of lightning, Lao-Ying's face lit up with a mischievous smile, he swung his staff right at her head.

"Ai!" Faster than she knew she could move, Ahndien shot her hand out and grasped the end of his staff, stopping it mid-swing. Now, something burned from within. The heat rose from her belly to her neck, her face, her scalp, her fingers.

"Yes!" The old man's eyes widened in an expression somewhere between wonder and dread. "Let it flow."

She gripped the staff and with all her might tried to push it back to Lao-Ying. But he held firm, clenching his teeth. "Come on! Do not let a feeble old man defeat you!"

At first she thought it was anger. But as she continued to press, she realized it was something stronger: Determination. She clutched the staff with both hands and with a final grunt, thrust Lao-Ying back with such force, it propelled him away.

He flew backwards.

For a moment Ahndien thought he might fall and hit his head. But instead, he transformed into a normal sized eagle, flew up and perched upon a tree branch.

// DO NOT STOP THE FLOW! LET IT HAPPEN! //

Still gripping the staff in her hands, she noticed the heat leaving her hands.

A golden light filled her vision.

The staff began to glow. First red, then white.

Then it burst into flames.

"What's happening?" She threw the burning staff onto the ground. But even as it left her hands, a stream of fire clung to it, like strands of tar. Her mouth dropped open as she lifted her hands to her eyes. Her palms were burning like kindling in a fire. But it didn't hurt.

// IT HAS BEGUN //

The more she concentrated on the fire in her hands, the hotter the flames grew. They almost felt solid. The more intensely she focused, the heavier they became.

// TRY THROWING IT //

Glowing white balls of fire pulsing in her hands, Ahndien turned and faced Lao-Ying. "At what?"

He spread his wings.

// WHY NOT TRY A MOVING TARGET? //

Not bothering to answer, she responded by hurling one of the fireballs at the eagle. It made a hissing sound as it launched through the air, a fiery tail streaming behind it like a shooting star. Lao-Ying flew off, but the fireball hit the tree branch and cut it off like a hot knife through a rice cake.

For the next few minutes, Ahndien marveled at her ability to conjure up fire in the form of projectiles and streams. She tested them everywhere she could without destroying all the trees and greenery around them.

"Just as I have foreseen." Lao-Ying now stood before her, in the form of the deceptively frail-looking old man. "Your time has come."

"I don't understand." The heat from Ahndien's face and hands dissipated. Her long hair which had been ablaze and floating as though under water returned to normal. "Is this my spirit potential?"

"Only in part, if all I have seen in my dreams is to be."

"What dreams?"

"Come, sit." He motioned for the mossy patch. She sat on the ground beside him. He pulled out the flask and offered it to her. "Thirsty?"

"My throat feels like sand." She took it and drank the entire flask without stopping to breathe. White columns piped from her mouth and nostrils. When finally she stopped, she wiped her mouth and exhaled a cloud of steam. "What about your dreams, Lao-Ying?"

"Ah, the dreams." He took out another flask and drank from it. Then he smacked his lips and wiped them on his sleeve. "For many years, I have forseen events in my dreams. At first, I didn't understand. But later—many years later, I came to understand. They foretell matters of Valhandra's Kingdom."

"The same Valhandra in Father's books?"

"Yes, child."

"It must be wonderful to see the future." But her excitement dissipated. "What if you don't live long enough to see it come to pass?"

"It is a blessing and honor to know what is to come." The old man's eyes began to shimmer. "And at the same time, it can be a curse."

Ahndien studied the creases in his face. Like the lines of an old parchment that had been rolled up and folded for many years, his skin betrayed his aged wisdom. Like Ah-Yeh. "Just how old are you, Lao-Ying?"

He smiled a bitter smile and shook his head.

"Well?"

"No. I will not say."

"But why?"

"It is foolishness. I would not risk your ridicule. It is enough to say that I am older than you can imagine."

"Ninety? One hundred?"

He shook his head.

"Oh, please tell me! I'll lose sleep if you don't!"

Lao-Ying murmured unintelligibly.

"What was that?"

He cleared his throat. "Never mind."

"Oh, but you must tell me!"

He shook his head. "No."

"Why not?"

He turned to face her, held both of her shoulders, a poignant smile floating to the surface like the air bubbles of dying fish. "You would not believe me."

"After all I have seen? I will believe almost anything."

"To be a seer, and the length of days I've been afforded is indeed a curse—knowing the fates of your loved ones years in advance, but not being able to do anything to alter their course—and believe me, I have tried. Watching friends, family, beloved rulers, and an entire people die over the years, while I continue to live? I serve Valhandra with honor. But this path is full of bitterness, and I wish..." His voice quavered.

At this, Ahndien stopped asking. Her heart ached for him, the man who reminded her so much of her Ah-Yeh, who had cared for her when her parents were busy with the many obligations of life. Ah-Yeh, who taught her to play the flute, to make silly poems that made fun of mean town officials, all the while maintaining a severe demeanor which she suspected no one but she knew masked the spirit of a little boy.

Lao-Ying took a deep breath, his chest puffing up, then breathed out slow and sad. "Ah, but you. You are the ray of sunshine breaking through the gray clouds of my life."

"Why are you so sad?"

"Do not be burdened, my child. You have much to look forward to."

"Can you tell me? Since you can see the future?"

Lao-Ying cleared his throat and took another sip of water. He wiped his mouth with his sleeve and said, "I can only see that which has been appointed for me to see. Such things tend to be for the benefit of others to know. But I bear the painful burden."

Ahndien gazed into his sagely countenance. At that moment she knew. A connection had been formed, a sort of trust that went beyond age or station. His eyes softened, as though she finally understood something he'd been trying to explain.

But she understood nothing.

Except that she would believe whatever he said, no matter how incredible. And she knew that he understood this. "Lao-Ying," she whispered earnestly. "How long have you lived?"

CHAPTER THIRTY-ONE

LAO-YING'S FACE seemed to crumble, like the last supporting beam of a collapsing house. The pain seemed to run deeper than the answer to Ahndien's question. He finally turned away and stared at the ground, where a lone tear had rolled off his cheek and fell.

"I have lived five hundred years."

Ahndien opened her mouth to speak, but nothing came out.

"I have seen my prophecies come to pass and know my place amongst the Elders, whom soon we shall see. But to have seen the things I have..." He sighed. "I have lived far too long."

She wanted to ask what he had seen, but didn't quite know if she ought to. Finally, after a long pause, she said, "Were we always like this? Poor farmers and peasants?"

"Is that how you see your father? A peasant?"

"He is a scholar. At one time, I believe he might have been a warrior."

Lao-Ying nodded. "As a people, we did not always live in the outskirts of Tian Kuo. Nor did we exist at the fringe of society. Once we were kings, who ruled the land in justice and mercy. Once we were a people who knew the truth."

Something came alive in her spirit. "What has happened since?"

"Four hundred years ago, the forces of Malakandor, by treachery exiled the four powerful Sojourner tribes and gathered them in the valley that lies between the great summits of Handara." He pointed over the top of the range, at whose foot they encamped. "By means unknown to us, they suppressed our spirit potential, our ability to transform and defend ourselves."

A deep pit hollowed out the center of her stomach from within. Ahndien thought about how helpless she or Lao-Ying would be if either of them could not use their powers. "That's terrible."

"I saw twenty thousand fall in one day."

"Could they not defend themselves?"

"I could only hide and watch. For Valhandra had purposed for me to go on, to strengthen the remnant of His people through the centuries, remind them of the prophecies that the one known as The Great Deliverer, would soon come."

"Twenty thousand. Killed in one day."

"They were consumed by the fire of Ashtoreth."

"What is—?"

"A force too horrible to speak of." He shuddered. "May you live never to know."

Gazing into the dying sun, Lao-Ying shook his head and sighed. "The streams that once ran through that valley flowed with blood. I felt like a coward hiding myself, but it was so ordained. My brothers, my children and grandchildren..."

Ahndien reached over and grasped his leathery hand.

"Lao-Ying. I'm sorry."

"And now, through five centuries, all I wish is..."

"Yes?"

"I have served Him with honor. What I wish is not unreasonable."

"What is it, then?"

"It does pain me so, going on like this without end, eternally waiting her return, eternally disappointed."

"Who?"

His eyes wandered, his lips quivered, and his breath shook. "Ah, the wishes of an old fool."

"Oh, Lao-Ying, please tell me what it is you wish."

With a sad smile, he held her gaze. Then, like a grandfather—or great-great-great-great grandfather—he kissed the top of her head. "I wish nothing more than to die."

Ahndien, full of understanding and sorrow, could not think of what to say. Her eyes blurred with tears.

Restoring a bold demeanor, Lao-Ying patted her hand resting atop his own. "Well, in any case, that barren wasteland beyond the Handaras is known as the Burial Grounds of the Ancients. While most Torians look upon it as a one merely named after folklore, the older ones remember. It has been quietly passed down to them that this place, where the bones of many an unfortunate traveler dries after being picked clean by scavengers, was the site of a most egregious injustice."

"Are there any more of us?"

"The remnant has been scattered. I know not how many we are now, but as a people, we no longer have a home, a kingdom." Lao-Ying sniffed and shut his eyes. "But all that is about to change. I have seen the signs and the time of deliverance draws near."

He stood up, stretched his arms and popped his neck a

few times and smiled. "And for that reason, we must rest so that tomorrow I can fly us both to the top the mountain, and meet the Sojourner's Council of Elders."

"And what of my father?"

"He will be there, if—" Just then, a like a rain cloud, a flock of ravens flew out of the mountains cawing and fluttering excitedly. Lao-Ying fixed his eyes upon them and his complexion turned white as rice. "—if he has escaped the Torians and survived."

CHAPTER THIRTY-TWO

HOT TEARS ROLLED DOWN the side of Render's face. He tried to wipe them, but his mail glove only spread the wet anguish across his skin.

Kaine stood over him for a while before he removed his helmet and gazed straight down at him. His labored breath and flashing eyes suggested a savage excitement Render had never before seen in his brother.

"On your feet," Kaine said. He reached down to help him up. "You fought valiantly."

Not only did this defeat confirm what Render had known his entire life: that his brother Kaine had always been the stronger of them, it meant that Render had failed one of the most basic, but compulsory courses in his training,

His arm ached almost as much as his heart as he staggered to his feet.

"Why so downcast, little brother?"

"I'll be sent back to Bobbington," Render said, removing his armor and throwing it to the ground. Kaine regarded him with pity, which to Render felt like the point of his sword between the ribs. "Or else, if I'm fortunate enough,

I'll be mending your shoes or baking bread in a year or two."

A weighty hand pressed down on his shoulder. Sir Edwyn's. His eyes betrayed more than a hint of disappointment. "We should go."

Render's mind was a spinning miasma. He shook his head as white specks danced before his eyes. To his right, his brother Kaine stood triumphant. To his left, Sir Edwyn urged him on, but couldn't seem to face him. Edwyn pulled Render's arm over his shoulder and helped him off.

As he limped, Render heard a sound far off in the distance. Beyond the citadel walls. He couldn't be certain, but it sounded like thunder. Yet, the sun shone bright and hot through clear skies.

Just then, a flash of black raced across the ground. Something brushed his legs, then dashed before him. Render squinted and stopped. There, two or three steps ahead on the cobblestone road, stood the black cat. She turned her head and eyed Render with intent. How she had found him in this vast citadel was beyond him, but for some reason, he was glad to see her.

"What is that accursed cat doing there?" Edwyn swung Render's sword at her. "Yah!"

"Sir Edwyn, don't!" But the cat merely stepped out of the way and continued to stare. Then it continued up the path.

Passing the rear of the fountain, they came upon a withered man, his back hunched over, dressed in sackcloth and waving his hands wildly. "...is coming, and is indeed here. For behold, the ordained son of heaven!"

Edwyn grasped Render's arm and tried to pull him along. But Render became too transfixed to move. The citizens gazed upon the old man with such interest, he simply could not pass this by.

"People of Valdshire Tor," declared the old man, who some were calling 'The Prophet,' though irreverently, "Citizens of the world..."

To Render's utter amazement, the old man spun around and pointed to him. "Bow before your true King!"

CHAPTER THIRTY-THREE

"TREASON!" some in the crowd began to shout. Others simply laughed and mocked the old man.

Oh, it's The Prophet!

He's lost his mind!

He's drunk, still others said.

Edwyn pulled on Render's arm. "Come along, now. Quickly."

The black cat rushed over to the old man whom everyone mocked. She glared intently at him and he took notice.

"I don't care," he said to the cat. "I know it is he, so I shall proclaim the truth! You and your perfectly ordained time—we have waited three millennia!"

The cat flattened her ears.

"Well lookie here! He speaks with animals, he does!" A woman in the crowd jeered.

"Do you not see? On his hand?" the old man cried, lifting both hands towards Render. "He bears the sign. The Great Deliverer!"

Render glanced at the birthmark. But before he could consider the implications, a barrage of half-eaten fruits and tomatoes flew from the crowd. One hit the old man in the cheek. Undaunted, though the muck oozed down his face, The Prophet's eyes flashed indignant. "Wicked, faithless generation! Have you not heard me prophesy from the Book of The Ancients?" And he shall come with lightning in his fist. He shall reign with an iron scepter and dash to pieces the corrupted rulers. Henceforth shall he reign with justice!" He turned and bowed to Render, a strange tenderness in his eyes. "Have mercy on us, O Great Deliverer. Have mercy upon us all!"

"What?" Render turned and stopped again. The old man fell prostrate and continued to cry out. "In the name of all that is holy. In the name of Valhandra!"

A deathly silence fell upon the crowd.

Render stopped, mid-stride.

Edwyn's hand dropped to his side.

Not one person moved. But the cat leapt over to the old man. And stood at his side.

"Traitor!" cried a man from amidst the multitude.

"He's a Sojourner!"

The crowd surged forward with a frightful roar.

Edwyn tried once again to take Render by the arm, but Render pushed him away and slowly approached the old man. Valhandra? He barely heard Edwyn shouting for Render to run, as the crowd rushed the old man.

Just as a blacksmith, reached him, Sir Mooregaard stepped forward and pointed a sword at his chest. "My good man, you behave as poorly as a Sojourner himself. Resorting to violence? Do you not see your hypocrisy?"

"But My Lord!" he stammered. "You heard him invoke the name. He's a Sojourner, he is!"

Mooregaard cast the old man a pitiful look. "So he may

be. But we do not indulge in violence as they do. Ours is a government of justice, of due process. He shall be handed over to the King's court, where any evidence shall be weighed for or against him. His fate lies in the hand of His Majesty, the High King Corigan." Mooregaard pointed his sword at the entire crowd. "Is that understood?"

At this, the crowd murmured.

"You, Centurion!" Mooregaard pointed to soldier wearing a red tunic with the insignia of the Order of the Scarlet Pendragon.

The soldier stepped forward. "My Lord."

"Take this man with all haste to the court of the High King's judge. See that he is treated with all due process and courtesy."

The soldier acknowledged the command and stepped forward. He grabbed the frail old man forcefully by the arm, causing him to yelp. "Come on, old fool!"

"Wait!" Render shouted, for something The Prophet had uttered stirred him. All eyes fell upon him. Even Kaine's, which widened with surprise and a hint of anger. But Render ignored them all. "I would like a word with this man."

"You'll have your chance to hear all at his trial," Mooregaard said.

But something told Render the trial would be no more than a formality, making official The Prophet's execution. With hastened steps, he strode over to the soldier holding the old man. "Please, I must speak with him now."

"About what?"

Render gazed at The Prophet whose countenance glowed far beyond one going to his death. Without taking his eyes from him, Render said, "About Valhandra."

"Render, no!" Edwyn cried, but was too many steps behind to stop him.

"Please, sir," Render said to the soldier.

"Begone!"

Render grabbed the soldier's arm. "You don't understand, this man—"

"I said begone!" The soldier struck Render with the heel of his hand so hard that he felt he would collapse. But he didn't. He held fast to the soldier's wrist.

A brilliant heat coursed through Render's veins. His teeth clenched at the sheer intensity.

Instantly, the soldier's face began to change. Indignation melted away, yielding to a grimace of pain.

Then fear.

Render's anger did not subside. The soldier shook wildly, tried to back away, free himself from Render's grip.

And then, before Render could comprehend what was happening, a blinding surge of bluish-white light flashed before him. A crash like a thunderclap filled the citadel. The hairs on Render's neck prickled. He was not prepared for what he found when his vision cleared.

Neither was anyone else, judging by the looks of sheer terror in their eyes.

Gasps, shouts and frightened cries flew up.

"By the scrolls of Malkor!"

"He's an alchemist!"

"Murderer!"

"Assassin!"

A charred heap of what remained of the centurion lay at Render's feet. His fingers, like claws twitched as smoke and flickering light rose up. Even his helmet had melted into an amorphous hunk of ore.

"No." Render let go. The arm, light as a twig, dropped dryly onto the blackened remains of the soldier. Even The Prophet blinked with an expression of wonder and dread.

"By all that is honorable and true," said Lord Mooregard

to Sir Edwyn, "What manner of science have you been teaching this lad? Why he—" a sudden look of cognizance fell over his face. He wagged a finger at him and said, "Of course. Of course."

Render stood, frozen in place, his jaw slack and trembling. What horrid thing caused this? Not even Edwyn seemed to understand. And presently, he seemed too consumed with what Lord Mooregaard was saying.

Kaine was leaning against a tree for support, the shock in his eyes palpable. Before Render knew it, a row of archers had lined up before him, crossbows drawn and aiming at him. As if he could run from this?

"In the name of the High King Corigan," said Lord Mooregaard, approaching Render with caution, "I hereby place thee under arrest."

CHAPTER THIRTY-FOUR

GOSSAMER VEILS DRAPED DOWN from the high vaulted ceiling enshrouding High King Corigan's bed in royal crimson. All torches had been long extinguished. All, save for the one above, which filled the area around his immense bed with a rose-coloured hue.

There, Corigan sat up, legs crossed, back against the padded head board. The train of his abandoned robe dangled to the ground. Before him, rested a wooden table just tall enough to reach his lap. Atop the table sat his goblet, filled and drained more times than he bothered recalling with Fire Orchid Wine, an exotic gift from the Eastern Empire of Tian Kuo.

"Your majesty has been careless," his guest said. She smiled and took an alluring sip from the goblet. With long, white fingers, she lifted her horseman piece, moved it across five spaces and captured his partisan. She lifted her eyes, their pupils black as ink, and smiled. Not once had Corigan even noticed her shift while seated in the bed and facing him.

"Leit is a game of patience, my illuminated one," he said, as he surrendered his piece to her. "Of strategy."

"Ah, but it is also a game of cunning, no?" Her hand, cold to the touch, sent a shiver through his blood. He quite relished the sensation for it excited him.

"Nevertheless. A game it is, and a game it always shall be."

She pursed her ruby lips. "You intentionally permitted me to dispatch your partisan. Was such a sacrifice made in the name of strategy?"

"Or perhaps, cunning?" Corigan lifted his siege engine, the piece with the emerald jewels, and captured her horseman. And her cleric and her siege tower as well.

The bed pulsed with her slowly erupting laughter.

"What now?" Corigan said. "You have lost your final line. And this amuses you?"

She took his hand, turned his open palm upwards and stroked it with her fingernails. Then she dropped the three pieces she had just lost into his hand, but they were too many to grasp. One of them dropped to the bed.

"Well?" Half a smile tugged the corner of Corigan's mouth.

"You well know, by now."

"Do I?"

"Apparently less than you realize, but yes. You do."

"Pray enlighten me then, my elusive, exotic beauty."

Placing her fan over the top of her bodice, she stared out the window and sighed. Her smile never fading—unnaturally so, but it aroused Corigan all the more—she sighed. "A game of cunning."

"Indeed, but what do you find so amusing about losing your key pieces?"

"Don't you see, Your Majesty?" Another sip of Fire

Orchid left her lips wetter and redder than before.

"I see many things, but this..." he tossed the captured pieces over his shoulder, put his hand upon hers and leaned in so close her cool, sweet breath touched his lips. "I prefer if you tell me. In your own words."

"This game of Leit, which you have taught me so well, oh High King, is more truthful than you or I."

"Oh? How so?"

She leaned over and brushed his ear with her lips and whispered, "You would never have penetrated my defenses, had I not desired it." And with that, she brought her executioner piece from behind her last two partisans and, through the opening that Corigan himself had forced, captured his Prince's Castle.

Corigan grit his teeth. Still two or three moves away, but once again, he had lost to her. The roots of his hair tingled. "You cheat!" He swiped the pieces aside and climbed off the bed.

"I have done nothing of the sort." She also stood, the hem of her silver gown alighting upon the ground.

"It is hardly fair, the way you distract me so."

"It is, nevertheless, a game." She fanned her bosom and turned her eyes towards the window again. "Did you not say as much yourself?"

"What I said—!" Finding himself in a deficit of words, Corigan paused. He calmed himself, lest he once again surrender the upper hand. "What I mean... that is to say, I..."

"You despise losing," she said patronizingly and placed her hand gently on his face. At her very touch, his anger ebbed, giving way to feelings far more dangerous. "Now look." She pointed out the window to the northern sea where a line of lights underscored the black horizon. "Once again, it is my move."

"How many?"

"Do not fret, Your Highness. Only half of my armada. And they have been instructed to stay clear of the citadel."

"But that is inequitable. I sent only a quarter of mine, and only to the remotest, most backwards villages to which you alluded to as your most troublesome!"

Again she laughed. This time it was more of a scoff. "Ah, yes. Xingjia. And you were so impressed with yourself for having dictated the terms to me." Corigan's face burned. He knew that his bridled rage only masked his humiliation for having been taken in by this dark, yet formidable temptress. "And now," she said, with feigned humility and a half-hearted inclining of her head, "I shall take my leave."

"But you said you'd stay till morning." Corigan's heart raced simultaneously with desperation and self-loathing. "We haven't yet had a chance to—"

Her countenance, always calm as the placid waters of a pond at daybreak, now hardened. Immediately, Corigan ceased his ranting. Her gaze like ice, her words like frost, she smiled but only from one side of her mouth. "You are just like Tian Kuo's dead Emperor—"

"Dead?" It seemed as though the entire ground had fallen out beneath him. His collar seemed to shrink, his back tickled with frigid drops of perspiration. This woman was far more lethal than he had ever imagined.

"Like you, he was weak, controlled more by his loins than his head! There is a reason he is no more. A very good reason."

Corigan dared not speak another word. For she had him at such a disadvantage anything he said would be rope for his own noose. "Perhaps then, it is indeed time for you to take your leave."

They stood, eyes locked, the High King doing all he

could to keep his head erect. And finally, her smile returned. Corigan breathed again.

"If all goes well, my dear King, I shall greatly enjoy your company in my palace. It is quite lovely in the Spring."

"Yes. Yes, of course."

She lifted the train of her gown, bustled it and went to the door, where no doubt on the other side, her ladies in waiting had been listening and giggling. "Let it never be said that The Empress Dowager Xieh-Suh of Tian Kuo is anything but hospitable."

CHAPTER THIRTY-FIVE

PERHAPS IT WAS EDWYN'S ADVOCACY—which Render imagined or at least hoped was passionate before The Honorable Judge Flogge—that afforded his incarceration to take place in his own room within Castle Mittelvald rather than a dungeon.

Render sat by the window, now covered with iron bars, and gazed upon the stars which dangled above in a heavy purple canvas. He was engrossed with what that old man, The Prophet, had said yesterday. More than that, with what happened to the centurion, an explanation for which escaped him utterly.

Hours had gone by without a word or sound from anyone but the guards who had delivered but one meal in a day and a half. Worse still was the silence, the isolation. Even the company of that black cat would have been welcome now.

The door creaked open.

The muscles in Render's neck tensed, anticipating a

guard placing a tray of food on the ground while an archer stood outside ready to shoot. But this time, someone else entered.

"Edwyn?"

"Quiet." He turned to the men at the door. "Guards, you may leave us, or wait by the door. No harm shall befall me, I assure you." They nodded, and backed away, never taking their firm gaze from Render even as they shut and chained the door from outside.

"How now?" Render's stomach churned as if it would dissolve itself. He looked for food in his mentor's hands. But there was none.

"Your trial before Judge Flogge is scheduled for tomorrow. I cannot say just what will happen. They believe you have murdered that soldier."

"Did I?" He sat and hoped Edwyn would reach into his robe and produce a roll or a potato. He did not. "That is to say, I did feel angry when he hit me, anyone would. But I could never kill anyone."

Edwyn sank into a chair, placed a satchel on the table. "They are investigating me as well."

"You? What for?" Perhaps there was a morsel somewhere in that satchel.

"Never mind. You are being charged as a co-conspirator with the old prophet for treason as well as murder. Don't you see? They think you are an infiltrator, a Sojourner. Because you spoke the name of Valhandra."

"Val—?" Render stopped, surprised at the freedom with which his mentor spoke that name which only yesterday seemed so unspeakable. "Honestly, I'm bewildered as anyone by what happened. It was as though a bolt of lightning had struck down the centurion."

"I couldn't see through that flash of light. But because of the way his body was so horribly burned, some allege that you employed the use of incendiary substances. Hid them up your sleeve, that kind of drivel. For that, I am being scrutinized."

"They think you taught me alchemy?"

Edwyn nodded gravely.

"I hate to ask you, and I know this may seem inappropriate," said Render.

"What is it?"

"Would you happen to have some food in that satchel?"

"How can you think of your stomach at a time like this? Do you not realize what is happening?"

"I'm being tried for treason, for murder. I'll likely be executed..." He stood and reached for the satchel. "If I don't starve to death first."

Edwyn yanked it away. "Try to take things seriously, young man."

"I regard dying of hunger with the utmost gravity. "

Instead of food, Edwyn reached into his satchel and produced a book. The same book of which Render had stolen a glimpse in Edwyn's library. "This is the Book of the Ancients that the old prophet quoted. Years ago the cover had been altered so as not to betray its owners."

"The Sacred Songs of Valhandra."

"Yes."

"So this is a book of Sojourner religion?"

"It is the last and only thing that connects me to my parents. As an only child, I had no other family. And like you, I was raised as a ward of King Rospican, father of King Corigan."

Render rubbed his sore neck and fought to ignore his stomach which all but screamed in protest of the neglect. "Your parents were Sojourners?"

"I was but a boy."

"The son of terrorists"

Edwyn's gaze wandered off into an unknown realm. "They slaughtered them in front of all the children. Every parent. Every brother and sister above the age of seven."

If there hadn't been enough to cloud Render's mind, there surely was now. His head felt as if it might burst. "So you are a Sojourner, by blood."

Edwyn's eyes glistened in the light of the dour moonlight, even as a low pitched rumble arose in the distance. It sounded like thunder. Right away, a chill clawed its way up Render's back.

"All they had to do was to say it," Edwyn said, his lips pulled thin, angry tears welling up.

"Say what?"

"Just a couple of words and I'd have grown up as a normal child, loved by his parents, not as an orphan."

The booming thunder grew louder, closer, more frequent. Light flashed into the room, casting a shadow the shape of the barred window. Render shifted uneasily. When would Edwyn ever come out of this sorrowful reverie? "You know, I think something's—"

"Why, oh why, could they not just lie? My parents didn't really have to renounce their beliefs. All they had to do was say they did!"

Render stepped over to the window. Over the citadel walls, towards the coast, light flashed in the sky, yet not like lightning, which would have been in the sky. A flickering amber glow began to rise up from behind the trees. "Something's happening."

"All these years, I have been taught to abhor the evil ways of the Sojourners, their terrorist activity, their backwards superstitions and their murderous zealotry. I have resented my parents for abandoning me as a small child for their fanaticism." He stood and slipped the book back into the satchel and handed it to Render. Confused,

Render accepted it. "But I have read the entire book, and though I regarded it as poetry, or at best, fiction, what I witnessed yesterday shakes my beliefs to their very foundations."

"What do you mean?" Render said. "The Prophet? The death of the centurion?" Behind him, out the window, the faint sound of people shouting caught his attention. He turned around to look. Before he could warn Edwyn to get down, Render leapt headlong at his mentor knocking him to the ground.

Just as a fiery explosion blasted open the stone wall of his room.

CHAPTER THIRTY-SIX

IT HAD BEEN DAYS.

Bai Juang had long since ceased getting sick at the putrid stench of bodily excrement that wafted with buzzing flies. He had seen the light of day briefly perhaps four times since the Torian soldiers hauled him away from his village and locked him in the back of a horse-drawn wagon.

Like livestock.

With barely a few holes in the wooden wall, just enough to stick a finger through, he could barely breathe. No one removed the bucket in which he was expected to eliminate—it could not keep from tipping over in the dark anyway. And the few times they opened the door was to toss a raw potato at him, or to slide a cup of bitter and gritty water in.

His bare feet had grown numb from exposure and constant chaffing against the splintery boards upon which he sat. His fingernails grew long and he constantly broke his own skin from scratching—something he didn't realize in the utter gloom unless a drop of sweat touched the open and most likely festering wound.

The only thing that kept him from giving up and killing himself, after watching his wife and son slaughtered before his own eyes, was the fact that Ahndien was still out there somewhere. She had one of his sacred swords, which she loved to carry with her when she ventured into the hills, but had she the ability to use it properly? Never had anyone thought she would need to, what with the Tianese line of defense that was supposed to have secured the village, outlying the central capital though it be.

If only somehow he could return to the Sojourner's Council.

Oreus or Hephesta might be able to divine the upcoming chain of events. If he could somehow bring Ahndien and that sword together with its counterpart before the council, they might just bring about a vision, a sign, any clue as to what should happen next.

But there was no way to tell which direction his captors were taking him, nor why they had taken him alive.

Right.

Alive.

If you could call it alive. His head spun, his lungs hurt, every joint in his body ached from the limited range of motion, as his hands and feet remained bound. From head to toe, the heat burning through his skin, the stinging sweat made him so miserable that death would have been a welcome relief.

He shut his eyes. For the first time since they'd taken him prisoner he allowed himself to drift off into a deep slumber.

He didn't know how much time had passed when a sudden jolt woke him up. Tingling and alert, Bai Juang's shoulders tensed at the muffled sound of people shouting outside the wagon. From the sounds of it, one of them was a woman. And a fierce one.

The chains that locked the door rattled outside.

Bai Juang coiled back, ready to strike out with his feet or head if necessary.

The door swung open and blinding white light stabbed his eyes. For the brief moment before it blinded him, he saw that in the midst of a deep purple backdrop, it was the moon.

Before his eyesight cleared, his captors threw a dark hood over his head and dragged him out onto the cold, damp ground. His knees scraped against twigs and stones, his feet sensed pressure, but nothing else.

"On your knees, Tianese dog!" The man's voice was rough, unrefined. Precisely what one would expect from a Torian soldier. A pair of hands slapped down upon his shoulders and forced him down.

The sound of a long sword whining as it scraped out of its sheath could mean only one thing. They meant to behead him. He thought about begging for mercy, but realized they were not the sort that would be moved by such pleas.

Instead, he held his covered head high as he could. His chest firmly set and shoulders back. He would never understand the mechanism to their taking him for days from his home, only to execute him, but he would meet his death with dignity.

The soldier made a loud grunting strain. Bai Juang knew the sound of a heavy sword lifting over its wielder's head, slashing heavily through the air like a large bird.

He clenched his jaw, and took one last breath.

CHAPTER THIRTY-SEVEN

LAYING STUNNED amidst the debris, it took only a moment for Render to surmise that the castle had been struck by a flaming incendiary cauldron from a trebuchet. Shards of the earthen vessel lay scattered around his room. A gaping hole had been smashed into the wall where the window once stood.

"Edwyn!" Acrid fumes from burning chemicals choked him as he cried out. Smoke stung his eyes. Though he could open them, he could not see a thing through the billowing clouds and searing flames.

"Here, Render!" He felt Edwyn's hand grasp his forearm and pull him to his feet. "We must find the door."

Another projectile hit the side of the castle. Render almost lost his footing at the impact. Through the crackling flames, the sound of crumbling stone and sand hissed. He clawed blindly for the door. "I can't see!"

The skin on his face burned, he wanted to open his eyes, but every time he did, the heat forced them shut.

Then came a heavy pounding.

"Guards! Let us out!" Edwyn cried.

Render found the door and joined in the pounding shouting. But to no avail. It had been chained. "Where are they?"

"Must have fled."

"Then we're trapped." A sinking sensation pulled at Render's innards. The only other way out was the hole in the wall. And a three story drop. The choice was clear. Burn to death or risk breaking their necks.

Something from above fell with a heavy thud. A rush of cool air from the floor shot upwards. A rafter from the ceiling had fallen and the floor from the room above them had opened.

"Quick," Render said, pushing his table under the opening. "Climb up!"

"You go first!"

"No, Edwyn, you're too heavy for me to pull up."

"Thanks a lot." The bulky Don stumbled to the top of the table and leapt up to the remaining rafter. Straining aloud, he pulled himself up through the opening in the ceiling. Choking on the smoke, he rolled away from the hole and reached his hand down.

The fire grew even hotter. Flames licked up from under the table. Its legs were burning. The opening above sucked out whatever little air came into the room from the gash in the wall and it only made the fire burn hotter. Render climbed up onto the table. Stretched his hand upwards.

Reaching.

Reaching.

Almost touching Edwyn's outstretched hand.

A slight groan from bending wood.

The table collapsed.

Render gasped as it fell out from under his feet. This

made him cough violently even as he anticipated hurtling down into the fire. But something yanked his wrist. Pulled him upward. Sir Edwyn snarled and huffed and strained as he pulled Render up through the hole in the ceiling.

When he emerged, Render rolled onto his back and drew a deep breath. There was enough fresh air in this room to breathe. But not for long. The flames from below continued to climb.

"Follow me," said Edwyn helping Render to his feet.

As they stepped outside, it felt as though a thousand fire ants were crawling up Render's back. His mouth fell open.

Up on the fourth floor of Castle Mittlevald, instead of staring across the cavernous foyer below, he was gazing at the heart of Valdshire Tor. The entire southern wall was gone.

"Come, come!" Edwyn urged. "We must get out."

They rushed down the winding staircase. But just as they were about to pass the third level. Render stopped.

Down the hall way, the sound of chains rattling and pounding rang out. "Render! Are you in there? Answer me!"

"It's Kaine," Render said.

"The stairs may collapse at any moment," Edwyn said. "We must continue."

"I can't leave him there, he's my brother." Render pushed away and called down the hallway. "Kaine! I'm here. Hurry!"

He looked up and came running. The smile on his face bore witness to his relief. "Render! I thought for sure you'd—"

An earsplitting explosion shook the ground. Kaine nearly stumbled. The door to Render's room blew open sending fragments of the chain clinking to the floor.

Flames roared out angrily through the door's fissures.

"Come on, hurry!" Render said.

"You're all right!" said Kaine as he arrived. He pulled his brother into a tight embrace and his weapons rattled against his armor.

"We must find Folen and Stewan," Edwyn said.

"Don't you think they'd have evacuated like the rest?" Kaine said. "Come to think of it, why haven't you both done the same?"

"House arrest," Render said. "The guards abandoned us."

Another incendiary hit the castle. Render never had much contact with any of the inhabitants, and the few he saw regularly, servants and staff members were nowhere to be found.

"Stop wasting time!" Edwyn rushed down to the second floor, where the twins resided. Render had never seen him move with such speed.

"Folen!"

"Stewan!"

They arrived to find their door shut. Edwyn grasped the door handle and pulled it away quickly. "It's too hot inside." With his hand wrapped in the loose fabric of his cloak, he tried the door again. But it was locked.

"We're too late," said Kaine.

Ignoring him, Edwyn grabbed a heavy chair from the wall. With a shout, he smashed it into the door once, twice, and finally on the third strike, the door burst open.

Flames roared out from the bedchamber. Render shielded his face from the searing heat. Bright amber and golden light flooded the entire room. If the twins were inside, there was no chance of their surviving. This did nothing to deter Edwyn from calling their names over and over.

One of the tall pillars out at the front of the castle began to groan and crumble. Before Render could draw anyone's attention to it, it fell with a ground shaking crash into the middle of the courtyard. As it fell, he took in the full panorama of the citadel. Strange, where was the royal army? As far as he could see, Castle Mittelvald seemed a lone target by the Tianese troops. Why was it that no other parts of the citadel had been attacked?

"We really must get out," Kaine said, pulling him by the arm. Then to Edwyn he said, "They may have escaped with the rest."

By the time they got back to the staircase, Render could see the enemy forces. They had begun withdrawing through the opening they'd made by ramming a large part of the citadel wall. Enemy torches faded back into the wood though the occasional flaming arrow flew back at what remained of the castle. Edwyn and Kaine had already entered the foyer.

Nothing could have prepared Render for what he found as he stepped through the rubble. The bodies of several members of the castle staff lay strewn on the floor, some with arrows sticking out of their backs, others soaked in puddles of blood.

Though Kaine leaned against the open space where the massive doors to the main entrance once stood, Edwyn knelt at a pile of hulking stone bricks. Both hands on his head, he rocked back and forth and wept. When Render came to his side, he realized why.

CHAPTER THIRTY-EIGHT

FROM WITHIN HIS HOOD, hot steam from Bai Juang's breath and tears nearly stifled him. He prayed the blow to the back of his neck would be swift and clean. But the next sound he heard was not what he had expected.

A swift whistle.

A flying arrow.

Coming straight at him.

He held his position, determined to die with dignity, whether by sword or by arrow. But the sound of it piercing flesh, cracking through bone, was not his own. Unless he had grown so numb that he could not tell.

The soldier standing above him let out a gurgling cry.

A heavy thud fell by Bai Juang's side.

He turned his head to the left, then the right, trying to discern what he could by sound alone.

Another arrow.

A second man, blubbering in fear.

Then another pained cry and thud.

"What is happening! " Bai Juang cried out. "Who are you?"

The reply came with a quick shove in the back as someone grabbed his wrists, slipped something between them and then cut the cords. He was free.

"Wait!" The woman's voice, smooth as satin, was furtive, urgent. "Hold still!"

Still on his knees, Bai Juang pulled the hood from his head. Gasped deeply as though he had been holding his breath underwater longer than he should. He turned to look over his shoulder.

A lady in a dark cape was cutting the rope that bound his ankles.

With that, He leapt to his feet.

A very large Torian soldier lay on his back, his mouth and eyes agape as though the last thing he saw were a ghost. Two arrow shafts rose from his chest, still as silence.

"Who—?"

"A friend." The lady, a fair skinned Torian who exuded aristocracy lifted a slender finger to her lips. Her ebony hair, shone in the brilliant moonlight which stung his eyes like needles. She held her head high, her chin tucked down and eyes, sharp as a bird of prey. Her crossbow at the ready, she searched the surrounding area. "We must go, quickly."

"How can I know where I am going when I don't know where I am?"

"Keep quiet!" She stepped over the second soldier, who in his death pose looked as taken by surprise as the first. Then she pointed through the tree branches. "There."

As his eyes adjusted to the moonlight, he blinked. Then blinked again. Through the tree leaves and branches it was unmistakable.

"Mount Handara."

How could his fortune have changed so drastically? Bai Juang rubbed his eyes and looked again. He could not help but smile.

"Yes, Bai Juang. I have come to bring you to the Sojourners Council."

CHAPTER THIRTY-NINE

No.

Words could not escape Render's mouth. With eyes wide open, a look of surprise and fear etched eternal into his features, Folen lay on his back, an arrow, the shaft of which still burned, protruded from the center of his chest. By his side, the upper half of Stewan's still body extended out from beneath a pile of enormous stones. Blood drew a dark line down from the corner of his mouth, his eyes, devoid of life, were still pooled in tears.

Sorrow upon sorrow fell upon Render. He never spoke to Edwyn about letting them go and visit their adopted parents. Had he done so, they might be in their loving care now. "What kind of soldiers would kill even children!"

"Tianese, Sojourners," Kaine said, through clenched teeth. He wiped his eye and peered out at the courtyard, where the fallen column almost blocked the entryway. His eyes widened suddenly. "Take cover!"

Because the Tianese troops had been withdrawing into the wood, and because the castle was all but demolished now, Render hadn't expected any further attacks. The explosion of the incendiary corrected that assumption.

A downpour of splintered wood, stone and dust followed. When he could see again, he perceived Kaine and Edwyn stumbling out of the castle, arms over their faces and coughing.

He was just about to run out to join them when he heard a faint sound. Like a child crying. A quick glance down at his feet reminded him it was neither Folen nor Stewan.

"Render, come on! Quickly, before the entire thing collapses!" Edwyn shouted back into the ruins.

But Render followed the sound to a door towards the castle's east wing. To his dismay, it became necessary for him to climb over the open-eyed body of a man servant crushed under a large slab of stone the size of a dining table.

It was from beneath that very slab that Render noticed a small white hand extending and flexing its fingers. Muffled cries emanated from the rubble.

He knelt down and found a boy trapped in space between the slab and the ground. The gap was not quite tight enough to crush him, but sufficient to entrap him. "Hello, are you all right?"

The boy turned his face. "I'm trapped!"

"Branson!"

"I can barely breathe. If this slab pitches one way or another, I'll be flattened!" A dark voice whispered into Render's thoughts, It'll serve the little monster right!

Partly because he wasn't certain how exactly to help, and partly because that voice had taken him aback so, Render stood frozen. Singeing heat from the flames encroached. The fumes provoked a fit of coughs.

"Render, get me out of here!"

He'd just as soon leave you to die.

"Would you stop floundering and do something!"

"Oh, do shut up and let me think!"

"Let you think?" Branson scoffed. "That'll be the death of me, for sure!"

Render rested a hand on the slab, which was alarmingly hot. As he leaned a bit on it to determine how firmly it was situated, the slab shifted.

Branson let out a howl. "You're killing me, you idiot!"

Forget him! Save yourself while you can.

Render pulled his hand away and began walking away.

"No, wait! Come back here this instant!" Branson cried.

As he neared the hallway, Render's eyes fell upon the heavy wooden beam that had fallen across a chair. With all his might, he grasped both beam and chair and pushed them, wood scraping against the stone floor, towards the slab.

Slivers pricked his hand as he pushed the lower end of the beam under the slab. Branson continued to mutter and complain, but Render ignored it. Not sparing a moment, he wedged the end of the beam in as far is it would go.

"Watch it, you dolt!" said Branson, slapping the wood beam set before his face.

"I don't know how long I'll be able to hold it up. So as soon as you can, roll out from underneath."

"Just. Be. Careful!"

Without answering, Render bore down with all his strength on the upper end of the beam. The slab did not budge. An endless stream of complaints gushed from Branson's lips. The fire grew so intense that Render could feel its deep beating, like wings of a gigantic moth.

Sweat poured down his face and stung his eyes. It's too late for him. Why should you die in vain? Render let out a grunt. "Shut up!"

At that, Branson stopped. Render leapt up and leaned his entire body atop the wood beam. This provided just enough leverage to lift the slab. He felt it rise off the stones which prevented it from pulverizing Branson. "Now, Branson!"

To Render's surprise, Branson sprung up into sight. Render pushed off the beam and let the slab down. Not to his surprise, the spoiled son of Lord Agon began to spew forth oaths. "Where are the guards, the military? How can they have all abandoned my father's home without so much as a—"

Render grabbed Branson's arm with enough force to silence him, if only momentarily. "Quit your jawing! We have to get out of here!"

This time, Branson obeyed and followed him into the hallway. The collapsing structures further encouraged him to listen. It was difficult to see through the dark billowing smoke, even when he wasn't shielding his face. But they finally made their way to the main entrance.

A wall of fire impeded them.

"We've been attacked and the portcullis hasn't even been lowered!" Branson said, glaring up at the archway.

"If it were, we'd have no way of getting out."

"And I suppose you're just going to walk through those flames?"

The ground shook. The ceiling above the hallway was coming down, one section after another. This sent a gust of searing heat right up against their backs.

"Not walk," said Render, grabbing Branson by the collar and belt. With a straining grunt, he heaved the boy off his feet and threw him through the fire. A second later he himself took three steps back, then jumped headfirst through the flames.

He shut his eyes, covered his face with his arms and

shouted as he blasted through the searing conflagration and out the door. If he had misjudged and the fire actually extended over the drawbridge, both he and Branson would be incinerated.

Render landed hard on his shoulder. The air rushed out of his lungs. He expected to find himself surrounded by the blaze, for the stench of burning hair and clothes reached his nose.

But when he lifted his head, he found himself next to Branson on the bridge. Safe and in the open air.

"Render!" shouted Kaine in the courtyard, waving his hands with excitement. "Over here!"

Just as they arrived at the courtyard, the western wall of the blazing castle came toppling down. Before they could catch their breath, Kaine hurried them towards the western gate where Edwyn paced about, craning his neck and peering out at the center of the citadel.

Without so much as a word, Branson broke away and ran from the Castle, shouting angry words about the cowards his father employed. He even complained about his father himself, who was nowhere to be found during the destruction of his home.

"There's gratitude for you," Render muttered.

"Hurry!" Kaine grasped Render's shoulders with both hands. "He'll be looking for me."

"What are you carrying on about?" Edwyn said, pacing around the perimeter, trying to see over the citadel walls. "Where is the royal guard? Wait here."

"You're marked for death, Render," said Kaine in a gentler tone, but with no less urgency. "Couldn't let that happen to my baby brother. So when the Sojourners attacked, I came for you. It's your only chance to escape."

"What?" The entire citadel seemed to be spinning. He held his head between his hands.

"If Lord Mooregaard finds me talking to you, he'll kill us both. Now run, Render. With all speed, run!"

Render hesitated. He saw the finality in his brother's eyes and could not believe it was so simple for him to sever his ties like this. "Aren't you coming with me?"

"I can't. Now stop being an idiot and go!"

"But The Prophet said...How will I ever know who... what I'm—?"

"Haven't you heard? He's gone missing. He must be the real traitor, a Sojourner spy." Kaine gave Render a brisk embrace, grasped his arms, turned him around, and with his foot, shoved his rump forward. "Now, get out of here before you get us both killed!"

"No!" Render shouted. "I have a chance at finding out who I am, what I was destined for. And now you—"

"You're destined to have your head lopped off, if the Tianese soldiers don't get us first!"

"And now, like you've always done, you think you can take charge of me, my life, my future?"

"Don't be stupid! Go!"

"Why, Kaine? What if I don't? What are you afraid of?"

Kaine's eyes grew large with exasperation. "I'm afraid you'll die!"

"Or are you afraid that maybe, just maybe, your little brother might upstage you? You heard The Prophet! Maybe I'm meant to be a king."

"You little fool! I don't care about any of that. Now get yourself out of the citadel before—"

"Before what!" Render reached over and pulled out Kaine's dagger. He pointed it at Kaine more out of rebellion than threat.

"Put that away! They already think you're—-Have you any idea how incriminating that looks?"

"Of course you'd say that," Render scoffed. "If you

wanted to get rid of me."

From the periphery, Render saw Edwyn running back to the courtyard. The sound of approaching hooves alerted Kaine.

"Oh no," Kaine said. "It's Mooregaard. Rend, please. Listen to me. Go while you still can. You have to believe me—"

Before he could complete his sentence, Kaine stopped and backed away suddenly. "Render, come away from there."

"Do you take me for a fool?"

"I said, get away from there. Now!" Kaine pointed in the air. An enormous marble pillar began to fall. Render stood frozen with fear. Kaine, however, rushed over, tackled him and threw him to the ground, shielding him with his own body.

Unable to see past his brother, Render squeezed his eyes shut.

The pillar crashed down and hit the ground where he had been standing. It split the cobblestone and sank halfway into the ground. Sand and dust and pebbles pelted the side of Render's head.

Kaine pushed himself off his brother and fell back onto his haunches. He touched his chest and looked at his wet fingers.

From his chest, a dark circle expanded quickly across his white shirt. Blood oozed down. "Render..."

"Kaine?" Still clutching the bloodied dagger upon which Kaine had fallen, Render got up and crawled over to him. His brother fell to his knees then onto his side, his eyes wide and mouth agape. Render slipped his hand under Kaine's head. It was heavy and limp. "No, Kaine, please. I'm so sorry.... I never... you just didn't... please, Kaine, don't."

Like smoke hissing out of a log in a dying fire, Kaine uttered his last word, "Run..."

"Kaine!" Mooregaard cried as he dismounted his steed.

CHAPTER FORTY

STAND, MURDEROUS TRAITOR!" Mooregaard dismounted his horse and glanced down to Kaine's lifeless body. "Is it not sufficiently egregious that you've aided the Tianese Sojourners in this craven attack? But now, you would kill even your own brother?"

Backing away, Render could not find an answer. Sorrow and remorse clutched his heart like a hawk's talons. The dagger fell from his hand and clanked against the ground. He stared at the blood on his hands. Tried wiping them on his pants, fearing it would never come off. "But...I didn't—"

"Silence, vile rogue!" Mooregaard's sword whistled as he drew it from its sheath. With clenched teeth and the tip of his sword shaking, he pressed forward, each step quicker than the last.

"He is not responsible!" Edwyn called out. He put himself between the Mooregaard and Render. "His brother's death was accidental, I saw it all."

"Stand aside, Sir Edwyn, this is not your affair."

"But it is." Edwyn's hand moved to the hilt of his own sword.

"Then you are a sympathizer and shall be dealt with accordingly." With his elbow, Mooregaard pushed Edwyn aside and pointed his sword straight at Render. "Stand clear. This one shall be shown all the mercy his fellow Sojourners showed their victims!

So transfixed was Render on his brother's blood between his fingers that he barely noticed Edwyn drawing his sword and striking it against Mooregaard's.

"Go, Render!" Edwyn cried out between blows and short gasps. "Fly to the East, quick as you can. Keep running!"

More present than his mind, his feet had already begun to move. But all Render could see was thc look of shock on his dying brother's face. All he could hear was Mooregaard's resonant invective: Traitor! Murderer! Vile Rogue!

He hid behind the collapsed wall, despite his tutor's command to keep running. Edwyn and Mooregaard exchanged few words as they battled. The contest was clearly mismatched and Edwyn quickly lost his footing. He fell to the ground on his back and dropped his sword.

Before he could regain a grip, Mooregaard stepped on his wrist and placed the point of his weapon right over Edwyn's heart. "So you've proven what I've always suspected: You're a Sojourner. A child after your parent's heart!"

Edwyn said nothing, only lifted a defiant chin.

Mooregaard crouched down and put his face up to Edwyn's. "And now, I offer you the same mercy they were shown."

"And I offer you this." Edwyn spat in his face and began to laugh.

Wiping his face with his sleeve, Mooregaard straightened up and said, "Say you are not a Sojourner and I shall spare you. Because we are friends."

"We have never been friends."

"Say you are not of those religious fanatics, those believers in Valhandra, and I shall yet spare you."

Their eyes locked for an eternal moment.

Edwyn puffed up his chest and said, "To be indebted to you for my life? To live a lie, now that I've seen the truth?" He scoffed. "I would sooner die."

"Then you have made your choice." Mooregaard pressed his sword in ever so gradually. Edwyn made no cry, no sound of agony. He remained so still one could hardly tell he was being killed.

Until he jerked upwards once and fell back, his head tilting towards Render with a vacant gaze.

Mooregaard wiped his blade with Edwyn's cloak and resheathed his sword. By now, a company of Torian soldiers had arrived. He stood looking over Edwyn's body, then to Kaine's and shook his head. Then to one of the soldiers he spoke and pointed towards the shattered opening in the citadel wall through which Render had run. Having finally gathered his wits, Render dashed off into the thick of the wood.

He would employ all he remembered to find a hiding place and evade capture. But of this he was certain: never again could he return to this land.

CHAPTER FORTY-ONE

BAI JUANG rubbed his arms tightly as he hid within the cave among the crags of the Handaras Mountain range.

No kindling, no food, no water.

It had been three days since he caught the rabbit and roasted it. But it had since been raining and all the wood around was wet. At the mouth of the cave, the wind howled. Bai Juang thought he heard the sound of his wife and son. Weeping as she had when begging for mercy from the Torian soldiers.

Kill me, only spare my son!

They made Bai Juang watch as they killed his boy and beloved wife. The images and sounds never left him. Now, all he could think about was finding Ahndien. But he could not do so alone.

"Valhandra, why have you forsaken us?" His words came out in a frigid stutter because his clothes clung cold and wet against his back, dripping with rain water. "You promised to restore your people. You promised a deliverer. And yet, we are being slaughtered like lambs. We, the last of Your remnant."

A peal of thunder so loud and terrible rocked the ground. The wind grew more fierce. Flashes of lightning lit the caves entrance in such rapid succession that it seemed to glow continuously.

And when the white light held in place, the thunder died down to a steady roll. The wind streamed evenly, almost singing. And as the sounds of the storm faded, from the emanating light at the mouth of the cave came a whisper. It echoed, not through the cave but within his spirit.

// BAI JUANG... //

That voice.

Unlike any voice he'd ever heard before, yet as familiar as one he'd known his entire life.

// BAI JUANG... //

"I am here."

The brilliant light entered the cave and filled it with such glorious beauty that he could no longer perceive or distinguish height nor depth, solid nor energy. But what he felt, what entered his body and soul, transcended all physical understanding, something that could only be described by one word: Joy.

// WEEP NOT FOR THY LOVED ONES, MY SON //

And at that moment, all the anger and hatred for the Torians, all the sorrow and tears for his fallen family lifted off of his chest like a millstone. He breathed in the cool, refreshing wind that blew his hair back, dried the stinging water from his open wounds and it made him feel....

Whole.

"My Lord, Valhandra. I have sought after you my entire life."

// IT IS WELL SOUGHT, MY SON //

"Thank you." It was all he could think to say, in the presence of The Supremacy—for it was all he could conceive of Valhandra's infinite nature.

// AND NOW, BELOVED SON. BEHOLD, I SHEW THEE THY DESTINY //

CHAPTER FORTY-TWO

BEATING HOOVES, the shouts of mounted soldiers, his own heart beating so hard it might very well burst out of his chest. Through tar-like mud and slippery leaves, with little more to light his way than fingers of dim moonlight, groping down through parting clouds, Render scrambled through the wood.

Despite his start, the Torian horsemen and their hunting dogs gained upon him quickly. His only advantage was the shadows. With his luck, he would run straight into the hands of the Tianese.

Every breath seared his lungs, every step impaled his calves like a hot skewer. What point was there in running, in delaying the inevitable? Where could he go? To the West, all of Valdshire Tor considered him a traitor and demanded his blood. To the East, the land of the people who attacked his home, he would not be spared. Perhaps the Sojourners were the only people who might receive him—if he could find any of them. Render shuddered at the thought of falling into league with the very people who had been so vilified throughout his entire life.

The worst part of his flight was the thirst. So parched were his mouth and throat that simply breathing caused him to cough. And that only made it worse.

Up ahead, he noticed a silver glimmer in the ground. It sparkled between trees and branches. A pool.

I'll stop to drink, he thought. And die at the hands of the soldiers, to be certain. At least I won't die of thirst.

Rather than slowing to a dignified pace, Render fell face forward into the mud, the pool some fifty paces away. Just then, the Torian soldiers came into view.

Three of them came to an abrupt stop. The hounds began to whimper and whine. The horses reared up and whinnied. Despite their riders' commands, they would not continue any further.

"Captain," one said. "We dare not go on."

Render lifted his head. They did not see him down in the muck.

"No, Jarod," said the Captain, his breath trembling. "I don't suppose we should."

Barely comprehensible, Jarod began to stammer. "It's here, isn't it?

"There's no mistaking it, just look by the water's edge."

Render tried, but from the ground, he could not see past the rock in front of him.

"Sire, I would rather not."

The third rider spoke. "Captain, I will support you if you claim that our quarry fell in."

The captain took in a shaky breath. "Who's to say he hasn't, Payden?"

Jarod cleared his throat. "What shall we do then?"

"By my counsel," said the captain, he and his horse backing away slowly. "We shall return at once and report to The Lord Mooregaard what each of us has witnessed:

The young fugitive named Render has fallen into the pool and..."

Both Jarod and Payden agreed and followed him away, the hounds along with them.

Presently, alone with the rustling leaves, the drip-drip-drip of fat, blood-like raindrops hitting the leaves around him, Render let out a slow breath, his first since the Tianese attacked Castle Mitlevald.

In the short time that had elapsed, his entire world collapsed. He'd seen Folen and Stewan dead, while that odious brat, Branson was saved. By Render's own hand, no less. Where's the justice in that?

And more disturbing still, Edwyn had given his life so that Render, an accused murderer and traitor could escape. For what truth had he died? Why would he allow himself to die in the very manner for which he'd resented his parents?

As Render stood up, his head became faint. The image of Kaine, vivid as daylight, eyes wide with surprise that his own brother would kill him, lodged itself the darkest recesses of his mind.

Traitor.

Murderer.

"No," Render staggered towards the pool. "It must be delirium. I'm dehydrated. Yes, that's all it is. I'm dehydrated. Water. That's all I need."

He stepped over a log. Not even bothering to look around, Render knelt by the pool, the water of which seemed utterly pure and reflective. Like a mirror. He cupped his hands and lowered them.

"My word!" Not even a ripple formed as his hands sank into the cool, refreshing water. The pool was so beautiful, it was almost terrifying. He lifted his hands to his mouth. Barely a drop leaked out, and those that did fell silently back into the pool, without that deep dripping sound one ordinarily hears. It was more of a hiss. As if it they had evaporated.

As soon as the water touched his tongue, Render gasped. It was by far the sweetest water he had ever tasted. Right away, he slurped the entire handful into his mouth and swallowed greedily. Then he went and drew another handful. And another. He could not seem to get enough. Nor did he desire to be satiated.

He was so engrossed in his frenzied drinking that he never heard the deep growl of the creature that leapt at him and knocked him over.

"What!"

Render's first instinct was to run back to the water. But when the creature let out a vicious snarl, he jumped back. When he saw what it was, he scampered back on his rear.

Looming before him was the largest, blackest, most terrible creature he'd ever laid eyes on. It stood over him, breathing in his face. A panther. From the way its deep green eyes fixed upon his, you'd think it had something to say.

Slowly and with great care, Render tried to inch away towards the water. But the panther slapped its mighty forepaw down onto his arm, tearing through his sleeve and skin. It bled slightly, but Render got up and backed away. Strangely, every time he tried to get near the water, the panther would lurch forward, warding him off.

"So this is your pool, then. I see." Render tried without success to sound unafraid. But a numbing chill tingled down his spine. Because when he looked around, he saw that the log he had previously stepped over had not been a log at all. It was the leg of a dead soldier. Render let out a gasp.

On thick black velvet paws, the panther approached. It

bore deadly white fangs and let out a deep, undulating growl as it looked around the pool. Render counted not one, not two, but nearly a dozen dead soldiers, Torian and Tianese alike, strewn around the pool, all in various stages of decay.

"Your work, no doubt." Render stared into the emeralds in the panther's head which had not yet released him. "For water, you killed them?"

The Panther lifted a paw and let out an angry growl. It pounded the ground with a heavy thump.

"I'll leave, if that's what you want." Render bent down and reached a hand towards the water. "Just one more sip and I'll—"

The panther roared and leapt right onto Render, knocking him off his feet. Its paw rested on his chest and it flashed angry teeth. Chest heaving, through wheezing breaths, Render said, "All right, all right. I'll leave!"

The odd thing about the panther's response was that it actually stepped away and permitted Render to leave. Stranger still, at least in Render's mind, was that this did not surprise him. Somehow, it seemed that he and the beast had come to an understanding.

"Well then," Render said, glancing back at the pool. "Thank you for the drink." He thought himself clever and bold to jest, when he should surely be dead, like those soldiers on the ground. But the thought faded as he walked away. It was then that he noticed something most peculiar about the dead soldiers.

One clutched a sword protruding from his stomach. Another, the hilt of a dagger which he appeared to have used to slit his own throat and wrists. And another still clutching his own wrist, which held the blade that he had used to gouge out his own eyes.

Now, not for fear of the panther that stood there like a

mythical dragon guarding its treasure, Render began to run. The sweet aftertaste of the water in which he had so delighted turned bitter. No matter how much he spat, he could not get the taste out of his mouth. Or his memory for that matter.

He would have continued to run, if not for the voice that whispered, "Murderer."

"Who's there?"

The voice came neither from behind, nor before him. Not from the left or the right. Thus disoriented, Render tried to convince himself that he was only imagining this. But before he could take another step, it came again. This time so close, the whisper seemed to be directly in his ears. But without an embodied breath behind it.

"You killed them all."

Render tripped back over a fallen tree trunk, his eyes wide with fear. Another corpse, a dirk lodged into its heart. Render grabbed the knife and pressed his back up against a large rock. He pointed the dirk before him. "Who are you?"

"Who are you?"

"Show yourself!"

With sardonic laughter, the voice faded away.

Then all was still.

Save the cold, weeping wind.

A dark cloud smothered whatever remaining moonlight there had been. With the resounding accusations, the cruel laughter echoing in his mind, he sat. When he was fairly certain he was alone, the full realization fell heavy upon him. Their faces haunted him.

Stewan.

Folen.

Sir Edwyn.

"Kaine," he murmured, and wept bitterly.

CHAPTER FORTY-THREE

THE TROUBLE with weeping out in the open is that you never know who might come your way and interrupt. With his knees drawn up and face buried in his arms, Render's heart flowed out with his tears. How could his only friends, his only brother be gone?

"I'm alone."

A cold breeze rushed by. Render pulled his knees in closer.

"Alone, yes."

That voice. Eerily familiar, yet not. It mocked him.

Render bolted up to his feet. Reached for his sword but realized he had none.

"Behind you."

He spun around and standing right before him was the most awful sight he'd ever seen. "You?"

"You, actually." It was as though Render was gazing into a looking glass. By all that made sense, this could not be. Yet, it was clear that this person embodied everything

Render knew of himself. His doppelganger, wore almost identical clothing, yet devoid of hue. In fact, its entire presence seemed translucent, like dark, gray tulle. He stood with his arms crossed over his chest. "Come now, Render. Let's not put off the inevitable. You know what you've earned."

"But I didn't—"

"Pond scum! You weren't worth anything at birth and you're worth even less now."

What horrified Render most was the familiarity, the intimacy of these words. The way they were spoken, personified. "What a fool you were to imagine that you could be anyone of significance. A painter? A poet or musician? Ha! You were at best a lowborn slave!"

"I'll not hear any of this," said Render. He shook his head, rubbed his eyes and walked away. "You're not real. Not even here. You're just a product of my distress."

The dark Render laughed. "Even now, you deny my existence? Well, I'll show you the futility of that effort. The sooner you admit the truth, the sooner we resolve this."

"And just what shall I admit?" He began to walk faster, ignoring as best he could the cruel accusations.

"That you're nobody. You're worthless." To Render's surprise, the ghostly double grasped his arm and held him back. "You cannot escape me any more than you can yourself."

Anger boiled up. Render withheld the words he felt like saying.

"That's right," said the double. "Ponder it. More and more. It's just that close to your tongue."

"I hate you."

"And I, you, sickly worm!"

"Shut up! Shut up! Or I'll—"

"Or you'll what?" The doppelganger slapped the back of Render's head. A stinging shock flashed down his spine. "You haven't got Kaine to hide behind any more. What will you do, eh? As if you could conceal your dark thoughts from me, you sniveling, whining child!"

Never had anyone incensed him as this ghastly reflection, never had Render felt such dark intentions so close to the surface. He never thought he'd act upon such barbaric feelings.

Until his doppelganger shoved him in the back of his head one time too many. Render swung around and, despite the fact that this ghostly double could not in actuality exist, grabbed his throat and snarled. "I don't care who you think you are, you're going to shut up and leave me alone!"

"Oh am I?" He laughed, unaffected by the fingers gripping his throat. "You're like one of those little lap dogs. You know, the kind that barks and snarls, but never really—"

"Shut up! Shut...UP!" Render thrust his fist square into the doppelganger's nose. The double fell back, and touched it, gazed at the blood that had dripped onto his hand.

"Oh, nice. Very nice indeed." Before Render could react, the doppelganger hooked his leg under Render's. Render tripped and fell back. The insidious version of Render fell upon him and began striking him in the face. Each blow sent white flecks of light into his eyes, shut though they were.

Render managed to turn over onto his side and deflect the blows. Then he clutched both hands around the doppelganger's neck and began to throttle him.

In the very same way, Render's double attempted to strangle him. The harder Render squeezed, the harder his double did. The double however, only smiled with satisfaction, whereas Render felt his eyes would burst out of his head. He reached for the dirk he'd lifted from the corpse. But it was no longer in his belt.

The doppelganger mocked him with cruel laughter. "You can no more kill me than can kill yourself! You haven't the strength nor courage." But Render would not let go. Soon, his vision blurred. His head began to swim. Try as he might, Render could not draw a single breath past the clamp on his throat. Tears of pain stood in his eyes. He was going to die at the hands of a specter.

CHAPTER FORTY-FOUR

THE CLIMB to the Assembly Hall had taken less time than Bai Juang had expected. Thankfully, this mysterious lady who refused to give her name had intercepted him from the clutches of the Torians. Clearly, she had a connection to the Elders, as no one but they and a select few Sojourner scribes—such as Bai Juang—knew this location.

"It was most fortuitous that you happened upon the Torians," Bai Juang said, leaning on the walking stick the Lady had brought.

"It was destiny. For we knew of your perils beforehand. I was sent to retrieve you." Then from beneath her cloak, she produced a sword and held it before his eyes. She handed him both the weapon and its sheath. Right away, by the markings carved into the blade he recognized it. His mouth dropped in wonder.

"Why, it's—"

"Yes."

He couldn't find the right word. But it felt like

"destiny." Bai Juang swung it around, whipping it through the air and felt a surge of power running through his body. Just like his sword back home.

The one Ahndien had taken.

His heart ached, felt as heavy as a large stone, cast into a murky pond.

"But why did you not come to our rescue when we were attacked?"

"I came as soon as we learned of it. Were the Imperial Troops of no help?"

"Nowhere in sight! My wife, my son..." His voice faltered.

The Lady put her hand on his shoulder compassionately. "Truly , I am sorry."

The moon had risen impossibly higher, larger. Above them, great winged creatures too massive to be ordinary birds flew blackly over to the Assembly Hall. A chilling gust blew over Bai Juang and made him shiver. "But what of Ahndien? My daughter must still be alive!"

"Yes, yes. We know of her." The Lady smiled, but the hood of her robe obscured her eyes, making it difficult to read her expression fully. "You will be pleased to know that she is safe in the care of the Elders."

At this Bai Juang grabbed her by the arms excitedly. "She is? Oh, Valhandra be praised!" He wanted to fall to one knee, kiss her hand and pledge his allegiance to her, but instead, he simply said, "Thank you. Oh, thank you!"

"Ah, but do you not long to see her?"

"Let us not tarry a moment longer."

"Follow me."

The night grew colder as they scaled the rocky hillside, thistles tearing at their sleeves. The crisp scent of pine hanging in the air gave him strength to go on, though his entire body ached from being bound for what must have been days.

"I haven't yet thanked you, my lady."

She continued to climb ahead of him. "What for?"

"For saving my life. For tending to my needs, the shoes, the refreshment. I'd have starved or thirsted to death, if they'd delayed another day."

"They were about to relieve you of your head, my friend. And that would never do."

Catching his breath, he paused and grasped a tree branch to steady himself. "In any case..." he drew a very long breath, stared into the shadow cast by her hood, under which only the fair tip of her nose and the edges of her crimson lips could be seen. "...Thank you."

She smiled, her porcelain teeth glinting in the moonlight. "And now, your presence is much needed in the council, even now as we approach the Assembly Hall."

"Needed?" For all these years, he had done nothing more than transcribe the occasional prophecies of Oreus, eldest of the Elders. Never before had he been needed during a council meeting. "To what do I owe this honor?"

She continued up the hill until they reached a level table land. There before them stood the stone walls of the Sojourner's Assembly Hall, upon which Bai Juang had never before laid eyes. The stone walls stretched up at least two stories but had no windows. Nor did it have a door.

They came upon a smooth part of the wall which looked as though a door might stand, if it were not solid rock. A lattice of symbols which resembled those found in the ancient tomes were etched along the frame.

The lady rested her hand upon the symbols and gazed at them for a while.

"How are we to enter?" Bai Juang said.

"This shall be the first test of your entry into the Council of Elders."

Bai Juang's eyes grew wide with astonishment. "Me? An elder Sojourner? But..but..how can that be, as I am less than seventy-five years of age?"

"Your time has come, Bai Juang."

The utter surprise and joy he felt almost eclipsed the ongoing pain of his recent loss. Only for a moment. Then he grew sober again. "Perhaps in joining the council, I will manifest my own spirit potential." He had given up on this years ago, because historically, if one had not done so by the age of seventeen, it was highly unlikely they ever would, no matter how diligently one sought the truth.

But who was he to question the judgment of the Elders?

"What must I do?"

She pointed to the symbols. "This portal can only be open by the hands of a true Sojourner. One who can decipher the symbols and one through whom Sojourner blood flows. It shall open by your spirit potential."

"I don't understand."

"You are a learned man, you've studied the scrolls. I have every confidence you will pass this test." A tinge of impatience infused her words, like a drop of ink dispersing into a clear glass of water. "Are you ready?"

"I am." And what a joy it would be to be reunited with Ahndien, who was waiting in the Assembly Hall.

The Lady pulled her hood down even further, such that her entire face vanished into the darkness of her hood. "As I speak the word, you must touch the corresponding symbol."

"Understood."

"Now, begin. Qalif. Sedha. Krohnus-Tarixa."

With each word she spoke in the ancient tongue, Bai Juang found and touched the correct symbol and they lit up briefly, as hot coals, then cooled before his fingertips could be singed. Faster and faster she spoke. But it was mere child's play for Bai Juang.

At last, a heavy bang echoed in the cavernous space behind the door which had just vanished as though it had never been there.

"Well done!" The lady patted his back, the way a mother would her child. "Through and through, you are a Sojourner!"

Amazed at what he had just done, He stared at his hands, which glowed for a short moment then returned to normal. A tingling sensation, like tiny needles pricking his skin ran from his fingers through to his spine and down to his toes. It made him shudder and gasp.

"Come along now, Bai Juang. Mustn't keep the Elders waiting."

"Yes."

Slowly, he followed her into the dark hallway and the stone door reappeared sealing him in. He never saw the lady pouring the grounded shikar stone powder into the flask of Dragon'sblood Wine.

CHAPTER FORTY-FIVE

HE WAS ABOUT TO DIE. At his own hand no less, albeit through that of his alter ego. Sheer madness, that what this was. It was only fitting, Render thought, considering that all who had already died were not nearly so deserving of this fate as he.

The doppelganger pressed down on Render's throat with such force it would surely be crushed.

Flailing, kicking, Render fought back. With his own hands, he also tried to strangle the doppelganger, but to no appreciable effect.

Darkness fell over him. Engulfed him like a viscous void.

He shut his eyes, perhaps for the last time ever.

A frigid tear trickled down to his ear.

The pressure on his neck finally relented. Which could only mean that it was over. No life flashing before his eyes, no golden light in the sky. He always feared he would die this way, alone, in the dark, his fate unknown. Just... a warm, mildly abrasive brush across the face?

// DON'T GIVE INTO IT //

"What?"

Surprised that he could open his eyes, Render glanced sideways. The doppelganger was gone. No hands strangling him, no evil eyes glaring. Just a soft cat's paw against his cheek.

// ARISE //

He did so. With a mixture of surprise and inevitability, he sat up and blinked. It was that black cat again. Swiping her tail from side to side, she gazed up into his eyes as though she were about to speak.

// NEVER COME TO THIS POOL AGAIN //

The voice was as intimate as a whisper in the ear, but Render glanced around the wood. "Who's there?"

// WE ARE ALONE, RENDER //

It was then that the cat placed her paw on his arm and he realized what could not be. It was the cat. "First a ghostly double, now a talking—? I've gone mad. Yes, that's it. I've gone mad, indeed!"

She stretched forth her forelimbs and began to do something that made the hairs on the back of his neck prickle.

With dried leaves crackling underfoot, her legs, her entire body began to elongate. Render blinked and rubbed his eyes. A warm breeze blew over him and ceased any trembling that he may otherwise have experienced

"You've not gone mad," she said.

When he put his hands down, he beheld the willowy figure of woman. Silver moonlight haloed her ink-black hair which flowed like the mane of a lion and alighted upon her shoulders. She pulled tight the belt of her black cloak and stretched her arms as though she had just awakened from a deep slumber.

Obscured by the shadows, her features appeared fair and fine, as far as Render could see. He almost failed to realize that his mouth hung open as she approached.

Render bolted to his feet. He backed away abruptly but found his back pressed up against the rough bark of an Arcani Elm. Sensing his apprehension, the lady stopped just an arm's reach away. Her face now visible in the pale sheets of moonlight, Render thought she must be the most beautiful woman he'd ever seen. And yet, from a cat she had become a person. Part of him wanted to reach out and touch her creamy face. Another part screamed for him to run. Run for his life. He might very well be insane, and this apparition might do worse than the last.

"Render." Her voice flowed like honey, dark and rich. Her countenance, simultaneously nubile and maternal.

"What are you?"

With elegant fingers, she reached out and touched his face as though it were an ancient relic. "Long have I awaited this moment."

CHAPTER FORTY-SIX

BUT, YOU'RE A CAT!" Render slipped away from her warm fingertips. Her long nails brushed harmlessly against his face. "I am going mad!"

The elegant lady found a large rock and took a seat. Her cloak unfurled and rested over her long legs. She clasped her hands and rested them on her lap as Render began to pace about.

"The doppelganger.... the panther....dead soldiers...how does this all fit?"

"I shall explain all to thee, young Render. But it would expend a prohibitive measure of time. No doubt you have many questions. Alas, time is of the essence. We must make haste and journey forth to the mountains."

"I'm not going anywhere with you."

"Tarry here and you shall not live long enough to manifest."

"Manife—?"

She stood, drew a velvet hood over her head, and offered her hand. "Come now. To thee, all shall be expounded. But we must take leave of this place at once. Corigan's soldiers may yet return. And we may encounter the Tianese warriors as they return to their ships."

"And just why should I go with you?"

With emerald eyes, she fixed a hard gaze upon him. "Because you know well that which has been placed upon your heart. As do I."

"And what pray tell would that be?"

Her fair countenance reflected the moonlight. "That you have been predestined for matters of great import—the magnitude of which, I daresay, you have yet to conceive. Not even within your own dreams."

Something rang true. Like a chord struck upon a well-tuned lute. "What do you know of my dreams?"

"Visions, my dear Render. Unto thee, have they been bestowed. Visions of your destiny. Of this entire world's destiny. Within thy spirit hast thou beheld the blazing zeniths. Those which you have depicted upon canvas."

"How do you know about that?" He said, and began to walk with her.

"I have been nigh to thee," she said and increased her stride. "Had you taken notice, you would have beheld me in the form of the cat, watching you work."

It was then that he remembered the first time he noticed her. Back in Talen Wood, when Bobbington had tried to kill her. So many memories. They all seemed different knowing that she had been there with him. Some of the memories caused his face to flush. He needn't resurrect them. "Where are we going?"

"Do you trust me?" she said, her countenance radiant.

"Trust you? I don't even know you."

She hesitated, a brief sadness passed over her lovely face. Then she breathed deeply and said, "I am Greifer."

Their eyes met. Remained inexplicably. As though each wished to say something to the other, but could not.

Greifer pulled her hood over her ebony locks and reached her hand out towards his. "Do you trust me?"

More than anything else, he felt too weary to argue or question her further. After all he'd witnessed, or perhaps hallucinated, he had just as much reason to trust her than not to. "I suppose."

"Then retrieve thy weapon." She glanced down, and there was the dirk that he had dropped in his scuffle with the doppelganger.

"We must journey westward. To those very mountains."

"Why?" What's there?"

Greifer turned her face forward and began to walk. "The Sojourner's Council."

CHAPTER FORTY-SEVEN

"WAIT HERE." The lady placed her hand upon Bai Juang's chest and it almost felt as though he could not breathe until she removed it.

"I want to see my daughter."

"And so you shall. But you must wait." She pulled out a wine flask, removed her hood and unfurled her glistening black hair. "Remain here until I return for you. Then you shall see your precious daughter."

That was all he needed to hear. His breath returned to him and he lowered his arched shoulders. "When I opened the portal...did that prove...?"

"You have manifested, yes. And you have proven most helpful."

"My Lady, of what do you speak?"

Without another word, the lady walked into the dark corridor, leaving Bai Juang anxiously awaiting his reunion with Ahndien.

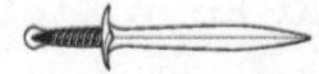

My Lady?

What did that Sojourner fool know of Lords and Ladies? Bai Juang believed that she had rescued him for the purposes of the Sojourner's Council, but had he known how she'd played him for the fool, he might not be so courteous as he had been heretofore.

She'd killed the Sojourner named Lucretia and taken on her form, but she needed another Sojourner—like Bai Juang, to help her open the portal and infiltrate the council.

She lowered her black hood, gripped the flask of ceremonial Dragon'sblood Wine in her hand, and walked the long corridor to the courtyard where the Elders had assembled. Her head grew light from the Shikar stones sapping her energy. She had to carry out her mission quickly, for if she kept them on her person much longer, they would drain the very life from her.

A couple of more steps and she would soon be upon the council.

Her heart fluttered, faint from weakness and afloat with anticipation for what she was about to do. She thought of Bai Juang, waiting for her like a foolish child, believing every lie she fed him. Perhaps she would keep him around, in case she had not regained her strength enough to operate the portals.

From the mouth of the corridor, a voice, strong and commanding resonated in the courtyard. She hid behind a stone column and listened to him speak. Oreus, the old fool.

He was addressing the entire assembly, prophets and elders, with joy in his countenance. And why not? The time for which they had all waited so many years drew nigh. Their deliverance from exile would soon be upon them. Their hope for generations.

If not for tonight.

Holding the ceremonial wine—Lucretia's part in the celebration—she entered the courtyard.

From what Bai Juang could hear—words of hope, hearty cheers, the Sojourner's Council had reason to celebrate. One phrase rang through that courtyard in the center of the edifice. A phrase that confirmed all he and the faithful remnant—wherever they had been scattered—had hoped for.

"The Great Deliverer!" They cried in unison.

Goblets and chalices clanked. Such an auspicious occasion. But more importantly, Bai Juang could not wait to see Ahndien—the last remnant of his family—to hold her close and not let go.

He leaned back against the rough stone wall, barely noticing its warmth to his fingertips. With his eyes shut, he sank down to the floor, exhausted from the long journey since his captivity. The voices of the Elders faded like an echo into the darkness of the corridor in which he sat, crouching. Resting.

At first, he did not notice the sound of words cut short.

Interrupted by a horrible strangling sound.

Strained groans.

Cries of agony.

Bai Juang sprung to his feet. Drew his sword.

"Ahndien!" His heart hammered within his chest as he dashed through the endless corridor. What he saw when he finally entered the courtyard nearly caused him to drop his sword. His knees felt like pillars of sand.

Before his eyes, the great elders, Oreus, Timea and Hephesta, lay on the ground, their eyes wide and mouths agape. Their limbs twitched perversely but death had already enshrouded their faces.

Kneeling above Oreus, her back facing Bai Juang, the lady in black drove a carved stone dagger into the chief Elder's chest, which rose and fell two more times then stopped.

Just then, a shadow so large it covered the entire outdoor courtyard in the center of the edifice darkened the entire area. The lady looked up and smiled. A mighty whoosh-woosh threw clouds of dust into the air, which got into Bai Juang's eyes, nose and throat.

The oncoming sound was so great it masked the sound of his coughing. When finally he opened his eyes, the shadow was gone. The moonlight struggled to penetrate the dust floating around him.

A mail clad knight robed in black stood by the lady. Neither of them took note of Bai Juang's presence.

"My Lady," said the Knight. "You have accomplished what no one else could have imagined."

"With your assistance, of course. The Shikar stones proved most effective."

"Had you any doubt?"

She shook her head and with her foot shoved Oreus' body such that it rolled onto its back, revealing a man of countless age. Now dead. Bai Juang could not imagine how this was possible. And why hadn't he transformed?

"Come now," said the Knight. "Let us return...fair Lucretia."

At this she smiled. "I no longer need that vile Sojourner name. And I do so prefer you address me by my own."

"But of course." He inclined his head, took her hand and kissed it. "Shall we take flight then, Lady Volfoncé?"

"As it please thee, My Lord Mooregaard."

Bai Juang hid behind a stone column trying to keep still. He could not permit his shaking breath to give him away.

However, his leg cramped and he could not help but shift his weight to the other. That slight motion caused his sword to scrape against the column.

He clenched his teeth.

In the dead silence of the courtyard, the tiniest scrape was loud as a heavy book dropping in a library.

The dark lord and lady both spun around.

Bai Juan swore silently.

If he ran, he would reveal his position. If he remained, they would find him.

Mooregaard murmured to Lady Volfoncé who replied, "The portal remains open, I no longer need him."

"The effects of the Shikar?"

"All but one piece disposed. I shall recover quickly."

Then with a series of heavy beating sounds, followed by the same wooshing wind that preceded his arrival, the sound faded into the night.

A cold bead of sweat rolled torturously down the side of Bai Juang's face. Right into his eye, where it stung wickedly. But he could not lift even a finger to rub it. He clenched his fist around the hilt of his sword, but there was no sound coming from the courtyard.

It was as though Lady Volfoncé and Lord Mooregaard had vanished.

He waited a moment longer.

Until he felt it safe to look.

Slowly, he moved around the column.

Quietly.

Steadily...

A sharp pain seized his neck. Before he could say a word, his throat collapsed in the fierce grip of Lady Volfoncé's claw-like fingers. She smiled in a way that looked more like a snarl. "Did you really think I'd forgotten?"

Still grasping him by the throat, she lifted him off the ground, his legs flailing. His eyesight began to dim. Unable to turn his head, he tried to search for Ahndien. His eyes swept the left-then right, left-then right.

But it was no good.

Wide as his eye were, he could only see blackness coming over him.

With his last bit of strength, as the air stopped flowing, he lifted his sword. No sooner had he raised it, than Lady Volfoncé plucked it out of his hand, as though it were a mere toy.

With her left hand, she reached into her cloak and pulled out a star shaped stone, its points sharp enough to cut through leather. "Behold, the bane of all Sojourners."

His sword fell into the dirt soundlessly.

The last thing he felt was a small cut in the side of his neck.

CHAPTER FORTY-EIGHT

DAY BROKE WITH THE SHRILL CRY OF A HAWK flying overhead. Render awoke with a jolt. His clothes stuck damply to his back. The sweet scent of morning dew clung to the air, belying the horrific events of the night before. Above him, small song birds warbled. Before him flowed a prattling stream.

It took a moment to regain his bearings. He sat up, shook the slumber out of his head and squinted as a sharp golden ray of sunlight cut through the tree branches and into his eyes.

"Where am I?"

The sudden realization that he was out of doors left him feeling vulnerable. Frightened. His dreams had been haunted by faces. Dead faces. Edwyn, Folen, Stewan. Kaine. It hadn't been a nightmare after all.

// ARE YOU AWAKE? //

"Greifer?" He wanted to turn in the direction of her voice, but her words rang not in his ears, but within his thoughts. Turning around, searching in every direction, he could not find that tall, slender figure enshrouded in black.

What he did find, however, was the black cat approaching with silent steps. With the agility of an acrobat, she leapt over a fallen tree trunk. She seemed larger than he'd remembered.

// YOU MUST EAT //

Within in her jaws, she carried an enormous fish, fresh as the morning itself. Her tail high and proud, she ambled past him and stopped by a fire which she must have started while he was asleep. While in her human state, no doubt.

"Why are you...? That is to say, why do you not...?"

// MY JAWS GROW WEARY FROM THE WEIGHT OF THIS LEVIATHAN. IF IT IS A QUESTION YOU HAVE, PRAY ASK IT QUICKLY //

"But I have so many." Render stood up and followed her to the fire ring.

As soon as Greifer set the fish down, it flapped violently and began to bounce towards the edge of a hill.

// CATCH IT, LEST IT FALL BACK INTO THE STREAM! //

Render grabbed a long stick. With three long steps, he overtook the fish and speared it just before it could roll down the hill.

// WELL DONE. SURELY YOU CAN PREPARE IT, AS YOU HAVE SO OFTEN //

"Just how long have you been watching me?" He took out his knife, held the blade over the fire.

// LONGER THAN YOU CAN REMEMBER //

After scaling and gutting the fish, which was surely as large as his thigh, Render hefted it over the fire, the ends of the stick suspended by two other tree branches driven into the soil. The salty aroma made his mouth water in anticipation.

Before partaking, Render cut the fish into small pieces. With respectful care, he placed a few onto a large leaf, and rested it on the flat surface of a rock. Greifer nodded her appreciation.

If Render had ever eaten a sweeter, more succulent fish, he was hard pressed to recall when. He shut his eyes and savored each bite. Perhaps this was no more than a renewed appreciation for life, this unexpected enjoyment of a simple meal.

"First question." Render wiped his mouth with his sleeve. Griefer lifted her head and began to wash her paws and face. "Mind you, it's not the most important one, but it's the one that comes to mind most presently."

// PRAY ASK //

"Why have you chosen this feline form, when it seems you can easily become a woman, as you were last night?"

// EASILY?//

She sat with regal dignity and gazed directly into his eyes.

// ON THIS SIDE OF THE VEIL, THE FORM IN WHICH I NOW APPEAR, IS THE ONE WHICH REQUIRES THE LEAST EXERTION. I RESERVE MY STRENGTH IN OTHER FORMS, A PANTHER, A HUMAN, FOR WHEN IT IS MOST NEEDED //

Render took another bite and forgot his manners as he

spoke and chewed concurrently. She was, after all, a cat. "I suppose what I'm asking is, what is your natural form? Human, a cat, a panther?"

// A SPIRIT //

"A spirit!" He almost choked on his food. When he stopped coughing he said, "You mean, you're a ghost?"

// NAY, FAIR RENDER. A SPIRIT IS NOT SOMETHING WHICH CAN BE TOUCHED WITH THY HANDS. NOR IS IT SOMETHING YOU CAN ONLY SENSE, SUCH AS A FOREBODING FEELING, OR A COLD BREEZE. AS A SPIRIT, I AM EVERY BIT AS REAL AS YOU, IN YOUR CORPOREAL FORM. I DARESAY, MORE REAL //

It took a while for Render to ponder this. Meanwhile, he continued with his meal until it was finished. He did not wish to trumpet his ignorance by saying anything else until he'd figured out what she meant. But he couldn't quite grasp her explanation.

"Greifer, would you favor me by taking your human form? I still find it difficult to believe I am speaking... or thinking to a cat."

// TO DO SO WILL EXHAUST ME, AND I SHALL BE LESS ABLE TO PROTECT YOU //

"Thank you, but I can take care of myself."

She gave off something that seemed like an ironic laugh.

// AS YOU WISH. TURN YOUR EYES AWAY, THEN //

He did so, wondering if perhaps in the daylight the

transformation would compromise her modesty in anyway. From the corner of his eye he looked and noticed soft white arms and legs.

"I did ask thee to turn thine eyes, did I not?" Greifer said aloud.

Embarrassed, Render spun his entire body so that his back faced her. "I... I'm sorry."

"You may turn around now."

In the morning light, Greifer looked many times more beautiful than he could have imagined. She wore a flowing black cloak over a mail shirt and black pants. Her verdant eyes shone every bit as bright and sharp and enigmatic as when she prowled as a cat. Long ebony hair rested over her shoulders. She smiled. "Does this form afford thee better comfort?"

Render's mouth hung slightly open. He meant to answer yes, but ended up nodding dumbly.

"Very well, then. If thou hast had thy fill, let us continue our journey as we converse." Her voice soothed him in a way that he could not explain. "I have as many things to tell thee, as thou must have to ask."

"How long will it take by foot?" Render gathered the remaining fish and wrapped it in leaves.

"To the Sojourner's Assembly? Five and thirty days, by my estimation."

"We'll be dead by then! If not by the hands of Torians, then the Tianese for sure. And who's to say that the Sojourners won't kill us?"

Already on her way ahead of him, Greifer laughed. "Verily I say unto thee, the Sojourners shall not harm even a hair upon thine anointed head."

"Oh? They didn't spare children like Folen, Stewan nor anyone else murdered in that cowardly seige."

At that, she stopped and turned to face him. "What of

thy brother, Kaine? Will he join you soon?"

"He can't."

"Surely thou hast not left him amongst the Torians? Not after everything he—"

"He's dead."

Immediately her countenance filled with pain. Her lips quivered. "How did this come to pass?"

Though it should not have mattered to this creature, Render somehow felt the sting of guilt and was too ashamed to tell her. "I keep trying to tell you, the perpetrators of all these cowardly acts are the Sojourners."

"Perhaps indeed I was too late." She said, her words echoing into a sad emptiness. "Perhaps thou hast been so indoctrinated that....Nay, Shamis foretold of even this."

"What are you talking about?"

"In due time, unto thee all shall be explained. But suffice it to say, what the Torians hath taught thee regarding the Sojourners, is not truth."

CHAPTER FORTY-NINE

RENDER'S QUESTIONS SEEMED ENDLESS even to himself. By late afternoon he decided that he had asked enough about the discrepancy between what he'd been taught about the Sojourners and what Greifer called truth. But thinking of the Sojourners as oppressed and persecuted twisted his understanding of the world. It was more than he could stand.

For the rest of the afternoon well until dusk, Render and Greifer exchanged few words. Once again, she transformed back into a cat because, as she had explained, her human form tired her exceedingly and would have left her too weak to help, should someone attack.

"And as I said before," Render said, rolling his eyes. "I can take care of myself, thank you."

Greifer simply regarded him with one of those cold stares only a cat can give.

"Thirty-five days on foot!" Render sat on a rock just before a ledge at the top of the hill on which they stopped. "I don't know why I'm even going along with you."

Greifer continued and peered down to the bottom of the hill.

// BE STILL //

"What is it?"

She shushed him with what sounded like a hiss. Render joined her, knelt behind a log and stole a look. Down at the foot of the hill, two roughshod men sat on the ground sharing a drink from a wine flask while their horses stood tied to a tree. They were laughing, belching and speaking with such coarseness it reminded Render of Bobbington.

Something odd caught his eye. Resting against a tree was a brown sack, its top tied with a dark brown rope. The oddest thing about this sack wasn't so much that its contents looked so strange, but that it moved. And it made quite a bit of noise, albeit it muffled.

"I'll bet he fetches a pretty price on the market," the larger of the two men said.

"If you ask me, he's a bit scrawny."

"But he seems sharp, for his age, anyway."

The smaller man shrugged. "He's a whole lot of talk, he is. Ah, he's not worth the trouble. Cut your losses, I say."

"Give him one more day, if he bothers you too much before we get him to the market, we'll slit his throat and dump him. How's that sound?"

"Fine. But you'll see. You're going to have to do it, not me. I don't like that part of this business, the blood and all that."

"And you think I do?"

"Don't seem to have no problem doing it when it needs doing. Serves you right. I told you he was going to be trouble from the first insult out of his mouth."

"We'll see if he's learned his lesson by tomorrow

morning. How's that? If he gives us any cheek, we'll cut our losses."

"And his throat."

They burst out laughing.

Render touched his neck and swallowed a lump. "Whoever's in that sack is doomed."

// TRAIN YOUR THOUGHTS UPON THE HORSES //

"The horses?" With an angry glare, Render hissed, "A person is about to be sold as a slave or murdered, and you're concerned with the horses?"

// THERE SHALL BE OPPORTUNITIES ENOUGH TO SAVE LIVES, RENDER. MANY LIVES. BUT IF WE DO NOT ARRIVE AT THE SOJOURNERS COUNCIL IN A TIMELY FASHION, COUNTLESS MORE SHALL PERISH //

"So, you mean to say that it's acceptable to sacrifice the lives of some to save others?"

// PRAY KEEP YOUR VOICE—//

"And how exactly do you judge whose lives are worth more, and whose are suitable to sacrifice?" Render hissed. "Would a slave be more suitable?" He tried to stand up and walk away, for this very discourse revolted him. But sooner than he could lift his head, Greifer placed a paw upon his shoulder. It surprised him that he could not stand up. The weight and force of her paw prevented it. He blinked and before his eyes, the slender black cat changed into that formidable panther, baring frightful fangs and emitting a low-pitched growl which Render could feel reverberating in his chest. Or perhaps it was his own heart, pitter-pattering in apprehension.

// YOU CANNOT YET GRASP ALL THAT IS REQUIRED. I IMPLORE THEE, TRUST ME //

One would imagine that a panther, as formidable as this, would make a great sound when it bounded over the log, over Render, and down the hill. But the only sound that Render heard was the whoosh of air as she flew over his head and bounded for the slave traders.

As soon as her feet hit the ground, twigs snapped. Leaves crackled. The traders started from their inebriated stupor.

"What? Who's there?" With surprising speed, one drew a sword, the other, the shorter, drew a crossbow.

"Greifer!" Render whispered.

// ASSIST ME OR STAND CLEAR //

CHAPTER FIFTY

BY THE STARS!" cried the larger sword-wielding slave trader. The shorter one screamed like a woman and fumbled with his cross bow. All the while, muffled cries emanated from the writhing cloth sack as the prisoner struggled in vain to pull free from the ropes that bound it to the tree.

Greifer roared and flashed fangs which bore a resemblance to curved daggers. Both horses reared up and screamed. Bewildered, Render gripped the edge of a branch so hard his fingers grew numb.

Down below, he could see Greifer, her sleek panther coat glistening in the amber light of the setting sun, her angry tail sweeping from side to side. Slowly, she approached both men and betrayed not even the slightest hesitation, armed though they were.

They backed away, stammering unintelligibly.

"I'm going to try to get on me horse and—" Greifer leapt over him. "Oh!" Now she blocked the path to the horses, leaving open the trail that led out of the wood and into the open road.

The taller man glanced over his shoulder, dropped his sword and flew down the trail.

"Wait!" called the other. "You cowardly worm! Don't leave me here alone!"

With great caution, Greifer approached him, even as he gritted his teeth, took a deep breath and aimed his crossbow. Unexpected pluck, Render thought. But the thought of Greifer getting killed gave him pause. She was the only person that could answer the many questions that plagued him. He could not allow her to perish. Moreover, if she was who she claimed, he owed her his life many times over.

"All right, you beast!" said the merchant. "It's just me and you then." He lifted the weapon.

Without a second thought, Render pulled out the dagger he'd lifted from the dead soldier. He concentrated his aim at the merchant's hand. In one swift motion, he threw the knife, sending it whistling through the air.

If he had not witnessed it with his own eyes, Render would not have believed what happened. The merchant let out a startled grunt. His crossbow clattered onto the rocks at his feet.

Now panting and wheezing, the wide-eyed merchant whined like a frightened child as Greifer stood upon her hind legs and planted her forepaws upon his shoulders. She glared down and growled at him, jaws ready to rip this throat out.

"No, please, no!" he cried, chest heaving with rapid gasps. His right arm dangled from the sleeve which Render had pinned to a tree with his dagger. Render climbed down and retrieved the fallen crossbow and pointed it at the pathetic little flesh merchant.

"I see you've met my friend," Render said.

"Your—?"

Greifer clamped her massive jaws around the merchant's right arm and pulled. This tore the fabric from his sleeve leaving a swatch fastened to the tree and fluttering in the breeze like a tattered sail. From the dagger which Render had thrown, smoke arose with tiny flames smoldering at the center.

Instantly, the man fell on his back, pinned by the mighty paws of the black panther. By the rumble of her growl, by the fire in her eyes, and by the same cool tingling sensation that traversed his spine, Render remembered how she had scared off Bobbington, that night at the cave, how she'd chased him from the pool with the dead soldiers.

"Please, kind sir," the merchant said. "Call off your...your...animal!"

"You must give your word that you'll never return."

"Yes. Yes. I can tell by your speech that you're of high born blood, you are. But what is someone of your princely stature doing in this rough wood, and so meanly attired?"

"Spare me your flattery and speculation, lest you try my patience beyond its limits."

The merchant bowed his head.

"Very well, then. You must also give your word that you shall henceforth cease this evil enterprise of peddling flesh."

"Young master," he said, stuttering. "Perhaps your tender age makes it difficult to see the harsh economic realities of it all. This trade of mine gives me no more pleasure than it does you. But I have a family to feed. It's an honest liv—"

"Hold your tongue, lest I cut it out!"

A repentant nod.

Render stepped forward. Slung the cross bow across his shoulder and retrieved the sword which the other trader had dropped. He glared down at the man whose neck now pulsed with trepidation, for Greifer's fangs now pressed into his skin, dimpling his neck with deep indentations.

"Now, arise. As a parting gift, we give you your miserable life. Make all haste and return to your family."

"It is well received, Sire." Greifer released the merchant but stood ready to pounce.

With the point of the sword under the merchant's chin, Render said, "Now go."

"Thank you, Sire. I give you my word, I'll never sell or trade another slave, for all my days."

Clearly, this was not one to be trusted. Render lifted his sword in a threatening manner. "On pain of our extreme disapproval, do not test us."

But the merchant had already begun to stumble down the trail and out of the wood.

"You were remarkable!" Render said, turning to Greifer. But she was not there. Not where he expected her to be, anyway. Render turned halfway to the left. Then the right. Then completely turned around and found Greifer, returned to the form of a small black cat. She regarded him with an aloof gaze, blinked twice and began to walk towards the horses.

"Did that take a great deal out of you?" Render said. "I mean, assuming the form of a Panther?"

// I SHALL RECOVER. BUT WE MUST HOPE FOR NO FURTHER CONFRONTATIONS UNTIL THE MORROW //

She stared up at the saddle of the brown horse. There hung a leather pouch, its flap slung open.

"There's this matter of the panthers I've previously encountered, Greifer." Render stepped up to the black horse which was tied next to the brown one. It blew out a breath and winced as Render stroked its mane. Soon, it relaxed and leaned slightly against his hand.

Greifer did not answer Render right away. Instead, she leapt up and climbed into the saddle pouch. After turning herself so that she faced outward, she draped her paws over the edge of the pouch and looked down at the squirming cloth sack by the tree.

"I nearly forgot." Render stepped over to the sack and knelt. "You in there. Hold still, I'm going to cut you out." He reached up and pried the dirk from the tree trunk. Then he slid the sharp edge under the rope coiled tightly around the gathered opening of the slave-sack.

With two or three attempts, the rope gave. Render pulled the sack down over the shoulders of the boy who had been captured. His face was turned to the ground and Render could not yet see it. Then he cut the ropes that bound his wrists behind his back.

Finally, he removed the gag by undoing the knot tied behind the victim's head. The boy turned around. His indignant and haughty eyes instantly betrayed him. But was this a ghost, or was it actually him in the flesh?

Render blinked to clear his eyes and to make sure he was not mistaken. "I say! Is that you, Branson?"

CHAPTER FIFTY-ONE

"OH, IT WOULD BE YOU!" Branson said, spitting out dust and shreds from the burlap cloth that had gagged him. "Untie me, at once."

"I've a good mind to put you back." Render stepped over to the tree where smoke still rose from the spot the dagger had pinned the slave trader's sleeve.

"No, wait. Come back here, immediately!"

Render glanced over to the horses and noticed Greifer asleep. "How can you sleep, now?" he whispered. "Aren't you the least bit concerned about this?"

Greifer yawned, lifted and shook her head, then rested it on top of her forepaws dangling over the saddlebag.

// THAT BOY WILL BRING THEE NO GOOD FORTUNE. YOU'D DO BEST TO LEAVE HIM HERE //

"Believe me, I am tempted." Nevertheless, Render did not heed her counsel and returned to Branson. "Hold out your hands."

"Be careful, you'll slit my wrists!"

"With my luck, I won't." With one swift motion, Render cut the chords and Branson's hands were loosed. Without so much as a thank you, he stood, shed the sack and undid the rope around his ankles.

Leaning on a tree, Render shook his head. "Why did you run?"

"As if someone like you could possibly understand."

"Very well, then. Perhaps it's best if we parted ways at this junct—"

"Have you anything to eat?"

Taken by surprise, Render reached into his pocket and produced some cooked fish, wrapped in a green Arcarni leaf. "Here." Branson snatched it from his hands and walked away eating voraciously, with all semblance of civilized manners thrown to the wayside. "You're welcome."

Through a mouthful of food, Branson said, "Do you want some kind of accolade?" He picked at his teeth and spit out a fragment. "Commoner." When he finished, Branson stared up the hill from which Render and Greifer had descended. "How ever did you escape?"

"I'm not certain. But I believe I had some help."

"Help? What help?"

Render stared over to the saddle bag where the black cat slept. Were she a panther now, standing at his side, Branson would certainly not treat him with such arrogance. But alas, she needed to rest.

"What happened to my accursed captors?"

"The slave traders? I sent them off. Did you not hear?"

"I was in a sack."

"What are you planning on doing?" Render asked, not so much because he cared, but because he was curious. "That is, after we have parted ways."

"Not that it's any of your business..." Branson's features

softened. "But I am going to... I need to find my father."

Images of Castle Mittelvald, the once proud home of the Lord Agon, crumbling in flames filled Render's thoughts. Again, the faces of Folen and Stewan, of Kaine and Sir Edwyn, all who had died that night during the siege, haunted him. "Aren't you concerned about the fate of your mother? Surely someone had survived that attack."

"Have you ever met my mother?"

"No, I—"

"Then you'd best not speak about things of which you have no knowledge." Instead of haughty disdain, Branson's eyes became bloodshot. His brow crumpled. He turned away and wiped his face with his sleeve.

Render still did not understand why Branson had fled, but it didn't seem worthwhile to pursue the question now. Cautiously, Render stepped over to him. "I didn't mean to pry."

"Just leave me alone, you imbecile!" He continued to mutter angry words as he climbed the hill.

// SOMEONE IS COMING. RESTRAIN THAT BOY OR HE WILL BETRAY OUR POSITION! //

Render turned around. Greifer leapt down and stared intently up the hill, then to Render.

// YOU MUST STOP HIM, I AM TOO WEAK //

Right away, Render went after him. "Branson. Hsst! Branson!" But he did not hear, or had chosen not to. Render dared not raise his voice because of the sound of hooves and men on foot, snapping twigs and dry leaves above and behind the thicket.

Just before Branson could reach the top of the hill, Render caught him by the ankle. Both of them slipped.

Branson opened his mouth to let out a cry but Render slapped his hand over it and muffled it.

They stopped at a tree and with a great rustling, Render pulled him behind its trunk. He put his finger over his lips and Branson wisely remained quiet.

Unwisely, Branson stuck his head past the tree to look.

Render yanked him back and hissed. "What are you—?"

Branson gasped, his eyes wild with fear. "We're going to die."

CHAPTER FIFTY-TWO

BEFORE RENDER COULD ANSWER, a chorus of deep growls had surrounded them. Branson's breathing became frightened hiccups. "R...Render...?"

In all directions, a sea of grey and black closed in. Puffs of white steam floated from the dripping jaws of every wolf in the pack.

"Don't move," Render whispered.

"C....can't move."

Feral eyes. Emanating from ivory fangs, and the smell of rotting flesh wafted over and evoked feelings of death. Brutal death. Some of the wolve's teeth were crimson-stained with blood.

In his mind, Render reached out to Greifer.

// WE'RE TRAPPED. YOU MUST TRANSFORM //

As if in reaction, the leader of the pack shot a glance down the hill to the horses. Render noticed that the saddlebag was empty.

// GREIFER! WE NEED YOUR HELP! //

Beneath the feet of the horses and from behind the tree to which they had been tied, the tip of her tail, not a panther's but that of a cat, protruded and then disappeared.

The wolf pack leader barked twice and three of the other wolves bounded down to the tree. The horses reared up and screamed at the attack. But why wouldn't Greifer respond?

A horrific cry from Branson turned his eyes back. One of the wolves had clamped its jaws around his neck. Still another bit down on his arm.

At the very same moment, the lead wolf lunged at Render. Out of sheer instinct, Render leapt into the air. To his surprise, he flew past the branches and found himself standing high above the entire scene, his feet planted firmly on a narrow branch.

Then came a dreadful voice. Strange and devoid of humanity.

// THE WAGES OF YOUR SINS ARE DUE //

A shriek from below.

Greifer, still a cat, flailed about helplessly in the jaws of a large black wolf. She hissed and spat, but could not free herself.

"No!" Branson cried out. A spot of blood expanded on his sleeve where a young gray wolf bit down.

And Render stood safely above the snapping, snarling, dripping jaws of the silver coated leader.

// YOU PLUMMET DEEPER INTO DEBT //

Frustrated and full of anger, at the voice, at himself, it

was never clear to him, Render gripped the handle of the dagger sheathed in his belt. He let out a shout and flung it at the wolf directly below him with such speed it, the blade would surely lodge itself deep into the dog's skull.

But it didn't.

As though the silver wolf had anticipated this tactic, it leaned to the left and the blade struck a root of the tree, where it flapped back and forth like a fish on the surface of sun-baked rocks.

// THEIR BLOOD SHALL BE ON YOUR HANDS AS WELL //

The voice could be described as nothing else but... evil. At that moment he knew. Branson and Greifer were about to be torn to shreds. A wave of hot desperation coursed through his blood from the center of his chest all the way to the tips of his fingers.

Without thinking Render leapt from the tree and let out a cry that echoed through the wood. Simultaneously, something like thunder boomed all around and a blinding flash filled his vision. Like it had, just before the centurion in the citadel had been struck down. Only this time, there was no question as to its source.

Suspended in the air which crackled and made the every hair on his entire body tingle, Render gasped as bolts of bluish white energy shot out from his hands to each of the wolves.

Painful howls went up.

Then cut short.

The whole thing had taken less than a few seconds, but when he blinked, he found himself standing on the ground, unaware of when his feet had made contact. Now, the blackened remains of six wolves, black smoke floating up from their twitching fur, surrounded him. White tendrils of light flickered and crackled round the carcasses. What remained of their eyes oozed out of their sockets. Red, swollen tongues hung slack from their once threatening jaws.

About eight feet away, Branson lay on his back, panting and stunned. His hair shot out in all directions, his cheek stained with soot. With eyes as wide as potatoes, he said, "What did you do?"

"I...I don't know, really." Render stepped over to him. "Are you all right?"

Branson shook his head. "Stay away from me!" His ingratitude came as no surprise. And there was good reason for him to fear. Render understood now what had happened back in Valdshire Tor at Hawthern Fountain, but this was not possible! There had to be a scientific explanation for this.

The internal discourse, however, was interrupted by the sudden thought of Greifer. Render leapt and soared clear to the bottom of the hill. When he approached, the horses stood bewildered. Instead of reacting with anxiety, as he approached, they bowed their heads as though with reverence, if horses were capable of such a thing.

Several paces from the crisp remains of the wolf that had seized Greifer lay the frail form of the black cat. "Greifer!" Render rushed over and knelt at her side. She was bleeding from a hideous gash in her foreleg.

Not sparing a moment, he tore a strip from his shirt and tied a tourniquet around it. "Why didn't you transform!" Render scolded, tears pooling in his eyes. "Why did you remain so helpless?"

// TOO WEAK... //

She lifted her head slightly, tried to turn her eyes to him.

"Don't." Render sat and gathered her into his arms. "I'm sorry. You needed to regain your strength, I understand. Can you transform now? Perhaps as a panther or a human the loss of blood would be—"

// SO COLD... //

By now, Branson was standing to the side, gawking at the carcasses. With a mixture of contempt and wonder, he stared at Render. "By the firmaments, it's just a cat!"

"Shut up!" Render lifted a fist. Branson stumbled back, arms shielding his face, and fell on his rump. Beneath his forearms, his mouth opened and closed rapidly like a fish, but he could not form any words. Instead he nodded in obedience and sat perfectly still.

"Please, Greifer. Hold on."

// YOU'VE BEGUN TO MANIFEST //

"Manifest? You mean—?"

// I MUST REST... //

By all Sir Edwyn had taught him about the medical arts, Render knew that he must stave off any possible infection. With the black cat still cradled in his arms, he searched the saddle bags. Finally he came upon a flask. With his teeth, he plucked out the cork and took a swig. Bitter. Strong. He spat it out but knew it could serve as an antiseptic. It would have to do.

"This will smart, just a bit." But Greifer's eyes were already shut. He poured a stream onto the pink and red puncture wounds which contrasted starkly with her sleek, ebony coat. She flinched one. Twice. Then heaved a sigh.

Though the twilight breeze began to chill him, Render sat down, lay Greifer upon his lap and removed his vest and shirt. He tore another strip away and dressed the open wounds. His leather vest provided little in the way of protection from the cold, but he put it back on, nonetheless. With the remainder of his shirt, he swaddled her and held her close to his body for warmth.

"Aren't you being a bit sentimental about that cat?" Branson asked, but this time, without a hint of disrespect.

Gently, Render placed her in the saddle bag, untied the white horse, and climbed into the saddle. "You are welcome to this other horse, Branson. I wish you well."

With surprising alacrity, Branson ran and mounted the brown horse, reached down to untie it. "You can't just dismiss me."

"Say what you will."

"I chose to leave." Branson scoffed. "And don't even think of following me."

Render glared at him. "You needn't fear that." He shook his head as Branson rode back into the wood, as if he'd forgotten the very perils from which he'd been saved. "You're welcome."

With one arm, he held Greifer in the saddle bag close to his side, sharing his warmth, and began riding towards the East. The sun blushed and fled towards Valdshire Tor and the west. But to the east, behind the zeniths of Handara, an amber glow illuminated the valley beneath the snow capped peaks, as if by a beautiful and terrible conflagration.

CHAPTER FIFTY-THREE

"WITH RESPECT, SIRE. Had you told me that your mistress happened to be the Empress Dowager of Tian Kuo, I might have advised you otherwise."

Bile rising to his mouth, Corigan threw a Leit game piece to the ground and it shattered. With a smoldering frustration, he glared at Mooregaard. "By your mouth, you say 'with respect.' But by your tone, your disposition, you contradict yourself."

"I beg your indulgence, Your Majesty. I live only to serve, to offer counsel." He bowed subtly. "Perspective."

Corigan snatched the queen from the Leit board and gripped it as if he could strangle the life out of it. "Then what is your perspective on this? How could I have allowed her to do this? For two years, she has deceived me. Two years!"

"You are but a man, Sire."

"And she has always abided by the rules. Never had she given even the slightest indication that she could be so...so...treacherous!"

"Corigan. No one could have imagined it. No one would dare call you...a fool."

"She promised not to attack the citadel. That is why... it was for that very reason..." Anger gave way to shame. Corigan swept the Leit pieces off the board and sat at the table. He pounded both fists down and the remaining pieces shook. "I stood with all of my active defenses, stationed outside by Puglehurst's township. That was the piece she won!" And they were not there to defend it, but to ensure that the enemy forces abide by the rules and not attack beyond the defined territory.

"Sire, the flag that flew from those cowards that attacked Lord Agon's castle..."

"What of it?"

"Have you not heard?"

"Heard what?"

"Surely you have been told by now."

"I tire of this babbling. Tell me!"

"The flag that flew over the attack bore the insignia of the Sojourners."

Corigan's throat went dry. "So she has finally descended to it. Sending the terrorists, to whom she gives comfort, to violate my kingdom."

Approaching with circumspection, Mooregaard cleared his throat. "Sire, they are a most terrifying force. And you have never engaged in full-scale warfare as your father did. No one would think you any less valiant if you did not retaliate."

"Silence!" Corigan bolted to his feet and stood face to face with his advisor. "For a counselor, you speak too freely."

"I am also your chief tactician. You would do wise to heed my counsel as did your father—"

"Who ended up dead on the battlefield while you strategized!" He stepped back and put his hand on his chest, as if doing so would calm the pounding within. "Have you any idea how long I have tried to find a civilized way of containing this conflict? For centuries our two kingdoms have spilled each other's blood. Then with the rise of the Sojourners we found a common enemy. My father's father had the wisdom to join forces with the Emperor of Tian Kuo to exterminate them."

"The Sojourners can never be completely exterminated. We can only do our best to control their spread."

"Have I not kept matters both domestic and exotic well-controlled? We've come to accept the fact that there has never been, nor shall there ever be peace between our nations. Let us be realists. Conflict is the currency of our economies. By relegating our warfare to the results of our Leit games, Xieh-Suh and I have spilled far less blood than any of our predecessors."

Mooregaard cleared his throat. "A worthy method, until now."

For a few minutes, the flow of time seemed to stand still. For all his political pontificating, one thought and image stood above it all: The Empress Dowager, that audacious commoner, that whore and pretender to the throne, laughing haughtily at him. It was humiliating enough to bear in the prison of his wounded pride, having allowed his primal urges and desires to blind his better judgment. But having his entire kingdom discover that their king, their ostensive protector, had unwittingly turned them over in a game of chance—no, strategy!—That would lay the foundation for an insurrection of unprecedented proportion.

"I must...MUST find a way to rectify this, divert their attention long enough to rise above this and prove myself a worthy ruler."

"I concur. But pray thee, Highness. Do nothing so rash as to attack blindly. Having proved her alliance with the Sojourners, the Empress Dowager is not to be underestimated."

"Nor am I." Determined to set a plan into action, any plan, he turned to his advisor, putting aside all feelings of offense, grasped his shoulder and smiled wickedly. "Mooregaard, prepare twelve legions. Leave behind three battalions to defend the citadel, that should suffice. Ready my fleet. We shall sail from the Northern Shore and fall upon those Tianese dogs in a southerly assault. Quick and with force. They shall know not what struck them. Is this not the best approach?"

"Not by my counsel." Mooregaard bent down and picked up the fragments of the Leit piece which Corigan had dashed. He tired to fit the pieces of the queen together but soon gave up and placed them on the board, broken beyond repair. "Such an action is, if you will, predictable. An army crossing East, straight across the peaks of the Handaras would be seen miles away, so what recourse remains but to land at their shores? But then, our entire fleet would be swallowed up before a single soldier set foot on Tianese soil."

"Is it any wonder my father chose you as his military advisor?" Sensing a unity of thought and purpose being forged between them, Corigan nodded with approval. "So then. What do you propose?"

With detached patience, Mooregaard righted and set the Leit pieces in an orderly manner on the squares of the board. "We should send our troops through the southern borders, around the back eastern woods, to the Valley of the Accursed."

A sudden chill rushed through Corigan's spine. "Are

you certain?"

"As you are not superstitious, you should fear nothing."

"It is not for myself." A weak grin. "Nor is it fear, but concern, rather. The troops may find it offensive." For to set foot in a place the Sojourners once called the Burial Grounds of the Ancients, would surely dampen morale, if not instill fear in those of weaker minds. In truth, this did frighten Corigan, but he would never admit it.

"It is for that very reason the Tianese would not expect us. Whatever remnants of the Sojourners there are will be easily dispatched by our troops."

"Yes. Yes. A masterful plan." But Corigan's present efforts were spent in trying to conceal his apprehension. Mooregaard had all but accused him of being a coward. He could not afford him any further reason to believe this to be true. "Very well then! Gather the troops. We shall require several days. Tonight, we march forth."

"By the time the Tianese discover our presence, it will be too late." Gripping the Monarch piece between his fingers, Mooregaard snapped the head off and tossed the broken shards besides the broken queen.

CHAPTER FIFTY-FOUR

HAVING EMPTIED THE WINE FLASKS and filled them with water, Render stared out at a sea of sand. The sun had risen not more than two hours ago and he had ridden his mare—whom he'd named Destiny—out of the wood and to the very edge of the Valdshire Tor. Before him, waves of heat rose up and reflective pools, which took the appearance of ponds that did not exist, glinted in the distance. At the horizon, a wall of mountains stretched upwards, white caps against a blue canvas. In the center, the grandest of all summits, Mount Handara. Though it stood many miles away, just seeing it with his eyes for the first time, gave him a sense of anticipation.

He put his hand on Greifer, who was awake now. Though she had slept the entire night, she did not show any sign of improvement. "We've reached the desert."

She lifted her head from the saddlebag and gazed out at the vast and desolate land ahead.

// FROM HERE, WE MUST TRAVEL WITHOUT INTERVAL. FOR BY NIGHTFALL, WE SHALL REQUIRE THE REFUGE OF THE HILLS //

"How long?"

// UPON HORSEBACK, HALF THE DAY //

"Are you well enough?"

She put her head back down, her emerald eyes vanishing into the darkness of her fur.

// I SHALL HAVE TO BE //

With a light tap of his heels Render rode forth, wonder and dread intermingling within. From his perspective, the mountains looked nothing like they had in his dreams. And yet, they felt so familiar. As if he were returning to a place to where he'd been, long ago.

As Destiny trotted out into the open landscape, a sound coming from the wood arrested his attention. It grew closer, louder. When he turned around, he saw, emerging from the shadows and branches, that which he would not have expected.

Pompous as could be expected, Branson came riding out into the open. Upon his horse, he matched stride with Destiny and spoke not a word.

"I thought you weren't coming with us."

"Just because I happen to travel on the same path doesn't mean I'm following you."

Render let fly an incredulous huff. "Right."

"The truth is, I was concerned about you."

This time, a full-bellied laugh broke out from his lungs. "About me!"

"I suppose it's a weakness of mine," Branson said.

"Invariably, I try to consider those with less fortunate an upbringing than my own."

"Indeed." Render clicked his tongue, shook his head and rode forth. "A nobler prince this world is yet to see."

"You may accompany me, if you wish." A self-satisfied, but entirely unconvincing smile stretched across his face, underlining his smug, half-opened eyes.

"Very well, then. I presume we share a common destination?"

"That depends on your definition of destination, but I assure you, common has no part in it."

"Whatever you say."

The truth was, Branson had gotten lost in the wood and resorted to traveling towards the setting sun, after a frightening night hiding and trying to sleep under his horse. Nothing could complete his humiliation more than coming upon Render, that freak of nature, that pauper who had no right whatsoever to have entered his home. Or what had been his home.

But now, with his home destroyed, and according to Father, with no one in King Corigan's dominion worthy of trust, Branson knew no other choice than to follow his father's instructions, should such a thing as the attack occur. He was to travel deep in the hills of the mountain range. The valley where history's bloodiest massacre had taken place. The Valley of the Accursed.

Despite his sorry attempts to exude the air of nobility, and despite the fact that he was in fact, son of The Lord Agon, Branson felt like a mouse. A very small mouse surrounded by hungry cats. Certainly, he must keep Render in check, lest he attempt to lord it over him, but there were times he wished more than anything that Father were there, so that the burden of his protection would not fall upon himself.

And why did Render ask so incessantly where he was going? He would have to be going in the same direction! That former slave could not be trusted with the truth, so Branson had to appear aloof and evade questions.

"We shall arrive at the foot of the mountain by dusk," Render said, pointing forward. "There we can stop for a meal and proceed into the hills for shelter."

Annoyed, yet comforted by his initiative, Branson set his eyes upon their destination. "Yes. Yes, I agree."

He would put up with Render's arrogance as long as he could. But for now, considering his mysterious powers that routed the wolf pack, Render might prove a useful ally in the crossing of the mountain range.

CHAPTER FIFTY-FIVE

GRATEFUL THAT THE ASCENT to the first resting place brought nothing more than a few scrapes, Render came upon a tableland partially surrounded by trees. This would be where they would set up camp. After he and Branson tied their horses, he started a fire. The sun fell over the Eastern landscape, painting the sky orange and violet over the snowcapped summits and well into the distance where lay the valley that separated the kingdoms of Valdshire Tor and Tian Kuo.

A crisp evening breeze wafted by carrying the scent of crackling embers, while a pair of doves sang a plaintive song.

Of course, Branson had already sat down by the fire, helping himself to the vittles Render found in the traders' abandoned satchels. He was pleased, however, to see Greifer leap gingerly from the saddlebag and alight upon the ground without a sound. She stretched her forepaws, one still bandaged, and lowered her body to the ground.

"Glad you're feeling better."

Branson turned around and shot him a queer look. "I'm not, actually."

"Not you." Render stepped over to the black cat and sat by her. Right away, she brushed her face against his arm.

// THE RESPITE WAS MUCH NEEDED //

"Of course," said Branson, a wry smirk twisting the corner of his mouth. "You were talking to the cat." He shook his head and continued eating.

For the rest of the evening, Render avoided speaking with him, which did not seem to bother Branson in the least. Griefer seemed herself again and Render spent the time attending to her and familiarizing himself with their camp.

When he discovered a small, empty cavern, Branson instantly claimed it for himself. "I am younger and more apt to becoming ill from exposure to the elements." And with that declaration, he went in, lay down and went to sleep. Not too far from the entrance.

Griefer made it clear to Render that she did not care much for the boy, but she suffered him nonetheless to keep their company.

"Come and sit by the fire," Render said and stretched out on the ground. The cat followed and sat next to him facing the flames. A wave of exhaustion fell over him. Though he had put his torn shirt back on, he shuddered as the cool breeze became frigid.

// IF WE BEGIN AT DAWN, WE SHALL CROSS TO THE EASTERN SIDE OF HANDARA AND ARRIVE AT THE SOUJOURNER'S COUNCIL BEFORE MIDDAY//

Render held his elbows tight, trying to stay as close to

the fire as he could stand. "Should we not send off a signal to let them know we are coming?"

// THAT WOULD NOT BE PRUDENT, FOR I HAVE SEEN ONE OF THE WOLVES ESCAPING, SURELY IT HATH REPORTED OUR PRESENCE//

"To whom?"

// TO WHOMEVER IT WAS THAT SENT THEM //

A strong gust blew from the top of the mountains sending a splash of snowflakes into his face. Render shuddered and rubbed the backs of his arms. "Won't we freeze to death at the summit, before we ever cross over?"

// YOU SHALL SURELY NOT DIE //

Too cold to argue, Render rested head down upon the satchel. He rolled onto his side and curled up, such that he faced the fire. All the while, Greifer sat still, staring out at both ends of the clearing, her tail twitching every now and then. "Good night."

Save for the snapping of the firewood, the cooing of the nocturnal doves and the moaning wind, silence enshrouded the entire camp. A stillness Render had never known. He opened his eyes and gazed into the countless points of light that sparkled in the heavens. Some flickered white, some silver, some even blue.

"Do you think there are other worlds out there, other people?"

// T'WOULD SEEM A GRIEVOUS WASTE OF SPACE, IF OURS WERE THE ONLY WORLD SO INHABITED. FOR ALL WORLDS ARE CREATED BY VALHANDRA //

"That name." Render's spirit quickened. Courage and dread arose simultaneously. "Why does it trouble me and stir me so?"

// HIS NAME IS HIGH ABOVE ALL NAMES. SO GREAT IS HE, THAT EVEN HIS NAME HATH POWER //

"You speak like a Sojourner." But this did not bother him. A curiosity, a hunger rivaled only by his life-long desire to know his parents, emerged from the depths of his soul. "I want to know of Valhandra. Why the sudden urgency, I cannot say. But the more I hear that name, the more I feel I have known it my whole life."

// NATURALLY //

He sat up and his heart began to race. In his mind, the name repeated, over and over. Valhandra. Valhandra, Valhandra, VALHANDRA! Holding his knees tight to his chest, Render began to rock back and forth. It felt as though his heart might burst. He held his head between his hands and began to groan.

Then, a warm touch to his face.

Assuming the form of a great panther, Greifer stood above him and laid the soft pads of her paw upon him.

// THE CURSE AFFLICTS THEE STILL . BUT YOUR TIME DRAWS NIGH. YOU MUST SOON ENTER THE CRUCIBLE //

The anxiety began to ebb, but his shivering became more tremulous than before. Render did not care to ask about this curse or crucible. He could learn more tomorrow. "I'm so cold.... so frightened."

Greifer lay next to him and curled closely around him.

// REST UPON ME, RENDER //

He did so and laid his head upon her side. The warmth that emanated flowed through him, comforted him. The shaking subsided. And finally, the long needed rest came over him.

Even as he drifted off, he faintly heard something most unusual from Greifer. A sweet sound. She was humming a song. A song that for some reason, he'd known for his entire life. But he could not remember where he'd heard it before.

Eventually, he fell asleep, oblivious to everything around him. Even to Greifer, who had transformed into human form and cradled his head gently in her lap, stroking his hair and singing that ancient song.

Canst thou remember
Canst thou recall
When once we surrendered
To dreams great and small...

CHAPTER FIFTY-SIX

BY FAR, THE GREATEST CHALLENGE that confronted Render—Greifer offered little assistance as a small cat—were Branson's unrelenting complaints. The morning sun rose up from the west and shone hot upon their faces as they walked the steep path towards the summit.

The air grew thinner and each breath took more effort. But Render was determined to follow Greifer's instruction. Something seemed right about meeting the Sojourner's Council, something that amidst all the recent alienation felt like a homecoming.

Stopping to rest, Render peered out at the highest of all the peaks that jutted into the sky. The peak of Handara stood obscured by a blanket of white clouds adorning it like the collar of a royal robe.

"There it is," Render said, wiping his brow.

"It's been there for eons, of course it's there." Branson said, twisting the side of his mouth. "One'd think you'd never seen Mount Handara before."

"Not this close."

Perched on a rock in front of both boys, Greifer stared at Handara for a while. Then she turned around and gazed up to the top of the trail.

// WE ARE NOT FAR. THE HALL OF THE SOJOURNER'S COUNCIL LIES JUST OVER THAT CLEARING ABOVE US //

"Branson, I suspect we are near to our destination. Why won't you tell me where you are trying to go."

"I don't trust you. We may very well be heading for the same destination, but it's possible that our purposes are not the same."

"Wouldn't it be better if we knew and settled our differences now, rather than later?"

Branson did not answer. He seemed too frightened to reason. Perhaps he sought the Council as well. If so, the members would surely mediate and resolve whatever issues needed to be resolved.

From his periphery, Render saw Greifer arch her back. He turned and saw her flatten her ears and take a defensive stance. A large shadow passed over them and the horses began to huff, and blow, and stomp their hooves.

"What was that?" Branson said, his eyes trailing the shadow as it flew past the ledge and dropped into the valley, even more massive than before.

Shading his eyes, Render looked up trying to discern what it had been. His vision adjusted and what he saw, gliding high up in the sky caused him to stop breathing for a moment.

"It's enormous!"

// TAKE THE HORSES AND FIND REFUGE IN THE CRAGS //

But Render could barely move, so enthralled was he by the figure hovering in a wide circle above.

"Looks like an eagle," said Branson. "But that's not possible. It's the size of an ox!"

"Run!" Greifer shouted, with her human voice, though she still appeared as a cat. In that instance, when Branson and Render turned to her, she began to transform into a panther.

Branson began to blubber like an idiot. Confused and scared, he pointed at Greifer and though his lips moved rapidly, nothing came out besides, "What...how did...where...?"

Nothing could move the petrified boy from where he stood, his feet planted into the ground and deep-rooted with fear. Not Render's words, not a strong yank on the arm. Nothing.

But when Greifer leapt over their shoulders, following the great eagle's motion, as it let out a piercing screech, Branson ran straight for the nearest opening in the rock walls.

// YOU TOO MUST SEEK SHELTER, RENDER //

"Absolutely not!" He mounted a rock and stood above her, his hands pointed towards the eagle, which was diving straight at them. "I can handle this."

// YOU HAVE NOT YET ATTAINED SUFFICIENT CONTROL OF YOUR ABILITIES //

"It'll have to do!" Even as he said this, a surge of heat spread from the center of his chest and radiated to his fingertips. Webs of crackling lightning stretched between them. The very air around him smelled like the fields after a thunderstorm.

Larger and larger the eagle's form grew as it blazed down at them. Both horses, still tied to a tree, screamed and reared up. Soon nothing could be seen behind the dark shadow cast by the eagle's massive wings.

He thought he heard Greifer again, but the words were indiscernible. Nor did the voice bear even the slightest resemblance, save for the fact that it sounded female. But Greifer was standing on her hind legs, her claws out and ready. In just another second, the eagle would be upon them.

Now, the ivory talons flashed into plain view, curved and savage looking, sharp enough to slice a horse in two. Render shouted to Greifer, "Run!"

CHAPTER FIFTY-SEVEN

BEFORE RENDER COULD summon the lighting, the massive bird swooped over his head, its talons grabbing at his neck. He leapt away and flew towards the trail.

Griefer let out a panther shriek and took a swipe at the flying beast. But it soared back up into the sky, preparing for another attack.

//TO THE TRAIL! WITH ALL HASTE! BEYOND THE HILLTOP, WE SHALL FIND SHELTER AT THE SANCTUARY OF THE COUNCIL //

Following her, for she had already bounded up the road, Render shouted for Branson, but he did not answer. "Bother him!"

Once again, the gargantuan eagle shrieked. But Render squandered not even a second to look back. At his side, the ground exploded sending pebbles flying into his face. Acrid smoke caused his eyes to water. The top of the hill stood less than twenty paces.

An undulating breeze and low-pitched flapping sound

told him that the eagle flew just above him.

Greifer leapt over the end of the trail and vanished from sight.

// QUICKLY! //

"I can't—!"

A series of fireballs shot down and hit the ground just before him, erecting a wall of fire which singed his face. Darkness fell over him like a heavy shroud.

But it was not only his sight that became disabled. He could hear nothing but the beating of his own heart. Even the smell of burning branches vanished. All he could perceive was the pain of talons slicing his chest like daggers.

He tried to call out, but his chest was too constricted even to breath. Then came the flapping of wings. The ground beneath him fell out. A rush of wind swept up from beneath him.

The eagle cried out and lifted him higher still. If it were to release him now, Render would surely plummet to the ground and have his skull crushed.

But he would not wait to be ripped to shreds by its claws or beak, only to be fed to its hungry young. Render grasped the eagle's leg. Its tough, leathery skin felt dry, but warm to the touch. With all the concentration he could muster, he focused on that skin.

A loud crack, accompanied by a blinding flash of light. The eagle began to convulse. But it refused to release him. In fact, it clutched him even more fiercely.

Once again, Render summoned the lightning. With a desperate shout, he released an even more powerful jolt. This time, black smoke flashed from the eagle's plumage.

A lattice of white energy wrapped round the eagle's body like the legs of a spider.

With great resistance, the eagle released him.

Render almost laughed.

He was free!

And plunging to his death.

CHAPTER FIFTY-EIGHT

TUMBLING THROUGH THE AIR, Render could hardly see or breathe. Too much wind rushed into his eyes, his nose, his mouth.

His entire body tensed in anticipation of breaking apart on the rocks below, or being impaled by tree branches. Squeezing shut his eyes, he braced himself.

But nothing happened.

Surely, he would have struck the ground by now.

// IT HAS BEGUN //

Render opened his eyes and found himself staring at the sky. The dark outline of the eagle fled into the distance behind the clouds that adorned Mount Handara.

When he rolled over, his entire body jerked again in anticipation of the fall, for there was nothing solid beneath him. Instead, as he opened his eyes, he saw and felt his feet hovering above the ground. It was as though he had merely jumped up and never landed. He blinked, unable to comprehend what had just happened.

Shielding her eyes, Greifer gazed up into the sky. She had assumed her human form and was clad once again in her black warrior's outfit.

"What happened? What's begun?"

"You have begun to manifest."

"Manif—?"

"Quickly, we must take refuge with the Council." She pointed to the entrance of the building—no doubt the Sojourner's Assembly Hall.

Render spread his hands to balance himself as his feet touched the ground, alighting with the grace of a butterfly. The moment he stood steady, Greifer grasped his hand. "The eagle shall return before long."

"But why? What does it want?"

"Quickly!" She pulled him towards a towering archway in the stone wall. In a distinct sequence, she touched several of the manifold symbols carved into the rock. Symbols he'd seen in his visions, in Sir Edwyn's books. When she finished, she stepped back.

To Render's amazement, the heavy slab vanished with a deep yawn. No door impeded their entrance, but a sense of dread seemed to restrain him as Greifer stepped forward.

"Why have you stopped?"

"I don't know...Something feels wrong. As though... I should not go in."

"Tarry longer and the eagle shall return, perhaps in greater force and number." She pulled his arm again.

"No, please. I... I'm.."

"I beseech you, Render, come."

There was no better way to say it. Render backed away, lowered his gaze to the ground. "I'm afraid."

She padded over and lifted his chin. "Courage." Her very touch soothed him as did her maternal voice. "For I am with you. Moreover, there shall be safety amongst the Elders. They have anticipated your arrival."

The portal wound like a maze and would have been completely dark if not for the strange golden light of torches that hung upon the walls. They seemed to glow, but not burn.

Finally, they arrived at the end of the hallway. An opening to an inner courtyard. Trees lined the perimeter and bright sunlight filled the entire area. He could not see over Greifer's shoulder. But he knew something was amiss when she gasped. "It cannot be!"

"What is it?" Render tried to peer over her shoulder, but she slumped against the narrow doorway, blocking his view.

"No!"

Finally, Render pushed past her and stumbled out into the sunlight. Strewn about the ground were the bodies of several large men, each dressed in peculiar clothing, somewhat warrior-like and resembling Greifer's. Each lay dead. Each twisted into an unnatural position that testified to a writhing, painful death. Frozen upon their countenances was the look of surprise and dismay, most incongruous for warriors as they appeared to have been.

He took a sharp breath and turned to Greifer. "What's happened?"

But she could only stand there, back against the wall, hand on her chest and breathing frantically. "No one could have...it is not possible."

To see her this way, unbalanced, immobilized by confusion and shock, only made Render more anxious. The grotesque state of the bodies spread around a huge tree stump urged him to run. But the threat of the returning eagle outside gave him pause.

And presently, the shrill cry of that very bird startled

him. The courtyard darkened under its growing shadow. Before he could speak, a barrage of fireballs hit the ground, causing the entire yard to burst into a quick burning flash. Like dry flames.

Alerted, Greifer transformed into a panther again. "We must depart from here."

He snatched a longsword from one of the fallen Sojourners, whose face was planted into the dirt, and ran after her towards the Assembly Hall's entrance. Behind him, something heavy hit the courtyard floor and rocked the ground. Flames exploded behind him showering sparks and heated pebbles at his back.

At last, he and Greifer found the door and exited the building. Render stopped at a tree, turned and said, "Can you shut that door again?"

With great panther paws, Greifer stood up and hit the etched symbols in sequence again. Flames lapped out of the doorway. The footfalls of several echoed from within.

The pounding of his heart nearly caused Render to stop breathing. "Hurry!"

Just then, a backlit figure emerged from the smoke. It was not the form of that giant eagle, which could never have fit in the narrow corridor anyway, but that of a person, slightly smaller than himself. Before he could say anything, a rush of wind and light came in from where Greifer had stood. The stone door remained open.

// NEVER MIND! RUN, QUICKLY! //

As fast as his feet could carry him, Render followed Greifer out. He turned his eyes back into the corridor just in time to see the dark shadow raise its hand. A bright glowing circle pulsed from it, each time growing brighter, from red, to blue, to white.

// STAND ASIDE! //

Frozen in place by the fear that had preceded his entry into the massacre scene, Render opened his mouth, but not a word came out.

At his side, Greifer was once again manipulating the controls.

The circle of white light burst and launched forward.

Straight at Render's face.

He raised his arms in a feeble attempt to shield himself, but it was too late. He felt the searing heat of the oncoming fireball on his arms, heard the rumbling of the conflagration.

Then came the sound of a muffled explosion. And a sudden cooling of the air. Render lowered his arms, forgetting any shame, and blinked. The stone door had materialized again. He struggled to catch his breath. "Whoever...whatever that is in there, it must have killed the Elders."

// I HAD NOT ANTICIPATED THIS. WHAT SHALL WE DO? //

"I don't know, I've been following you. You're supposed to know!" How could she be so uncertain?

But it was a futile debate.

From the inner courtyard, at the center of the building, more fireballs launched out and arched down towards them. The eagle's shriek resounded over their heads.

This time, there was no escape.

CHAPTER FIFTY-NINE

THE ONLY WARNING came from the fiery projectiles, but even those were not enough to prepare Render for what happened next. So quickly had the eagle swept down upon them that he could not warn Greifer.

The bird fell upon her, knocking her to the ground, her paws making a heavy thud.

Render leapt forward. But before he could reach her, two projectiles struck him simultaneously. One in the belly and one in the head. He fell to the ground, his newly acquired sword clanging onto the cobblestone.

His shirt had been singed, his head a bit burned as if by standing in the sun too long. But he was still alive.

From the ground he could only see and hear Greifer shuffling about and snarling. When he looked up, he marveled at how she had overcome the eagle's clutches and had sunk her fangs into its neck.

"Get up!" Someone said, apparently a second assailant standing above him. Young but fierce, she spoke in a strange accent. Furtively, he reached for and wrapped his fingers around the hilt of the sword. Then he leapt up, and to his amazement, flew well over the trees, and landed a short distance from his attacker.

An exotic young lady, who stood poised to strike.

From her open palms, a circle of white flames smoldered at her fingers. Raven hair fell half over her face. Her chest rose and fell, anger seething in her large, almond-shaped eyes. Somehow, he felt captivated by her. But then she let out a shout and hurled another fireball at him.

Barely reacting in time, he ducked. The fireball screamed over his head and struck a tree trunk, splitting it into two. The burning halves hung limp as they disintegrated into ashes. Greifer's struggle and the brown-eyed beauty—every bit as mysterious as she was dangerous—vied for Render's attention.

Now, the girl, whom he surmised was Tianese—for the Tianese, he'd been told, were darker of skin and peculiar in an alluring way—approached him in a threatening posture.

Render raised his sword. To his surprise, it crackled and glowed with energy. "Who are you?"

"Murderous barbarian!" She hurled another fireball at him, this time aimed straight at his face. Render swung the lightning-charged sword and deflected it. Her entire body began to glow. Hot red, then blue.

Then white.

"I should have known it was a Torian swine!" She stretched out both hands and shot a line of fire onto the ground. The flames circled around him and rose up as a wall, entrapping him.

Apparently, she knew not the extent of his abilities. Render smirked and leapt straight up out of the blazing snare.

Only to meet her fist.

The blow to his jaw surprised him almost as much as her deadly beauty and strength. Dropping his sword, he hit the ground with such force that he slid across the ground, stopping between Greifer and the eagle. Still fighting, the giant bird's talons flew straight down at his face.

He rolled out of the way, but could not escape without incurring a gash in the ear by the bird's razor claws. He gasped in pain. With his eyes shut, began breathing rapidly.

And then stopped.

His vision blurred. A burning sensation gripped his throat, cutting off his breath. All he could see was the white hot figure of the Tianese girl standing above her. Pushing down on his throat with force.

Greifer growled and snapped her jaws. The bird let out a shrill cry. Not far from his bleeding ear, claws and talons scraped on the ground seeking purchase. The sounds of struggle began to fade. Nothing stood in his vision but the blazing white before him.

Even that faded.

Weakly, he reached out clutching for his sword. She pinned his wrist down as well. Searing pain coursed through his entire body. For a moment he heard that voice. His own voice. His doppelganger. The curse.

// YOU CAN'T BEAR THE PAIN. END YOUR SUFFERING BEFORE YOU ARE *BURNED* TO DEATH. GIVE IN, COWARD! DIE QUICKLY! //

CHAPTER SIXTY

// DIE...//

THAT GHASTLY VOICE. Most frightening to Render was that it was his own, only darker. It echoed in his head, knew intimately his thoughts, his fears. Knew just how to accuse him, reducing him to a frightened child.

// DIE!//

No! Render struggled to speak. But the Tianese fighter's hand clutched and pressed down on his throat with even more force. It felt as though his eyes, his blood, his innards were boiling. Was this how she had murdered the Elders in the Assembly, burning them from the inside? Then Greifer's words came to him: Even His name hath power...

The Tianese continued to send searing heat into his body. He could not die here, not when he had come so close to meeting his destiny.

// DESTINY? THEY ARE ALL DEAD! *THAT* IS YOUR DESTINY //

Even his name...

And then, from deep within, it emerged. Flooded Render's thoughts. The words formed. And a tingling surge enveloped him. The ground trembled and the rolling of thunder filled the sky.

Stop.

Stop!

"In the name of Valhandra!"

A blast of pale blue light.

A roaring crash.

As if swatted away like a gnat, Render's attacker flew off of him. For a moment, a blinding wash of light and floating sparks flooded his vision.

He rubbed his eyes and blinked.

All fell silent.

When everything cleared, he found the girl lying on her back, stunned and moaning. Her hair bloomed outwards, smoke rising from her clothes. Render got up and grabbed the sword. Before she could arise, he pressed the tip against her throat. "Be still, treacherous assassin."

She gasped and hissed and spoke through clenched teeth. "Blasphemer of His name! You killed them!"

"I've killed no one..."

She tried to lift her hands, but Render pressed the sword in ever so slightly.

"...yet."

Rising to her feet—human feet—Greifer brushed the long black hair out of her face and gazed with amazement down at the ground. The giant bird of prey was gone, but in its place... "Wait, both of you!" Greifer shouted. "Strive no further."

At her feet, an old Tianese man, perhaps this girl's grandfather, sat, rubbing his bald head, his eyes wide and staring up at Greifer. "Is it...?"

Her mouth fell open. An incredulous smirk stretched across her face. "Lao-Ying?" She reached down and helped him to his feet.

"So it is you, Greifer!" They were holding each other's arms now. "I cannot believe this. We had all thought you'd—" He turned to Render and then back to her. "Is that him?"

Greifer nodded. "Render. Pray release the girl. Methinks a grave misunderstanding hath occurred."

The girl turned her eyes to the old man. "What's the meaning of this, Lao-Ying?"

"They are not our enemies," he said. "We share a common cause."

"But they killed—"

"No, Ahndien." The old man sighed. "That is not possible."

Render withdrew the sword and offered a hand. "As I said, we killed no one."

She glared at his hand as though it were a fetid piece of carrion, then by her own efforts stood up. "Nor did we." Like the final flames of a log, flickering and refusing to die, the anger in her eyes continued to burn.

Until a sudden noise alerted the four of them. Each whirled to the trail, ready to strike.

"No, wait!" Branson cowered and shielded his face. When they realized it was only the boy, the lowered their hands and weapons.

"Oh, it's you," Render sighed. The incessant coward had a way of popping up like a weed at the most inopportune moments.

"I say! What goes?" The boy looked simultaneously

apprehensive and annoyed. "That cat—that is to say—that panther, and that enormous bird. How did they all do that?

A short interval of silence.

Then the four carried on as if Branson had never appeared. Ignoring him, they gathered together and told the stories of their respective journeys to the now defunct Sojourner's Council. Render marveled at how this frail man could transform into that formidable bird of prey. And that Ahndien had ridden him as an archer rides a horse.

As Lao-Ying spoke of the moment he and the girl had arrived, Ahndien, who heretofore had seemed to possess a heart of granite, began to weep. Bitterly, she sobbed and shook her head. Render turned to Greifer and the old man.

"Xing Bai Juang, the fifth and newest elder, who was murdered with the rest of them, whose sword you hold..." Lao-Ying pointed to it. "He was Ahndien's father."

CHAPTER SIXTY-ONE

"BUT HOW DO YOU KNOW this was your father's sword?" Render stood guarded, but his heart softened when he saw this lethal and altogether beautiful girl weep. Nevertheless, the fact that she had nearly incinerated him encumbered the fullness of his compassion.

Ahndien reached for the sword at her side. It rang out as she unsheathed it. Out of instinct, Render stepped back and swung forward the sword in his hand. Almost quicker than he could see, Ahndien slashed at him and their blades clashed, making an otherworldly, almost musical sound.

"Behold the chord struck." Greifer pointed to the symbols carved into the blades of both swords. Behold the markings. They bear an uncanny resemblance."

"Like those." Render pointed to the ones she had touched to open the portal to the Assembly Hall.

Lao-Ying nodded and regarded him gravely. "They are of the Ancient Sojourner lexicon."

"Can you read it?"

The old man gazed at the writing and read as though reciting.

First, Render's sword: "Two weapons of war..."

Then Ahndien's: "...One instrument of peace."

The last symbol of the phrase on Render's blade looked identical to the first on Ahndien's. He pointed to them. "What does this say?"

"It means: United."

Two weapons of war—UNITED—One instrument of peace.

With a grunt, Ahndien threw her sword down. It stuck a rock on the ground sending sparks into the air. "If they didn't kill them, then who did?" she shouted.

At that moment, a frightened but very determined Branson stepped forward. "Killed?"

"Who is this child?" Lao-Ying said, asking aloud what everyone else seemed to be thinking. Render explained as much as he could before growing weary of Branson's terse and haughty interruptions and corrections. But then the boy said something that drew an unexpected reaction from both Lao-Ying and Greifer.

Lao-Ying cleared his throat with a raspy cough. "Agon? The Lord Agon, son of Refalla, son of Lusera?"

"Yes, yes. It's all public knowledge. Why should this surprise you so?"

"Was not his coat of arms the Red Gryphon?" Greifer said. Branson stepped forward and lifted his closed fist. On his finger, he wore a signet ring. Render leaned forward and saw the icon. A winged lion, with the head of an eagle.

Lao-Ying and Greifer regarded each other with unspoken understanding. "Yes, I did see it," the elderly man said.

"Alas, Agon." Greifer lowered her head.

"What are you all blathering about?" Branson pushed forward and rushed to the portal. He began to slap the etched markings on the doorframe, "He's in there, isn't he?"

Neither of them replied.

"Take me to him, now!" Now with both fists clenched tight, he pounded on the stone door. His voice broke into a shrill cry. "Right now! Right now!"

As always, demanding, condescending. Render had just about had his fill with this child, spoilt by indulgence and privilege. "Oh, do shut up, you petulant little beast!"

But Branson only buried his face in his hands and leaned his head against the wall. For the first time, in all the time Render had known him, Branson wept.

"You're as callous are you are obtuse!" Ahndien hissed at Render, as she brushed past him and bumped his shoulder. She went over to Branson and put a consoling arm around him. Her words were hushed, but her demeanor soft, compassionate.

Soon, Greifer and Lao-Ying gathered around the boy and they spoke so quietly that Render could not discern a word. After a brief exchange, Greifer opened the door once again and Branson along with his entourage walked in.

"That's just wonderful." Render heaved a sigh and followed behind them, hoping whatever it was that had so engrossed them with Branson's outburst would eclipse all else. Before he reached the end of the hall, which opened to the courtyard where all the fallen Sojourner Council members lay dead, Render heard Branson let out another cry.

"No! Father, no!" And the weeping resumed. At the entrance to the courtyard. Greifer took the boy who wept into her embrace. Ahndien stared away, angry tears rolling down her face.

It seemed the only person willing or able to speak with Render was that old eagle-man. He was crouched down with his hands upon the heads of two fallen Elders, his eyes solemnly shut.

"What has happened?" Render asked, with quiet humility. In response to his presence, Ahndien whipped around, trudged away from him and sat upon a stone bench with clenched fists.

Lao-Ying opened his eyes and stood. "We arrived shortly before you, Ahndien and I, expecting to seek counsel from the Assembly. Her father had been taken prisoner by...we are not even certain who it was that took him after the raid on their village. The last thing we expected to find was her father dead, along with all the Elders here."

"Who would do this?"

"We thought it was you."

"Why would I want to—?"

"It may have been the Torians, or Xieh-Suh's people. What's even more puzzling than who, or why, is how."

Greifer directed Branson to sit with Ahndien, then came to join the discussion. "They have both lost their fathers. We do well to afford them time to mourn."

Lao-Ying nodded and regarded the bodies strewn about the courtyard. "I have never prepared myself for this."

"Nor have I."

"It was simply not within the realms of possibility."

Intrigued as Render was by it all, one question refused to stay put in his mind. He turned to Greifer. "Why have we come here, in the first place?"

"It hath been so ordained, long ago."

Lao-Ying was now gazing around the courtyard, his lips

moving silently, his finger pointing from one body to the next. Suddenly, he stopped, recounted, then turned back. "But one is missing. Besides The Lord Agon and Ahndien's father, there should have been five Elders."

Branson ran over to the body of the fallen Sojourner. "Father!"

"Wait!" Ahndien ran after him, but not in time to stop him from turning lifting the black cape that bore the Red Gryphon insignia off of its face.

"But...this is not my father!"

Greifer and Lao-Ying gathered around and marveled. "Are you certain," the old man asked.

"Without a doubt." He laughed nervously. "This Sir Nolin, his right hand...My father is still alive then!"

"This is puzzling," Greifer said. "We are without direction and must seek out the shrine of Valhandra. Or truly, all shall be lost."

The old man straightened up. His eyes opened wider than before and his woolen eyebrows crumpled together. "With respect. I must disagree. It is now clear that we must find the fifth elder. He alone holds the answers we seek, he will know who is responsible for this massacre."

"Now, more than ever, we should seek Valhandra's counsel."

"You wish to seek him?" Lao-Ying set his jaw firm and narrowed his eyes. "Where was Valhandra when our villages were attacked, women and innocent children slaughtered? Where was Valhandra when his faithful council of Sojourner Eelders breathed their last? Seek him? I think not!"

Render stepped between them both. The etchings in the pair of swords flashed in his mind. UNITED—One instrument of peace. "We mustn't fight amongst ourselves or we'll be doing our enemy's work for them—whoever they might be."

"Lao-Ying?" Ahndien, the cold-hearted warrior, now looking more like a frightened girl, approached, wiping her eye and sniffling.

"Come, child." He stretched forth his hand. "We must find the missing elder."

"But we came here to seek the council, to seek the wisdom of Valhandra's prophets."

"They sought him as well. And now? They're all dead!" Lao-Ying threw his arms up. The sleeves of his white robe flowed open and he began to transform. Sleeves and arms into vast wings. Sandals and feet into formidable Talons. "Come, Ahndien. I've seen enough."

But she did not. Nor did she answer.

"Please, Ahndien. We have been mistaken. For half a millennium, we have misplaced our faith!"

Render tried to grasp at one of his wings. "No, Lao-Ying, wait!" But Lao-Ying, now fully in his eagle form, screeched and snapped at his neck with his curved razor beak.

The eagle tilted its head, gazing straight into Ahndien's eyes. She shook her head, her lips quivering and silently mouthed, "No."

Letting out a mournful cry, the eagle leapt and flew into the sky. The clothing of the dead Sojourners ruffled in the breeze as wind kicked up leaves and sand, obscuring the air with a cloud of dust.

Render marveled that Ahndien had remained. She kept watching as the great bird's form grew smaller and smaller into the clouds. There was a sadness in her eyes, but at the same time an immovable determination.

Once again, in the recesses of his mind, swords flashed, the smooth deadly sound of blades striking. And then the image of the symbols etched into the blades, which he now recognized and understood:

Two weapons of war—UNITED—one instrument of peace.

CHAPTER SIXTY-TWO

IT STRUCK RENDER as unexpected how everything changed in so short a time. Within the hour, he and Greifer had defended themselves from supposed enemies only to find that they were not. And now with Lao-Ying's flight and the revelation of Branson's Sojourner heritage, the one thing needed to complete Render's absolute confusion now happened before his very eyes.

Ahndien knelt over her fallen father, weeping and trying in vain to stir him. Greifer went and stood over her. The shadow she cast over him and onto the blood stained ground did not match her human form. It was more like that of the great panther. Had this been a month ago, it would have made Render stare in wonder.

When Ahndien took notice of her, she stood, turned and sank into her arms. With a motherly caress to the young lady's head, she held her, her eyes condolent. "There, child."

A few minutes passed, and Ahndien regained her composure. Courage steeled her countenance and she went over to Branson, who sat on the large tree stump, staring up into the clouds.

"He'd been away so long." Branson wiped his eyes and sniffed. "King Corigan was always sending him to battle somewhere, and as soon as he returned, he'd send him out again."

"How did you know to come here?" Greifer asked him.

"He had been acting strangely since last year when my mother died—they say she was lost at sea. From then, he became suspicious, not trusting anyone. But he would always say to me, 'To the hills, the tallest summit by Handara.'" If anything were to happen, if he failed to signal me for longer than a fortnight, I should at all costs come here."

"So you knew there would be an attack on the castle!" Render said, remembering the last time he saw his brother alive.

"I knew nothing of the sort! It was three days past the time I should have left." He straightened himself up and wiped his face. "And what happened here? Where is my father?"

Until now Ahndien stood quietly, her eyes squeezed shut, her lips quivering as she uttered silent words. Until... "Render."

Surprised, he answered, "What is it?"

"My father managed to escape the Torian raiders and find his lost sword, the one you now hold. How do you suppose he overcame them?"

Fire? Lightning? These were abilities that Render had only begun to manifest, though he had no explanation for them. "I don't know."

The crying was over now. Her tear-softened

countenance toughened once again and she stood. "Father often spoke to me of the Sojourner's spirit potential. All my life, I thought he was entertaining me with fairy tales, children's stories and legends. But after all I've experienced, all I've witnessed, especially today, I know it is real."

At this Render became animated. "How long have you been able to...?"

"Just recently. Lao-Ying had been training me."

"Quite well, I'll daresay." He glanced down to the hole burned into his shirt. "How you managed to survive the lightning I conjured is beyond—"

"And what about you? I struck you with my worst." Ahndien ran her hand through his hair. "Not even one singed."

At this point, Greifer stopped her pacing and said, "I must retreat to a quiet place and...and think."

"Wait." Ahndien stepped forward. "There's so much I want to ask you. So much I need to—"

"Perhaps later, young one." And with that, she became a black panther once again and stepped outside, her tail whipping back and forth.

Branson groaned. "Oh, I do hate when she does that."

In response, Ahndien touched Render's arm gently and said, "I think I should talk with him, he's distraught and frightened."

"If you only knew him the way I do."

"After Lao-Ying left like that, I am not certain I know anyone anymore."

"Go ahead. I'll see if I can find Greifer and bring her back so we can decide what to do next."

"What do you think we should do?"

Render glanced over to the dead Elders in the courtyard. "Let's give them a proper burial."

The sun blazed high over the treetops and burned away the fog in the valley below. Many a song bird twittered and Jicaba beetles sang, all as if nothing remarkable had happened here. No battle to the death with unearthly powers, no massacre of Sojourner Elders, no loss of fathers.

And the fact that both Ahndien and Branson's fathers had been Sojourner Elders, one Torian and the other Tianese, should have struck Render as odd, or at the very least, coincidental.

It did not.

Instead, it made him think about his own father, whom he had never known. Yes, Kaine had always said that Father had been killed that same night in which mother...

// RENDER //

But who was this? The voice that entered his thoughts, his very soul, was not Greifer's. She was nowhere in sight, anyway. Nor was this the voice of his doppelganger. No, it seemed much more powerful, fearsome, and at the same time, it drew him.

He didn't even think to answer. He just allowed his feet to take him to where it seemed the voice emanated. Pebbles crunched beneath his feet, a hot breeze, like that which rushes from a freshly opened oven flew into his face.

Render continued to walk towards the edge of the chasm, towards the face of Mount Handara.

// RENDER //

With each step, he heard a smaller voice in the back of

his thoughts. What if it were the voice of his enemy, the doppelganger, or some other form of evil intent, luring him to the edge of the precipice, only to have him fall and be dashed to pieces?

Doubts notwithstanding, he could not resist the call. He didn't want to. As he neared the end of the ledge, a white rush of steam—a cloud perhaps—rushed up from the valley below, right before his face.

But he didn't flinch.

Now the voice called again, but this time it was heard echoing throughout the valley, across the manifold summits of the mountain range, causing even the ground to shake with its magnitude.

"RENDER."

With a loud whoosh came a column of fire that burst through cloud. And before him was what could only feebly be described as a brilliance, like that of a star, pulsing with...with life, energy, supreme wisdom. It was as if the sun itself had descended and now confronted him. But that too would be but a child's description of what he could never quite put into words for the rest of his natural life.

Filled with awe, and dread, and excitement, Render stepped forward, not realizing until he nearly slipped that he had been standing on the edge of a cliff. He took in a sharp breath and watched broken pieces of the ground fall eternally. He never heard them hit the bottom.

The light before him swelled, as though taking a deep breath. With profound rumblings, the mountains quaked, causing pieces of rock to crumble and fall all around him.

"COME FORTH, RENDER."

One step further and he would fall over the edge. Instead, he leaned as far forward as he dared. "Here I am."

"VERILY, I SAY UNTO THEE, RENDER, THOU

MUST STEP BEYOND THE LIMITS OF THY IMAGINATION."

Surely, he did not mean...But if this were who Render knew he must be, then..."Forgive my ignorance, but...are you—?"

"I AM."

From the bottom of his feet to the very ends of the hairs upon his head, he felt a tingling charge rush through his entire body. Even his bare hands began to glow, pure and white. The light from the great white flame smoldering before him enveloped him.

"REMOVE THY SHOES AND CAST THE OUTER GARMENTS FROM THY SHOULDERS, FOR THE GROUND UPON WHICH THOU STANDETH IS HALLOWED."

Render obeyed. And though any question in his mind as to whose presence he stood before faded, he still felt the compulsion to ask. To speak His name.

"Then it's true. You're—"

"I AM HE. WHO FORMED THE WORLDS BEFORE ALL THINGS CAME TO BE. YEA, BEFORE I LAID THE FOUNDATION OF THIS, AND ALL WORLDS, I AM. BEFORE YOUR SUN GAVE THIS WORLD LIGHT, I AM. BEFORE THE FIRMAMENTS LIT THE NIGHT, I AM."

Terror, excitement and recognition surged through him. Render fell on his knees and buried his face into the ground. Even His name has power.

"Valhandra."

CHAPTER SIXTY-THREE

ALL AT ONCE, at the uttering of His name, something within Render changed. He could never quite say what exactly it was, but it seemed as if the white light, unadulterated and omnipotent entered him. Only one word to describe it came to mind: TRUTH.

And so it was.

"ARISE AND FOLLOW ME, RENDER."

When he opened his eyes, Valhandra's light had moved further, deeper into the expanse above the valley. Towards Handara's summit. This was Valahandra, and yet, it could not be. Not completely, in any case. For he knew the glowing sphere of light in and of itself could never fully encompass the entirety of Valhandra's being. It could only have been a manifestation, a supreme condescension. As a story is to its author.

"FOLLOW."

His knees threatened to give out, but Render stood and gazed down. So high up was he that he could not discern what it was that spread across the barren wasteland in the valley below.

One thing he did know: Another step forward and he would be dashed against the rocks, never living to see the end of his fall.

"Sire, I...If I move forward, I shall surely—"

"LOSE THY LIFE, AND FOLLOW ME. THUS SHALT YE FIND IT."

He wanted nothing more than to obey. But at the same time, the thought of being smashed to a bloody pulp made him hesitate. "Sire, I must go back and bury the Elders."

"LET THE DEAD BURY THEIR OWN," came the reply, in a fatherly tone which Render found he could barely resist. "FOLLOW ME AND FIND YOUR LIFE, YOUR IDENTITY. YOUR DESTINY."

"I...I truly wish to obey. But..."

"COME!"

The sphere of Valhandra's light shone brighter, grew larger and appeared nearer, though it was not. A great sea of clouds flowed into the valley, covering it like a blanket. No longer could it be seen from where Render stood. The clouds rose up such that it surrounded him utterly. All that could be perceived now was Valhandra's light, shining through the white mist.

"COME."

Render stretched one foot over the edge and began to lose his balance. Immediately, he planted it back on the edge of the cliff and shuddered. "Sire, I...I cannot."

"DO I NOT KNOW THY FEARS, DEAR CHILD? TO LIVE AND DIE WITHOUT PURPOSE? OR THAT THOU SHOULDST NEVER KNOW THE TRUTH REGARDING THY MOTHER AND THY FATHER?"

Legs growing feeble again, Render knelt, which seemed a most appropriate posture.

"AND DO I NOT KNOW THY MOST PROFOUND

DESIRES, CREATIVE DESIRES, TO MAKE SOMETHING OF GREAT WORTH WITH THY LIFE, TO LEAVE THY MARK UPON HISTORY?"

"Yes."

"AND WAS IT NOT I THAT PLANTED THESE DESIRES WITHIN THINE HEART?"

"And my fears?"

"THOSE ARE OF THY CORRUPTED NATURE, WHICH IS COMMON TO ALL, UNTIL THEY HAVE COME TO ME AND EXCHANGED IT FOR A NEW NATURE. THEREFORE, AGAIN I SAY TO THEE, COME."

Fear, corrupted nature? And what of that desire, planted by the Almighty Himself? Render had never before known what if felt like to be understood, to be known completely, the way a swordsmith knows his handiwork, a painter his subject, or an author his characters. He felt naked. And unashamed.

He hadn't noticed until now that he was standing in the illuminated mist with one foot dangling over the precipice. He began to move his other foot when he faltered. Let out a terrified gasp. "Sire, forgive me. I cannot!"

"I AM VALHANDRA, WHO CREATED THEE. WHO WATCHED AND WEPT WITH THEE AS THY BROTHER KAINE DIED IN THY ARMS. AND I AM HE THAT PUT THE LIGHTNING IN THY HANDS. WOULD I NOT KNOW WHAT THOU CANST AND CANST NOT DO?"

Lightning flashed brilliantly through the mist. "COME!"

To resist now seemed as sensible as walking face first into a closed door, while another door stood wide open next to it. Render shut his eyes.

// SIRE //

As he stepped off the ledge, he felt a sharp twinge cutting through him, from the heart, straight to the head. Beneath his feet now, nothing stood. Wind howled and wind rushed past his ears, through his hair.

He was falling.

CHAPTER SIXTY-FOUR

DESPITE THE RUSH OF WIND, the giddy sense of weightlessness, Render was not afraid. Not entirely. If this was the manner in which he was to meet his end, having heard the voice of Valhandra, seen his face, or a reflection of it anyway, it was well enough.

Somehow, death seemed not so frightening as he had imagined. Perhaps, when his body struck the ground, it would happen so quickly that he would barely feel any pain. It's not so bad.

"OPEN THINE EYES." The voice seemed closer now, intimate. Render obeyed, expecting the ground to come rushing up to crush his body into fragments. Instead, when he looked, his heart leapt with a jolting start that went to the tips of his fingers.

"BEHOLD."

"But... this is not possible!"

"FOR MAN, IT IS IMPOSSIBLE. BUT WITH ME, ALL THINGS ARE POSSIBLE."

Was he dreaming? Or perhaps he had already struck the

ground and died. For when he gazed down, the clouds had parted and beneath him stretched across the valley. And about a hundred paces away, the edge of the cliff from which he'd stepped off.

"But how is it that I am not falling?"

"FOLLOW ME." Like a shooting star, Valhandra's luminescence blazed towards the summit of Mount Handara. With nothing more than his will, Render followed, unaware that the shadow he cast below was far too massive to have originated from someone of Render's youthful stature—a dark form with large bat-like wings and a jagged edged tail.

"I..I'm flying!" He spread his arms as though he were a bird, but realized he didn't need to do anything but desire to fly.

When they arrived at Handara's snow capped peak, Render held his position. Exhilarated and breathing deeply, he smiled. Suspended in the air, a hot jet of wind blowing in his face, he no longer saw the rocks or the earth below, nor the sides of the mountains. But in the center of the glowing light, he beheld what appeared to be moving images, faces of great lords, kings, emperors, cities flowing with prosperity and peace. He also saw bloodshed, battles, and men, women and children fleeing in droves from burning villages. And as all this went on, time, in his own plane of existence had not so much stopped as it had paused. Paused so he could look upon the images Valhandra now displayed in what could only be described as a borderless rectangular window.

"This world, and all the creatures in it," began Valhandra, "is my handiwork. Moreover, they are my children, whom I love." The window turned dark until all was black, save a pinpoint of silver light. That light grew until it filled the window utterly. And in a flash, it was gone. In its wake lay terrestrial spheres, stars in the firmaments. Render dared not breathe. "By my word, have I wrought manifold worlds. And upon a precious few have I bestowed my favor. Yea, there shall be other worlds yet to be born, but none until this, unto which thou hast been called, hath been redeemed."

Over the one sphere, a crystal-like globe, lush with green and alluvial continents between the liquid sapphire which flowed between them. Render understood to be his own world, and marveled at this view from the heavens.

But presently, an ominous shadow fell and enshrouded the land and sea. The shadow came not from outside, but from within. As drops of ink taints water until the entire goblet has turned black.

CHAPTER SIXTY-FIVE

BEHOLD, THE BEGINNING." Valhandra's voice resounded. "From its birth have I blessed this world with freedom, wisdom, beauty and limitless bounty. All were one in spirit and purpose and harmony.

All at once, Render's senses fell away. It was as if he no longer inhabited his body. All was light and word and knowledge and wisdom.

But one of my creatures—not terrestrial, but celestial in origin—purposed within himself to travel a path which I, Valhandra had not ordained. Malakandor, the chief messenger, of whom I considered myself a father, had allowed evil to take root in his heart. To corrupt and foul from within that glorious spirit which had been given him, beautiful above and beyond all created spirits.

"O my Father," said he. "Grant what I wish, for I am thy beloved son."

"Indeed, thou art so."

Malakandor, already darkened in spirit, came forth. "Grant that I would have dominion over this new world. For I am created in thy image, and shall thus rule over it as thou wouldst."

"Take heed," said I, "For what thou asketh, cometh not from a pure heart, but from pride and greed."

"But it is my birthright."

"My son, it is not for you to rule, but to prophesy a divine and most honorable appointment."

At this, Malakandor, who had served faithfully through the ends of twenty-five hundred worlds, grew indignant. With great fury he rushed forward. "Then thou hast misappointed me! Beyond prophet, beyond envoy am I, for I possess power of which thou has no knowledge."

But nothing is hidden from me. Though Malakandor believed otherwise, whether by self-deception or the blindness of lust, all knew that Malakandor had turned his divine abilities towards darkness and manifested that which can only be so by choosing to abandon one's design, one's destiny.

"My son," said I, "As with all my creation, this world was born of love. Wouldst thou defile it by thy greed and lust for power?"

"Behold! The people, how restless they grow! They long to see, and not rely on mere faith. They seek empirical evidence of their deity, and yet, you do not reveal yourself. How then, shall they know their purpose and destiny?"

"They know. For I have written and set eternity on the tablets of their hearts. Within their spirits, they long for their creator. They long to become all they were meant to be. And the evidence they seek is in the heavens, in their books of law and prophecy, and most importantly,

Malakandor, through the message thou hast been ordained to send them at such a time as this—when they grow so restless."

"They desire a monarchy! To rule with strength. To lead them into an age of self-discovery, self-reliance and self-determination. Surely, they have the right— "

"They know not what they ask. Verily, I say unto thee, even thou knoweth not what thou asketh."

"But I do."

"To rule a world, thou must drink of the cup which maketh he that drinketh it worthy. But bitter is this cup. Only through the denial of thyself, sacrifice, and unconditional love for my children, shall anyone be given to rule."

At this Malakandor scoffed. "Such weakness! I shall do no such thing. Nay, I shall rise up like the morning star. I shall take that which pleases me. I shall rule with the power which even thou, O my great father, cannot contain."

"Not so, my son. Look to thy brother Kronis."

"He is but a feeble and obsequious lamb!"

"Yet by his sacrifice, his obedience and love, he rules all the worlds I have birthed and have yet to birth."

This caused Malakandor's heart to burn, for he hated his brother. "Compare me not to my brother! This world shall be mine. The people desire me and I will rule over them, even now!"

"Though by force thou taketh dominion, thy reign shalt not be legitimate. For no authority can be taken, only granted. And only to the worthy."

"What do I care for your legitimacy, your worthiness, when I have all the power I require? I am beyond such insignificant rules."

"Nevertheless, thou shalt not rule."

"How will you prevent me, old fool?" Malakandor raised his hand. Fire streamed forth as a sword and he pointed it to his Father's heart.

"No more canst thou take my kingdom than thou canst take my life." Valhandra spread wide his hands, and with open arms, stepped forward.

And behold, Malakandor plunged the flaming sword into my breast. Not resisting I fell.

Triumph maliciously burned in Malakandor's eyes. "Lo, I shall take this thrice-accursed world, as I have taken thy very life!"

Presently Kronis entered into my court. "What manner of treachery is this!" He cried lifting his hand towards his brother. Glowing white and blue streaks of lightning crackled.

But I, Valhandra, wounded and appearing rather powerless intervened. I reached up and grasped Kronis by the arm. "Suffer him to live, for it shall be but for a season." I turned to Malakandor. "My son. Thou hast taken nothing. For I have freely given it. But not for thy sake." I heaved a sigh, shut my eyes and then, before Malakandor's very eyes, vanished.

CHAPTER SIXTY-SIX

BUT YOU COULD NOT HAVE DIED," Render said, still suspended somewhere in time and space. "You're still here."

"Indeed, before the first grain of sand slipped through the hour glass, I was. I am, and am yet to be."

"But Malakandor—"

"He believed he had killed me because he wished it so."

"And Kronis? Where is he?"

Then Valhandra did something Render never expected. At first it sounded like thunder. But as he spoke, he realized that Valhandra was laughing gently. "He is nigh, my son. More than thou canst imagine. But he attends to many worlds, and his time here hath not yet come."

"Well, then what happened to Malakandor, did he end up ruling?" Render thought it might be so, because the current condition of the world, what with all the bloodshed, slavery and evil. Still, some things simply did not add up. "There are three, maybe four rulers, four kingdoms, not one."

"So you say. But presently all rule under the fist of Malakandor. Some knowingly, others not. For when Malakandor descended, he scattered my faithful and devised maleficence with those that demanded his power. To the East and the West, did he divide the central kingdom. To the North and South did he establish his own throne."

"I have heard tales of the giants of the North and the mysteries of the frozen South." Frightful tales which without thinking in detail were sufficient to cause a shiver to run down Render's back. "But you say that the Eastern and Western kingdoms were once united?"

"T'was once, when my chosen people established my tabernacle. They who in faith, sought my presence regardless of sight or evidence. They traveled as the four winds took them, from the ends of the entire world to seek me."

"Hence the name, Sojourners."

"Yes. But Malakandor drove them out, and the remnant were sold into slavery, or indoctrinated to revile my very name. In the East, he appointed oracles to be emperors and priests, those that espoused and worshipped his dark powers. My chosen remnant in Tian Kuo practices their belief in secret, for fear of torture and death."

With the inevitability of a perforated wine skin, Render felt as though his mind would burst. Not comprehending all that Valhandra said, he sensed that he had always known, always understood. And that this was merely a way of...remembering.

"And what of the West? Valdshire Tor? And their perpetual warfare?"

"Yet another of Malakandor's machinations. For at the time of the great schism, he agreed to grant full dominion to the Eastern Emperor and the High King of the West, upon one condition: That they utterly drive out the Sojourners and remove the very memory of them. And that they never permit the people of their kingdoms to reunite. Yea, the very memory of the era of peace and prosperity, when they knew me and enjoyed my favor, hath been expunged from their history, from their minds."

"How did the remnant survive this long?"

"Because I am with them. And amongst the people, I still have ancients, prophets and prophetesses who serve, as I had intended Malakandor to before his fall."

"But why did you permit this? Why did you not destroy Malakandor and all his followers? Why not erase every trace of evil?"

Again, the thunder rolled, Valhandra laughed. When he answered, he seemed neither angry nor impatient, but endearing, as though explaining something very simple to a child. "Dost thou perceive me as so narrow? So controlling?"

"I don't understand."

"Had I desired to create automatons, hollow beings without spirit or soul, I might have stopped him. Had I created any of my children devoid of free will, how then could they truly love me as children their Father? That shall not be forced. Nay, love must be borne of free will."

"But Malakandor ruined your entire world."

"Nothing is ruined, my son. For my plans are not as those of man. They cannot fail. I am the one true creator. And though my creatures, of their free will, chose the path they desire—some of which stretch longer and are rougher trodden than others—all lead ultimately to their intended destiny. And behold, I was, I am and shall always be the same."

The more Render listened to His voice, the more an unspeakable familiarity and recognition filled him. It connected to a visceral sense of his identity, but at this moment, he could not say just how. It welled up and drew his emotions, his thoughts, and his determination towards Valhandra, the way a Moshla is drawn to its spawning grounds.

"And now, the question for which thou hast waited thy entire life."

The question? Could there be only one? There was so much more that only He could answer: Render's future, that overwhelming need to live a life of significance, of purpose. What lad his age cared for such weighty matters? And yet, it had been seeded in his heart for as long as he could remember. But he also desperately wanted to know about his past, his father, his mother, people who were to him but a dim memory, and yet...

"All of thy life is summed up for such a time as this."

"Sire?"

"Even so, it is not an end, but a beginning. For thou hast been called to a manifold purpose and before the sun sets on that day, thou shall witness it come to pass."

A brisk gust of mountain air rushed at him and in that instant, he found himself surrounded by the white clouds again. But he could hear the wind, the birds singing, the leaves rustling. He was back.

"My son, I have chosen thee to unite my people and reestablish my kingdom."

"But the remnant, they are scattered."

"For this you have been called. Even now, by Malakandor's design, The Empress Dowager of the East has betrayed her covenant with the High King of the Western Kingdom. Though she believes she will prevail and conquer the West, Malakandor's intent is that both kingdoms destroy each other."

"Would that be so awful?" Considering how both rulers

have persecuted the Sojourners, and how they had deliberately hidden the truth, revised history and thrown their people into darkness, it seemed this might prove a fitting fate.

"As a father hath compassion for his son, so have I for all of my children. I would not that any of them should perish. But they must seek truth, not the lies of Malakandor, who, above all else, is a devourer, a cunning deceiver."

"Would it not be better for the Sojourners?"

"Nay. For Malakandor will once again raise up a new generation that knows nothing of the sins of their ancestors. And their wickedness and iniquities would surpass those of their fathers."

"What can be done then? Their armies are great..."

"They shall be united, Render."

He blinked and gazed upon the vision: both armies clashing, fierce warriors on both sides falling. "Impossible."

"You and Ahndien shall make it come to pass."

This stopped all the questions floating in his mind. "How can this be?"

"Not only shalt thou prevent their demise, thou shalt do far greater things than thy mind can conceive. Together shalt thou vanquish the forces of Malakandor, the might of whose own army far exceeds that of both Kingdoms."

The thought of confronting even one army was enough to make Render's stomach clench. "But what can the two of us possibly do, alone?"

At this the blazing white sphere swelled, as though taking a deep breath. "Thou art not alone. All shall come to pass, but not by thy own strength. By mine. Look into the valley, Render. What seeth thou?"

"I do not know."

Warm and paternal, Valhandra's light enveloped him. "Behold, the last battleground of the Sojourners prior to the exile. Look closer still."

By his mere will, and without any strain of the eye, the valley's ground became enlarged in his sight. "I see...desolation. Barren land."

"Thou seeth the surface, presently. But henceforce thou must see beneath, within. Behold, the final battleground of the Sojourners, who once reigned in justice and truth, who defended truth to the end."

Render had wondered why this place, which seemed nothing but red dirt and sand, devoid of any markers, held any significance these days. How could it have ever been anything but a wasteland?

"This, my son, is where Malakandor wishes to destroy both armies. To desecrate hallowed ground with blood betrayed, as he had ten generations ago. But thou shalt thwart his plan."

"Forgive my ignorance, Sire. But how?"

"Unto thee, all shall be revealed. Yet at the appointed time."

He knew not what Valhandra meant. But a thought, some unspeakable words were planted in his heart. And though superficially he could not discern their meaning, in his spirit Render knew that what mattered was the will of their author. Not only did the name of Valhandra have power, His words did as well.

To Render, those words which he was commanded to speak—at the appointed time seemed sharp as a double-edged broadsword, cutting through flesh, bone, straight to the soul.

"Speak the words I have placed within thee. And you shall see my glory."

"Sire, I am afraid. Ahndien, Greifer, Branson and I. We

are few."

"Fear not. Only believe."

CHAPTER SIXTY-SEVEN

ONLY BELIEVE.

And with that final exhortation, the light burst into countless shards which spread and grew so bright Render could not open his eyes. And yet, rather than frighten him, it caused him to gasp in delight.

Now enveloped completely in what he could only describe as pure joy, the surge from that burst infused his entire being. A tingling sensation coursed through his blood as he shut his eyes and yielded to it.

Once again, time as he understood it stood still. Only, he sensed motion. Not the kind of motion one feels when running, falling, or riding upon a horse. Whatever it was, it caused his head to grow light. Like a warm blanket, golden sleep fell upon him and for the first time in his life, Render felt something he'd never felt before.

Peace.

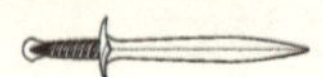

It was the sound of Branson, shouting with confused excitement that woke Render from what felt like a long slumber. Considering where he found himself when he opened his eyes, his back and neck should have ached frightfully. But they did not.

He sat up and found Ahndien lying across from him, deep asleep. From a quick glance through the snow frosted branches, he perceived a sphere-like cloud, glowing and rising up from Handara's peak.

Valhandra.

"Well? Are you going to just sit there, or are you going to help me down?" It was Branson calling out, but from where, it was unclear.

"What? Where?" Render shook Ahndien's shoulder and she stirred slightly.

"Oh..." The Tianese girl who earlier had almost killed him blinked and sat up, rubbing her eyes. Her voice and entire demeanor had changed. "How did we get here?"

"Wake up, you two!" Branson called out again.

This jarred Ahndien. She sat up, rubbed her eyes again and called out. "Where are you, Branson?" Both Render and she peered around the black barks of the trees and the edges of the rocks. Surely in the open area beyond the thicket, if he was there, Branson would appear clearly by contrast with the snow-covered ground.

But he did not.

"Up....HERE!"

A ball of snow came hurtling down and splattered over a fallen tree trunk. Render gazed up in the direction from where it flew. "How did you get up there?"

Crouched low and seated up at the very top branches of a Yuccah Pine, Branson waved at them, shaking snow off the branches beneath his feet. "I don't...you wouldn't believe me if I told you."

Both Render and Ahndien stepped over to Branson's tree. Render could not help but let out a laugh. "We've got all day to listen."

"Get me down from here, now!"

To Ahndien, with a mischievous grin: "I suppose you could burn the tree down and—"

"No! No!" Branson said. "Not a good idea!"

"Well, I still would like to know how you got up there." Render shaded his eyes and looked straight up to the top. "It must be thirty feet up. Don't tell me you climbed."

"I didn't climb. Will you please hurry up!"

"Oh come now," Ahndien called out, clearly amused. "Tell us! Hurry, because I have such a story to tell you about what just happened to me."

"As do I," said Render. "How did we all get here? Weren't we—?"

"If I tell you how I got up here, will you do something to help me down?" Branson called."

Seeing him up there helpless as a kitten was too precious an opportunity to squander. But after a slight pause, he finally relented. "Yes, then. Tell us and I'll help you down."

With a deep sigh, Branson said, "I leapt."

At the same time, Ahndien and Render both said, "You leapt?"

"How's that possible?" she said.

"Honestly, I don't know. Render, you said you'd help me down. Now make good on your word!"

Render folded his arms across his chest.

"Please?"

"Well all right, but we all must exchange stories about what happened just before we got here." Without a second thought, Render reached one hand up and before he realized what was happening, flew straight up towards

Branson.

The lad's eyes grew wide. "Render, how did you...?"

"I don't know." He reached out and took Branson by the arm with surprising ease and tucked him under his arm like a bundle of kindling. "It feels like something I could always do."

Flying down proved more amusing than up because of the way Branson screamed like a little girl, his hands covering his eyes. "We're going to die!" Stopped and hovering mere inches from the ground, Render simply could not resist. "Well, if you are not happy with my service..." He held him away and let go of Branson.

Eyes still covered, he shrieked, not realizing how close to the ground he already was. "No!"

Branson came down with a gentle bump in the thick snow. With all four limbs splayed across the ground, he writhed and grabbed and gasped. When he opened his eyes, he glared up at a laughing Render. "I don't appreciate that!"

"Consider that repayment for the way you've been from the start." He held out a hand to help him up. At first Branson hesitated. But eventually, a smile cracked across his face and he took it.

For the next hour, Render, Branson, and Ahndien shared their stories. Render first explained how he had met Valhandra. But for some reason, he could not recall all that he had seen and heard.

"All I know is that I am supposed to—"

"Unite two kingdoms which have been mortal enemies for centuries." Ahndien grabbed Render's hand and gazed straight into his eyes. "He told me the same."

"What did you see?" Render's entire body grew warmer, despite the cold air and snow. And it was not coming from her fiery abilities. It came from within. Thankfully, the redness of cheek that must surely be apparent now could easily be attributed to the cold.

"Many things. I saw my past. I saw a great battle. And I saw..." Ahndien turned away.

"What did you see?"

"Yes, do tell us," Branson said.

But she put her hand to her lips and shook her head. Her eyes glistened. A stray tear fell to the ground and a tiny cloud of steam rose up from the tiny crater in the snow it created. "I am not to speak of these things. He has commanded me not to say a word to anyone."

"Do we win the battle?" Render desperately wanted to know.

"I did not see that far."

"Do we fight alone?"

"Again, I did not—"

"Will anyone come to our—"

"Either I saw nothing or I am forbidden to speak about it!" Her tears became angry and at the same time sad. "Don't you understand? Valhandra has not given us evidence. It is not for us to question, but to obey."

Branson muttered something.

"What was that?" Render said.

"And to believe." He looked up and suddenly, wisdom enshrouded his face. A wisdom beyond his tender age. "It is not for us to question, but to obey and believe. That's what He told me as well."

CHAPTER SIXTY-EIGHT

FROM WHERE HE STOOD, Render could only surmise that they were now far from the Sojourners Assembly Hall. Ahead in the distance, the dry brush swayed, the golden sand shifted across the vast expanse of the barren wasteland, the winds of which groaned painfully in the valley below.

"What is this place?" Branson said, standing on Render's left and gazing at down at the desolate valley.

On Render's right, Ahndien answered. "The final battleground of the Sojourners. This is where the last generation of Sojourners made their stand."

"But how did we get here?" Branson wanted to know. "It was at least three day's journey."

"By His command," Render said, not even sure how he knew it, but it was true. "We are to go down into the valley. And find the ancient shrine."

Branson shuddered visibly. "Oh, it's dreadful down there. Just look at all those bones!"

Beneath the surface of the sand, there were countless

ridges and ripples. Upon a more careful look, Render saw. Dried bones, skulls, rib cages. "Yes, I see."

"It is called the Burial Grounds of the Sojourners," Ahndien said, also gazing down into the wide expanse at the foot of the Handaras.

"I see no graves," Branson complained. "Just a bunch of old, dry bones beneath the surface of the sand! It gives me a chill just thinking about being down there."

"I don't much care for it myself," said Render. "But we must go. It is by His command."

Just then, in the form of a black cat, Greifer scampered into their midst, dashed though a thicket and behind a tree. A moment later she emerged tall and beautiful, robed in black, her glistening ebony locks flowing over her shoulders. "Valhandra be praised, I have found thee."

Render's heart leapt. "But, where have you been?"

"Why, searching for thee, of course."

Ahndien went over to the elegant lady, touched her sleeve. "How long has it been?"

"From the moment I returned to the Assembly Hall to find you all gone? Three days. And three nights have I sought thee by thy scent."

Branson laughed. "I thought you were a cat. Not a dog."

"A panther's nose is far superior." She stepped over to Render, put a warm hand softly on his face, and tilted her head as she gazed into his eyes. "By thy countenance, I can see. Thou hast changed."

Her touch warmed him to the soul. "Changed?"

"Thine eyes testify to it."

"To what?"

"Thou hast been called. By Valhandra."

"How did you know?"

"I know the look, the glowing of the countenance. It was once common for princes when they came of age and calling. In thine spirit hath He revealed thy destiny. Young friends, pray tell me what you saw."

Render explained all he had been shown. Ahndien and Branson did as well, but it became clear that Valhandra had revealed much more to Render than the other two. "How are we to defeat an immortal army, much less unite two warring people?"

"I do not know. But if Valhandra hath so ordained it, you shall prosper indeed." Griefer inclined her head, and kissed the top of his. "And whatever be thy lot, I shall ne'er leave thy side."

If ever he had imagined what it would have been like to have a mother, this sense of security, her complete belief in and support for him, this far outshone any such notion.

Ahndien took hold of his hand. "Nor shall I."

Branson grabbed his shoulder and gave it a brisk shake and squeeze. "I'm with you too."

"Then on to the Ancient Shrine of Valhandra," Greifer said to Render. "Indeed you are ready."

At that moment—and he wished it would last forever—Render felt certain that together, they could overcome any adversary, any force, natural or spiritual. And he knew what he must do next.

CHAPTER SIXTY-NINE

RENDER..." A distinct warble infused Branson's voice as he stood at the edge of the precipice overlooking the valley. "I think you should see this."

"What is it?" Render stared in the direction in which Branson pointed but did not know what he was talking about. "I don't see—"

"There!" Ahndien pointed sharply. "In between those two peaks!"

Well into the distance and coming from the East, a black column of smoke rose into the air. It moved toward the valley. Render took a deep breath, then let it out, the tension in his chest palpable. "Ahndien, what do you make of it?"

"I've seen this before. It's the Tianese Imperial troops."

"How far?"

"They'll probably set up camp in the mountains tonight and set their warriors in position."

Branson cleared his throat nervously. "For what?"

"That." Render saw it as they spoke. He turned to the West, where dark clouds cast a black shadow over the woods on the edge of the desert and pointed it out. "Those lights flickering, a long string of them. Torches. Troops. Horsemen. By my estimation, there must be at least ten legions. If I've learned anything about Torian strategy, they must believe they can take the high ground before the Tianese reach Handara."

"Do they not know the tactics of their opponent?" Greifer hissed and began to transform again.

Branson jumped back. "Would you stop doing that. It's getting to be more than my nerves can handle!" The black cat leapt up onto Branson's shoulder, then over to Render's.

"What will we do?" Ahndien said. "It'll take us till tomorrow to get to the Shrine. We'll never get there in time."

"Not on foot, we won't." Render gazed down the cliff, down to the thousands of dry bones, then it caught his eye. A small door frame carved into the limestone by the hills. The Ancient Shrine of Valhandra. "But if we fly..."

"Fly?" Branson and Ahndien said at the same time.

Greifer jumped from Render's shoulder down into his arms. She then squeezed into the opening of his vest where she rested tight and secure. Render smiled, put his arms out and wrapped them both around his friends. "Do you believe?"

"Are you mad?" Branson cried.

"Render, let go!"

An unprecedented boldness surged through him. A strength that had been instilled by the words of Valhandra—the same unknowable words which he must later invoke to bring about the help needed to defeat the forces of Malakandor. Render tightened his grip on

Ahndien and Branson and leaned over the precipice. Out of fear, they held onto him all the more tightly. "I said, do you believe?"

"Render...!"

Before either of them could answer, yes or no, Render pulled them with him.

Straight over the cliff.

CHAPTER SEVENTY

AFTER A FEW SECONDS of screaming and squirming, Branson went limp. It made it a bit more difficult to hold him under one arm while Render flew over the mountain range. But for some reason his arms felt stronger during flight, and it made holding him and Ahndien easier than he would have imagined.

"Render, I...This is remarkable!" Ahndien hugged him tighter as they soared over the snow covered treetops, making a circular descent.

He tilted his head down and found her gazing at him with an expression of awe and anxiety.

// I WON'T LET GO, AHNDIEN. DON'T BE AFRAID //

// I'M NOT //

She smiled and pressed her face against his chest, perhaps to hide her face from the chilling wind, perhaps for another reason. It didn't matter much right now. He was flying. And it felt like something he'd always known he could do.

Greifer remained still in his vest, though her claws gripped through his shirt. He could sense her confidence in him. If he weren't so enraptured with this experience, he might have found it odd. But this was freedom. Freedom beyond anything he'd dreamed of all his life as a slave.

"You'd better put us down soon," said Branson. "I think I'm going to be ill."

Render let out a chuckle, as did Ahndien. Their eyes met.

For some reason, though she smiled, a poignant expression filled her eyes. Until now, the strongest emotion they'd ever displayed was anger. But this sadness, mixed with something else, something that seemed to establish a connection between them, made her even more beautiful than Render had bothered to notice.

Something was happening, though.

Even as they came nearer to the foot of the valley, where many a rock jutted from the sides of the hill, and reddish-gold sand rippled like waves in the sea, Render felt something unfamiliar as he held Ahndien's gaze.

When they finally arrived, he made sure to land gently. First he let go of Branson, who swiftly ran behind a rock and began to throw up from the nausea of flight.

Greifer leapt out of Render's vest and padded over to check on Branson.

But Ahndien remained in his arms.

"What is it?" he asked. "You have this look in your eyes."

Quickly, she turned away. Though she'd loosened her grip, she didn't not let go of his arms. "I don't know what you mean."

"It's like, you know something. But don't want to say."

Now, she pushed away, but slowly. "I was just...I was impressed with your ability to fly. There is so much to this spirit potential it can be overwhelming."

Her eyes glistened with shiny tears. Ahndien turned and wiped her eye. She was not telling the truth. But he did not press the issue.

In human form, Greifer returned with a very pale looking Branson under her arm. She motioned to a rock. "Sit, child." Then to Render she said. "Since the days of old, every Sojourner prince has been sent from the Council of Elders to the sacred shrine of Valhandra." Then pointed to the tall opening in the rock face. The borders of the rectangle opening resembled a large portal, with ornate carvings in borders around it.

"You, Render were to have gone before the council and prepared for the age old tests."

"What tests?"

"I know not. But this much I do know. Not every young Sojourner—prince, warrior, oracle—that hath entered returneth alive." She looked into Render's eyes with concern. "But you must prevail. With or without the preparation of the elders. It has been so ordained."

Render bowed his head. "I know. And I am ready."

Ahndien opened her bag and pulled out what appeared to be dried fish. She offered it to Greifer, who frowned and shook her head. "Thank you."

Then to Render. "You'll need your strength. Eat."

The last thing he could think of was his stomach right now as he stared at the imposing portal to the Ancient Shrine. "Branson will probably appreciate it more."

"I prefer my food cooked."

From her open palm, the fish in Ahndien's palm lit up in

a moderate fire. The fish sizzled sending up a mouth-watering aroma. Now Render reconsidered her offer, but she tossed it over to Branson, who bounced it from one hand to the next, back and forth.

"Ooh! Hot! Hot!"

Without announcement, Greifer strode past them, over to the archway of the shrine's entrance. She bowed then for a while spoke in hushed tones such that the only word Render could discern was the name of Valhandra.

A few minutes passed. Neither Render, nor Ahndien said a word. They just watched. Eyes shut, her lips moved as though speaking, Greifer nodded as though listening to someone speak. Finally, she turned around and let out a long breath. "Yes, Sire. I understand," she whispered and opened her eyes.

"What was that?" Render asked.

"It is as I thought." Greifer approached and place her hands on his shoulders. "Though the shrine lies in ruins, there shall be no deviation from the past."

"I don't understand."

"Tonight, when the sun falls over the Eastern summits, you shall enter the shrine and do as those before you have."

"And what is that?"

"Free yourself from all that hinders you."

He released Ahndien and stepped over to Greifer. "Hinders me from what?"

"Your destiny."

CHAPTER SEVENTY-ONE

WITH THE SPREADING DARKNESS over the valley came a frigid wind that at times howled through the rocks. Branson sat as close as he could to the fire which Ahndien had started with the dry bush that jutted out from the ground.

He still complained a bit, but not as much as he might have back in Valdshire Tor. Nevertheless, Render understood his apprehension concerning all the skeletal remains out in the center of the valley. They too made him uneasy.

"At least they aren't anywhere near this part of the foothills." Ahndien said, trying to cheer the boy.

"Oh...I don't like it. I don't like it one bit."

The thought of the last Sojourner army, meeting their demise in great numbers did little to inspire Render. He was but one person. How could he accomplish what Valhandra had charged him with?

The flames from the bush grew weak.

Greifer stood and stretched. "The hour is upon us."

"Yes. I suppose it is." Render also stood. But a tug on his hand stopped him from leaving just yet. It was Ahndien.

"Please be careful, Render." Fire danced in the deep pools that were her eyes. She was indeed so beautiful that Render almost wanted to forego the entire destiny matter and stay here with her.

"I shall. Promise."

"Here, take this." She handed him her sword. "Now you have the two weapons of war, united."

Following, then walking past Greifer, Render approached the archway which—no matter how much light from the fire lit the inside—looked as black as death inside. What lay beyond was not revealed to Render. Only that he must enter and find the written words that matched the unknowable one which Valhandra had set in Render's spirit.

Words of victory.

He drew nearer to the opening and squinted as he looked inside. It didn't seem possible, but the void became darker still, with every step forward.

Behind him a deep guttural growl reverberated. Greifer had once again become a panther.

They arrived at the mouth of the Shrine.

Just as he stepped into the gloom, something repelled him with unexpected might. It almost knocked him off his feet.

"What was that?" Without thinking, Render drew his sword. Bright white energy crackled like lighting from the blade.

He stepped forward again. Slashed into the darkness.

A silent, but equally powerful blow struck his weapon.

Sparks flew.

The invisible force shoved him back even more violently

than the first time. Greifer let out a snarl and bore her fangs. A cold tingling sensation crawled up Render's back like the spindly legs of a scorpion. His heart raced, his throat grew dry. Nothing worse than an invisible enemy.

On the verge of panic, Render shot his hand forward and a bolt of energy cracked through the air lighting up the area in a brilliant blue-white array. But as soon as it reached the obscured doorway to the shrine, it was deflected and sent right back at Render.

It hit him, hurtling him back several feet and onto his back. He let out a pained shout. The smell of his singed hair and clothing rose up with smoke from his body.

It felt as though he'd hit that spot in his elbow that sends numbing needles into his hands. Except this sensation traveled throughout his entire body, like swarms of fire ants nipping at his skin from within.

// YOU ARE NOT WORTHY TO ENTER //

That voice. It jolted Render back to his feet, though his joints and neck felt sore. "I come in the name of Valhandra!"

"Render?" Ahndien called out.

"Keep back!" Greifer replied, having transformed back into a woman. Then to Render: "To whom do you speak?"

"It's...It's him...I mean...in a manner of speaking..."

// ONLY THE RIGHTEOUS MAY ENTER //

"Who, Render?" Greifer whispered.

"It's...my own voice." His shoulders slumped as he turned his back to the shrine and began to walk away. Of all the opponents he'd faced, this one—his doppelganger—seemed the most impossible to defeat.

How could he overcome someone who retaliated in the exact manner in which you attacked it, and with equal force?

Greifer blew out a terse breath. "Your own voice. When did you first encounter it?"

"At the pond, with all the dead people. That's when it started."

"The Pool of Madness."

With both hands leaning on his sword pointed into the ground, Render sat on a large stone. His entire spirit deflated. He knew what the doppelganger would say and do. He could not escape the condemnation and accusations, because they came from within. "I'll never get past him. I've failed Valhandra.

"Nay, Render. You shall surely *not* fail."

"But I have."

"Did you drink from the Pool of Madness?"

"Yes, don't you remember?"

"And did you die at thine own hand, as did those soldiers at the pool?"

Her words came from behind him, yet they entered his heart. Render lifted his head. "But how is it my doppelganger has followed me here?

Willowy and warm, Greifer stood behind him and wrapped her arms around him. "I have only seen one prince confront his dark nature thus. And he had become the last Sojourner King. A doppelganger lives within the hearts of us all. On this side of the great veil, no one is ever free of it. The dark nature continually strives to resurface. But you, O chosen son of heaven, you must vanquish you inner darkness once and for all."

"But how?"

"Arise." She took him by the arm and helped him to his feet. "Cast off all fear, all pride, for they are one in the same."

"I...I don't understand."

Pushing him toward the dark archway, she whispered, "The Spirit of Valhandra has called you, and He goes before you, ne'er forget."

"How am I supposed to do this?"

With alarming strength, she pushed him right to the door. "By His spirit and truth."

"But—"

Echoing in the darkness, Render's doppelganger laughed—low and diabolical. It was the laugh of madness, of pure evil. And death. A bead of sweat rolled into the corner of Render's eye. He wiped it with the back of his hand and took a deep breath.

It wasn't courage that propelled him into the unknown. Nor could it have been the knowledge that he would overcome this most insidious of adversaries. It was that quiet voice in his spirit, the words sown like seeds by Valhandra, that impelled him.

Render unsheathed the two swords.

And moved forward.

CHAPTER SEVENTY-TWO

//...NOT WORTHY... //

THE DOPPELGANGER'S VOICE could not be heard outside of his own mind. But the trepidation Render felt was nevertheless real. He stepped forward to the opening of the archway and saw nothing in the utter darkness.

He did, however recoil at the moldering gust that blew out from within: the smell of death. Back in Bobbington's house he'd cleared away many a dead mouse from the cupboards, but this reeked of a thousand very large, very dead rats.

"I'm not afraid of you." Render said under his breath, for he knew it made no difference how loud he spoke to a creature that existed in his own mind.

// TURN BACK, YOU CANNOT FACE WHAT LIES WITHIN //

"It is you who cannot face what lies within me."

The doppelganger mocked him with another gust of rancid air which flew into Render's face.

// MANY HAVE ENTERED WITH DELUSIONS LIKE YOURS...FEW HAVE RETURNED //

"Then let me in, if you dare." But behind his bold words, his heart trembled. Was he about to join the rotting corpses within? It didn't matter. Because if he didn't move forward, his own dead bones would probably join those out in the valley, under the sand.

// COME, THEN //

He glanced over his shoulder. Greifer had returned to her panther form and paced about, her tail swiping side to side.

It was no use. The doppelganger knew Render was afraid, despite his strong speech. Swords pointing forward, he approached the entrance. Sparks from the tip of his weapon lit up the area in brief flashes such that the Sojourner symbols etched into the towering limestone door frame could be seen, one character at a time.

He stepped past the point where he had been repelled and anticipated another attack. The first instinct was to strike first into the darkness, as he entered the threshold. Ready to hurl a lightning bolt from his sword, he coiled his arm back. But he stopped himself.

Any attack he made would only be met with equal force. That was just the way the doppelganger worked, feeding on his fear, his hate, his anger and sending it back. How could he defeat this dark reflection of his inner nature?

A few more steps and the darkness swallowed Render completely. At which point did this cave become a shrine? The solid objects beneath his feet could only be bones.

The dull, damp stench confirmed what he could not see: corpses in various stages of corruption.

// MANY A PRINCE HAS FALLEN BEFORE ME //

The voice was different now. Not so much his own, but something much blacker, more sinister. An ancient evil.

He came to a point in the gloom where the deadened echo of his footfalls scraping told him he was now in an enclosed area—a small alcove by the sound of it.

The only thing he heard over his own uneven breath was the thrumming of his pulse in his ears, and a high-pitched whine, barely discernable. For a brief eternity, nothing stirred.

All at once, the roar of the ground and mountain walls moving startled him. But as far as he could tell, nothing had actually moved. A dark red hue lit up the entire area which was now filled with smoke, or steam, or some kind of rancid mist. A hideous stench reminiscent of dead mice and Bobbington's breath.

// YOU MAY YET TURN BACK //

The voice filled his heart with dread. Every bone in his body wanted to do just that.

"You'd like that, wouldn't you?" But it was the voice of Valhandra—not even His words—just the echo, that resonated in Render's spirit and kept his feet planted in the ground.

// LEAVE, WHILE YOU CAN //

"Not until I've done what I've come to do." Exactly what that was, Valhandra had not said. Render could only take it on faith that he would know when the time came. Or die in the attempt.

The voice became external. "You are a foolish child..." It resounded in what now sounded like cavernous cathedral.

He gripped the sword so hard his fingers ached. "Show yourself...for what you really are!"

From deep within the cloud it spoke, the voice familiar, yet gravelly. "I am what you refuse to look at. A mirror."

"You're not me!"

"Oh, but I am. I'm your true nature." All at once, it was upon him, over him, before him. The mist cleared just enough for Render to see, before his face the black, scaly texture of a wall—no, it was too uneven...

Instinctively, Render jumped back and flew, slamming his back into the wall. All around him, in a crimson light, the cloud dissipated revealing the beast that stood before him. Its vicious talons curled around and dug into the limestone floor making a dreadful sound like a rock scraping against glass.

Well above him the beast's head loomed, its gaping mouth spewing sooty smoke. It reeked of rotted bones and burnt flesh. It coiled back. Render barely leapt out of the way as it blasted a stream of fire from its mouth.

He shouted and dove to the ground. A sharp pain pinched at his ankle, and then spread up his leg. His pants had caught fire. Without a second thought, he ducked behind a wall and fell to the ground, throwing whatever sand he could find on his clothing and patting it rapidly.

"You cannot escape me any more than you can escape yourself!" The beast said.

From behind the wall, the shadow it cast in the next room betrayed its form. Jagged wings, a serpent like tail, a bearded reptilian head. It stood on its hind legs and walked erect like a man—a twenty foot tall man—and approached the doorway behind which Render hid. He had never expected to see a real live dragon. They were supposed to be mythical creatures, the stuff of lore, nothing else.

Thankfully, the fire on his leg went out.

Each breath the dragon drew made a sound like that of a huge bellows. When it exhaled, the entire room lit up. Render felt the heat emanating through the doorway.

"If you leave now, I'll spare your worthless life." The dragon said this even as it lurked ever so close to the door. "There is no need to die a meaningless death."

Run? That might be a wise thing to do. But then, he'd never know the purpose for which Valhandra had sent him. "You're lying!"

"Am I?" A thunderous rumble filled the chamber as the dragon laughed. "How can I lie to you if I am your true nature? You who deceive yourself. Run now, or come in. Choose, while you still can!"

Render tried to stand. But it felt as though the bones had been removed from his legs. When he finally got to his feet, propping himself up on his sword as though it were a cane, he turned back toward the mouth of the shrine. His breath shook, his heart raced. Every fiber in his body implored him to run. Nothing in this horrid place would make it worth suffering at the claws, and teeth of that mammoth dragon.

He turned to the opening of the shrine, where Greifer, Ahndien and Branson waited. From outside, white light bathed the corridor and filled his heart with comfortable feelings. It certainly beat the sense of death and dread that awaited in the room behind him.

He took a step toward the safety of the moonlit skies.

Then he heard a whisper.

// COURAGE, MY SON //

It wasn't Greifer. It was...

A thousand words, even more thoughts that had been sown into his soul began to sprout. He recognized the voice, though he did not remember the words which were now flowing in his mind, so quickly he couldn't even form them into coherent thoughts.

But in his spirit, he began to comprehend. Enough so to react.

Just then, the entire corridor lit up in blazing red and yellow. Render swung around, swords slashing through the air.

But before he made contact, his entire body was seized by a force greater than he'd ever experience in his life. His chest was so constricted that he couldn't even breathe. His arms, completely immobilized. Dull pain grew more intense with each attempted breath. He looked down, realized that the dragon had grabbed him in its hand and lifted him off the ground.

He wanted to shout for help but felt his ribs would crack like burnt twigs if he inhaled. That is when the dragon lifted him up before its hideous face. Its scales were black as death. With vermilion eyes, it glared at him. Its diamond shaped pupils narrowed.

"You should have run." It said, its breath many times hotter than the heat of a furnace. Render had to shut his eyes because of the acrid smoke and intense heat.

"Open your eyes, BOY! See what you are made of. I am your spirit potential, I am the darkness within you that you know so well. I know every wrong you've committed." It held him close to its face. "Serve Valhandra and you shall be nothing. Serve me..."

"No!"

The snapping just above his stomach must have been a rib. A sharp pain drove like a spear into his body.

"Accept your true identity and find your peace. I will make you the bright and morning star, a king above all nations." It drew another hissing breath. As it spoke, though its breath stank of death, Render relaxed and ceased his striving. Still clutching his torso, the giant dragon relented slightly.

"What will Valhandra make you? His slave? Will you cower before Him, do his every bidding as you did Bobbington? I will give into your hands the empires of this entire world!"

At that very moment, Render's vision grew dark. Would he die here, just like that? Is this what Valhandra had sent him for?

// I SHAN'T BE A SLAVE, EVER AGAIN! //

"Yes." The dragon smiled, with terrifying teeth. "You see the truth now." It set him down on the ground and released him. Render staggered back and caught his balance. He gasped deeply, wheezing a long breath, then taking a series of short ones.

Now, before him stood his doppelganger. Render, as a young boy. And in Render's own voice, he said, "Valhandra is a liar. What can he do for you? Look, I can give you your heart's desire."

Then the young doppelganger turned and ran to the opposite side of the wall. Smoke still obscured the outskirts. Yet beneath an amber light stood a beautiful woman, with long ebony hair and fair complexion. The young "Render" ran into her arms. "Mother!"

The woman stroked the young doppelganger's hair lovingly and kissed his head. Then she looked up and spoke to the true Render. "I'll restore the memories Valhandra stole from you, my son."

Render's eyes blurred with hot tears. A sob ached in his chest and he wanted to cry, "Mother!" for he had missed her so, his entire life. He longed to know her, even if she was just the memory of her, just an illusion.

Mother stretched forth her hand. "Oh, my son. How I have missed you."

Everything that made him who he was could be summed up here. Valhandra had never said anything about Mother. Never mentioned a word about the things that really mattered. Was He even who claimed?

"Take my hand, my son. And we shall never again be apart."

And then, despite all he'd been taught, not regarding anything he'd heard in the presence of Valhandra, like a moth drawn to fire, Render took a step towards her.

CHAPTER SEVENTY-THREE

WITH EACH STEP RENDER TOOK, time seemed to leak away like water from a cracked jar. It was not his own will that moved him towards the image of his mother, but he did not think he could resist it. He wanted to see what she looked like, know the scent of her hair, feel the touch of her gentle hand, hear the soft words of unconditional love only she could speak.

"Mother?"

"Yes." She smiled, so warm, so accepting. "Come, my son."

As Render stretched out his hand, he didn't realize that the doppelganger—the younger version of himself—had vanished.

At last, the desire of your heart will be fulfilled. All of who you are, and all you ever wanted to know, stands before you.

"Give me your hand, Render," she said in a comforting, maternal tone.

Only a few more steps and he would be forever reunited

with her.

A sound echoed through the corridor behind him. But Render hardly noticed. At first it reminded him of a bird.

Then the tones became musical.

Mother's face remained pleasant. But her voice became tense. "Come along, now Render. Give me your hand!"

But the sound, the song playing in the shrine's corridor drew his eyes from Mother's image. He stopped, turned his face to the music.

"Render! Do not be distracted. Take my hand. NOW!" The anger in her tone startled him. He turned around, and though what he saw nearly made him gasp, he pretended that the shock of it had not in fact snapped him out of the trance.

"Yes, mother." He took another step, but realized now that the beautiful woman calling him "son" had black scales growing all over her bare arms, her neck, her face. Her elegant fingers grew long and curved into claws.

The music grew louder but it seemed only to be in his mind. It was a familiar song, a song he must have known his entire life, but could not say just what it was.

Fire raged in his chest. It overwhelmed the pain of his cracked rib.

"Quickly, Render," the scaly beast in Mother's black gown said, extending her claws. Render recoiled at what he'd thought had been the memory of his mother, now transforming into a reptilian apparition. "We haven't much time!"

And then, from within him, everything burst to life. The song, the words sown into the soil of his heart, the sudden clarity and courage at seeing the beast for what it really had been all along.

Still feigning his trance, Render reached out his hand.

"Yesssss," hissed the beast. Now growing slimily, its

scales gurgled as it rippled out of the gown and into full dragon form.

Before it could react, Render swung his sword with such speed and force, it whistled as it cut through the smoky air. The beast let out an angry roar just as the blade came slashing down, slicing off its left hand at the wrist.

The beast roared and grew to full size, towering over Render. It struck him with its right fist, sending Render flying back at a wall. But a blue ball of light engulfed him and cushioned him from the impact.

Render set his feet back down, and stood tall.

Slowly, he raised the point of his sword at the hissing monster.

Slowly, he raised his eyes up to the beast.

And slowly, a bold smile emerged onto Render's countenance as his hands began to glow with crackling lightning. All trepidation and emotions over the false images vanished. He was looking into the glassy eyes of a black dragon twice the size of an elephant.

And he was not afraid.

The dragon let out a fierce roar and spewed forth a column of fire. But Render merely lifted his sword, drew a circle in the air and a blue-white shield appeared before him, deflecting it until the dragon had expended its breath.

Then Render leaped into the air and soared high above the smoke. He landed on the back of the dragon, whose arms, though he stood erect on two legs, were too short to reach around to pluck him off. Render spun around and grabbed the neck of the dragon between his knees, mounting it like a horse.

The dragon flailed about, reaching wildly at its back, spinning around so many times its massive tail crashed several times into the walls, sending up sprays of dust and rock.

It panted nervously, spewing flames with each breath.

Render tossed his sword over his shoulder so he could grasp the beast's neck with both hands. It was so thick—thicker than a Colossus Pine—he could not get his arms around it. But he dug his fingers in between the scales, which felt cold and wet, like raw mussels or clams.

The dragon threw itself down. Tried to roll over on its back and crush Render. But Render sunk his fingers in so far he could feel the hot, soft flesh under the dragon's scales. He sent a buzzing current of energy into it which seemed to paralyze the dragon.

It howled in pain. Hissing like water poured on red hot lava rocks, it said, "You can't kill me! It'll be the death of you, all your dreams!"

In that very moment, Render recalled the dead soldiers at the pool of madness, how everything they did reflected back on themselves.

More of the planted words bloomed into life. Now, they blossomed, one at a time.

// TRUTH //

// POWER //

// HIS NAME... //

Even the name has power.

"By the name of Valhandra...!"

The dragon wailed in pain.

Then, with each subsequent word, Render sunk his fingers deeper into the dragon's soft flesh, popping off scales which fell to the ground.

"You...

...are...

...not...

...ME!"

Impossible thought it may be, a thunderclap filled the temple. Blue light flashed, almost blinding Render. Like spears, some seven lightning bolts launched from the air and into the sides of the dragon.

They penetrated its scaly armor and looked like solid silver, protruding from its body as black blood oozed from the wounds. As the dragon convulsed, the bolts sizzled and snapped angrily, humming like a swarm of hornets. Render jumped down, as it was now lying on its side, its limbs twitching violently, its red tongue turning dark blue.

This continued for another second and then the shining bolts drove all the way into the beast until they vanished. The dragon's entire body lit up. A final spurt of fire dribbled out of its gaping mouth. Then a long strand of black smoke.

The glow from its body remained bright for a while longer. Then a most remarkable thing happened.

The dragon's body transformed into the form of Render's mother, who's beautiful face looked pathetically at him. She reached out her bloody stump and untransformed claws and pled. "Render, my son. Please..."

But when the forked tongue slipped out and lay across her face, Render had to turn away. He could not stand to look upon that perverse image, an insult to his mother's memory.

It let out a choking shriek, full of hatred and anger.

Render turned his head back and watched in disgust as it writhed and turned into the form of a black panther, his brother Kaine, Ahndien, and finally, Render himself.

And then, like the last ember of a dying fire, the light died.

CHAPTER SEVENTY-FOUR

RENDER SENT a lightning bolt into a large stone which caused it to glow, illuminating the chamber.

When the entire area became visible, he beheld what could only be described as an ancient assembly hall covered in dust, cobwebs and broken rock. This entire place of worship had been carved into the mountain walls and must have been a sanctuary for the Sojourners during the years of their systematic extermination.

Apparently, it had become a site for some sort of sinister proving ground. Still, why had Valhandra sent him here? Was it just to destroy that dark voice that had accused him all his life? There had to be a greater purpose.

The hall stretched far into the shadows, at least two hundred feet in every direction. The fight with the dragon had only been at the entrance. He stepped over to where the dragon's body had finally transformed into that of a young man's.

In its place now lay a small heap of ashes.

There seemed to be a thin layer covering a small rectangular slab.

Render reached down to pick it up, expecting it to be hot. But it was actually quite cold to the touch. He held it away from his face and blew off the ashes. In his hand, he held a stone tablet with writing in the ancient Sojourner lexicon.

He should not have been able to interpret it so easily, but it was as though it had been written in his own native tongue. On it, he read:

"When thou standeth alone surrounded by thine enemies, prophesy to the valley, from whence cometh thy help."

The images from his and Ahndien's sword came to mind:

Two weapons of war—UNITED—one instrument of peace.

Somewhere in the recesses of his mind, the depths of his spirit, a sense of purpose and destiny came alive. A bright azure glow filled the entire assembly hall, casting shadows on the bones of several princes from ages past, unsuccessful at overcoming the dark spirit of the entire tabernacle.

At that moment, he knew. Something had been unlocked. Something ancient and powerful, terrifying and beautiful. It was the message on the slab, coming together with the unspeakable words Valhandra had planted into his heart.

The valley.

From whence cometh thy help.

Thy destiny.

Render now realized that the blinding light came from his body. It glowed like the sun, and yet he did not burn. Then, before him against the wall arose a shadow which at first made him gasp. The shadow of a dragon, its enormous wings unfurled, its razor sharp talons outstretched, and powerful tail swinging. But just as soon as Render drew a surprised breath, the fear vanished.

As did the shadow.

He stood tall, picked up his sword, sheathed it besides Ahndien's.

The hour was at hand to unite the peoples of their kingdoms, and to face the forces of Malakandor. He took three steps towards the exit and paused.

"But am I ready?"

The very thought resounded in his mind as though it were the wide open assembly hall.

// INDEED YOU ARE, MY SON //

Render smiled, threw his shoulders back and marched right past the bones scattered through the corridor. He knew not exactly what the future held.

But he knew who held the future.

CHAPTER SEVENTY-FIVE

WHEN RENDER EMERGED from the shrine, the moon had dropped behind the mountains. Over the Eastern peaks, a faint amber hue infused the otherwise purple horizon. The first thing he noticed as he stepped outside was how fragrant the air had become. No stench, no dust, just the sweet smell of Tianese jasmine and other desert flowers.

"Render!" Ahndien called out. She ran over to him, clutching a wooden flute. "Are you—?"

"I'm all right." She threw her arms around him and held him so tight, so long, he wondered when she would ever let go. But then, instead of pulling away, he sank into her embrace, holding her tight. "I'm all right."

Finally, she pulled back and gazed at him, her eyes brown and wide. "I thought you might..." she turned to Greifer, who had assumed the form of the black cat again. "She said that only one other person in the last two thousand years had ever come out alive."

In her feline form, Greifer came over and circled Render's legs, pressing up against them and purring.

"It was horrid." He glanced back into the entrance of the shrine, which looked as dead and dark as it had when he first arrived. "And at the same time, wondrous." Sitting with her on a rock, with Branson and Greifer on the ground, Render went on to tell them all that had happened inside.

When he got to the part when he killed the dragon, Greifer became a woman again. "Did you say, dragon?"

"Yes." Render shuddered. "I never knew they existed, at least not in our world. Hideous thing, that. To think, it was trying to make me believe that a dragon is my true nature."

"I wouldn't mind that," said Branson. "Just imagine, no one ever daring to bother you, scaring your enemies away with nothing more than your breath..."

"Don't you already do that?" Render smirked.

Branson stuck his tongue out at him.

"Anyway," Render said, grinning at Branson. "If I never see another dragon again, it will be too soon."

Greifer stood with her back to the young ones, her watchful eyes on the hills. "In some cultures, the dragon is seen as a symbol of evil." She wrapped the black cloak tightly around her shoulders. "But it is not always so. Nevertheless, dragons are most rare. As rare as princes that emerge victorious from the shrine."

"Well, there's no recorded history of anyone ever seeing them." Branson's voice trembled. His teeth began to chatter as a dewy cloud from the mountain floated through the valley and turned the air biting cold.

Ahndien flicked her index finger, and a small fire bloomed from the ground—though there was nothing that could burn in the sand. A flame rose up and burned like a torch.

"Thanks." Branson rubbed his hands together and then fanned out his palms to warm them.

Despite what Greifer had said about dragons, it didn't

change how Render felt. "All the same, I'll be happy never to see another one in my lifetime." He turned to Ahndien, who now leaned back against his shoulder. From what little he could see of her face, she seemed sad. "What's wrong?"

Snapping out of whatever had been consuming her thoughts, she turned around and forced a weak smile. "Oh, nothing. I'm just glad you're safe."

"You're not fooling anyone." Render put his hand on her shoulder and rubbed it gently with his thumb. "You've been this way since Valhandra—"

"Please!" She stood up, threw her flute into the sand, and walked away. Just let me be!" Walking past Greifer, she disappeared round the corner of a rock formation. In the quiet of the night, her muffled sobs kept leaking through what must have been her hands.

Render got to his feet, bent down to pick up her flute, and started for the rocks behind which Ahndien wept. But Greifer held up her hand.

// LET HER //

// BUT I WANT TO KNOW WHAT'S MAKING HER SO SAD //

// TO EACH THEIR OWN PATH, RENDER. WHEN READY, SHE SHALL EXPLAIN //

He leaned a shoulder against the rock wall and waited. The smooth surface of Ahndien's flute warmed in his hands. With a heavy sigh, he shut his eyes. All he wanted to do was to comfort her, to let her know that he'd never let anything happen to her. But she would not let him know what it was the troubled her so. And this, despite his ability to fly and summon lightning, made him feel powerless.

Greifer padded away, leaving him there.

Ahndien grew quiet.

Taking a deep breath, Render stood away from the wall. "Ahndien, please. Talk to me."

To his surprise, she came round the corner and appeared before him. Her eyes still shimmered, but a peaceful smile now graced her countenance like the soft blanket of winter's first snow. She put her hand on his chest, and leaned into the crook of his neck. "Forgive me. I was...I was just thinking of my family."

"Of course. How obtuse of me." He handed her her flute, held her close and kissed the top of her head. Then he turned her around to look her straight in the eye. "Are you sure there isn't anything else?"

At first she held his gaze, silently. Then she looked down, took back her flute and said, "Did you hear me playing?"

"While I was inside the shrine, about to be killed? Yes, I think so. Why did you do that?"

Again, with the poignant smile. "He told me to."

"Valhandra?"

"Back when we experienced the visions. He'd shown me this, what I would do. Did it help?"

"Yes, I believe it did. I was about to lose my mind and will. But when I heard the song you played...such a familiar song...Play it for me again, won't you?"

She shook her head. "I was in some kind of trance. At least that is what Branson and Greifer say. I have no recollection of the song. I barely remember taking the flute from my pocket."

"It doesn't matter," he said, taking her hand into his. It felt cool and moist, as though she were frightened. "What matters is that we have a calling, a destiny to fulfill. And I will never leave you, nor allow any harm to befall you."

With sincere appreciation in her eyes, she nodded. Like a tiny diamond, a tear fell from her eye. Neither of them noticed that when it hit the sand, it sizzled and a tiny jet of steam rose from the ground. "I know your heart, dear Render. And that is what matters."

He didn't think much about what she said, because his heart felt near ready to melt. There was something they shared that transcended race and station, something far deeper and more powerfully binding than any politics or society could weave. Something he knew in his soul.

They were Sojourners.

And they were meant for each other.

Heretofore, Render had never imagined a girl's lips so close to his, much less those of a Tianese. But it seemed so inevitable now. She shut her eyes awaiting his kiss.

"Render!" Branson shouted. He would have struck him with a small bolt of lightning, if his voice hadn't sounded so panicked. Both he and Ahndien rushed over. "What is it?

Pointing over into the distance, Branson's finger shook. "There."

Perched as a panther atop a nearby crag, Greifer's tail swished tersely. She stared without flinching at the sight which unfurled like an unholy flag.

From both sides of the valley streamed unending lines of torches, the ominous clinking of wheels, horses whinnying.

// BEHOLD, THEY COME...//

CHAPTER SEVENTY-SIX

IN THE DISTANCE, the deep and steady beat of Tianese war drums beat like the heart of a great beast. It was a sound Ahndien had heard only twice. First, when she was a child of four, maybe five years of age. But then, it had been a welcome sound. The Imperial Guard marching by the hundreds through the land, gracing the borderlands in a show of strength and the promise of protection.

The second and last time she'd heard them was when she was ten; the Imperial Guard had rushed to her village's defense during a daybreak raid by a battalion of Torian soldiers.

So where were they when the Torians came and killed Ah-Ma, Shao-Bao and everyone back home? They were supposed to be their protectors.

To the western hills her gaze fell upon the legions of people she'd always considered the enemies of her people. But now that Valhandra had shown her everything, she knew it was not them. No. In fact, it was not against flesh and blood she needed wage war.

"What are we supposed to do?" Branson grabbed Ahndien's arm.

"It shall be revealed to us in time," she said, patting his hand. She meant to comfort him, but the sound of her own voice did not sound convincing, even to herself. She knew what was to come. Valhandra had shown her, told her: No matter the cost, Ahndien, thou must do all thou canst to ensure that Render, the great deliverer of my people, prevaileth.

Valhandra never showed her everything. This, she suspected was by design. He only revealed what she needed to know for the next step.

Render climbed to the top of a rock and shielded his eyes from the blaze of the morning sun, its rays now slashing through between the manifold peaks of the mountain range. Down below lay the desolate valley.

Unflinching, he stood still and watched.

"Render?" Ahndien tried to call out to him, but only a pitiful whisper emerged from her lips. Tears stood in her eyes because she knew her time was short. She knew the cup she must drink. And she knew not what would happen afterwards.

From the East, an ensemble of Tianese trumpets blasted a fanfare which cut through the valley and echoed eternally. Five notes, five trumpets, a chord of doom. A cold gust of air blew straight into Ahndien's face, chilling her blood.

CHAPTER SEVENTY-SEVEN

LIKE SWARMS OF HORNETS, the Tianese forces charged down the hills flooding the dry ground until they covered the space they occupied with the red of their uniforms. Against the ground, they looked like a pool of blood, ever-expanding yet never absorbed by the sand on which they flowed.

Render tightened his fists. He stood upon the rock looking down into the valley. He and Ahndien were charged with bringing peace to the people of these two warring nations, to unite them as the symbols on their swords dictated. As Valhandra had commissioned them.

With an equally fierce roar, the Torian troops flooded into the valley as well. So vast was the barren land that even after both armies got into position—there must have been tens of thousands on either side—a great distance still stood between them as they began to get into formation.

"Render." Branson stood behind him, his breath shaking. "Do you know what we're supposed to do?"

Images flashed through his mind: The hot orange

flames rising from the valley that he'd painted back in the castle. The black dragon he'd slain back in the shrine. And then, from a vision in his mind.

The faces of warriors, both Torian and Tianese.

They ceased fighting and stared into the sky.

Fear seeped into their eyes like blood spreading in clear water.

Then fear turned into unmitigated terror.

Greifer, now a black panther stood at Render's left. She pressed against his side, as she had in the cave back in Talen Wood, and leaned warmly against it.

// HAS VALHANDRA TOLD YOU WHAT MUST COME TO PASS? //

"I do not see it yet. But He said all will become clear to me at the right time."

Ahndien flanked him on his right, sword at the ready. "How can anyone unite them?"

The question lingered in his mind like the morning dew on blades of grass. He was never given all the answers, nor the exact mechanism to how he should accomplish this impossible task.

But he knew where they must position themselves, before the first arrow flew; that much Valhandra had revealed. Down in the valley, in the open space between which both armies encroached, stood a solitary tree. Its branches bore neither fruit nor leaf and may well have been dead for many years.

"We must go down there," Render said, pointing into the eye of the brewing storm.

// THE WIZENED OAK, OF COURSE //

Greifer transformed into a cat, leapt into Render's arms and climbed into his vest.

Branson laughed nervously. "You mean, right in the middle of those armies?"

"It has been ordained." Render reached his arms around Branson and Ahndien who had already pulled up close to his side. Without another word and without looking back, he lifted off with his three companions into the air, and down into the heart of the battleground.

CHAPTER SEVENTY-EIGHT

SEATED UPON HIS BLACK STEED, Lord Mooregaard fell back to make way for King Corigan. His majesty looked ridiculous, he and his horse completely covered in plates of steel glinting in the morning sunlight. He was supposed to be a symbol of strength and leadership, not clad like one of his subjects in the Torian cataphract.

This, Your Highness, is why your kingdom is forfeit this very day. You are a coward, not a ruler.

Corigan rode out before the legions, tried several times to lift the visor from his eyes, and finally removed his helmet. As he blathered on, Mooregaard sensed the apprehension in the troops. They knew the ground upon which they stood. And the superstition of ghosts and spirits in the Valley of the Accursed did nothing to mitigate the fear that grew in the hearts of the thousands of Torian soldiers, all charged to fight to the death in service of their King.

At last, Corigan rode over. "Well, My Lord Mooregaard, this is a fine situation we've run into! Did you not anticipate it? Did you not foresee?"

"All things are possible in war, Majesty. We can only—"

"Where is the element of surprise then! We should have crossed into the mountain range, taken the high ground facing the East and plucked those Tianese dogs off like insects. But now? They are already in the valley and show no sign of retreat. What do you say about that now?"

Mooregaard restrained the wrath that brewed within. Since the day he was weaned, he'd suffered Corigan's petty tantrums and wanted nothing more than to give the brat his due. But he must be patient. "Your Excellency, I pray thee, do not despair. For I have indeed prepared for this contingency. Even as we speak, the Lady Volfoncé has arranged a hidden company of warriors who, once we have drawn those Sojourner sympathizers into the battleground, will close in from behind. We shall then crush them, as though they were locusts, trapped in a sack!"

At this, Corigan's countenance lit up. "Really?"

"You didn't think I would allow the entire military forces of your great nation to be caught unawares, did you?"

"Well, I—"

"Courage, my king. Your hour approaches! Take your place and lead your people to victory."

"Yes. Thank you, my good and faithful counselor." He rode off to the front, strength and resolve renewed in his eyes. As he exhorted the foot soldiers, archers, armor-clad horsemen on their armor-clad steeds, his voice resounded with the contrived pomposity. Pride. Little did he know how this flaw in his character would prove to be fatal.

It was clear to Mooregaard that the King's empty words did nothing to inspire, but rather incited more fear and hatred in the hearts of the multitudes. Hatred for their cowardly king, hatred for Tianese and Sojourners.

Fear.

Hatred.

Kindling for Malakandor's altar.

In just a little while, the two armies would converge. And the two rulers, both bent on each other's destruction, would be the firstfruits offered up to Malakandor.

For all the years of denying the preternatural, fear and true terror—the very things Malakandor demanded had diminished greatly. Hatred alone would not satiate the unquenchable thirst of the Dark Ruler of the world.

For this reason, Mooregaard and Lady Volfoncé had answered his call. Today, they would offer the souls and bodies of Valdshire Tor and Tian Kuo's entire military to Malakandor. In exchange for this bloody sacrifice of at the very least sixty-thousand, Malakandor would grant new dominions to them both.

Volfoncé would become the dark ruler of Tian Kuo, Mooregaard of Valdshire Tor. They would rule by terror and bloodshed, stirring up both fear and hatred to Malakandor's satisfaction. This would seal their immortality, and both countries would grow to forget the preternatural powers that once terrified them, at which point, the cycle would be repeated: The myths about Sojourners as their common enemy, the wars between their two kingdoms, until the next millennial sacrifice to the great Malakandor.

"Men of Valdshire Tor!" Corigan cried, with a raised gauntleted fist, "Arise and seize your victory!"

Half hearted shouts and fists flew into the air.

Mooregaard rode to the front lines. "Who is with his Royal Highness?"

At that, soldiers roared and rattled their weapons. Corigan nodded with appreciation to Mooregaard, then replaced his helmet and pointed his sword forward.

To the Valley of the Accursed.

He led the battle cry as he charged forth.

CHAPTER SEVENTY-NINE

LIKE A BLACK WIDOW SPIDER, the Dowager Empress stepped forward, twin swords in her hands. Cold and impassive, her eyes bore straight into those of Lady Volfoncé.

But Empress Xieh-Suh knew her as Lucretia. Lucretia, the almond-eyed Sojourner traitor who allegedly killed off the last of those infernal barbarians, once a threat to her reign because of their ridiculous faith and philosophy of peace. Without blood it was impossible to rule a nation the size of Tian Kuo.

Xieh-Suh scoffed. To think, Corigan actually believed they could avoid bloodshed by playing the lives of his people by means of that childish game Leit?

The fool.

By her charm and deceptive beauty, Xieh-Suh had caused the downfall of countless men and rulers from her days as a slave girl, to a royal concubine, and finally as the wife of the Emperor—a weak man, like Corigan.

Lucretia (the form of whom Volfoncé now took) bowed deeply as the Empress approached. "Daughter of Heaven."

"You have done well, Lucretia." Xieh-Suh touched her shoulder and then lifted her chin. "When I have crushed the Torian army, and their child-king, you shall be duly rewarded."

"Just as they were taken by surprise when we sent your troops to raid Valdshire Tor under the Sojourner banner, so shall they fall under our assault here in the valley. Death shall fall upon them suddenly."

"As it had the Sojourner's Assembly?"

"All dead, O Great Empress."

"I envy your..." She paused to find the word, "Skill."

Lucretia grinned crookedly and shaded her eyes from the glare of the sun. Across the alluvial planes straight into the blackness of the Western woods, she saw the shaded area among the trees where Mooregaard prepared his portion of their offering to Malakandor.

Empress Xieh-Suh—none the wiser—had entrusted Volfoncé-as-Lucretia with the fate of Tian Kuo's military forces. A double portion for the great Malakandor.

With both nations stripped of their armies, nothing could stop her and Mooregaard from taking the thrones from the weak-willed Corigan, and the treacherous but ultimately powerless Xieh-Suh.

Ironic.

Despite all the mistrust that festered between the King and Empress, they had both entrusted their lives and kingdoms to the very two that would tear it from them.

"Do you stand with me, Lucretia?"

"You know what I am capable of."

Through dark lips almost black as poison, Xieh-Suh smiled. Indeed, the Empress had witnessed her shape-shifting abilities, her uncanny speed and precision in killing. Yet she had never seen Lucretia's most deadly abilities.

But she would.

Soon.

CHAPTER EIGHTY

EVEN AS RENDER FLEW THROUGH the air, the two armies flooded the valley like spilled ink; the red of Tianese troops and the black of the Torians.

"We're too late!" Branson said. "They're like two colonies of ants fighting! Once they've started, nothing can stop them."

Render ignored his words, so determined was he to get to the wizened oak before it truly was too late. Greifer pressed a warm paw against his heart.

// COURAGE //

As they alighted on the ground by the dead tree, from both sides the sound of countless hooves stormed through the valley like a thunderstorm. To the east and to the west, thousands upon thousands of horses, foot soldiers and large engines of war surged forward.

Beneath his feet, the sand shifted over what must be bones. Bones of the centuries-old Sojourners. If he gave it any more thought, he might lose his nerve. The very thought of...No, he must not think on it.

"What are you going to do?" Branson said, trying to find somewhere between Render and the tree. Ahndien clung to his arm drawing shorter and shorter breaths as she stared out at the onslaught. Greifer, now transformed into a black panther, paced around the three of them, her tail slashing the air.

Render's heart pounded almost in rhythm with the hooves charging from both sides of the wizened oak. Tawny clouds of dust flew up around the approaching armies. Render touched the stone tablet in his vest pocket. All he knew was to speak into the valley. But was this the moment of which Valhandra spoke?

"Render?" Ahndien whispered with palpable anxiety. If he didn't act soon, they would be trampled in the battle, if not first killed by the first arrows shot from either side.

Speak to the valley

He shut his eyes, pictured himself in the only position in which he could be seen or heard: High above the armies. When he opened his eyes, Render found himself about twenty-five feet from the ground. A dark cloud had spread over the valley and the thundering hooves died in midst of the clouds.

Flashes of lightning crackled within the pewter clouds which had gathered above. His hands glowed. Bluish-white energy pulsed from his fingertips. Through his clothes, the same azure illumination thrummed visibly.

Then he opened his mouth to speak. "TORIANS! TIANESE!" The unnatural profundity and volume of his own voice startled him. And, by the looks of it, caught the attention of the two armies as well. They both stopped in place, every eye gazing up at him.

An aura surrounded him as he floated above the battle ground, just a few dozen yards from the wizened oak. And from his dear friends.

Ahndien gazed up at the sky turned dark. In awe, she beheld Render—dear Render, whose very soul was now knit into the fabric of her own—hovering god-like above the valley. Surely he is the Great Deliverer of which the prophecies foretold. And at that moment, she briefly forgot that he was her friend, and saw him as royalty above all worldly authorities.

Perhaps there was hope, after all.

Perhaps the people of the two nations would see the truth and cease their striving.

Perhaps Valhandra had taken the bitter cup from her.

Another flash of lightning and for that instant, the darkened sky turned as bright as the morning, though the clouds had swallowed up the sun utterly.

"HEAR NOW THE WORDS OF VALHANDRA."

A rolling thunder peal erupted into a loud crack, filling the entire valley below with a brilliant white glow. Though Render was fully aware of what came from his mouth, the words he spoke seemed not his own. He felt like a musical instrument in the hands of a master musician. A powerful conduit of thought and feeling.

"THUS SAITH THE ALMIGHTY ONE: WAR NOT AGAINST ONE ANOTHER. FOR THIS IS THE WILL OF MALAKANDOR, THAT YE DESTROY ONE ANOTHER. PUT DOWN YOUR WEAPONS AND JOIN HANDS AGAINST THE DARK RULER OF THIS WORLD."

As the thunder ebbed into the distant hills, a dead

silence filled the valley. Render felt a presence so powerful coming over him like a mantle. Valhandra had spoken through him. Surely they would drop their swords and arrows and take heed.

Instead, he heard a familiar voice cry out, "Ignore this trickery and attack!"

Before Render could return to rescue his friends, a thousand soldiers, horses and weapons rushed into the center of the valley.

Towards the wizened tree.

CHAPTER EIGHTY-ONE

WITHOUT THOUGHT for anything else, Render dove back down to his friends. Greifer bore her fangs, her ears flattened back. Ahndien kept a trembling Branson behind her, but trained her eyes on Render as his feet touched the ground.

// STAY CLOSE, RENDER //

// WE HAVE TO LEAVE! //

// NO, THAT'S NOT WHAT VALHANDRA SAID! //

Ahndien was right. But far as Render knew, he was to stand and prophesy to the valley.

From whence cometh thy help.

He had failed!

Now, with the roar of two armies closing their grip on the valley of dry bones, what else could he do to bring them out of their lust for blood and into unity? He stood a better chance of holding back the flow of Leviathan Falls.

"Blast them, Render!" Branson shouted. "Use your lightning!"

But that would do nothing to accomplish his calling. And could he possibly stop them all? "Closer, everyone! We're going to fly out of here before—"

A sickening sound severed his words.

An approaching whistle.

From both sides.

"Get down!" Render dove at Ahndien and Branson, knocking them to the sand, where pale shin bones clattered about. From the corner of his eye—but more from the screaming over his head—he perceived thousands of arrows flying over them from both the Torian and Tianese archers. Some collided, spun and tumbled in the dust around them.

He looked up, but Ahndien pushed him down. Kneeling, she lifted her hands and wove a ring of fire about them. It blazed so bright Render had to turn away. The arrows that hit the fiery ring fell to the ground in small piles of ash and molten ore, still glowing red.

It seemed to go on forever, but eventually the first wave of Torian foot soldiers passed them by and proceeded to launch their assault on the oncoming Tianese troops.

Swords clashed on the eastern side of the valley. Horses galloped, pounding the ground and causing it to quake. Ahndien let out an exhausted breath and lowered her hands. Seizing the opportunity, Render rose to his feet and peered to the melee. But the rhythmic beating of war drums and horns drew his attention back to the approaching Torians.

The next wave—a solid wall of Torian warriors—marched over at a relentless pace, spears, swords and arrows at the ready. Perhaps he could make an appeal to King Corigan, as a citizen of Valdshire Tor. But he abandoned the thought, when he caught a glimpse of the black-armored knight, riding on an ebony-colored warhorse.

Lord Mooregaard.

Even at this impossible distance, their eyes met.

"Behold!" Mooregaard cried out to the Torians. "It is Render, standing with a Tianese spy! He has betrayed us all by warning them of our attack!"

"That's a lie!"

But his voice could not be heard over the angry soldiers' shouts, who now doubled their pace as Mooregaard rode forth, his sword glinting in the sun which broke through the charcoal clouds.

"Traitor!"

Before Render could move, a flash of black flew past him. It went out so quickly, he could barely distinguish the head, the powerful legs and thc tail. Greifer let out a snarl as she rushed into the open plane at Mooregaard.

"Greifer, wait!"

Lifting up one hand, Mooregaard commanded the troops to hold their position. All the while, over on the other side of the wizened tree, Tianese and Torians fought to the death.

Mooregaard raised his sword to strike the panther, but was not prepared for how swiftly she fell upon him. He let out a grunt as she knocked him off of his horse.

Then, grabbing his right wrist in her powerful jaws, she shook it so violently that he could do nothing but strain and groan and drop his sword. He began shouting oaths and thrashing about in pain, but the great panther only bore down more until he ceased struggling.

Render intuited her words to Mooregaard.

// COMMAND THY MEN TO TURN AROUND, OR BE RELIEVED OF YOUR ARM! //

Chest rising and falling, his teeth clenched, Mooregaard lifted his other hand from the ground. With her massive paw, Greifer pinned it to the ground and throwing a puff of dust to rise up around an upturned skull in the sand.

Then, without a hint of a warning, he swung himself around—arm still caught in the panther's jaw—and rolled over such that he freed his other arm.

Before Greifer ever noticed, Render saw it.

He shouted out.

Too late.

In one swift set of moves, Mooregaard dropped his hand, caught a sharp stone that fell from his sleeve, then thrust it at Greifer's neck.

She let out a startle hiss and caught his hand in her jaws.

Mooregaard shouted in pain and dropped the stone blade. The white of his eyes made them look as though they had grown twice their size.

But the panther released him and staggered away. A small trail of blood oozed from her neck and down her black fur.

"Greifer!" Render tried to fly over to her.

As though she already knew the outcome, Ahndien caught him by the arm. "You can't help her now!"

All of existence slowed before his very eyes. Greifer fell (though it seemed she floated) down onto her side, writhing in pain. But the struggle was short-lived. Her head went down. Emerald eyes gazed vacuously in Render's direction as her breathing grew more rapid.

In that short instant, which may as well have lasted an eternity for all Render knew, he remembered the black cat that had been with him since he was a small boy and slave in Bobbington's house, the panther in that Talen Wood cave, the cat that never left his side from his days in Castle Mittelvald and through the entire journey to the present battle.

A dagger of anguish pierced his soul.

Was this what it was like to lose his parents?

And then, the normal passage of time resumed.

Mooregaard rose to his feet, grasping his wounded arm. He glared down at the dying panther and drew his sword.

"No!" Render pulled free from Ahndien and flew straight at the black knight. But no matter how swiftly he flew, he could not arrive in time to stop it. Mooregaard knelt on one knee, put his hand gently on Greifer's jet black head, and then raised the sword over her neck.

CHAPTER EIGHTY-TWO

RENDER LAUNCHED HIMSELF straight at Mooregaard and drove his fist into his jaw. The black knight's head swung to the side. His sword fell to the ground. Render wasn't certain if the crack of bones and ligaments came from Mooregaard's face, his own hand, or both.

Render landed square on his feet expecting his opponent to falter, at the very least. But Mooregaard merely turned his face back and glared with such malice, it made Render stumble back.

The black knight advanced. From beneath his mail shirt, pulled out another sharp rock resembling a long spear head. "Come on!" He thrust it at Render's chest.

Render jumped back and raised his glowing hands at him. But the light and heat dissipated. He blinked in confusion.

// BEWARE, RENDER //

Greifer's thoughts...faint, barely discernable.

// SHIKAR ...SUPPRESSES... //

The power flowing through Render's entire body surged, then ebbed. The radiance in his hands dimmed at the thought. He stumbled back, intimidated not only by the thought of the Shikar stone and what it had done to Greifer, but by the malevolent look in Mooregaard's eyes.

"Don't prolong the inevitable. Come and die quickly!" Mooregaard rushed at Render again.

A blue and white bolt flew from Render's hands. Mooregaard lifted his arm to shield his face, but the lightning dissipated before it even reached him. The young Sojourner stared at his hands, then to the ground where Greifer lay, breathing heavily and dying. His heart sank.

In the distance, thousands of Torian soldiers stood, brandishing swords and spears as they cheered their commander, who smugly wielded his sword in one hand, and the Shikar blade in his other.

"Come now, don't waste my time. I promise to kill you quickly and painlessly." Mooregaard stood with the sharp Shikar stone pointed at Render's throat.

But before either of them could react, something whisked through the air above them. A fierce shout, then, in a loud clatter of armor and weapons and shields, something struck the black knight, causing him to fall to one knee, his helmet covering his eyes.

Whatever it was that hit Mooregaard, it flew straight up into the air again. Render took the opportunity to swing the point of his own sword just beneath his opponent's chin. Searching for the thing that had just saved his life, Render beheld, but he could not believe his eyes.

It was Branson.

"How do you like that, you stinking pile of cow dung?" Bounding into the air in repeated leaps, Branson leaped over horses and spears, kicking over soldier after soldier as he descended then bounced back into the air. Like a very large and mischievous frog.

In wonder, Render took a few steps back and could not help but smile.

But Mooregaard took the opportunity to stand, recover his sword and signal the second wave of his troops. He raised his weapon, and pointed over to the growing battle in the center of the valley. His men let out a roar and charged forward.

Back to his senses, Render brandished his sword, lightning crackling about the length of its blade.

Ahndien ran over and took Render by the arm. "You have to leave this place!"

She was right. Whether or not the troops meant to crush Render, Greifer and Ahndien, or to join the melee in the center of the valley, they would be killed. Barely able to hear his own voice above the din of the oncoming troops, Render turned to Greifer. "I can't just leave her there!"

"You'll be killed!'

// FLEE, RENDER. GET THEE TO SAFETY //

// I WON'T LEAVE YOU! //

At that very moment, Mooregaard removed his gauntlets, threw them to the ground, and with eyes glowing red like burning coals, thrust his open hands at Render and Ahndien.

A great gust hit them, hurling them back about two yards until they hit the ground.

Too winded to speak, Render tried to stand.

But a series of wind blasts kept knocking him down.

It was Mooregaard. He kept attacking them with gale force air bursts. While doing this, he took his sword in his other hand, held it above Greifer and prepared to deal her a final blow.

Just before he thrust it down, an errant brown horse came charging through the dust cloud. It let out a wild neigh and with its head rammed Mooregaard so hard he went flying into the air.

To Render's surprise, Mooregaard did not fall.

Instead, he righted himself mid-air and flew straight up into the sky and towards the raging battle. Though surprised, Render turned around and ran back to Greifer.

But as he did, he saw the most peculiar thing.

The brown horse, which looked too old and worn to fight in a battle, stood over the wounded panther. Render strode over, eyes wide in wonder. Ahndien following close behind and they witnessed the horse transforming ever so gradually. First the head, then torso such that he resembled a man, then finally all the limbs pulling in as he reared up on the hind legs and stood erect and clothed in a hooded brown robe.

The man seemed familiar to Render, but the hood he wore obscured his face. He knelt down and now, Greifer had also begun to transform. But not into a black cat. She was taking the form of a woman.

"Render," Ahndien said, touching his shoulder. "Please, we must go. Valhandra has said—"

"Not yet!" His words caused the man to turn his head. His hood dropped and straight away, Render knew who it was. The Prophet! "But how did you—?"

He held up a hand, interrupting Render's words, and knelt by the panther. "She's been grazed by a Shikar stone. It will only prolong her suffering."

"Render..." Greifer called out, laying on the ground and gasping for breath. She reached out her hand. "Draw nigh..."

Warm tears stood in his eyes and blurred his vision. He knelt and took her hand, which felt unnaturally cold. "Please Greifer, you mustn't..."

"Let it not be for naught, dear prince—" she grimaced, arched up. "There is....still hope..."

"I won't leave you."

"Go and...fulfill your destiny."

His face looking younger than possible, The Prophet inclined his head to Render with reverence. "I shall remain by her side as long I can, O Great Deliverer." He took Greifer's other hand and caressed her face. Then when he lifted his head, his eyes regarded Render with mixture sadness and dignity. "Your mother and I are exceedingly proud of you."

"What?" Render fell to his knees and choked back a sob. "My mothe—? Why didn't you—?"

"Beloved son." A poignant smile tugged at the corners of her lips. She reached up and touched Render's face tenderly, then glanced over to the Prophet. "Behold, thy Father."

"You're my father?"

A thousand questions flooded Render's mind threatening to burst like a breached dam. And at the same time, understanding and acknowledgment filled the recesses of his spirit.

There was so much he wanted to ask, so much he needed to reconcile. Yet the rising clamor of the battle forbade him. As did Ahndien's barely contained urgency. With otherworldly understanding, the Prophet looked Render in the eye, made a connection of recognition which traversed time, and said, "You must go. Now."

CHAPTER EIGHTY-THREE

IT WASN'T THE DREADFUL SOUND of the soldiers crying out in terror that caught Render's attention. Nor was it the sudden cessation of the clanging of swords. It was the biting cold gust that came rushing up his back.

Ahndien grabbed his arm. "Fly!"

Taking her in his arms, Render did so, leaving Greifer and the Prophet—his mother and father—in the skeleton-strewn sands of the valley. Down below, thousands of soldiers stood with their faces pointed into the sky, their arms and weapons slack at their side, and mouths agape.

It took a moment for Render to realize what they were staring at. Finally, at the sound of a struggling woman, he turned in the direction of her voice.

Arms firmly wrapped around Render, Ahndien said, "It's the Empress!"

"Treachery! This is treachery!" Suspended in the air, a woman clad in mail, with flowing scarlet scarves streaming in the wind, strained and flailed about, unable to control her upward ascent. She clawed in the direction of another woman who also hovered in the air not far from her.

But this woman seemed entirely at ease as she floated.

By the way she maneuvered her hands towards the Dowager Empress, it was clear that she wielded a supernatural hold on her.

"Treachery for treachery, vile she-dog!"

Right away, Render knew the voice. It was Lady Volfoncé. And before the Empress could utter another word, Volfoncé clapped her hands together sending a percussive wave through the valley. Instantly, the Empress's body exploded into thousands of tiny shards of flesh and bone. A sickly red spatter fell to the rocks beneath her.

Render whinced at the sight, too horrified to speak.

Ahndien turned her eyes from the monstrous sight. "It's the people we must rescue," she said.

Somehow Render understood. He remembered. For this too had been revealed to him by Valhandra in his encounter.

Mooregaard stood on a precipice over the valley. With his left hand twisting in the air, he commanded a whirlwind to encircle both armies. The wind howled and threw up a curtain of dust in around them. It spun at such a speed that frost grew on every soldier, Torian and Tianese alike. When they tried to cry out, they coughed and fell to the ground trembling from the cold.

"What's happening?" Ahndien said.

"He's freezing them." Render flew at Mooregaard but stopped midflight as the black knight lifted his right hand, directing a stream of air enclosing King Corigan. The King looked like a frozen piece of meat, curled up into a ball, white frost and icicles forming on every edge. Perhaps he was dead already.

"And now, fools of the East and West, behold! How your mighty rulers fall!" All the while spinning the frigid air around the soldiers of both kingdoms, Mooregaard made a fist with his right hand and then thrust it at Corigan.

Tiny frozen pieces of what was once the King's body flew in every direction, raining down over his cowering army. The sound evoked fine crystal shattering.

"Oh no. This is impossible." Mooregaard and Volfoncé were a far worse manifestation of evil than even the black dragon in the ancient shrine. "I...I can't face them," Render whispered, an internal chill creeping down his back.

"But you can!" Ahndien pressed her face into the crook of his neck. "I know you can."

"No. They're too powerful."

"You don't have to face them alone. I'll help you." Warm breath rose up. Her tears moistened his chest. "No matter the cost, I won't let them hurt you."

In the short time this had taken place, Volfoncé had flown over to Mooregaard's side. She stood, hands on her hips and smiled crookedly.

Ahndien turned her head and looked. "We have to stop them, Render. I think they're about to do something even worse."

"Oh great Malakandor!" Mooregaard lifted his hands and stretched them out over the immobilized armies. "Hear our supplication, oh great one."

Volfoncé held out her hands in the same direction. "At thy bidding, we offer these souls to thee. Now, according to thy word, bestow upon us, thy servants, the reign of these two kingdoms!"

"Accept our sacrifice, Malakandor!" Mooregaard's voice resounded through the valley. "And establish thy dominion through thy servants!"

At those words, the earth beneath them shook. The ground beneath the paralyzed legions began to glow. The wall of wind encircling them became a wall of fire, tightening slowly. In moments it would swallow them all.

"Do you see that, Render?" Ahndien's voice quavered. "They're all going to die. The entire military of both kingdoms. There'll be no one to stop them."

"All right then." Render took a deep breath, pressed his forehead gently against hers, and said. "But what have you withheld from me? What did Valhandra tell you?"

"Now is not the time."

"I can see it in your eyes. What I fear most—"

"Think not upon it. By Valhandra, you are the Great Deliverer, do not let such thoughts sway you."

With that, he embraced her, then flew straight down at the two infernal agents of Malakandor.

// PLACE ME ON THE PRECIPICE BEHIND THEM //

"Be careful." Render approached the cliff.

Before he knew it, Ahndien leapt from his arm and landed square on her feet just as he came within striking distance of Mooregaard and Volfoncé. Lightning crackled to life from Render's hands. This alerted them.

Mooregaard sneered. "Ah! Malakandor has delivered the final portion of the burnt offering. Straight into our hands!"

He sent a chilling blast straight at Render.

With his arm, Render shielded his face.

He squeezed his eyes shut.

A bone chilling blast bit into his skin.

CHAPTER EIGHTY-FOUR

AHNDIEN SET HER FEET upon a rock above the Torian knight and his female accomplice that had used their abilities to kill the Torian King and the Empress of Tian Kuo. She caught a glimpse of the Torian reaching for the pouch at his waist from which he'd produced the stones that had mortally wounded Greifer.

Now, seeing that this Malakandor-serving Mooregaard could manipulate the air and objects Ahndien knew what she must do. Even as he reached inside, Render began his descent, hands glowing blue and white, lightning crackling from the tips of his fingers.

Before Mooregaard could pull out the sharp stones and hurl them like arrowheads at Render, Ahndien summoned all her energy and sent a blast of fire straight at the pouch.

It flew from Mooregaard's hands and burst into flames. In an instant, nothing remained but ashes drifting to the ground. Both Mooregaard and his partner turned around in surprise and looked up at Ahndien.

In that moment, Render let loose a web of lightning which enveloped Mooregaard and the Lady beside him.

They cried out in pain, faltered, but quickly launched themselves into the air.

Mid flight, their bodies stretched out grotesquely as they transformed into two enormous vultures. Brown plumage, sickly pink heads, curved yellow beaks. Their wingspans exceeded that of Lao-Ying's as an eagle.

If only he were here to help.

Right away, Ahndien formed a fireball and hurled it at them. It nearly grazed them. Now aware of both her and Render, they flew down into the valley.

She reached out to Render. It made her anxious to be apart from him right now, when she was so close to the moment Valhandra had shown her in her vision. At all costs, she had to stay by him. To the very end.

// COME GET ME, RENDER //

In a brilliant flash, Render came to her side. "They're about to sacrifice both armies as a burnt offering to Malakandor!"

Once again, she climbed into his arms, preparing for flight. "Do you have a plan?"

"I'll take Mooregaard. Watch for Volfoncé, she may slip from view and catch you unawares."

Ahndien pointed down to the wall of fire surrounding the frozen masses of soldiers. Some of them twitched, many of them looked like frosted statues. They were fully conscious, but completely immobilized.

Like scavengers, Volfoncé and Mooregaard flew about the top of the gigantic fire ring that stretched across the golden expanse of sand.

"Ready?" Render took hold of Ahndien. Somehow, their thoughts connected. Just how much he saw into her heart, her mind, she could not tell.

Dry wind blew through her hair as Render flew into the valley, faster than she'd ever seen him do. If she herself could fly, things would be so much more efficient. As it were, she had no choice but to hold on and try not to fall. "The fire's closing on them!"

Render nodded. "Almost there!"

Why they should care about saving these people escaped her. Yet, it was the will of Valhandra, spoken directly to them, connecting their destinies like the inscription on the swords strapped to their sides:

Two weapons of war—UNITED—one instrument of peace.

The hairs on Ahndien's neck began to prickle as Render's entire body crackled with energy. Her hair unfurled and floated around her as though under water.

White light flashed in the clouds above.

The two vultures that were Mooregaard and Volfoncé now remained suspended above the hapless troops. Righted, they appeared to be standing mid-air, side-by-side, with wings outstretched.

The flames shot up suddenly and began to close in faster.

"Hurry, Render!"

He released a bolt and sent it straight at Mooregaard.

Mooregaard leaned back as it nearly grazed his head. He glared and, with the flapping of his wings, sent a powerful blast of air that hit Render and Ahndien like a stone wall.

She barely heard him calling for her as she slipped from his arms and plummeted into the valley of dry bones.

CHAPTER EIGHTY-FIVE

I AM NOT MEANT TO DIE THIS WAY!

Wind rushed up mercilessly as Ahndien fell hundreds of feet within a sliver of time. She squeezed her eyes shut in anticipation of hitting the ground and shattering into pieces.

But instead of the thud of fatal impact, a piercing screech filled her head. It wasn't the ground that came up under her. It was something massive, warm and powerful, yet gentle.

She opened her eyes and found herself straddling the neck of a mammoth bird, its silver crest and brown feathers as familiar as the back of her own hand.

"Lao-Ying?"

// TAKE HOLD QUICKLY, FLEDGLING //

"Lao-Ying! You came back!" He turned to the right and swooped down. Ahndien wrapped her arms around his neck. Diving headlong, Lao-Ying sped as though attacking the ground. Before she knew what he was doing, something landed behind her on his back and he swooped back up just a few feet from the ground.

The startled voice belonged to Render. "Where did you

come from?" They were now behind Mooregaard and Volfoncé, who were looking to the left and to the right searching for their crushed bodies on the ground.

// WE MUST ATTACK FROM BOTH SIDES //

Ahndien gave Render a quick smile. She touched the side of his face with tenderness she never knew she had. "Are you all right?"

"Yes." Not wasting a moment, he embraced her, took a deep breath and leapt from Lao-Ying's back. A thunderous clap jolted the air as Render flew.

Aglow like a silver-tipped arrow, Render drove straight between Mooregaard and Volfoncé. Ahndien and Lao-Ying followed closely. Render brought his hands together cupping a ball of energy that sizzled to life between his palms. From it a streak of lightning lurched forward and split into two, striking both Mooregaard and Volfoncé. They changed back into human form and fell to the ground, though not from a sufficient height to injure them.

Right away, the flaming wall surrounding the warriors of both kingdoms fell. Render turned to face them as they lay on the ground, still as statues. But Volfoncé, still lying on the ground next to her dazed partner lifted a hand, pointed at a large rock, causing it to levitate. She meant to hurl it at Render's head.

"Look out!" Ahndien called, just as it flew at him.

In an instant, Render drew his sword which shone with a dazzling blue light, spun around and sliced at the oncoming rock, which was several times larger than his head.

It split just inches before his face. The halves fell to the ground with glowing molten ooze bleeding from the edges.

Just then Lao-Ying landed, pinning both Mooregaard and Volfoncé under his powerful talons.

// CLIMB DOWN, AHNDIEN //

She obeyed. Before her feet even touched the ground, Lao-Ying launched into the sky, gripping his prey between his claws.

// FREE THE CAPTIVES. I WILL HOLD THESE TWO AS LONG AS I CAN //

She ran to Render's side. He stood before the entire host of Torian and Tianese warriors, who trembled and blinked—for it was the only movement they seemed capable of.

"I don't know what to do."

"We haven't much time," Ahndien said, filling her palms with a fresh plume. Then she noticed the frost encrusting the soldiers' helmets and fingertips. Right away, she sent a monumental pillar of fire into the air above the entire multitude. The blaze overhead lit the entire area like sunlight. The heat could be felt pulsing in the air around them all.

"Wait, what will they do if you free them?"

"We have to bring them together!" Ahndien sent another surge into the air. One of the Tianese soldiers started to move his fingers, which began to close around the shaft of his spear that lay in his open palm.

Render called out into the valley. "Hear me now! You have all been betrayed."

From the corner of her eye, Ahndien noticed Lao-Ying's flight becoming disjuncted. He seemed to be struggling. But the motion beneath her drew her attention back. "Render," she whispered, still keeping the flames burning hot above them.

All throughout the ground like ripples in the water, soldiers of both armies began to move. There must have been ten thousand of them, or more. Over to the far right and out of Render's view, a Tianese pikeman pushed himself up to his elbows, then to his knees, then to his feet.

// RENDER... //

Ahndien strained to keep the pillar ablaze.

Continuing to address the troops, Render did not heed her thoughts. Or perhaps did not perceive them. "See with your own eyes. This war has been contrived. As was your conflict against the Sojourners!"

The pikeman grit his teeth, pointed his spear at Render's neck and charged at him with great speed and ferocity.

Ahndien stopped the fire and gasped.

// RENDER! //

CHAPTER EIGHTY-SIX

THIS WOULD BE A FIGHT TO THE FINISH. He knew the two vile agents of Malakandor by their true identities: Mooregaard and Volfoncé. Gripping them in his talons, he regretted his years of inactivity pining in the hills as a hermit, all while these two immortals had not yet been defeated. But he had refused to go out and find them.

Now, they had succeeded in doing precisely what he alone might have been able to prevent, had he not disobeyed Valhandra. So many years ago, he'd all but forgotten.

Until today.

In the time Lao-Ying had left Ahndien to wallow in self-pity and hide himself from Valhandra—as though such a thing were possible—The Great Father of the Sojourners had appeared to him in a vision as He had—until recently—for centuries.

Thou shalt receive that which thou hast sought, and find the ending for which thou hast longed.

After centuries of waiting for the promised return of his

beloved, he had all but surrendered to the idea that it would never come to pass. And through the years, possessing the advanced knowledge of all the death and suffering that would befall his friends and loved ones through the ages and not being able to die himself, Lao-Ying had grown bitter in his immortality.

But just yesterday, Valhandra had granted his request:

I shall suffer thee to die, as your heart so desireth.

Now, facing death for the first time in half a millennia, Lao-Ying struggled to stay aloft, as Mooregaard and Volfoncé pried themselves free. The old hermit who had once been a prince felt something altogether unexpected. Something he'd not felt for hundreds of years.

Fear.

But not for himself.

He only knew what Valhandra had told him. Render and Ahndien must fulfill their destiny. To bring the warring kingdoms of Tian Kuo and Valdshire Tor into unity. And to reestablish the Dominion of Valhandra's people. Protect them at all costs.

As they loosed themselves from his grip, rather than fall, the traitors of both kingdoms flew outward. Just as Lao-Ying had anticipated, they transformed into spirit creatures of hideous aspect. A pair of massive vultures.

With one flap of his wings, Mooregaard sent a powerful gust that knocked Lao-Ying out of his flight path. The vulture turned to the frozen troops below and hovered over them.

Eagle that he was, Lao-Ying quickly recovered and drove down with all his might. He pointed his beak at the middle of the great vulture's neck. His attention was divided and it hadn't expected Lao-Ying to return so quickly.

One stab.

Pierce the center.

Should have done this two hundred years ago.

Just moments before he reached Mooregaard, Lao-Ying hit what felt like a wall of stone. Only there was nothing before him. He went tumbling to the golden sand, his vision darkening.

// OLD FOOL! DO YOU STILL SERVE A DEAD KING?//

It was the fatally alluring voice of Volfoncé. She had thrown up a wall of air as solid as rock. Lao-Ying's ears rang in pain which manifested in the smell and taste of blood in his mouth. Plummeting, he let out a cry, but no sound came out.

As he hit the ground, a dull pain went through his back and extended to his extremities. He opened his eyes and saw nothing but a blur of muted color and specks of dancing light. Instead of his wing, he saw the outline of his hand, fingers curled in agony. Pain ravaged him—not of the body, but of the realization that he'd failed to stop Mooregaard and Volfoncé.

Failed to protect Render and Ahndien at the moment they needed him most. He stretched his bloodied hand towards them. Before he could form his next thought, a sharp pain went through his ribs and shoulder.

Then with an atrocious screech, the cruel curved claws of the giant vulture dug into his sides. Volfoncé lifted his frail human form into the air. A gritty gust of wind tore against the open wounds on his neck and arms.

Try as he might, he could not muster the strength to transform.

His vision cleared enough for him to discern the valley

below, Render and Ahndien struggling to free the frozen warriors, Mooregaard in human form conjuring up a whirlwind of sand.

And the rocks below, upon which Volfoncé meant to dash him to pieces.

// AND NOW, OLD MAN, BEHOLD THE POWER OF MALAKANDOR AS YOU DIE //

CHAPTER EIGHTY-SEVEN

THIS IS USELESS!

What good was talking to statues? Paralyzed soldiers bent on killing each other, and probably Render himself, if they were able. Without knowing how long Lao-Ying could hold Mooregaard and Volfoncé off, Render began to doubt his ability to do anything useful.

Speak to the valley...

He may as well be speaking to the rock face of the hills.

// RENDER! //

Ahndien's distant call filled his mind. He turned around and instead of the beautiful Tianese who he'd come to love, he saw a snarling Tianese pikesman charging at him with a spear.

Just before the point of the spear reached his vest, Render flew into the air. The pikeman, still stiff as he thawed in the fire Ahndien cast around the frozen multitudes, thrashed his spear about, and finally lobbed it at Render. But it fell limply to the ground. The pikeman shivered and hugged his arms trying to stay warm.

Relieved he hadn't killed the soldier, Render sighed and flew over the thawing troops. In the distance, something odd began to happen. It first appeared to be a swirling dust cloud. But then, even as Ahndien called out to him, the sound of howling wind overwhelmed her voice. Each grain of sand turned black until the cloud itself changed from gold to slate.

"By all that is sacred!"

Beneath Render's feet, the troops began to stir, thanks to Ahndien's warming fire. But a more ominous threat approached. Render felt it in his blood.

In one brief moment, three things happened. Render couldn't react quickly enough to do anything about it. First, an enormous vulture flew by with the elderly human Lao-Ying in its claws. Then Ahndien let out a shout directing Render's eyes back to the black cloud, which settled to the ground across the valley.

Finally, from within the cloud emerged what could only be described an army of shadows. Ethereal, black, and but for the outline of men on horseback with weapons drawn, featureless.

There must have been thousands of them coming at the Tianese and Torians, who were too weak to defend themselves.

"Get up, everyone!" Shouted Ahndien at the staggering warriors. "Look alive, they're coming!" But those that were able to stand stumbled and fell again. Their limbs were too rigid.

Render shot a line of lightning straight into the oncoming horde which for sure outnumbered the two armies they were attacking.

The lightning passed through them as though they were nothing more than a dark vapor.

Then came the first arrow from a mounted archer.

Black smoke trailing as it flew, it seemed nothing but a shadow.

Until it pierced the first Torian soldier's chest.

CHAPTER EIGHTY-EIGHT

MOOREGAARD LAUGHED subtly as legions of the demon horde sprung to life. Pure spirit-creatures, nothing could stop them from destroying all the pitiful Tianese and Torian warriors, who were like sheep going to the slaughter.

They would then swallow them up in flames. A pleasing sacrifice to Malakandor.

The covenant would be upheld: The middle kingdoms would be Mooregaard's and Volfoncé's to rule in perpetuity.

Streams of black smoke took bodily form and rushed out to the center of the valley. Render and that feeble girl had no recourse whatsoever.

Mooregaard shouted into the valley such that his words echoed repeatedly. "Valhandra is dead!"

Lao-Ying watched in horror as the demon horde drove at the royal troops under Render and Ahndien's guard. Nothing could stop them, neither lightning nor fire.

Smoke-like arrows struck down the soldiers, dozens at a time.

// DIE IN THE BITTERNESS OF YOUR FAILURE //

Blood oozed from Lao-Ying's ribs as the points of Volfoncé's claws dug in. She dangled him over the jagged crags. He felt his life pouring out. This was not how he had hoped to die. Not before he was to behold his beloved once again. That was the entire reason he had accepted his fate as an immortal, the reason he'd suffered half a millennium. To be with her again, even in the lifting of the eternal veil.

Valhandra, if thou still livest, grant thy servant but one last effort...

Lao-Ying squeezed his eyes shut. He clung to his last shred of faith even more firmly than he did to Volfoncé's claws.

Faith.

The power behind the spirit potential.

And then something wondrous happened.

Like the rush of hot air from the opening of a fiery furnace, energy flowed through his body. He saw. He intuited. He began to transform.

With a final surge, Lao-Ying swung his bare feet up just as they turned into talons. He dug them deep into the monstrous bird's belly and punctured the flesh with a fierce grip.

Instead of an angry screech, the pained gasp of a woman came out of the vulture's beak. Its yellow eyes widened in shock as it let out a shriek.

Then they fell.

Turning over and over, neither the vulture nor the eagle relenting their grips.

Lao-Ying struggled to right himself, but could not catch the wind under his wings.

// WRETCHED OLD MAN, WE'LL BOTH DIE! //

"I am prepared," said Lao-Ying smiling calmly in his heart as only an eagle can. "Are you?"

Right away, the balance of power shifted.

The violence in Volfoncé's eyes turned to fear. Black pools which once boiled haughtily, now darted from side to side as she tried in vain to flap her wings and catch the wind.

They fell faster and faster, the razor sharp points of the rocks jutting up beneath them.

Lao-Ying struggled until he found the strength to spread out one wing. This caused the two of them to turn over one more time, and now he angled his weight just so the air rushing up prevented Volfoncé to unfurl her own wings.

Then came the crack of bones.

The sinking of petrified stone points into flesh.

A strained cry.

Cut short by the hiss of expiring breath.

Lao-Ying rolled across the enormous aviary form of Volfoncé and pushed himself up with human hands. From the vulture's neck, bent at a perverse angle, and the stillness of its breast, he knew she was dead.

He climbed down, careful not to cut himself on the sharp rocks, and wrestled himself to his feet. Blood poured from his punctured side, but it was not the pain that sent him down to his knees. It was the chill of blood loss.

He was dying.

He had stopped Volfoncé, but would not live to see the

promise for which he had waited over the past five centuries. And worse still, down in the valley below, he beheld a ghastly sight now threatening Render and Ahndien. Something he had not seen since the fall of the Sojourners at the hands of Malakandor's legions.

The demonic cloud.

CHAPTER EIGHTY-NINE

THE MANIACAL LAUGHTER stopped just long enough for Mooregaard's words to echo into the valley. "Valhandra is dead!"

Render shuddered at the thought. It must not be so. Yet, where was He? Why did he not come to help at this most desperate moment? Render glanced around. The few soldiers that could actually move stumbled and backed away. They cowered as the dark horde rushed forward like a demonic swarm of locusts. Their smoke-arrows pierced many who tried to flee.

He could sense the mass panic amongst the thousands of immobilized fighting men of the two kingdoms, many of whom murmured, groaned and screamed in terror, but could not move.

Speak to the valley...

Was it his imagination? His memory playing tricks?

Apart from the charging demon horde, which howled unlike anything he'd ever heard or would ever want to hear again, there was nothing in the valley but dying soldiers and the dry bones of fallen Sojourner warrior, centuries dead.

Where was Valhandra now?

// SPEAK TO THE VALLEY...AND PROPHESY //

"Sire?" The voice within resounded unmistakably.

Valhandra.

Render lowered himself to the ground, even as the thundering hooves of demon horses filled the air. A smoke arrow screamed past his face carrying the stench of decaying flesh with it.

// SPEAK AND DO NOT FEAR, RENDER, FOR I SHALL GIVE THEE THE WORDS //

He shut his eyes, facing the onslaught which would overtake them all in moments. The ground began to shake, rattling the thousands upon thousands of dry bones in the dust.

Then, a pulse of light filled his chest—it was not blazing hot, but cool, refreshing. Render's mind and soul became clearer than it had ever been in his life. It was as though he could see for miles unobstructed, hear things clear over the mountains, and smell the fragrance of Valhandra's presence. The pulse rose up to his mouth and his tongue became loose. It practically moved on its own, though he seemed to already know the words.

"Warriors of truth! Arise!"

At this, a mighty cry of opposition rang out from the dark horde, just a few hundred feet away. At first Render wondered if the Torian or Tianese soldiers would receive these words. But as he spoke again, he realized that it was not they that he addressed. Light shot out from his mouth as he spoke again.

"Rise up, warriors of spirit and truth!"

The light spread like a mist and raced out into the sand, straight at the demon horde.

"THUS SAITH THE KING OF ALL KINGS! THUS SAITH VALHANDRA!"

Demon horses screamed.

Thundering hooves stopped.

White light, the inspired words from Render's mouth, enveloped the entire valley. The demon hordes stopped dead.

Everything faded into a dreadful stillness.

A beauteous terror filled the entire valley.

And then it began.

CHAPTER NINETY

IT WAS NOT THE BLINDING LIGHT.

Nor was it the sudden cessation of the hordes.

It was the melodious tones of a Tianese flute that flooded the valley. From behind the white veil which enveloped nearly everything within an arm's reach, Ahndien emerged, her lips pursed over the end of her instrument.

She played a simple yet haunting melody that seemed to cause the hills to tremble, the ground to shudder.

Render turned and regarded her. Of course it was her. Who else could be responsible for such an otherworldly sound?

Head held high, her brown eyes fixed Render with a courageous smile as she strode past him. Then she looked sharply into the light-filled expanse. Render followed her into the cloud.

The cloud grew manifold tendrils, supernal and restless. They wove under and around the innumerable bones on the ground, caressing them, lifting them into the air.

Ahndien's song grew louder. Stronger.

Render didn't realize that he'd stopped until the words returned.

// SPEAK TO THE VALLEY...FROM WHENCE
COMES THY HELP //

With one punctuated note, high and shrill, Ahndien's song stopped.

But the music continued.

The echo of one flute became a chorus of many.

Though Render didn't understand, yet in his spirit he must have comprehended fully, for it drove him to speak again.

"ARISE, IN THE NAME OF VALHANDRA!"

At the sound of the name, a bristling wave of grunts flooded through the ranks of the demon forces.

The fingers of light lifted hundreds of thousand bones into the air. Render could not believe what he saw. Nor could the weakened human warriors behind him, for they gasped in wonder and fear.

Ahndien came running back to Render's side. She put away her flute and exchanged it for her father's sword and pointed to the peaks of Handara. "Over the hills..."

A blazing ball of white fire shot through the air and rushed towards them.

On closer observation, Render saw that it was a mass of small, bird-shaped light entities, flocked together as one.

The demon warriors stepped back as the flock rushed past them. The few who did not move out of the way soon enough disintegrating into ashes.

"Get down!" Render grabbed Ahndien by the shoulders and jumped forward. The flock hit the ground and exploded in the midst of the host of bones, now fashioned into the skeletons of thousands of creatures.

Render lifted his head.

Before his very eyes, flesh and sinew stretched around the bones quicker than he could observe. In an instant, the valley teemed with life: Eagles, tigers, bears, men and women girded for battle.

Before he could even blink, legions of spirit creatures haloed with white light stood ready. This seemed to enrage the demon horde though none of them dared take a step forward.

Render blinked in amazement. He had finally done as Valhahdra had commanded and spoke to the valley. From whence cometh thy help.

In the distance, Mooregaard transformed into a giant vulture once again, flew into the air and shouted at his demon army. "Why do you hesitate? By Malakandor, destroy them all!"

The hordes charged forward with a horrific battle cry—something that resembled the shriek of mountain lions and the howl of wolves. For a brief moment, the sky darkened with thousands of smoke arrows flying at them. But this time, the resurrected warriors threw up a wall of fire, extinguishing all but a few.

From the ranks of resurrected Sojourner troops, a tall and formidable man with flowing white hair, a silver breastplate and shield—upon which was emblazoned a royal blue dragon—turned and approached Render and Ahndien and pulled them to their feet.

At first glance, from the wizened face and sagacious eyes, the man seemed hundreds of years old. But from the powerful arms, sturdy posture and chest, he could well be a young man, but a few years older than Render. He inclined his head.

"Hail, Great Deliverer! Mikahl, High Commander of the Sojourners reporting. I await your command."

Even then, the demon horde fell upon the front lines. A furious battle ensued. Beasts of light wrestled, twisting and writhing against the dark shadow hordes. Mikahl did not so much as blink.

Render looked to Ahndien and nodded to the hapless Tianese and Torians. Understanding, she agreed. "Yes."

"Very well then, Commander," said Render. "Assemble a battalion to protect the Tianese and Torians. If they become ready to fight, employ your best judgment."

"Sire." Mikahl turned, put two fingers in the corners of his mouth and blew a loud whistle. Right away, a flock of seagulls—much larger than usual—formed a line before all the human troops.

Had he blinked, Render might not have witnessed them transform into a solid wall of mail-clad warriors, swords and crossbows at the ready.

Gently placing a hand on the back of Ahndien's head, he pulled her in close and kissed her. "You should stay here."

"I am charged by Valahandra to protect you. I will not leave your side."

"You could die. Did He consider that?"

She turned her eyes downward. For a moment it seemed she might change her mind. But then lifted her face and with the same blazing glare as when they first met she said, "I only know what He told me. And I will obey."

He knew better than to argue with her.

"Then we'll die together." Render took her by the hand, but to his surprise, she began to lift off the ground by her own power.

"You shall surely not die," Ahndien said, as he flew up and joined her. "You've a kingdom to deliver and establish."

Aloft, with Ahndien by his side, Render drew his sword, gave Ahndien a grave nod, then to Mikahl—who also raised his sword, indicating to the remaining Sojourner troops they were to join the battle.

"And now," Render said, all Sojourner eyes fixed upon him and ready to engage, "For Valhandra!"

A mixture voice both of human and beast, the Sojourner battle cry shook the air. "For Valhandra!"

CHAPTER NINETY-ONE

FLYING DIRECTLY INTO THE BATTLE, Render took heart. The glowing Sojourner warriors, resurrected from ages past must have been spirit creatures because only they could effectively combat the demon horde. No human mortal seemed able to stop them as they passed through solid matter. Mikahl, however, led the charge and repelled the first wave.

By Valhandra's wisdom, the help had come.

But could they stop Mooregaard and the unending stream of demon warriors pouring out of the black whirlwind? As they hovered over the battlefield, swords held out, both Ahndein's and Render's blades touched, his crackling with bridled azure lightning and hers ablaze like a long golden torch.

"They're coming!" Ahndien said, her voice taut with dread.

The next wave of smoke spewed out of the whirlwind, past the ground battle, and straight at Render and Ahndien. The dark smoke snaked out at them, then dispersed into countless bats the size of hawks. All round them Render could see nothing but blackness. All he heard was the shrill shrieking, the relentless flapping, as they engulfed them.

He could barely breathe.

The rancid stench of decay and of blood choked him. Even before he could swing his sword, Ahndien began slashing into the swarm. Every few seconds the fire from her sword sliced an opening in the flying pitch, affording a ray of sunlight to come through. But it never lasted more than a moment. Even more bats filled the space.

Render shouted in pain as one of them bit into his shoulder, piercing his shirt and skin with its fangs. With his left hand charged with power, he grabbed it. Instantly, it turned to ash. But the wound from its bite still burned with pain.

He continued to slash at the bats, each time cutting open a swath of sunlight, each time watching the blackness fill it again. They could continue this for a while, but it kept them from the real battle below.

Ahndien strained and shouted as she struck dozens with each stroke. "I can't stop them, Render!"

From the corner of his eye, through the opening in the swarm, he saw the vulture. Mooregaard, ominous and massive in size, slowly hovering towards the Tianese and Torians. "We've got to get out!"

As though in response, the swarm closed in even tighter. Bats fluttered in his nose, ears, hair. They bit into his neck, arms and legs, faster than he could burn them off. But he kept his eyes on Ahndien.

She fought them off well with her sword until a dozen of them knocked or pried it from her hands. It fell silently into the black stream which swallowed it into the whirlwind.

Render sheathed his sword, flew straight at Ahndien and

wrapped her in his arms. "Shield yourself."

"You'll burn!"

"Just for a moment."

"No!"

// AHNDIEN, PLEASE. IT'S OUR ONLY WAY OUT! //

The swarm became like a solid wall, closing in on all sides, biting, pulling on hair and clothes with sharp teeth. They would tear the flesh from their bones if this continued.

"Trust me," Render said. "Just one quick burst."

She agreed, then hid her head in his chest.

The swarm was so tight around them he could hardly breathe. Each time he tried, it constricted even more.

// ONE BURST, AHNDIEN. READY? //

He felt her nod tightly.

// NOW! //

In a flash of blue and gold light, a deep thunderclap that deafened Render's ears momentarily, Ahndien's fire melded with his lighting. The collision of forces detonated. Heat, lightning and fire shot out in all directions. The energy sphere exploded, incinerating the swarm in an instant.

It also sent Render and Ahndien flying back in opposite directions. Render remained aloft, but Ahndien seemed to have lost consciousness and plummeted into the melee below.

Eyes still stinging from the smoke and smell of burnt hair and bat flesh, he fought the backwards momentum. Tried to fly over and catch her. But he was too far. She would be dashed against the rocks or killed in the midst of the swords, spears and arrows. "Ahndien!"

Then, out from behind the rocks, along the outskirts of the valley, a singular body came bounding at incredible heights and speed. It was Branson!

Bouncing off the heads and shoulders of the unsuspecting demon warriors, he knocked them to the ground before they even knew what hit them. He gave a loud whoop and caught Ahndien in his arms just yards above the fighting.

"Follow me!" He said and pointed his chin to the eastern edge of the valley. "Mooregaard's over there!"

Fully recovered, though tiny needles prickled every inch of his body, Render flew after Branson and Ahndien, who was now awake and able to fly on her own.

It was difficult to discern if the Sojourners or the forces of Malakandor were winning. Thousands of both had fallen. The Tianese and Torian troops, now released from their enchanted frozen state, cheered and rattled their armaments behind a fiery line of Sojourner spirits. "Let us fight!" they shouted. But their natural weapons would have no effect on the mist-like demon troops, no matter how real they appeared.

"Hurry, Render!" Branson led them to a rock ledge which overlooked a secluded area below. As Render alighted, he touched Ahndien's face tenderly. Her hair was singed and dark burn marks covered the edges of her clothes, but she was otherwise unharmed. He turned to Branson.

"Why, you're like some kind of..."

"Don't even say it. All my life, I knew there was something special about me. I just never expected to manifest the spirit potential of a blasted frog!"

Ahndien kissed his cheek. "Frog spirit or not, I'm grateful."

He wiped the moisture off as though it were poison. "There'll be none of that, now!"

"Where's Mooregaard?" Render whispered.

"Down there."

He glanced down but saw nothing but sand. But from beneath them, under the space over which the precipice hung, a whooshing sound caught his attention. All he could see below was a flash of light. Then came the smell of sulfur and smoke.

"What's he doing down there?" Render asked, unwilling to fly out before knowing.

"It's..." Branson's eyes lit up in a mixture of joy and fear. He leaned over to take a look over the edge. "Why, it's..."

"What, Branson? What is it?" Ahndien said.

"He's fighting Mooregaard, but something's wrong. We've got to help." Branson stretched his neck again and almost fell over the edge.

Render caught him by the collar and pulled him back. "Once and for all, who or what is fighting Mooregaard?"

Branson's lip quivered. "My father!"

CHAPTER NINETY-TWO

TRAITOR!" cried the tall and imposing knight as Render, Branson and Ahndien descended quietly to the ground and hid behind a rock. Clad in shining silver armour, a crimson shield in hand, he thrust his sword forward at Lord Mooregaard, who stood in human form.

From the sword, a stream of fire blasted straight at the black knight but he simply waved his hand and snuffed it out with a mighty wind. It threw his opponent back two steps. "Ah, Lord Agon," Mooregaard said, with alarming calm and an unnerving smile. "Thou shewest thy true colors. I have always suspected you to be a Sojourner."

Render looked to Branson and whispered, "You're the son of a Sojourner."

Agon pointed his sword at Mooregaard and glared. "You know nothing but treachery! You've betrayed your people, blamed every atrocity on the last of our people. But it was you and Volfoncé behind it all!" He sent forth another fireblast.

Unimpressed, Mooregaard held up a hand and deflected

it back.

Agon held up his shield.

"Where is Volfoncé, anyway?" Mooregaard asked himself pensively gazing past Agon.

"No doubt reaping the rewards of her betrayal, if there is any justice!" Another blast of fire. This one came a bit closer to its target before Mooregaard once again extinguished it.

"Out of my way, fool! Cease your annoying ranting and I will make your death quick."

Branson almost leapt out. Render caught his arm and prevented him. "Spring too soon, and you'll lose the element of surprise."

"We have to help him!"

"And so we shall, but at the precise moment, when Mooregaard is vulnerable." Render loosened his grip when Branson seemed to understand. Ahndien put her arm around the boy's shoulders.

"Just as Mooregaard transforms, we'll strike," Render said.

Mooregaard stepped forward, annoyed at being cornered in the rockface. With a wave of his hand, he threw a blast of wind at Branson's father and knocked him off his feet. He dropped and landed with his knee pressed into Agon's breastplate. From Mooregaard's sleeve, a dagger slipped out and fell into his hand. He pressed the point into Lord Agon's throat.

Branson hissed. "He's not going to transform."

"Wait!"

But Render was too late to stop him.

Branson leapt into the air and shouted with more ferocity than anyone could have imagined.

At the sound of it, Mooregaard turned and glanced around. "What was that?"

From about fifty feet in the air, Branson crashed down onto his shoulders with all his might. This knocked him to the ground and off of Lord Agon's chest. The dagger tumbled and sunk tip-down into the sand.

Branson sat on the ground kicking Mooregaard repeatedly in the head.

"Branson!" His father cried.

"I've got him, father!" He continued to kick with such rapid force, Mooregaard could not even get to his feet. Every time he tried, Branson kicked him down. In vain, the black knight groped for the dagger, but each time he did, Branson kicked him, pushing him just out of reach.

Though it seemed to weaken him significantly, Mooregaard, prideful to the end, only laughed with each blow.

Render and Ahndien flew forward calling for Branson. Even his father shouted for him to stop and escape. But Branson refused. The frenzied state that besieged him would not permit him. He punctuated each kick with a word:

"You vile!...Piece!...Of!...Dung!"

Mooregaard stopped struggling. Even as his fingers wrapped around the dagger's handle, his body went limp.

"Die...traitor!"

And finally, Mooregaard ceased moving altogether.

Branson stopped kicking and looked at Mooregaard's still body, his head turned to the side revealing open, lifeless eyes.

"Ha!" Momentarily, Branson's own eyes glowed a venomous green hue. "Ha-ha!"

Render took a step forward. "Branson, come away from him. Carefully."

"You're dead, Mooregaard! Dead, dead, dead!"

"Son..." Agon approached cautiously. He seemed

disturbed by the display of unmitigated hatred from his child.

But the anger in Branson's eyes soon became tears. "Father...I obeyed your command...went to the mountains...I never knew we were—"

"Son, look out!" Agon rushed forward, threw his son behind him.

Sooner than Render, Ahndien or Lord Agon could react, Mooregaard grasped the dagger which lit up in a deadly green glow, and hurled it straight into Agon's chest. With a sickening clank, it penetrated the silver plating and sunk straight into his heart.

Still reaching forward with his sword, Agon fell to his knees. A fiery blast flew from his weapon, but as soon as it dropped from his hand, the fire died.

"Father, no!" Branson shouted and tried to leap into the air. But Mooregaard caught him by the foot, stood up and threw him aside like a cover-worn book. He grunted as he landed in the sand and skidded to a halt.

Render drew his sword.

Ahndien did the same.

Something from within—an impulse from perhaps the swords themselves—caused them to cross blades. In an instant, a stream of fire and lightning shot at Mooregaard.

He dodged it by leaning slightly to one side. The surprise on his countenance betrayed him for a moment. But the malignance and haughty look quickly returned. "So *you* are the Great Deliverer?"

Right away, the same accusing doubt that confronted him at the Pool of Madness and in the Shrine of the Ancients returned. Before he could steel up his nerves it sapped his strength.

The blades separated.

While Ahndien continued to hurl fireballs with her left

hand and columns of fire with her sword, Render's sword flickered and returned to its natural state.

Mooregaard extinguished Ahndien's attacks with the fingers of his left hand and stepped forward menacingly. "Render? The slave boy? The little whelp of the very dead Sir Edwyn? Thou art neither a deliverer nor great!"

Mooregaard's words sunk into his soul. His legs softened like unbaked dough. He could not even take a step back.

Ahndien blasted twice as much fire at Mooregaard, but now, with the twist of his wrist, a vortex formed in the air and sucked up every bit of air and fire. "Render, fly!"

"I can't...move!" Render's teeth chattered as they had on those frigid winter nights in Bobbington's cottage. The vacuum and frigid air immobilized him as it had the human troops.

"Thou art nothing." Mooregaard locked his gaze upon Render's eyes like a serpent mesmerizing its prey. "Thou hast been deceived to think thou wast anything but a lowly slave!"

With a feral cry, Branson leapt in the air and came down at Mooregaard. But the black knight lifted his right hand, made a circle in the air, which caught Branson like a noose.

Branson strained, clawed at the invisible cord that wrapped around his neck as he hung suspended in the air.

"I can't continue..." Ahndien screamed, "Oh! Render!"

Then Mooregaard cut off her words by hanging her up in the air like Branson, by the neck with an invisible cord of air current.

"Nothing, do you hear? You have delivered nothing but the pitiful mortals of both kingdoms into my hands. Their unbelief makes them more pleasing a sacrifice to Malakandor. And your death will prove to my new dominion that faith in Valhandra is futile. None shall testify to any of these wonders they will all be dead! Generations of mindless, faithless people will be mine to rule. And all because THOU ART *NOTHING*!"

// NEVER MIND US, RENDER. GET AWAY IF YOU CAN! //

Render ignored Ahndien's thoughts and lifted his eyes to Mooregaard's. "Yes." He nodded, his eyes glancing up to his beloved and to Branson, gasping for breath, powerless to escape.

Even His name has power.

"On my own strength, I am nothing." He then trained his thoughts like an arrow, and aimed straight for Mooregaard's skull.

// BUT I AM AS *VALHANDRA* SAYS! //

Render's entire body exploded with lightning. From every particle of air, he sensed the energy rushing into his body, lending its power.

Accumulating in force.

The sky turned black, just above them.

Every hair on his body stood on end.

Mooregaard's smile faded.

He took a step back tentatively. The black knight's form began to change.

But Render focused all the energy flowing through his body into his hands. He could move one arm. Then the other.

Then Mooregaard took his demonic form. First the wings, then the deadly beak. He rose up to the size of an elephant and began to flap. The wind came as a torrent.

Ahndien and Branson dropped to the ground.

And just before Render discharged the lightning surging within him Mooregaard flew into the air. This would be his most powerful blast ever, he could tell.

But then, just before he released the bolt at the hideous vulture, something rose up into the sky behind it.

Something which made the vulture seem insignificant in size and dread.

Something more terrifying than anything he'd ever imagined.

The power drained from Render's body as he stared in terror.

CHAPTER NINETY-THREE

FROM BEHIND THE GREAT VULTURE, a dark figure many times its size fell upon it. Its words were clear as speech in his mind, and no doubt, to all who were present.

// MOOREGAARD! YOU HAVE EXPENDED MALAKANDOR'S PATIENCE. HE HAS SENT ME TO PERFECT THAT WHICH YOU HAVE LEFT UNFINISHED //

Astonished, the vulture turned to find a massive black dragon (similar, yet many times more horrific than the one Render defeated.) It clutched the vulture's throat with the talons of its foreclaws. It appeared as shadow-like as the demon warriors, but its effect on Mooregaard's vulture-form was palpable.

"I pray thee mercy, Ashtoreth!" Mooregaard cowered in his human words, which blended hideously with a vulture's screech. "Behold...I have prepared the...the sacrifice!"

// YOU HAVE SUFFERED THE SOJOURNERS TO RISE AGAIN! MALAKANDOR PERMITS NO SLUGGARD TO LIVE, MUCH LESS REIGN //

And with that the black dragon shot fire and tore the burning Mooregaard to shreds. It devoured his vulture body as he screamed in agony. Bits of smoldering flesh, blood, and black feathers fell to the ground all around Render, Ahndien and Branson. The nauseating fetor and gurgling screams afforded them a moment to run to Lord Agon.

While the ghastly feeding frenzy took place above them, Branson crawled over to his father, whose chest rose and fell rapidly. Render had seen this in the last gasps of his brother Kaine. It brought back such sorrow, he could barely look on.

"Father," Branson sobbed. "I'm so...sorry."

The Lord Agon, now fallen, his life pouring out like wine from a broken flagon, put his hand on his son's face. "Be strong, my son. And forgive thy father for withholding too much...Truly...I have never...left you..."

Branson took his father's hand. "I...Father, I have always believed you...forgive my doubt and impatience!"

Gently, Agon pulled him down to his chest and kissed the top of head. "Do not fear, my son. For you have only begun to see the truth."

He turned to Render, who knelt at his right hand. Then, taking his arm, "I have fought the good fight, O Great Deliverer. With kindness, pray remember my son, when...when...."

Render put his hand on Agon's shoulder. "I shall, My Lord."

And then, after one final gasp, The Lord Agon breathed his last. The tightness in his brow relented. A look of peace, like he'd seen the end from the beginning washed over his face. His eyes shut as though in a sweet slumber.

"Father!" Branson wept, pressing his face against his beard, baptizing it with his tears.

"I'm sorry, Branson." Render said, still aware of the horror that continued above them. He turned to Ahndien who already knew what they both needed to do. Then back to Branson. "Stay here with your father."

Still holding his father's hand, Branson nodded.

Sun light flooded the ground as the shadow dragon's form dropped a single claw—the last remains of Mooregaard—to the ground, and looked to the valley for Malakandor's sacrifice.

Ashtoreth let out a hideous shriek and turned her head just slightly to stare at Render with a malignant vermilion eye.

// I SHALL SAVE YOU FOR A CONFECTION //

As it flew off, the demonic dragon's cackling laugh echoed throughout the alluvial hills, sending a chill through Render's blood. Had Ahndien perceived its threat? Regardless, he must do everything in his power to stop Ashtoreth.

Render leapt into the air and hovered above. But Ahndien hesitated. He could see the fear in her eyes. "Stay here with Branson."

She too flew up to his side. "We have not yet fulfilled our calling. Let us go now."

Somehow, he knew. She must be by his side, though it pained him to see her apprehension. Against his own heart he agreed, took her hand, and raced to stop the demon dragon.

Ashtoreth blasted a stream of fire at the humans and the

Sojourners guarding them. It snuffed out the protective wall of fire suddenly, and formed yet another fiery ring even more frightful than Mooregaard and Volfoncé had done. This was a warning shot, something to terrorize them before Ashtoreth scorched and consumed them. At the sound and glow of the blast, all the demon warriors in the front line flew up over the heads of the Sojourners like a cloud of locusts to the ever tightening fire ring.

The flames climbed so high Render could not see over them.

Ahndien pointed to the hills on the Tianese side of the range. "We can approach from the East."

As they flew behind the summits of the Handara range, Render's entire body began to tingle at the sight. It was as familiar now as it was when he first painted it back in Castle Mitelvald.

The fire cast a red and orange glow over the peaks. Like the sun setting over the Eastern Mountains. Yet they faced the West, where the sun should rise. This was the very scene he'd painted while under Sir Edwyn's tutelage.

Now, out of Ashtoreth's line of sight, Render and Ahndien flew straight to the fire trap.

"They're closing in!" Ahndien pointed to the black demon swarm following Ashtoreth. A few of them shot straight through the fire untouched and fell upon a line of Tianese archers. As the archers fell, their arrows flew lamely into the air, some striking their fellow soldiers. The ensuing sound of the demon hordes tearing flesh from bone was even more horrific than Mooregaard's demise.

Render shut his eyes momentarily.

// GRANT US SUCCESS, VALAHANDRA //

With all his concentration, he conjured up a mighty bolt

in both hands. "Distance, Ahndien."

She backed away.

Then, striking his hands together, he sent a broad wave of lightning straight over the oncoming demon horde. A roaring thunderclap followed drawing all eyes below up to him.

To Render's surprise the wave covered the horde. Crackling like embers in a fire, webs of white light crawling over their bodies like flashing insect legs, the demons toppled and fell to the feet of the Sojourners.

"Finish them!" Mikhal commanded.

As the demons fell, their bodies became pale and solid. He caught sight of some, their eyes wide with fear as the Sojourner warriors routed them with spears, swords, fire, and Valhandra only knew what other powers they possessed.

"You've done it!" Ahndien grasped his arm and for the first time today, a hopeful smile escaped the confines of her rueful countenance. But that hope was short-lived. For at that very moment, a very irate Ashtoreth turned her furious eyes towards them and roared.

Even from a distance of several hundred yards, she seemed as large as a battle ship, her head the prow, her wings like its tattered sails. Render could feel the heat of her anger as she flew straight at them.

Her shadow covered dozens of human soldiers, cowering as her accursed fire ring constricted. Those unfortunate enough to be standing at the edge were charred immediately and fell to a blackened heap as the fire passed through them.

Heart pounding, chest tightening, Render turned to Ahndien. She hovered by his side and gripped his arm intensely. "Get to safety, now!"

"I'm not leaving you!"

The heavy percussion of Ashtoreth's wings beating the air felt like waves crashing against a rocky shore. It made his ears pop. "There's no sense in both of us dying! Now go!"

But Ahndien would not release him. "Think of something else. I am staying!"

"Why are girls so stubborn!" Render gasped as the heat of Ashtoreth's fire blast flew over their heads. "Fine. Let's give her two targets, then!"

At that, they flew in opposite directions just as Ashtoreth's next blast hissed through the space they had just vacated. Even through his leather vest and shirt, the heat burned his skin.

Render threw a bolt of lightning at the colossal demon dragon. But in his panic he could only muster a short burst. The bolt bounced straight off of her inky scales.

Wings flapping up a wind storm in all directions, Ashtoreth turned her massive head and bore blood-stained fangs. She blew out another column of fire. Render flew up and managed to escape it. But the heel of his shoe was burned straight through exposing just a small part of his flesh. It hurt worse than he thought possible.

Higher he flew, one hand pointed down and eyes locked on the demonic dragon.

Ashtoreth pursued upwards.

Good.

When they leveled off, she stared and her neck bobbed repeatedly. By her fangs and eyes, Render could see she was laughing. She hovered there for a while, the way a cat crouches just before it pounces on its prey. Which was exactly what Render wanted her to do. Anything to draw her away from Ahndien and the people they were charged to unite.

"Foul-breathed, chicken-lizard!" He struck his chest

with his fist, then sent three blasts of lightning straight at her face. She blinked, shook her head, and cackled. But Render continued to taunt. "I'm right here! Come and get your 'confection,' if you dare!"

Now, Ashtoreth's insidious laugh became an audible snarl. Her diamond-pupiled eyes narrowed at the insult. She roared, fanning out half a dozen barbed horns that framed her scaly face. Then, faster than possible, simultaneously stretching her neck and lurching forward, she shot out her head and lunged at Render.

It was all a wash of blackness and scales and decay, overwhelming him. Then a sharp pain stabbed his left arm. When he opened his eyes, he found himself in the jaws of Ashtoreth, her teeth clamping down around his shoulder and upper arm.

Render cried out as unspeakable pain enveloped him. It was as though she injected acid or venom into his body with her fangs. He could barely hear Ahndien shouting his name over the rumbling breaths of the demon dragon.

Focusing all the pain into a massive charge, he released a burst of lightning. This shook the Ashtoreth slightly, but only made her clamp down harder.

He felt a bone snap, followed by an unbearable dull pain that ran amok through his body.

Again, another lightning burst.

And another.

Ashtoreth still did not loosen her grip. She only paused her crushing jaws to inhale deeply. The incoming air—frigid by comparison with the outgoing breath—rushed past him as he struggled in vain to free himself from her jaws.

Then came that sulfuric odor. And the rumbling that came from within the belly of the beast just before she belched out a lethal flame. Flapping her wings wildly,

Ashtoreth began to roll as an alligator does before it dismembers its prey.

She was about to crush his bones, incinerate and devour him as she had Mooregaard.

CHAPTER NINETY-FOUR

NOT ONLY DID the teeth grind against the bones in Render's arm, but the heat and acidic saliva dripping into his open wounds burned with intense pain. It was so overwhelming he could not muster the strength to retaliate with even the slightest spark.

Hovering over the glowing hills, Ashtoreth held him in her jaws and gripped his limbs against his body with the foreclaws of both hands. She only need pull in any direction and pluck off an arm or a leg and begin feeding on it like that of a roasted pheasant.

// INSIGNIFICANT MITE, YOU HAVE FAILED UTTERLY. WHERE IS YOUR HELP NOW? //

Her jaws loosened just enough for her to laugh. A series of ever increasing guttural convulsion rippled up through her throat. Puffs of acrid green smoke choked Render as he tried in vain not to inhale.

But it was futile.

He had failed indeed.

And would now die in that knowledge.

It was almost as painful as the teeth sinking deeper into his arm, as he dangled like a wounded mouse from the mouth of a cat.

A black cat...

Greifer...

Mother... would she live long enough see her son torn to ribbons by the hideous demon dragon?

The entire world turned dark. Or were his eyes just shutting, his body relinquishing and accepting his fate?

Ashtoreth laughed and pulses of heat washed over his face. At this close range, one blast full would burn him to a crisp.

It's over.

But his face did not burn.

Ashtoreth's claws loosened their grip. Her entire head swung up, to the left, to the right, up again. Dizzy from the shaking, Render opened his eyes.

A bright white flame blazed above. But not from Ashtoreth's mouth. It was on top of her head.

Above the bloody fangs, above the dripping snout, and clear past the reptilian eyes, the residue of white flames splashed out from behind the dragon's horned collar, which opened and retracted, opened and retracted frantically.

Muffled explosions accompanied by flashes of light burst out just above the dragon's head.

In that instant, Ashtoreth screamed.

Render fell from her jaws, the blood-soaked sleeve of his shirt tearing off and remaining like floss between the fangs. Immediately he flew back, gaining a safe distance above her.

To his surprise, Ahndien straddled the demon dragon's neck. Over and over, she formed what looked like spears of white fire in her hands. Drove them into Ashtoreth's skull, her ears, through the fleshy horned collar.

Render shot a bolt of lightning, but the pain in his arm caused him to wince. He missed by a great measure. The bolt struck the rock face, sending up a shower of pebbles, smoke and dust.

With each fiery blow Ashtoreth swung her head wildly. The dragon snapped its jaws at Ahndien, blew steams of fire all over, grabbed behind her neck but could not reach her.

After suffering repeated fire spearing, her ebony scales began to open. Green blood oozed out. Ahndien shoved her fist into the opening.

A blast of fire and bright emerald blood erupted from the opening, splattering Ahndien's clothes and face. Ashtoreth roared and flew straight up, sending Ahndien tumbling down the dragon's saw-edged spine.

"Hold on, Ahndien!" Render flew over and upward in pursuit. Hanging by one hand from one of Ashtoreth's spine plates, Ahndien swung a foot around, then her other hand, and climbed up again.

For a dragon the size of a battle ship, Ashtoreth moved with alarming speed. As Render flew after her, cold wind rushed through his hair, across his face and stung the open wounds on his arm.

Ashtoreth reached her apogee and leveled out. Like a bucking horse, she kicked, arched and dove all about trying to shake Ahndien off of her back. Render took that opportunity to shoot another bolt of lightning. This time, it stuck her in the very jaw that had entrapped him. Knocked her head to the side.

Then the dragon did something no one would have expected. Leaning to the side so that her jagged spine—onto which Ahndien hung—would hit, Ashtoreth flew straight for the rock side of the mountain.

"Oh no" Render muttered. "Ahndien, let go!" Render flew with all his might. Just as the dragon slammed her massive back into the rocks, Ahndien leapt off and flew out of the way.

Just a dozen or so yards away, Render threw another bolt at Ashtoreth. But she swooped down after Ahndien and it only singed the tip of the dragon's tail.

However fast Ashtoreth could fly up, she flew down many times faster. Render followed, but the dragon was already above Ahndien. He reached out to her in his mind.

// ABOVE YOU! //

Ahndien screamed in terror as the hideous jaws snapped at her heels.

Willing himself to fall or fly faster, Render gained upon the demon dragon.

Just a few more yards.

Flames burst from Ashtoreth's mouth. She'd caught Ahndien in her jaws. But were the flames from the dragon or Ahndien?

Like a thousand castanets, the clacking sound of loosened scales fluttering in the wind grew louder. Render could just about reach her.

The tip of the tail.

A few more feet.

Now inches.

Now...

Render grasped the tail. Sinking his fingers as deep into the scaly flesh as he could, his entire body began to glow and hum as he accumulated all the energy he could for a powerful discharge.

Suddenly, all the weight, speed and force of the

gargantuan black dragon yanked him down. But Render would not let go.

"Let her go, foul demon!

At this, Ashtoreth snarled. The sound, like that of a hundred tigers.

Ahndien called to him.

// GET AWAY, RENDER! //

// NO! //

// YOU'RE NO USE TO ANYONE DEAD! //

Diving headlong, Ashtoreth shook her head back and forth like a rabid dog with its prey in its jaws. The ground was coming up fast. A dragon of Ashtoreth's size might be able to withstand hitting the ground at this speed, but the impact would crush Ahndien instantly.

// I CAN'T JUST— //

// YOU MUST, RENDER! //

Then it happened.

Cold from the core of Render's body, a huge surge of energy, as unstoppable as the Mighty Rapids of Jutundra expanded outwards. It threatened to burst out of every inch of his body. He squinted and gritted his teeth containing it, focusing it all into his hands.

Then...

A deafening thunderclap.

Blinding azure light.

From where he fell, Render did not see the manifold strings of lightning connecting with his hands from the four winds. An explosion haloed the diving dragon, illuminated her entire body such that her black scales flew off of the greater part of her body. With a deafening explosion, the halo glowed and shot outwards until it winked out with a frightful flash.

Only from a great distance could it be seen; a huge mushroom-like cloud rising into the sky and beneath it, a ring expanding in all directions.

Ashtoreth's tail stiffened. Her entire body convulsed.

The explosion knocked Render back.

He barely caught his balance and he came crashing into the sand, a great distance from the deadly fire ring, the shouting Sojourners and human warriors trapped behind it. Render hit the ground hard and rolled on his side more times than he could recall.

He stopped just in time to witness the dragon strike the ground.

The entire valley quaked from the impact.

"Ahndien!"

The dragon lay in the midst of a cloud of dust, its four legs twitching uncontrollably. But its jaws were empty. Only a red forked tongue hung out, flitting with each bodily tick. Sparks of light crackled from the soft, exposed skin where black scales once shielded.

But Ahndien was not there.

He called for her again.

Then, a faint moan.

It was her!

CHAPTER NINETY-FIVE

SO THIS IS WHAT DYING IS LIKE. Lao-Ying managed to drag himself to the edge of the hill overlooking the valley, which seemed to blaze like a bonfire, its orange flames licking out over the mountain peaks.

He labored for every breath.

Five hundred years.

Only to end like this.

All he had suffered had been in vain because the one for whom he waited did not appear. But Valhandra had made a covenant with him. And five centuries should be no different from five days with The Almighty, His word must be true. If this was the true Valhandra who granted his immortality back then, and granted his death just a few days ago, then he could not have lied. The covenant must be fulfilled.

Lao-Ying shook his head and laughed bitterly. Perhaps he was not nearly as wise as his many years led him to believe. Trusting Valhandra came with no guarantees of receiving whatever you wished for. He should have known.

His fingers ached. Even flexing them open to grasp the limb of a dead Yascha Tree jutting out of the pale rocks hurt. Pulling himself to a seated position, he leaned against the tree and turned his face to the valley.

Through tears and stinging perspiration, he discerned nothing but two figures on the ground next to...Ashtoreth!

Horror of horrors! He knew the insidious demon dragon might re-appear, but never suspected it would be this soon. She lay there as though dead.

Upon a more careful look, Lao-Ying made out the two figures below. Render and Ahndien. She was injured, unable to stand. They appeared unperturbed by the presence of the gargantuan dragon, because it lay unmoving.

But that is precisely what Ashtoreth would do to lull them into a false sense of security. He tried to shout out to them but could not find the strength in his lungs. Nothing but a feeble whisper came out.

// AHNDIEN! YOU MUST BOTH GET AWAY FROM THERE, NOW! //

But there was no reaction. She was not perceiving his thoughts, perhaps because of the distance, perhaps because of his weakened state. Summoning all his remaining strength, he tried to transform. But he could barely stand. He grasped the tree and fell to his knees.

CHAPTER NINETY-SIX

AS THE DUST CLEARED, Render saw Ahndien, pushing herself up with her arms. She had freed herself and landed about ten feet from Ashtoreth's head. He rushed over to her, pushing past the dust and green smoke rising from the fallen dragon's nostrils.

"You've got to help them, Render. Don't worry about me."

He arrived and knelt beside her.

Gathered her in his arms.

She buried her face in his shoulder, her breaths stuttering as she tried to hold back sobs.

"Can you stand?" Render asked tenderly.

She pushed back, sniffled and glanced at her legs. "I think they're broken." Reaching her hand up, she touched Render's face with fingertips that nearly singed his cheek. But he didn't care. She was alive, and he would not let her out of his sight again.

Just then, Ashtoreth heaved a heavy sigh.

Ahndien gasped.

Render turned sharply, extended a crackling hand in the dragon's direction.

But the light that glowed from Ashtoreth's eyes dimmed, even as the lids remained open. All the smoke that streamed from her mouth and nostrils turned black, then faded.

One final jerk of the head.

And then with a long hissing sound, her chest rose up.

Then deflated.

The last puff of smoke stopped. As did her breathing.

Ashtoreth was dead.

"By Valhandra! You've done it, Render!"

He turned to Ahndien and kissed her forehead. Caressed her shoulder. "We did it."

"Look!" Ahndien pointed to the middle of the valley. "It's coming down!"

And so it was.

The wall of fire that had encircled the Tianese, Torians and Sojourners began to fall. Even though the charred remains of hundreds whom it had consumed could be seen, a deep sense of relief filled Render's entire being.

Now that the people of both kingdoms had seen the truth, they would surely unite and embrace the resurrected Sojourners and the remnant in this part of the world.

Ahndien whispered to herself. "But this is not how..."

"What's that?"

She met his gaze and blinked. "It's nothing." With pained effort, she pulled herself over and leaned against him. "Your time has come, Great Deliverer. Go and speak to your people."

An anxious grin tugged the corner of his mouth. "I'm not leaving you here..." he pointed his chin to Ashtoreth's still body "...with that."

"Just go. They don't need to see you with a peasant girl with broken legs."

"To me, you're a princess. Here, let me carry you."

She shook her head. "This is your first appearance before them. It would not be proper."

"But—"

"Render, please. I will fly over quietly after you."

"Are you quite certain?"

She gave him a scolding look. Go.

"Fine. But I do so under protest."

Finally, the smile returned to her face. As he stood and began to walk, she still gripped his hands until he noticed the pull against his fingers. Render stopped and turned around.

Ahndien smiled, squeezed his hand lovingly. "I am so proud of you."

"You are just as much their deliverer, as I. If not more so."

And with her eyes, she told him such that he understood. Even without hearing her thoughts. But he chose to respond with words.

"I love you too."

In that moment, just as he turned his head and walked past the lifeless head of the demon dragon, a most dreadful thing happened.

He sensed it. Then heard it. It can't be! He barely heard Ahndien cry out.

"Render, look out!"

Render swung around.

Ashtoreth lifted her head and opened her jaws. At this close proximity, the blast of fire would kill him instantly.

But Ahndien came flying through the air straight at Render, her broken legs dangled at an unnatural angle. She shoved him out of the way just as Ashtoreth blew out a huge fire blast.

Render tumbled to the ground and could only sit up in

time to watch it happen.

Ashtoreth enveloped Ahndien with a storm of fire so intense a wake of glass formed rising out of the sand. Ahndien's body burst into flames and burned as bright as the sun.

CHAPTER NINETY-SEVEN

SHOUTING IN ANGUISH, Render flew straight to the flames where Ahndien's body burned like an effigy. But the fire grew and grew and was much too strong for him get close enough to help her. His hands burned as they groped into the fire seeking anything, a hand, her elbow, any way to rescue her.

But there was no possible way for any person to survive such an intense conflagration.

She was gone.

All his fury rising up, Render launched himself at the mocking Ashtoreth. He drew his sword and blasted lightning at her.

But it only absorbed into her scales, causing her body to glow, her eyes to burn brighter. The rumbling sound under his feet was actually Ashtoreth cackling a giant dragon's laugh.

Then he came directly before her.

Condescendingly, she lowered her face such that her eye, which was about half his height in diameter just blinked at him.

"Didst thou think it so easy to smite or subdue me?

Cower before the right arm of Malakandor! "

"I'll tear you apart, foul beast!" He plunged the sword into her eye. But it turned into molten steel when it touched. Render dropped the pommel as it seared his hands.

Again, Ashtoreth laughed. She had merely been toying with them. Like a cat plays with a mouse before finally killing it.

She lifted her head, took one imposing step forward, her claw coming down and tearing the leather vest on his chest. She drew a thin scarlet scratch against his skin as his shirt tore open.

Render backed away, but Ashtoreth towered over him. Lightning crackled at his fingertips. But it was useless now. He was powerless to stop her.

The flames of Ahndien's pyre burned stronger still, warming his back. Ashtoreth took another step forward, prolonging the inevitable just to be cruel. She snorted two jets of fire from her nostrils and shot a stream right in front of Render's toes.

Render leapt back.

The flames from Ahndien's pyre whooshed and rose up, as though someone had poured a vat of spirit wine upon it.

Ashtoreth swung her massive head down and snapped her jaws just inches from Render's face.

He stumbled.

Fell on his rear.

Got up and backed away more.

He could not fly. The fear within paralyzed him.

Ashtoreth glowered down. Behind Render, the fire burned so fiercely it would surely consume him as it had Ahndien.

And then, with the flames of the pyre licking at this back, something reached into Render's soul. It made no sense whatsoever. But in his spirit, he knew there was no other choice.

Ashtoreth inhaled deeply, preparing the blast to burn him to death.

Then Render fell backwards...

Into the raging fire.

CHAPTER NINETY-EIGHT

SICKENED BY HIS INABILITY to help, Lao-Ying watched in horror as the fire which devoured both Ahndien and Render effloresced into a raging sphere of light. It was as though the sun itself had descended into the valley.

A cold tear streamed down his face. Unable to hold onto the tree any longer, he fell sideways, all the strength leaving his five hundred year old body. He leaned his against a boulder, drawing on the last bit of his energy to keep his eyes open.

Alas. Mei-Liang, my Spring Blossom. I have waited in vain.

A pang clenched his heart at the realization. But he resisted the whispers in his spirit that said, *Valhandra has cheated you!*

"Though He slay me...yet will I trust in Him..." he murmured, his very breath fading.

With a triumphal roar, Ashtoreth stood erect on her hind legs, reached her forelegs into the air, cruel curved talons outstretched, and flew up. The wind from her beating wings sent clouds of sand at the ever blooming conflagration that had been Ahndien and Render. The demon dragon cocked her head at the sight, then let out an atrocious cackle that sent a chill through Lao-Ying's expiring body.

The entire world became a darkened blur. He began to gasp his final breaths. *Forgive me, Ahndien. I have failed you.*

Try as he might, he could not keep his eyelids open.

Just as they fell, a burst of light, accompanied by thunderous detonation shook the hills and the ground beneath him. With a grunt, Lao-Ying opened his eyes, for a moment forgetting that he was about to die.

Somehow, he found the strength to keep his eyes wide in wonder.

Even Ashtoreth craned her neck and looked down in astonishment.

A most wondrous thing happened.

All at once, the visions and dreams Valhandra had given him over the centuries flashed in his mind. Even before it completed, Lao-Ying's chest and belly bounced in laughter.

From the center of the blazing pyre, where Ahndien and Render had been incinerated, it arose. Though it had been five centuries since he'd last seen it, it was unmistakable.

First the fiery crest.

Then the smoldering head, the golden eyes shining like the morning star. The crimson plumage.

Then with a cry as terrifying as it was beautiful, the Feng Huang, the Millennial Phoenix that Valhandra had promised Lao-Ying he would live to behold arose from the pyre. She spread her flaming wings and rose up. It was about half the size of Ashtoreth, who flapped her wings wildly and backed away in surprise.

The Phoenix parted her beak and from it arose the most beautiful pentatonic song. It resounded through the mountains and valley so that every warrior below stopped and looked up. The song drew a sublime pang from Lao-Ying's soul where it had resided all these years.

He reached his fingers out hoping to feel the warmth of the beautiful firebird, whose spirit had encapsulated his princess, his love eight dynasties ago as she sacrificed herself for her kingdom. "Mei-Liang..."

Ashtoreth flared out her hood, all nine horns radiating around her neck, and roared. She sent a massive blast at the phoenix. But the firebird absorbed it and the flames from her wings seemed to grow stronger.

The demon dragon rushed at the the phoenix and snapped it jaws at her neck, but the phoenix flew away so quickly that her opponent slammed against the rocks, sending an avalanche down the hill.

A refreshing cool wind preceded the phoenix as she flew around the hills toward the crag where he lay.

// COURAGE, MY FRIEND //

A voice he had not expected. "Ahndien?" Even in his fading consciousness, he smiled. But of course. Though he'd not seen her transfiguration in all his visions, it made sense in a way he could not explain.

As she passed, their eyes met. Beneath the burning gold veil enshrouding the Phoenix, he could see the same brown eyes he'd come to know. It was her!

The Phoenix blinked and shot up, streams of fire in her wake. As she righted herself, she turned to the pyre from which she'd emerged and let out a call that resembled that of both trumpet and bird.

Lao-Ying wrestled with his breath, trying his best to stay alive and witness the end of this conflict.

Valhandra...grant that thy servant might live but a moment longer...

In her glorious phoenix form, Ahndien hovered in the air.

Again, the ground shook.

From the way the entire mountain range rumbled beneath him, and the streaks of lightning that shot out from the blazing pyre, he recalled the details of a vision he'd long forgotten. Something he'd envisaged before he'd been granted immortality, but never paid it mind.

Until now.

The Great Deliverer.

Now, he could die in peace. Though the desires of his heart had not been granted, he knew that he'd fulfilled his destiny.

As the tones rang out, Ashtoreth swung her head to Ahndien's phoenix form, then to the pyre. Agitated, the demon dragon flew at Ahndien as she sang her powerful song. Almost outshining the flames of her entire body, the phoenix's eyes shone brilliantly. So transfixed was she on the blazing pyre that she didn't notice Ashtoreth rising up in attack.

Lao-Ying tried to reach out in his mind. Warn her. But his eyes went dim and he could not even hold his head up any longer. He only heard the haunting scream of the demon dragon growing closer and closer.

CHAPTER NINETY-NINE

HIGH ABOVE THE GROUND, the song resounded. Unlike anything any living being had heard. The cry of the phoenix instilled courage in some of the human soldiers, and terror in others. It was strangely alien, and at the same time primal as one's first heartbeats from within the womb.

Flames and lightning flashes emanated from the blazing pyre out of which the grand phoenix had arisen. The mountains trembled.

Above, Ashtoreth flew straight at the phoenix and clasped her massive jaws around its neck. Ahndien's entire body burst with such a blast of fire, the heat could be felt in the valley below. But Ashtoreth did not relent.

The two tossed and tumbled through the air, Ashtoreth trying to break the firebird's slender neck. Bursts of fire scorched the skin from the black dragon's face, melting it until some of it oozed down, exposing white eye sockets and deadly teeth. Still, the demon dragon clamped down and thrashed its head wildly.

The phoenix let out shrieks, its body burning hotter and

brighter. From gold to a white hot blaze.

And then, from the quaking ground, out of the smoldering pyre from which Ahndien had transfigured, a most glorious form arose. First, its snout, then the crest of its head. It was covered in scales that resembled translucent rubies.

Finally, the arms, jagged spine and tail.

It unfurled its massive wings and let out a roar that shook the entire valley.

These were the final images that would fill Lao-Ying's mind. All he had believed, all which had been revealed to him over the centuries, must surely come to pass. But even then, he could not be certain that the prophesied rise of the Cobalt Dragon and the Phoenix would bring about the end for which he had longed.

In the span of a few seconds—or hours, he could not tell how precisely time was passing—Render perceived his soul, his very essence penetrating what could only be described as a veil. A veil between the physical and the spiritual realms. It made no sense at all. And yet it made complete sense.

Through the fire that should have consumed his physical body, he sensed Ahndien's presence. Yet she was strong, not burning to death. But there was nothing around him but power and presence.

In the very moment he detected her, he reached out.

// AHNDIEN, WHERE ARE YOU? //

// OH, RENDER! IT'S GLORIOUS! //

The joy in her words was unmistakable. Her spirit rose

up and out of the blazing splendor that enveloped them. That was when he realized that his entire body had begun to transform.

The way he'd seen Greifer...his mother, turn from a small cat to formidable ebony panther. But this was different. His hands begin to grow along with the rest of his body. Blue scales formed on his skin.

His fingers became powerful talons.

Then, all at once, he burst out of the pyre. Rising so high off the ground he almost thought he was flying. Yet his feet were still sinking into the sand. When he beheld his shadow cast by the high afternoon sun, he understood.

The massive head, tasseled beard.

The powerful tail and bat-like wings.

When he stood and stretched out his arms, he saw the shadow of the enormous dragon he had become. Not for a moment did it bother him, for long before he could comprehend this in his mind, something within his soul had known this to be his destiny, all along.

High above him, he saw Ahndien. She too had transformed, but into a beautiful firebird. But the demon dragon had caught her in its jaws and shook her violently.

// ASHTORETH! //

Render cried out. The sound of his roar echoed through the valley like a thunderclap. Wings beating, he leapt into the air and flew straight up. Sand shot up and whirled as it might in a dust storm.

In an instant, Render was upon the demon dragon. She ignored him and continued to bite into the blazing phoenix's neck. Despite her own flesh, burning away, Ashtoreth would not release it until she'd crushed it.

Render wrapped his dragon claws around Ashtoreth's

throat.

With a mighty blow of her wing, she struck Render in the snout. Ignoring the pain, Render flew higher up and pulled Ashtoreth's head upward.

She turned, released her grip on Ahndien and sunk her fangs into Render's foreleg. The Phoenix fell, a plume of fire trailing out of his periphery. Then Ashtoreth sent a stream of fire onto Render's hands.

This too caused immense pain. But to his surprise, the scales seemed to protect him from serious damage. Even as the fire burned his hands, Render tightened his grip, pulled Ashtoreth higher.

Higher.

And then, focusing on his talons digging into the demon dragon's neck, he summoned all the energy he could. As a dragon, it seemed infinitely more potent.

From every direction in the sky, a lattice of blue and white lightning converged on his hands. A terrible humming and sizzling sound ensued. Ashtoreth's entire form glowed brightly.

She let out a horrid shriek, released Render's arm and tumbled tail over head into the valley. Trails of flickering lightning webbed around her body.

But she was not dead.

Before hitting the ground, she straightened out, and at low altitude flew straight at the entire army of Sojourners, humans, and demons. Her wings beat angrily through the air, sending percussive shock waves that rippled in the sand and carved a visible wake.

The phoenix flew after Ashtoreth and hurled several fireballs at her. Each exploded on her back, charred the scales and burned for a moment, but ultimately became extinguished.

From Ashtoreth's bleeding jaws, she launched a

horizontal column of fire straight at the demon horde standing in surprise. They evaporated into wisps of black smoke as she flew through the ranks of those that had not gotten out of her way. Like a swarm of black pestilence, the remaining demon horde followed.

The horrendous sound that arose from the demon dragon resembled the growl of a lion and the wicked laughter of a woman. Render flew after Ashtoreth. Clearly, she no longer concerned herself with her physical body. Only one thing mattered to her now.

// SHE'S CLAIMING THE TROOPS TO SACRIFICE TO MALAKANDOR //

Thousands of arrows and spears flew at the dark dragon, whose shadow covered the ground like a cloud. But they merely bounced off her iron scales. Even the blasts of energy and fire from the hands of the Sojourners seemed to have no effect.

If Render did not overtake her soon, she would complete the task of which Mooregaard and Volfoncé had failed.

To his amazement, even before he reached the Sojourners and humans, a great column of fire shot out of the ground a few hundred feet in front of the troops.

Ashtoreth dug her hind claws into the ground and stopped, just as the Phoenix burst into full form. Her fire burned away many more of the demon horde that had not stopped in time to avoid it. Ahndien was now mostly fire now, with a reminiscence of a bird's form within. From the tips of her flaming wings, golden fire shot forth and wrapped itself around Ashtoreth like a rope. First around her legs, then her wings. As though solid, the fire cords tightened around her and she fell to her side as she tried to wrestle them away.

She parted her jaws preparing to blast fire at the troops. But Render landed, his dragon-clawed foot stepped down and shut her mouth. Thrashing ferociously, Ashtoreth freed her jaws and snapped at Render's leg. But as soon as her fangs touched it, lightning burst around her jaws, sending her head snapping back and convulsing.

// YOU CANNOT TRULY KILL ME, LITTLE MINION OF VALHANDRA //

Ashtoreth snarled.

// I WILL CONSUME THE ENTIRE SACRIFICE WITH ONE BREATH //

Ahndien's fire cords continued to stretch out and bind her limbs, her neck and tail. But before they reached her jaws, Ashtoreth leaned her head over, got a clear view of the Sojourners and human soldiers, all standing outside of Ahndien's protective fire.

The demon dragon scoffed. Her eyes glowed. A verdant hue emanated from her open jaws. The familiar sound of sizzling foretold the imminent blast of fire, aimed straight at the sacrifice to be offered to Malakandor.

Reacting quicker than he could have in his human form, Render, as the Cobalt Dragon, sent a wave of lightning at the sand in Ashtoreth's trajectory. It burned so intensely that a molten substance rose up, glowing. In just moments, a wall of solid glass stood in the way and deflected Ashtoreth's blast, sending fire out in every direction. None of it reached its intended target.

Ashtoreth had been subdued.

For the moment.

How could they stop her completely?

Could he actually kill a demon dragon, a being that was every bit spirit as it was physical?

In the instant he considered this, Ashtoreth sprung up, knocked him over and launched her entire body headfirst at Ahndien. The surprise caused Ahndien to release her fiery bonds. As the demon dragon leapt up and fell upon her, all the flames around the phoenix winked out, leaving her vulnerable.

Ashtoreth pinned the phoenix under her talons and coiled back her neck to deliver a deadly strike.

// I SHALL TEAR YOUR THROAT OUT AND THEN FEAST UPON YOUR ENTRAILS! //

Render got up, but it took longer than expected because of the unfamiliar mass of his dragon body. Ashtoreth's jaws were descending quickly at Ahndien's neck. Her entire phoenix form began to shrink. She was transforming back into a human!

A tiny flame smoldered from the tips of her wings, pinned to the ground by Ashtoreth's four feet. But that flame stretched upwards, hovering just over the demon dragon's head.

Even as Render lunged forward, from his foreclaws he sent a thin string of lightning not at Ashtoreth, but at that singular plume that burned from Ahndien's fading phoenix claw.

When the lightning touched the fire, it was as though he touched her hand.

Simultaneously, an unimaginable surge of power flowed from and into his entire being. He sensed her presence, her being, her fears and determination. And he knew that she sensed his as well.

// ACCURSED FOOL! THE ONE YOU SERVE IS DEAD! //

Even as Ashtoreth's words reached them, she drove her fangs down at Ahndien's throat.

Render and Ahndien pulled the connected energy line straight up.

In a flash, accompanied by the sound of flesh and bone severing, the fire and lightning cord of the dragon and the phoenix cut through Ashtoreth's neck. The black demon's head fell off and tumbled into the dust.

Its body convulsed as it rolled over next to Ahndien.

Black blood that at first oozed like a viscous tar evaporated into a mist which drew the remaining demon horde, howling like the wind back into the open neck of Ashtoreth's dying body.

The head snapped its jaws vindictively, its eyes defiant, until they too were extinguished like the last bit of fire from its jaws.

And then, silence fell over the valley.

The dark cloud, which had actually been smoke from the demon horde blanketing the sky, yielded to the sun.

When the dust cleared, Render had returned to his human state.

Hundreds of yards away, he barely heard the cheers and shouts of triumph from the troops as he took several solemn steps towards the firebird, which stood regal, its head high and wings unfurled.

Glorious flames danced around her frame and warmed Render's face as he came as close as he could without getting burned.

He reached up to touch its feathers. "Ahndien?"

The Phoenix turned its head sideways and gazed at him with one eye.

// SHE IS NOT HERE //

His heart sank. A pang of regret impaled his chest. "Were you not—?"

// THOU STANDETH BEFORE THE FORM OF THE PHOENIX SPIRIT, A SERVANT OF VALHANDRA. AND WITHIN THYSELF RESIDETH THE SPIRIT OF THE COBALT DRAGON. THIS IS THY SPIRIT-POTENTIAL, DEAR RENDER //

"But what of Ahndien?"

// UNTO HER, HAD VALHANDRA GIVEN THE CHOICE. SHE CHOSE TO SACRIFICE ALL FOR HER PEOPLE, AS DID OTHER PRINCESSES OF HER KINGDOM BEFORE HER. IN DOING SO, SHE HATH SAVED HER PEOPLE AND FULFILLED HER DESTINY //

Tears welled up in his eyes. He hadn't expected to lose Ahndien like this.

// BUT REJOICE. THOU TOO HAST FULFILLED THY CALLING //

There was nothing for which to rejoice. Ahndien was gone. And he had only just begun to understand that he loved her. Loved her more than anything or anyone.

Before he knew it, tens of thousands of Torians, Tianese, Sojourner humans and spirit beings stood before him. Row after row, they knelt in the fiery glow of the great firebird.

Wiping the tears from his eyes, Render looked up at the Phoenix. "I would give anything to be with her again. Even for a moment."

// MY SPIRIT ARISES ONCE EVERY MILLENNIUM. YET FOR THE FAITHFULNESS OF ONE, HAVE I RETURNED AFTER FIVE HUNDRED YEARS. FOR SUCH A TIME AS THIS. AND THIS, TO HELP YOU DEFEAT THE PLANS OF MALAKANDOR. TO BRING THESE TWO GREAT NATIONS TOGETHER. AS ONE //

"Yes, I...I understand." Valhandra never promised him happiness, nor long life with Ahndien. Render knelt down from fatigue, shut his eyes and bowed his head. "I shall honor and submit to the wisdom and authority of The Almighty."

Penetrating warmth enveloped him. Through his eyelids he sensed a glow above. The sound of fire grew as though fanned by the wind.

And then, something alighted upon his shoulder.

At first when Render looked up, the brilliance of the phoenix's blazing wings and glowing plumage blinded him. He blinked and reached for that which had touched him. It was the soft hand of the one who now stood before him, rimmed by golden light, her head haloed.

His vision cleared and there she stood, adorned in a gown white as snow, her body whole and unbroken. She smiled even as every inch of her body's outline shone. Filled with awe and wonder, he nearly forgot about the joy he felt at seeing her alive, standing before his very eyes.

"Ahndien?"

"It is I." Her voice took an otherworldly quality that resembled music and glory and light all at the same time. "Thou hast proven worthy, my friend, O companion of mine heart. Unto thee hast Valhandra bestowed the following honors."

For as long as he could recall, he'd yearned to come to

the valley, to the Handaras. For such a time as this. Valhandra had placed that desire within his heart.

"Because thou hast submitted to the path set before thee, the Spirit of Valhandra has inhabited thy life. His hand is upon thee. Thou shalt live to see the manifestation of the Cobalt Dragon Spirit in thy being yet once more."

"And now..." From her side, she drew a flaming sword and touched his shoulders, first the right, then the left. It sent a thrill through his entire being, reaching past bone and marrow straight into his spirit. He knelt and bowed his head. "Arise, Sir Render the Dragon-Hearted!"

The entire host let out an awesome cheer that went on without end. At the very moment Render stood, a stream of lightning leapt from his chest straight into the air. There it formed the ethereal outline of the Cobalt Dragon, the form of which Render had occupied not ten minutes ago.

A collective gasp went up into the valley.

At the same time, a column of fire stretched up from Ahndien's form, reaching up to the Phoenix. First the Phoenix alighted upon the ledge of a hill where a lone tree stood, then out of its blazing form walked what appeared to be a lady of great nobility, young with flowing ebony hair, attired in the clothing of royalty.

At least that was what it appeared to be, for in the moment that Render blinked, she stepped out of view, leaving nothing but the tree.

CHAPTER ONE HUNDRED

THE SOUND OF THOUSANDS shouting for joy. What better way to be ushered though the veil? Lao-Ying had wondered many times what this moment would be like and now it had come. He could no longer feel his hands or feet or any part of his body. An incredible lightness came over him as he lifted off the ground while his expired body lay still on the ground by the foot of the tree.

And then, a flourish of white flashed before him and consumed his mortal body with light. From that light, a figure emerged. Even before he could utter the name, his spirit leapt for joy.

// MEI-LIANG! MY SPRING BLOSSOM! //

There she stood, more beautiful than he'd ever remembered. Her ebony mane shone with glory, the train of her white robe emanated heavenly splendor, and her gentle eyes, full of love, met his.

// MY PRINCE //

Prince? He'd lived as a hermit for five centuries, but hearing her address him so was as fresh as the days when he'd competed for her hand and affection. Lao-Ying flexed his fingers and looked at them, then his arms. He too was aglow. But he felt as strong as the day she gave her life for her people, and became the Millennial Phoenix.

In this state of existence, words seemed almost superfluous. He stepped over his expired physical body as though it were a tattered garment, rushed over to Mei-Liang, took her in his arms, kissed her without thought of when he would let her go.

In an instant, five hundred years evaporated like the morning mist that blankets verdant fields with dew. It was like awakening from a dream. Suddenly, physical life as he'd known it was but a distant memory, an echo of this reality.

His journey was complete.

CHAPTER ONE HUNDRED AND ONE

AS THE COBALT DRAGON and the Phoenix Spirit flew into the sky, a blanket of white clouds drew over the valley offering a refreshing shade from the otherwise oppressive heat from the sun. Thousands of soldiers and Sojourners in various states of physical form stood and watched.

But to Render, only one thing in the crowd mattered.

As soon as the light withdrew completely from her body, Ahndien slumped into his arms like a cloth doll. "Oh! Where—?"

"Are you all right?" Render smiled, delighted to find her fully restored to her body.

"I think so." She stood, gazed in wonder at her legs which were no longer broken, her dazzling robe and then at the great throngs gathered about them.

Render wrapped his arms around her and held her so tight he didn't want to let go. "Valhandra be praised!"

She seemed slightly confused.

Render suddenly remembered. He was probably too late. He released Ahndien. "Wait here, I've got to find Greifer."

She nodded. "Hurry."

He strode forth, pushed past the warriors and quickened his pace. As he made his way back to the place where he'd left Greifer and The Prophet—his mother and father—many hands reached out to shake his, or to pat him on the back. But in his rush, he ignored them.

Someone grasped his arm. It was Branson. His eyes were red, but his countenance bright. "I saw him, Rend. I saw him taken up!" A brave smile stretched across his face.

"Your father?"

Branson nodded. "I finally understand. He did all to protect me, to protect everyone."

"Truly, he was a noble soul."

"Is." Never before had Branson appeared so adult, so brave. "He is, Rend."

"Quite. Quite right."

He held out his hand to shake Render's. "Thank you. For everything."

As soon as Render extended his hand, Branson assailed him with a strong embrace, held him tight. "Thank you." Standing there amidst the rough and battle-worn warriors staring with stern, proud countenances, Branson appeared for the first time, not so much like a boy, but a young man. Render grasped Branson's shoulder. "Would you go and attend to Ahndien, please?"

Branson nodded dutifully and went.

And finally, he arrived at the wizened tree where he'd last seen...was she Greifer, or Mother? And was he The Prophet or Father? How should he address them?

Lying in the old man's arms, the folds of her black robe glittering and turning pale before Render's eyes, she lay gasping for her final moments of mortal life. With fingers outstretched she called to him.

// MY SON... //

He ran to her, every doubt dispelled, every hindrance subdued, and cried out, "Mother!"

Falling to his knees before her and the man whom she called his father, Render took her hand, pressed it to his face and bathed it in his tears. "Oh, Mother. I have only now learned who you are." And yet, it felt as though he'd always known. The way she'd looked after him all his life. In the form of a cat, in the form of a panther, and now in the form of a dying, yet all the more beautiful woman.

"Ne'er have I left thee, my son..."

"This is too much to bear! I have only just—" And he wept. Abandoning every bit of dignity he might otherwise have grasped as one just knighted, he wept openly. "Oh, dearest Mother..."

Slowly, she reached up, touched his face and wiped a tear from his eye with the tip of her little finger—just as she had done when he had been but an infant. He knew that but for a fleeting moment as his Spirit glanced through time.

// LET NOT THINE HEART BE TROUBLED, DEAR SON. WE SHALL MEET AGAIN, WHEN THE VEIL HAS BEEN TORN DOWN FOREVER. AND THEN, FACE TO FACE. FARE THEE WELL, GOOD KING //

She drew one final breath."

"Mother!"

// FAREWELL... //

Still draped over her husband's lap, her body began to glow, a cloud of bright light swirling about her. Her frame transformed into that of a panther, then a small cat, then streamed up into the sky and shot over to join the light which surrounded the Cobalt Dragon and Phoenix spirits, high above the valley.

Render expected a torrent of sorrow, a flood of tears.

But neither came.

Instead, an odd sense of joy and anticipation filled his heart. "Father?" He turned to the man, who had appeared now and again in the squares of Valdshire Tor, spewing forth words perceived as folly, but were in fact words of destiny.

"'Tis true, good lad." A broad smile broke across his countenance, even as his own form began to glow. The long white hair drew shorter, growing darker, and deeper in hue. The wrinkles in his face smoothed out and the slump in his back straightened out. Frail limbs grew taut with muscles of a man a fraction of his apparent age. Soon, he was all light and somewhat translucent.

"Why have you never come for me, Father?"

"Because like your mother, I had already died. But Valhandra had permitted that we guide your steps as spirit creatures, all your life until now. Hence the ever-present—"

"Cats."

"And horses." The light he emitted was so strong Render had to shield his eyes. "I was killed as a man, protecting our colony of Sojourners, even before they had killed your mother. Yet, as a spirit being, I had been appointed elder of the Sojourner's Council and given the designation Cerbeus."

"You were The Prophet."

"I took that form to keep watch over you whilst you lived in Valdshire Tor. It took all my discipline not to intervene when you were arrested..." his chest bounced as he laughed, "...when you tried to *protect* me."

Though he'd only met his father and mother moments ago, his heart was blessed as though he'd known them his entire life. This no doubt because Valhandra's plans, His very existence and all who dwelled within its power, transcended time and place.

"And now, dear son..." His entire frame burst into light and ascended to the sky.

"Father?"

"Follow the light!" The dazzling star-like spirit of his father—Cerbeus, The Prophet—flew over to the place where he'd left Ahndien and rested behind her.

Render stretched his hand up, laughing with delight and shouted. "Father!"

// FOLLOW THE LIGHT! //

CHAPTER ONE HUNDRED AND TWO

FATHER'S LIGHT joined with the same brilliance into which Mother's had. When it did, the Dragon raced over the Western Hills.

The Phoenix to the East.

Render pushed through the multitudes, eyes filled with wonder and never letting the flying lights out of his sight. Finally, he arrived at the front where Ahndien and Branson stood waiting.

"Did you see that?" Branson pointed into the sky. His mouth opened, but no other words came out.

Ahndien wrapped her arms around Render's. "It's beautiful!"

On opposite sides of the valley, the stately Dragon and Phoenix burned with regal glory. Then, like two mighty weapons of war, they converged until the tips of their wings touched.

What followed could only be described as a dazzling array of pyrotechnics. Like shooting stars and fireworks, lightning and flames lit up the sky until all you could see was the light emanating from the great spirit manifestations.

The Dragon and Phoenix outlines were no longer visible, but had become one mass of brilliance.

"Sir Render! Sir Render!" The Sojourners shouted, and rushed over, lifting him and Ahndien onto their shoulders. They brought them to a large rock and set them down. Branson pumped his fist in the air repeatedly and joined the chant.

Delighted and somewhat confused, Render turned to Ahndien. "What's happening?"

"How should I know?"

The cheers continued, now joined by both Tianese and Torians alike.

"You spoke as though you understood everything that was happening."

"I did? When?"

"When you...Oh bother, didn't you just knight me?"

"That wasn't me speaking."

"What do you mean, it wasn't you?"

Before Render could say another word, a peal of thunder rang out. Lightning flashed across the sky directly above them. And then the clouds drew together into the form of yet another dragon, which descended slowly. This one so pure and white, it almost hurt the eyes to behold him. By its demeanor, it seemed gentle as a lamb. But by its majesty, no one could doubt that it could devour nations, if it so chose.

Then the unmistakable voice of Valhandra echoed through the sky. Every knee bowed, every head inclined in joyful reverence, as the white dragon descended towards the rock upon which Render and Ahndien stood.

Valhandra spoke as the white dragon alighted upon it.

"THIS IS MY SON, IN WHOM I AM WELL PLEASED. HEED HIS WORD."

Ahndien leaned into Render and whispered, "Is that...?"

"It must be."

One of the Sojourners shouted, "Praise be the name of Kronis, son of the Most High!" Then the rest of the Sojourners continued to repeat the chant.

"Son of the Most High!"

From the looks on the Torians' faces, it was clear that they feared the great dragon. For before this day, none of them believed such creatures existed. Nor had they believed in anything as the spirit potential.

But judging by their sincere genuflections, it was clear they now did. Though in truth, no living creature could help but to bow at the white dragon's magnificence.

Kronis lifted his mighty head and spoke as a man, his voice resounding and profound.

"My good people, stand and behold thy great deliverer. Sir Render the Dragon-Hearted."

All rose to their feet lifting triumphal fists and swords into the air. They roared in appreciation. "Long Live The Great Deliverer!"

"He and Lady Ahndien of the Phoenix Heart have fulfilled the prophecy and set you free from the bondage of Malakandor. Young though they may be, yet do not despise them for their youth."

The valley erupted in a collective shout. "No!"

"For they have been sent to establish a new kingdom. A kingdom of mercy and justice. A kingdom of truth and faith. By these attributes shall it be ruled." Kronis lowered his head such that his great emerald eyes gazed deeply into Render and Ahndien's. To them he spoke directly.

"Art thou ready to rule this great people, my young prince?"

"Pr...Prince? A few months ago, I was but a slave. And

just moments ago, I was made a knight. Now, you ask if I am ready to—?"

"Dost thou perceive thyself as ready, Sir Render?"

He lowered his gaze, ashamed of how he must answer. To have come this far, only to be thwarted by his own inadequacy. Why would the Son of Valhandra ask such a question, the answer of which He surely knew? "Sire...I—"

"ART THOU READY?'

Both Render and Ahndien took a step back as the words shot out of Kronis' mouth, glowing with power and light.

Render screwed up all his courage and looked Kronis in the eye. "No, Sire. I don't feel ready at all."

If it were at all possible for a dragon to smile, Render could not say for certain. But that is exactly what Kronis seemed to do as he replied.

"Thy humility is evident, Sir Render. Thy obedience and valor proven. Thou shalt receive counsel by my hand and spirit. And behold, thou art indeed ready."

Render bowed deeply. "Yes, Sire."

Kronis turned to Ahndien. "And thou, Daughter of the Eastern Song. The beauty of thy spirit is evident to all on this side of the great veil. Because of thy willingness to lose your life for the purpose of Valhandra, unto thee shall be given length of years, prosperity, and the joy of thine eyes."

She inclined her head. "Sire."

"Art thou ready to embark upon a great adventure, with Render by thy side ever more?"

Her porcelain face flushed slightly as she looked to Render. But the fire in her eyes that he'd known from the day they'd first met told him that she was, in fact, more than ready. This delighted Render more than anything he could imagine. Ahndien looked up at Kronis. "I am, Sire."

Kronis dipped his head in approval, blinked

affectionately and nudged Render as gently as he could (for the nudge of a great dragon is like the shove of a dozen strong men) towards Ahndien. "Behold, thy hearts and destinies do I weave together, here and on the eternal side of the great veil from today until it is torn asunder."

The great white dragon lifted his head and stood erect on its hind legs. He stretched forth his arms around Render and Ahndien, and addressed the multitudes.

"People of Valdshire Tor and people of Tian Kuo, I give you King Render, The Dragon-Hearted and Queen Ahndien of the Phoenix Heart!"

Cheers and blessings for long life rang out.

Kronis stepped forward to the center of the rock and stomped his foot. It sent an awesome quake through the land. "And upon this rock, do I establish this new Kingdom of Petrus, the unified dominions of the East and West. And I declare that the forces of Malakandor shall not prevail against it."

The cottony clouds above parted as blades of golden light stretched down onto the rock, the place upon which Render and Ahndien would begin their reign.

Kronis stretched out his wings and rose into the air.

"Blessed are you, King Render and Queen Ahndien. Unto thee is bestowed the heritage of Sojourner Kings. I charge thee and thy house henceforth to do what is right in the sight of Valhandra and to unite the Southern Kingdom and yea, even the great and terrible Northern Kingdom. Thy children are blessed. All their endeavors, though they prove costly, shall ultimately prosper."

And then, with a mighty wind that flushed the valley from the flap of His wings, Kronis ascended past the clouds. Render and Ahndien marveled as they looked into the beams of light that shone down upon the rock of the newly established Kingdom. As though behind a golden veil, five figures appeared, each smiling with approval in their human form: Lao-Ying who looked like a young man now, and the beautiful Tianese Princess who was adorned in an ancient royal gown, Render's mother, his brother Kaine, and his father. But it was mother's words that reached him.

// WELL DONE, MY SON. UNTIL THE VEIL IS TORN FROM THE HEAVENS, FARE THEE WELL //

And with that they all transformed into pure light and went up with the beams, into the sky following the path of Kronis.

Thus was the kingdom of Petrus established. And thus concluded and began the first of many adventures in the quest for the reunification of the Sojourner kingdoms.

ACKNOWLEDGEMENTS

It has been said that treating the release of a new book as though it's the birth of a child is not truly professional for a writer. It's just a widget, a tool that helps you earn money. Well, as a professional writer, I do see some truth to this, especially because it is becoming more and more important these days for writers serious about their careers to be objective and business-minded.

However, I cannot help but feel a sense of natal joy at the release of *Once We Were Kings*. You see, about four years before its completion, my son and I were enjoying *The Chronicles of Narnia*, by my literary hero C.S. Lewis. Knowing that I was a writer myself, my son said, "Daddy, will you write me a book?" I could not refuse. His innocence and simple faith in me compelled me to reach past my comfort zone of writing Suspense and Thrillers and start writing epic fantasy.

I have chosen the pen name Ian Alexander in honor of my son. It should be noted that this book is dedicated not just to him, but my beautiful daughter as well. My entire family has been nothing less than supremely supportive in my aspirations as a writer. The sacrifice they made to afford me this opportunity to pursue writing full-time is one of the greatest gifts I have ever had bestowed upon me.

There are so many people to whom I am indebted, and despite my best efforts to acknowledge you all in this section, I shall have to beg your grace for not listing every one of you here. But know that in my heart, I am convinced that I would not have made it here without you all.

I would like to thank my copyeditor Christy Giangreco, who has now worked on three of my novels and for this one put up with hours of foreign fictitious fantasy names and names of places. I would also like to thank Anna Steinbauer of Austria, who painted the stunning cover art for this book.

No writer is an island, despite what it often feels like. I would also like to thank my Online Writing Trio members, Susan Wingate and Michael Bellomo for all their encouragement, not just in the process of writing this book, but in my writing career in general. I've learned so much from you both. I would also like to thank Dean Wesley Smith (my first editor ever) and Kristine Kathryn Rush, my mentors in writing and the publishing business for years. The effects of their generosity and wisdom will remain with me always and I can only hope to pay forward as much as they have poured into me. And of course, my fellow Fall 2009 Master Class alums, who have given me invaluable feedback and cheered me on as I embarked on this journey of writing.

I would be remiss if I neglected to honor the people from The City Church San Diego, my second family. Pastors Jerry and Tami McKinney, the Business Owners Prayer Group, Tom Giangreco, Patrick and Connie Montoya, Chris and Carol Essex, Kerry Layton, and my connect group members, Brandt and Jennifer Strieby, Reza and Kathy Namvar, Ken and Lisa Lako, Cary and Tammie Gilmore, Tom and Trish Vesneski, and Farshid and Marisol Farokhi. Also, my very close friends and relatives William and Ckristina Sutjiadi, Michael and Patricia Goh, Stephen and Vivien Tseng. Thank you all for your fervent prayers through some of the most challenging times of my life.

In all my books I wish to honor the memory of my mother, Anna, as well as my father Paul, who at the time of this note continues to race across the planet preaching and teaching the good news of Christ at the age of 83! God bless you always.

Of course, I must save the best for last. I want to thank and honor my beautiful wife Katie for standing by me all these years from my first short story sale to the publication of this book. You are my muse, my best friend and my wonderful helper in life.

And now, let it be known that in the saga of the Sojourners, the scribe Joshua Graham shall be known henceforth as Ian Alexander.

A NOTE FROM THE AUTHOR

Thank you for taking the time to read *Once We Were Kings,* one of the most personal books I've ever written. Some of you may already know me by the suspense fiction I've written as Joshua Graham, and for some this is the first you've ever read.

Did you know that you could be responsible for this book becoming a bestseller? This happens by word of mouth. So again, if you enjoyed this book, won't you please recommend it to your friends and family? One day, when *Once We Were Kings* becomes a bestseller, you can say that you made it happen!

And, if you enjoyed this book enough, may I also ask you to kindly leave a review at Amazon.com, BN.com, Smashwords, or wherever you purchased your copy? If you're on facebook, would you kindly leave a review on the official facebook Nook and Kindle fan page too?

I would love to connect with you on the internet as well.

Please "like" my facebook page and leave me a note!
http://on.fb.me/IanAlex

My website(s)
www.ianalex.com
www.joshua-graham.com
www.facebook.com/j0shuaGraham
www.twitter.com/j0shauGraham
Twitter: @IanAlex77

www.ingramcontent.com/pod-product-compliance
Lightning Source LLC
Chambersburg PA
CBHW020617310726
48979CB00008B/1520/J

* 9 7 8 0 9 8 4 4 5 2 6 1 3 *